Barely Living Alive

For my aunt and godmother, Debbie Gosalvez. You have given me more confidence that anyone should be allowed to have. Thank you for always believing in me.

Barely Living Alive

SC ALBAN

Published in the United States by Creative James Media.

www.creativejamesmedia.com

978-1-965648-04-9 (Paperback)

First U.S. Edition 2025

Chapter One

GIO

"Katarina! Katarina! Where are you?"

I ran through thick, grey fog. It hung on my skin, in my mouth; heavy and wet. Where the hell was I?

"Katarina!" I screamed. Panic ran through my veins, chilling my blood. "Katarina!"

My chest tightened, squeezing my heart as it beat at an alarming rate. This couldn't be happening. It *couldn't*. My fingertips rubbed circles at my temples as I tried to remember every detail before everything went black. We were together, I had found her. She remembered me. We had won, damn it! Love had won! So where was she?

No, this wasn't right. Something was wrong. What was I not remembering?

I closed my eyes and pushed far into my brain until I could feel it. It was there, just out of reach, but I couldn't quite place it. What had happened? Just a little closer ... I could almost touch it.

Gone.

"No!" I yelled at no one. My heart thundered in my chest,

my breathing quickening to keep pace. Losing my temper wouldn't help the situation. I had to get control.

I opened my eyes and looked around. The fog was so thick I couldn't see more than two feet in front of me. Though all I wanted to do was keep moving until I had Katarina in my arms, it would be useless to continue blindly. I stilled. I had to think. One deep breath. Two. A final one to regain my bearings. I tried again. If I could just remember the last time I saw her, maybe the missing pieces would fall into place. I brought my hands to my side, closed my eyes, and let my memory take over.

It was night. Tall redwoods reached up to the sky like fingers. I sucked in a breath. I remembered how the moonlight sliced through the trees, creating brilliant streaks against the forest backdrop. She was in the clearing, sobbing. Her body was hunched down on the soft ground. I could hear her agony through the raw, unrestrained grief, each breath hitching painfully. It broke my soul. With steady steps, I had approached her slowly. Carefully.

Oh Goddess, her face! He had hit her. Damn, bastard. A feeling of hate in its most pure form oozed into my being. Alessandro would *pay*. I pushed the feeling down for the moment. I'd save it for later. Right now, I needed to remember.

I took another breath. The images appeared again in my head. Fuzzy at first, then sharper with each passing second. I had shown her the serum. My stomach clenched as it all came flooding back. She had looked up at me, past my eyes, into my soul. She had *trusted* me. I watched in my mind's eye as she drank from the vial, her body doubling over as it took effect.

And then, we had kissed.

My hands pressed my chest over my heart as the next memories danced through my mind. I gasped. She had felt ... tasted ... just as I had remembered. I squeezed my eyes tighter as we tumbled and turned and melded into one on the forest floor. She knew me, had called me by name. I had called her by hers.

Katarina.

She was so much more than I had remembered. Every life she had ever lived, every existence she had suffered through, every experience her soul had encountered over the centuries all the way to present day, had come to the forefront of her consciousness all at once. Thousands upon thousands of memories remembered and she still had said my name. She had remembered *me*.

I took a deep breath and pushed further into my recollection. Where was she now? What had happened? The answer was somewhere inside me, I just had to think. I had to focus. If I could just remember, I could figure out what to do next. I had to find Katarina. The fog pressed in around my body and wrapped around my limbs with its wispy, soft fingers. It pulled and tugged me gently to my left. It wanted me to follow.

Was it a good idea? Probably not, but I decided to follow the fog's lead anyway. What choice did I have? Standing around wasn't helping my situation, it wasn't putting Katarina in my arms. On hesitant feet, I stepped into the gentle direction of the fog. One foot after the other until I was walking steadily through the mist, blind to anything that lay beyond the two-foot buffer between my body and the ominous grey wall.

I pressed forward until the air began to lighten. A few more steps carried me beyond the condensation and into a small forest clearing. The fog had retreated, leaving the space untouched, its tendrils clinging to the edges like a spectral border. My eyes swept the surrounding wall of mist—there was nothing beyond, only an impenetrable expanse of shifting grey. But still, I recognized this place. This was the clearing where Katarina and I were last night. I was back. I scanned the space, looking for any trace of her. Nothing. I tried to step forward but couldn't. My feet wouldn't budge. It was as if they were frozen in blocks of ice, locked in place at the exact spot where I had entered.

I opened my mouth to call her name, but no sound escaped. The muscles in my forearms tensed. Why couldn't I speak? A creeping dread settled over me as I grasped the reality of the situation I was in. I wasn't in the physical world. There could be no other explanation for what was happening. What kind of magick was this?

Alessandro.

Had he somehow done this? Had he cast a spell to trap me somewhere between realms? And why was I the only one here? Where was Katarina? Was she even alive? Panic seized my throat, and I swallowed hard.

Think, Gio, think.

The thread. Of course. I threw my energy out and searched for the thread the Strega Onesta had conjured tethering me to her centuries ago. Frantically, I searched for the invisible line that connected her soul to mine. Again and again, I threw out the connection but couldn't find it. Had Alessandro finally figured out a way to break through the Onesta's magick? Had *he* won, after all? I clenched my jaw. No, it wasn't possible. I refused to believe that.

Frozen in my own body, a prisoner within my own skin, I stood helpless. Then—a flicker of movement to my right. My breath hitched as Katarina burst into the clearing.

"Katarina!" I tried to shout, but no sound came out. My lips formed the word, yet the silence swallowed it whole.

She didn't see me. She didn't even look in my direction. Instead, she stumbled forward, falling to her knees at the center of the clearing. A strangled sob tore from her throat, her body shaking with grief.

I fought against the invisible force holding me, straining, pushing—nothing. My feet remained fused to the ground; my existence reduced to a mere shadow.

So close.

She was right there, within reach, yet utterly unaware of my presence. I was nothing to her. A ghost. A whisper lost in the wind. Destined to watch. Helpless. Silent. Unseen.

Her sobbing seemed to go on forever before another figure caught my attention. As the person slowly approached, I saw her sit up and turn. My eyes widened as I realized the person who approached was me. *I* was there. How was this possible? How could I be standing here, and watching myself there? It made no sense. Every part of me went still as I watched—watched myself step deeper into the clearing, Katarina rushing to meet me. The moment played out with an eerie familiarity, each movement a whisper of something I had already lived.

Recognition struck like a slow, dawning horror. Yes. Of course. This wasn't real. This was a memory.

But how?

How could I be standing here, outside of it, watching my own past unravel before me? And yet, that seemed to be the thought of least importance. Since I awoke in this place, wherever it was, I had been struggling to remember, and now, here was my chance. If I wanted to know what happened last night, it appeared all I would have to do was be patient and watch.

As I watched Katarina and I unfold before my eyes, our interaction playing like a scene from some long-lost film, a rush of emotion lifted me—buoyant, all-consuming, like a balloon swelling toward the sky. This was our story. Written, directed, and lived by us. The intensity of it burned, searing through me until even my bones ached.

I couldn't look away. We lay tangled on the forest floor,

lost in each other. Then—she smiled. Soft. Content. Utterly at peace.

My heart clenched, doubling in size.

Until this moment, I had forgotten that she had smiled. How? How could I have lost something so small, so precious? A detail so delicate yet powerful enough to break me apart?

For an instant, it didn't matter that I couldn't move, or speak, because I could see. I watched us lay there together; my hand had gently brushed a loose strand of her hair from her face. She was so beautiful, so happy.

We both were.

And then, the air shifted. Her face changed. Her eyes widened, surprise ... fear? Something replaced the contentment in her expression, though I wasn't sure what. Suddenly, I saw him. Alessandro emerged from the tree line. His right hand grasping a sword.

Two easy strides. One quick thrust. I flinched in my spot as I watched. He had run the blade through my body. I lunged toward his figure, but I was still frozen, trapped on the edge of the clearing forever watching as the man I most despised made simple work of destroying me with a sick smile on his face.

The air around me pressed down, thick and suffocating. I rolled my shoulders, a feeble attempt to shake off the weight of it. I had never given much thought to death—how it would look, how I would look, sprawled across the forest floor. You'd think after four centuries, I'd have been better prepared. But I wasn't.

Was I dead?

I stared at the grotesque scene before me. My body lay face down in the dirt, arms twisted at unnatural angles, motionless, lifeless. I didn't remember dying, yet how could I deny it? I *looked* dead.

I pressed my hands to my chest, to my stomach, to my arms—solid. Whole. I *felt* no different. Was this death? Had I endured four hundred years of suffering, waiting for my curse to break, only to be murdered by the very soul who had condemned me in the first place?

This can't be real. It must be a spell.

Even as the thought formed, I knew it was a lie. This was real. The truth sat heavy in my bones. A dull ache throbbed deep within me, right where the blade had pierced. The pain pulsed, growing hotter, sharper—searing through my heart. Instinctively, my fingers clawed at the spot where the wound should have been.

I had to get out of here.

Desperation surged through me, and I fought against whatever force kept me rooted. I *had* to move.

And then I saw him.

Alessandro.

Taking Katarina to the ground.

"No!" I mouthed, still silenced, though in my mind my voice screamed. *"Fight, Katarina, fight!"*

I was a wild animal, caged. I thrashed about, my soul frantic, trying to free myself from my invisible prison. It was no use. I stood planted, absolutely sickened, forced to watch the gruesome story unfold before me as Alessandro pinned her to the ground with his body and proceeded to take down his pants.

My stomach turned. I was wrong; I wasn't dead. I was alive. Alive and living in hell.

TEARS WELLED IN MY EYES, spilling down my cheeks in thick, unrelenting streams. *Katarina, my love, I'm so sorry. I'm so sorry. I'm so sorry.* The words echoed in my mind, a desperate, useless prayer. I wanted to turn away, to shut my eyes against the horror unfolding before me—but something deep inside refused to let me.

If she had to endure this, then I would endure it with her. My pain was nothing compared to hers. I owed her that much. I *would not* look away.

Just when I was certain Alessandro would take what he wanted, the air shifted. A new presence. Willem. And Claire.

The clearing tensed. The fog, once lingering at the edges, began to slither inward, creeping between the trees, curling around the scene like a living thing. My vision blurred. Shapes distorted. From the periphery, I saw Willem step forward, cautious, controlled. Claire lingered in the shadows of the treeline—was that a gun in her hands?

The mist thickened, swallowing details, reducing everything to outlines and shifting shadows.

I turned back to where Katarina and Alessandro had been. Two figures remained—one standing, the other kneeling. My pulse pounded. *What was happening?*

I searched for Willem again. He stood frozen, his hands raised. *Surrender?*

The fog pushed deeper into the clearing, rolling in heavy and unrelenting, threatening to consume it all.

Like a woolen shroud, preparing to bury the scene entirely.

No, not yet. I need to see what happens. Katarina!

My eyes darted back and forth between where Katarina and Alessandro had been to where Willem and Claire were. I could just see a trace of outlines as I struggled to break free from my vantage point. A bright flash ignited from Willem and Claire's spot. Did the gun go off? Had someone been shot?

Immediately, my glance flew to where Katarina and Alessandro had stood. Though the fog blanketed the space, I could still make out the faintest outlines. Just. A form way too big to be Katarina slowly staggered backwards with an uneven, wobbly gait, before dropping out of sight.

Had they killed Alessandro? Was he dead? Where was Katarina?

The fog rolled in with greater force, thick and efficient in its cover, and pushed the scene entirely away. I desperately scanned the area around me, trying to capture a small glimpse of my friends, of my love, but there was nothing to see. *No!* I couldn't make out anything. I thrashed about, willing myself to move. Then, without any warning, my feet released from their spot, and I stumbled forward.

"Katarina!" I called out, my voice now back. It echoed in the mist. *Please hear me.* "Willem! Claire! I'm here! *I'm here!* Where are you?"

Silence.

My mouth hung open, gulping desperate heaves of air.

Still silence.

"If you ever want to see Katarina or your friends again on the earthly plane, you'll have to do a lot more than just scream their names, you know."

I spun around, my eyes widening as I came face to face with someone I hadn't seen in over four hundred years.

Chapter Two

KATARINA

Nothing seemed alive. Everything was dull and grey. Nothing seemed real anymore. I felt as if I were trapped in a horrible dream, a dream where I could neither go farther into its depths nor wake up. A limbo nightmare.

Gio had been in a coma for two weeks. I had sat by his side for every one of those days and nights, listening to the beeping of the machines, the ticking of the monitors. I had eaten, slept, showered, and prayed, all in the confines of his ten-by-ten hospital room. I couldn't help but hold the guilt of his condition on my shoulders. It was, after all, my fault he was there in the first place.

Fourteen days. In that excruciating span of time, his condition hadn't changed. The doctors had said that it was good news, a sign that he didn't need more intensive medical intervention. But I couldn't agree with their sentiment. I couldn't get excited. I wanted him *awake*. I wanted him in my arms. I wanted him to kiss me and hold me and tell me that everything was going to be all right, because as I saw it, everything had fallen to shit.

I stood in my bedroom and touched the cold window that looked out over the park next to the house I had shared with that monster, my breath fogging the glass as I rested my forehead on the smooth pane and watched busy children play. As the chill from the outside air seeped in through the glass and cooled my forehead, I remembered the moment when my life had started this tragic loop.

Four hundred years ago, I had been betrothed to a very powerful, very dark, Strega. Back then, our people had been known for blurring the thin line between Goddess magick and sorcery, and Alessandro was one of the most powerful.

But I was young and powerful myself. And I wanted to be free. Free to live my own life. Free to make my own choices. My father had been different. He had grown up with the Strega Onesta and had instilled in me a balance that many of my mother's clan lacked. While we tended to believe in the tenets of the Old Religion, his clan was more progressive. He showed me there were other ways to live, other ways to be. It felt natural for me to seek out those options as I grew older and matured. I had wanted a different life, one filled with love and light, one worth living.

Giovanni had been the answer to my prayers. It was love at first sight. He was nothing like Alessandro. Nothing like *any* other Strega. He was human through and through, and I felt beyond any doubt that the Goddess had sent him specifically to me. *Il mio destino.*

We had intended to run away, but Alessandro had discovered our plan and put into action what would become the timeless mess that our lives evolved into. The night Gio and I were to steal away, Alessandro intercepted us, slit my throat, and cursed Gio with immortality.

As Alessandro saw it, I was his— would always be his— and Gio was going to take what he owned. So, according to old Strega law, his actions were justified. My death was simply a consequence for turning my back on my bloodline. To force Gio to live an immortal life without me was merely a lawful punishment for interfering in Ilmalo business. It would have worked too, if the Onesta had not intervened and altered the curse just enough to give Gio and I another chance.

A tiny tweak in the magick allowed me to be reincarnated over and over until Gio could find me once more. The catch? I had no idea who I was from lifetime to lifetime. Further complicating matters, Alessandro intervened yet again. If he couldn't have me, no one would. He used the same magick of immortality on himself and thus began this epic game of cat and mouse with me as the prize.

Life, death, rebirth. Life, death, rebirth. Life, death, rebirth.

Eleven cycles worth. Well, that's how many had come back to my memory ... so far. Since my Strega powers returned, there was no telling what my mind would recover.

A high-pitched scream brought me out of my thoughts, and my attention was pulled back to the park where the children played tag. I swallowed hard and pushed back the tears that dared to spill down my cheeks. The pain of centuries stretched its long arms and legs inside me, pushing against my creaking bones, threatening to tear open my skin as I thought of Gio lying in a sterile hospital bed.

I don't remember all the details of the night Gio went into a coma, only that no sooner had the curse been lifted and my memories started coming back, than Alessandro had run his blade through Gio's back, leaving him for dead. True to form, my bastard husband then tried to take me right then and there, with Gio's limp body lying on the ground beside us. I shuddered. He would have succeeded if it hadn't been for Willem and Claire.

I closed my eyes. Willem and Claire. Now that was something I could've never anticipated. If they hadn't been by

Gio's side through this current life cycle, I very well could have been bonded to Alessandro for eternity. There is no question about that. Luckily for me, Claire's magickal abilities as a Watcher, and Willem's time with the Onesta were enough to get us this far. They'd helped Gio find me. They'd kept one step ahead of Alessandro, so that Gio and I could be together. They'd stopped Alessandro from forcing himself upon me.

My heart skipped erratically, desperate to put the pieces together, as I replayed that horrific night in my head. I suppressed the urge to vomit.

Claire had shot Alessandro. The bastard fell over two hundred feet and landed on the jagged rocks below. There was no way anyone could have survived such as fall, and yet ... The police had told me his body had been carried away by the ocean, that most likely it would never be recovered.

But I knew better.

Alessandro didn't die. I didn't know how; none of us did. All we knew was that he wasn't dead. He wasn't dead, and Gio was trapped in a coma. Taking a steady breath, I pushed away from the window and felt the numbness resonate through my entire body. Looking over my shoulder, Dave sat on my bed, trying to talk me into staying in Freestone, but that wasn't going to happen. No way in hell. I walked over to the closet, grabbed a small bag from the top shelf and stuffed a small box of crystals into it.

"Kate ... *Katie*! Are you even listening to me?" Dave asked.

I took a deep breath before even acknowledging him. It wasn't his fault; he had no idea. He had no clue that I'd been waiting by Gio's side for fourteen long days. He'd just known I hadn't been home when he came by to pick me up for work. That *Alex* wasn't either. That I couldn't been reached. That I had, essentially, disappeared. But enough was enough. It was time for action. Today was day fifteen. As difficult as it would be, today was the day I tied up loose ends. Today was the day

I'd let Dave go. It was also *the* day I was going to take up hunting. And Alessandro had better start running.

"Kate, I know that everything is upside down, but hey, I'm—"

"Dave, please stop. You won't change my mind about this. I've made my decision. It's final. I'm leaving."

"I don't understand this. Where'll you go? Where are you staying?"

He continued to talk, but I didn't hear a word he said. Not really. I returned to the closet and began pulling clothes off their hangers. I wasn't sure exactly what to grab, just that I needed to grab things.

"Claire, did I bring a big black bag downstairs?" I yelled.

Dave looked at me with frustration.

"Just slow down, would you?" He grabbed my arm as I passed him. His fingers gripped my bicep a little too tight. I could feel the intensity of his energy as the adrenaline flowed through his blood.

I reflexively yanked my arm away. A couple weeks ago I wouldn't have given another thought to the touch, but ever since my husband had made it excruciatingly clear he would rather see me dead than alive, I'd become a bit sensitive. That, and the fact that my continually reconnecting powers made that simple inoffensive touch nauseating. My stomach lurched.

"I'm sorry," he said. Fear sliced his tone as he quickly brought his hands to his chest. "I didn't mean anything by that. I'm sorry. It's just that ... Look, I can't imagine what you must be going through. I mean, I had a suspicion that Alex had his issues, but ..." His voice trailed off. "I had no idea things could get so bad. I mean, a murderer? A fucking *psycho*? I ... I—just talk to me, please. We can work through this. You don't have to leave. Let me help you."

I saw real pain in his eyes. Far past his striking blue irises, veiled under worry, hidden behind guilt, the pain one feels when they're about to lose something they love lurked like a shadow behind a lamppost. I only saw it for a moment, but there was no mistaking its presence. It was unquestionably there. Unfortunately for Dave, I was counting on that pain to help me manipulate the situation.

Because the truth was, I did feel guilty leaving. Dave was an important presence during this lifetime. Our friendship would leave a lasting impact on my heart. But compared to Gio, he was very low on my priority list. Especially when my murderous husband was still alive and probably devising plans to destroy everything I lived for.

I took a deep breath and paused. Hell, it wasn't his fault that everything had fallen apart. A shiver ran up my spine as I remembered how things had gone down in the clearing. Gio and I had made love under the moon, and Alessandro had run a blade straight through his body. I winced as I remembered the sound of the steel as it pushed through his flesh. If Willem and Claire hadn't shown up in time and shot him ... I couldn't even begin to imagine what the outcome would have been. Not like it ended with a happily ever after. Not at all. The memories made my determination to find Alessandro even stronger.

"Yes, Dave. I *do* have to leave. I can't stand it here any longer." I took a deep breath, hoping I'd be able to get through the next few minutes without vomiting over the floor.

Since I'd come into my full powers, everything around me had become amplified. I could feel the energy thrumming. It'd been many lifetimes since I had felt the full power of the Strega flow through my blood. The fact that I had been a true daughter of the Goddess, from one of the most powerful lines of both Ilmalo and Onesta magick, did not help to quell the intensity of the sensation.

Both my parents had been powerful Strega, my mother's

family being one of the most influential among us. It was her father, my maternal grandfather, Vincenzo, who'd led our clan through most of the fifteenth century. And as true to the Old Ways as he was, his power was feared by all. It ran deep to an evil core, an evil that my mother embraced and nurtured, hoping to pass it on through her bloodline. And she probably would've, if not for my father.

Also, from a long and distinguished line, my father's bloodline did not follow the path of most practitioners. During the Age of Cleansing, my father's clan was taken prisoner and thrown to the fires. My father, just newly born, was spared only because his mother had begged local clergy to take him, hide him, and care for him.

The clergymen had tried to raise him as a Christian but soon realized that the magick coursing through my father's veins was too strong to change. At the age of thirteen, they released him from their care. They sent him to a local sage, a solitary practitioner, who directed him in the old ways and taught him about the good in the world.

The sage worked with him for two years before confessing that she knew where he would find his true people and sent him to the Strega. My father was welcomed back into the clan like a prodigal son returned. Not long after that, he was immediately taken by my mother. Though they had far different inclinations about the true path of the Strega, my father's ability to capture my mother's affection was unparalleled.

The Strega Ilmalo council was divided. How could they let one of their most powerful bloodlines be coupled with what was, in their opinion, a diluted one? His connection to humans made him weak and vulnerable to feeling sympathetic to their plights. Some on the council wanted to be rid of my father; others wanted to keep him but not allow the union. For four nights, the council debated and, in the end, decided to allow the marriage utilizing my father as liaison to the outside world. His compassion and understanding of how things worked outside the Strega camp could prove useful to their long-term survival.

Centuries later, I was experiencing the effects of two powerful Strega, the thick, unbridled prowess of a more visceral magick coupled with an ageless compassion for humanity and hope; molten velvet contained within a cool, crystalline sheath.

That duality molded me into the Strega I became. Neither good nor evil, I was born as something new: an angel capable of revenge. A do-gooder until things went awry. My justice was my own. I did not go out in search of creating chaos, but if chaos came to me, I would not hesitate to commit whatever it took to justify my being.

"At least tell me why? Why do you have to leave with those two strangers down there? I mean, who are they even?"

I blinked twice and stopped packing. I stood in front of Dave, clawing onto whatever semblance of composure I could maintain, trying my hardest to find the part of myself that would not let my emotions get the best of me. Would he try and physically stop me? I bit the inside of my cheek as anger flared. He wouldn't. He *couldn't*. Even if he thought about that route ... I wouldn't kill him, but he wouldn't stand in my way. The truth of this new reality, who I was, felt thick in my throat as I tried to swallow. It was hard to accept, this version of me. But if I had learned anything in this lifetime, it was that I knew better than to make promises to myself I couldn't keep. And the sooner I could accept all of me, the easier the transition back to my Strega self would be.

But I wasn't worried about Dave interfering. I could feel his heart. He loved me. He was scared *for* me. His intentions were pure, and it was all I needed to hold the fire in my blood back and trap it deep within its aqueous casing. Again, I took a deep breath and tried to steady myself.

"Dave, do you have any idea of what it's been like the past nine years? Do you have any idea what it's like to be a prisoner in your own home?"

He shook his head. "I know, I know, I—no. You're right. I have no idea what it was like." He moaned as he covered his face with his hands as he sat down on the bed. "I wish I could turn back time and be there to pick up on all the signs I missed. Don't you think I'm hating myself right now thinking about it. I mean, maybe I could've changed something, maybe I could've helped. I should've. I mean, I should've known something was going on when you started up with that Gio guy. But no, I just kept on living in my own little world. I just didn't ... see. I-I'm ..." His voice fell.

My heart froze at the mention of Gio's name. I pushed down my hackles. I would be no use going on the defensive. How would I even explain that Gio was not just *some guy*? Especially since I knew it wouldn't get me anywhere close to where I needed to be. I closed my eyes, crushing back the tears that had surfaced in the millisecond since his name had been uttered.

"Dave," I said gently, forcing my hand to rest on his shoulder, "this isn't your fault. There is no way you could have known. Alessan ... Alex was very skilled at what he did. He fooled a lot of people ... me included."

Dave kept his hands over his face. I took another deep breath.

"Look, I know I don't have to leave here, but I really need to get out of this house for a while, you know?" I looked around the room in disgust, focusing on the brown accent wall where a picture of Alex and I hung. It had been taken on a trip to Ensenada before we married. I thought back to how he wouldn't let anyone speak to me while we were there, how he almost got into a fistfight because he thought a waiter looked at me too long, how we went back to the hotel ... Oh, Goddess, why didn't I see it before? My stomach heaved at the thought of the nine years spent as husband and wife. I shook my head, forcing myself back to the present, and focused on Dave. I needed to make this believable. I needed *him* to believe me so he could let me go. "I just need a break from all the questions, all the stares and whispers, you know?"

I sat next to him carefully, on the edge of the bed, not wanting to absorb any residual memories the fabric of the duvet might be holding. Slowly, I let my guard down. I wanted to connect with Dave. My friend. I wanted him to know that I wasn't abandoning him. I could feel the guilt he held for things he'd had no control over. It just wasn't right.

"Why leave, Katie? Where will you even go? Why don't you come stay with me for as long as you need to. I just don't get why this rush to get out of town. And now there's this Claire person and ... Willem? I mean, who are these people? You've known them for what? Five minutes? *I've* known you for almost a decade. You're my best friend. I-I love you." He sounded scared even as the words were coming out. "I've always thought that maybe in another life, or—hell, if circumstances were different in this one, it'd be just you and me, you know? But now ... now, I'm realizing ..."

He ran his hands through his hair, letting them rest at the back of his neck for a moment before they fell into his lap.

I placed my arm around his shoulders and tried to comfort him. What could I tell him? That no matter what life I lived, it would always be Gio? Yeah, right.

"Claire and Willem are good people, Dave. I know it's impossible, but please try not to worry. I'm fine now. I'll be okay. Everything will be fine. And to be honest, I don't know where I'm going or what I'll do, and that's okay. I just need a break. But I'll be back." I placed my head on his shoulder.

Exhaustion began to kick in and I felt myself begin to melt into his form. "As soon as I can. I promise."

"You shouldn't make promises you can't keep, my love."

My eyes widened as Alessandro's voice filled the room. I tried to stand, but my legs wouldn't move. I glanced up at Dave. He turned his head to face me, a twisted, familiar smile spreading across his face. *Jesus.* I jerked back, but before I was out of reach, his hands were around my neck.

"Did you actually think you could get rid of me that easily, you fucking whore?" My breath caught in my throat as Dave's hands squeezed. Panic seized me as Alessandro's voice came out of Dave's mouth.

How was this possible?

Frantically I reached for something to get hold of, but my arms wouldn't move. I felt my entire body immobilized as I watched in horror as Dave's face began to transform into Alessandro's.

What the hell was happening?

"There is no one to help you now. It's just you and me, *Katarina.*"

I clawed at the hands around my neck as Dave's eyes became more and more like Alessandro's. Slowly, my friend's features were transforming into my husband's. Fear turned to instinct. Panicking would do no good. I stopped fighting and concentrated. I pushed the fear away, I ignored the pain around my neck. I forgot about needing air and that if I didn't get some soon, I would surely die. No, if I were going to escape, I was going to need to focus on other parts of me. Parts of me that I had not used in centuries. Parts of me that I was afraid of. My inner Stregheria.

I closed my eyes and focused on that hot, molten part inside of me. I teased it from my bones, from each cell, and slowly let it spread throughout my body from my deepest center out to my farthest extremities. The heat touched every part of my being, and it only took a second to realize that I was smiling even though I was desperately in need of air.

The power. Every cell in my body both feared and welcomed it. It filled me up and emptied me, let me fly and buried me deep within its bubbling void. It'd been an eternity since I had truly felt who I was, and in that moment, I was satisfied. I almost forgot that Alessandro was about to kill me.

"You were never good enough for me," Alessandro's voice hissed through Dave's teeth, pressing his two thumbs deeper into the crook of my neck.

In less than an instant, I was back in the room. I focused on the pain in my throat and led the heat in that direction. I told it to find the cause and obliterate it. Immediately, the heat responded, gliding through my body, weaving in and around my bloodstream, up to where Dave's hands clutched my neck. I pulled the hot energy up from each leg, in from each arm, from every finger and toe and rounded curve, up to where it was collecting near my windpipe. In my mind's eye, it grew, a collective ball of energy, heavy in mass and intensity.

When it was as large as my fist, I slowly let it rise to my throat, filling my neck completely. I carefully pushed the heat outward until it gently resisted against Dave's hands. I hesitated. I didn't want to hurt him, but Alessandro had left me no choice.

"I'm so sorry, Dave," I thought. Then, with every drop of will in my body, I shot the heat past the resistance.

I felt sick to my stomach as I felt the energy slice through Dave's hands with ease. Instantly, Alessandro's hold on Dave was broken and his hands released my neck. Oxygen flooded my lungs like rusted needles, and I blinked hard, trying to adjust.

Dave screamed. Alessandro was long gone, but the terror was still present as I rushed to see the damage I'd done to my friend's hands.

Both Claire and Willem were in the room before I could reach him.

"Katarina!" Willem yelled as he rushed in, ready for the worst.

"It was Alessandro," I shot back crouched next to Dave.

"What do you mean? Where?" Claire immediately looked around; her face drained of any color that had been left after running up the stairs.

"He's gone," I answered in a rush, adding, "First, Dave. Then I'll explain."

Willem and Claire joined Dave on the carpet, hunched down near the foot of my bed. His hands were closed into fists near his head as he whimpered. Claire approached him first. She cautiously knelt beside him, her hands assessing his aura.

"Dave, can you hear me?" Her voice was soft, and I knew that she was using her magick through her tone to soothe him.

She looked up at me. "His aura has been seriously affected. Alessandro's dark signature is everywhere. I need to cleanse him immediately if he's got any chance of healing at all."

I wrung my hands. "Do what you need to do. Anything. Do you understand? *Anything.*"

"I will," Claire promised. "Willem, can you make a *non memorabor* draught? Or something close. Anything that will help him forget is a blessing right now."

"Aye. I'm sure I can find everything in the kitchen. It'll take just a few minutes. I'll get right to it." He took two strides out of the room and bounded down the stairs. A few seconds later, I heard him rummaging through the kitchen, opening cupboards and drawers. I sat next to Claire.

"What can I do?" I looked at her expectantly.

"Just stay near. If I need you, I'll let you know." She closed her eyes, each deep breath she took a deliberate choice.

Dave was still curled into a ball on the floor of the room whimpering. He looked so small as Claire began to trace her hands around the shape of his body. Her healing energy resounded with bold, pulsating vibrations. It built and grew, and I knew it would be just moments before she began to pull the black energy from his aura. Thank the Goddess above.

I inhaled deeply. Alessandro's scent was still fresh in the room. It coated the walls, dripped from the ceiling like acid rain, creating a bitter stench. How had he taken over Dave's body like that? To hijack a living body with a soul? And could he do it again? There was no way he could harness that much power on his own. He had to have had help. But who?

A snake of cold slithered through my blood as an inkling of how he had attained the needed power leached into my brain. I fought against the idea. I would not resurrect old demons. Not unless I had to.

I brought my attention back to Claire. She diligently worked on Dave, and I could sense a state of peace wash over him. My muscles finally relaxed. By the time Willem returned with the draught, Claire had Dave in a deep meditative state.

"Will he remember anything?" I asked Willem.

"Aye." He smiled slightly. "Just not anything that happened today or maybe even the past few days, for that matter. I'd recommend we head out of here soon, before he comes around. You can leave him a note to settle him down."

Well, damn. I supposed it was for the best, but I still felt bad about leaving Dave without saying goodbye. But I couldn't risk staying. Alessandro had shown me just how dangerous sticking around could be. I couldn't stomach it if anything else happened to Dave because of me. I was a danger to be around. Dave would be better off this way.

Claire and Willem loaded the car with our few belongings while I quickly scrawled a note to Dave explaining I'd gone to visit some old college friends. As I signed my name and folded the paper in half, a chill crept up my spine. What type of magick was Alessandro tapped into? It was old, that was for sure. I wasn't entirely certain of what he connected with or how he did it ... yet, but I'd find out.

At that moment, we were leaving. Finally. I pushed into my furthest memories and tried to come up with a clue that might lead us to where Alessandro was. A place to start. Nothing. Oh, well. I wasn't too concerned. After all, there was one thing I was certain of. No matter what, I *would* find Alessandro. And once I found him, I would kill him.

Chapter Three

GIO

"It's you," I said breathlessly. "How can it be?"

Like everything else in this godforsaken place, it didn't make sense. Standing in front of me, plain as day, was the man who had bought my figurines those many years ago in Florence. I knew it was him. I would recognize his eyes anywhere, green with flecks of gold, just like Katarina's, his daughter.

"Like I said, if you ever want to see Katarina or your friends again on the earthly plane, you'll have to do a lot more than just scream their names."

My palms began to sweat. *Fuck. This can't be it. It can't be him.* He held his ground, nearly six feet tall, and stood there clad in his simple attire looking at me. Every bone in my body told me who this man was, and still, I had to know for certain. It just couldn't be. That would mean that—

"Who are you?" I said, though I knew the answer.

"I think you already know who I am, Gio. But how about you call me Jack? Just seems more familiar as we're practically family." He pulled his lips into a tight half-smile. "You know, I thought I'd never see the day when we'd meet again. I truly was hoping you'd win, but such are these things …" He trailed off in a heavy sigh. "We were all rooting for you over here, you know. And, really, who could have anticipated this?" There was a short pause. "Not quite fair, is it?"

He began walking past me into the fog. What the hell was he talking about? I couldn't process what he meant, everything was all happening so quickly.

"Wait! What do you mean?" I yelled as I ran after him, struggling to keep up through the thick haze.

Jack waved his arm to his left and the fog wafted away, clearing the forest.

"Now, that's much better," he said as he admired his work. He walked up to a redwood and placed his nose close to the bark, inhaling deeply. "There's something magickal in every tree, every bush. A real-life force. Strong magick. Most humans don't take the time to really appreciate the gifts that are among them, you know. I never quite understood that."

He continued walking.

"Jack, wait! I need answers."

"I know, son, I know. But first, you must come with me. Now that you've seen what happened that night at the clearing, you'll be better prepared to deal with what's going to happen to you next." He paused for a moment, waiting for me to decide if I was going to follow.

It didn't take long for me to choose.

"Let's go," I said as I hurried to catch up.

Jack turned and led the way to a small clearing surrounded by stones. Seven stumps surrounded a large fire pit.

"Come, sit." He gestured to the stump on his left.

I walked slowly to the flattened log and positioned myself facing the pit. As soon as I sat, flames erupted from the center.

Jack spoke, "Ancestors, we are here to honor and obey you. We humbly ask for your assistance in the grave matter of Giovanni Rossi's fate. Please come forth and lend counsel."

As the flames grew higher and higher in the pit, shadows began to dance in the heat's core. My breath caught as the shadows within the flames began to take human shape and emerged one by one from the pit, each one taking a seat on the remaining five stumps.

The forms sharpened and I saw their faces. Altogether there were two men and three women. Each wore a neutral, sheer wrap that hung loosely around their bodies. Flowers adorned the women's hair. An intricate silver pendant of a sprig of rue with various charms among the branches hung around their necks.

"Cimaruta," I whispered.

The word appeared in my head, though I wasn't sure where it had come from. As soon as I had said it, I could feel something shift inside of me. I looked at Jack.

"What is it?"

"You know this word, Gio, because you have our magick in you now," the woman sitting across from me spoke. My eyes darted in her direction. Though she was sitting, I could tell that she was a tall woman. Lithe and lean. Her golden hair had jasmine woven throughout its thick waves that hung down past her bosom, covering what the thin piece of fabric did not. In the center of her chest, about four inches in diameter, hung her cimaruta.

"I don't understand," I uttered.

"Dearest Aurelia," Jack said quietly, "He does not understand what the potion has done. And he cannot yet move forth before he understands where he is. This is why I have asked for your assistance."

Aurelia nodded, a pensive expression painted her face. "Then let me explain. The sooner we can get you back to Earth the better. Katarina will need you alive if Alessandro is to be stopped."

My heart sank. It fell into my stomach and rolled in the

acid that began burning me from the inside out. There was only one explanation to this madness. The hard truth, the truth I didn't want to admit.

I didn't make it that night.

Katarina had made it. She was alive. Alessandro had survived, as well. But after living over four hundred years, day after day, minute by minute, hoping and praying, striving to prove that love would indeed conquer all, despite the deep blackness of the moments in which I had wanted to give up, but did not, I, Giovanni Rossi, was finally dead.

Chapter Four

KATARINA

T he hospital was our last stop before we headed out. After pulling into a parking space near a Pistache tree, its red and yellow leaves reaching up to the sky like flames, Willem turned off the engine. We sat in silence; no one moved. I'd never been to Venus, but I imagine that the atmosphere of the car at that moment would have rivaled it. I could barely breathe. Claire was the first to speak up.

"Katarina, we don't have to leave." Her voice was cautious. "No one would think any less of you if you wanted to stay until Gio wakes up."

"We don't know when he'll wake up, Claire. I can't just sit here and do nothing," I snapped.

My stomach rolled over. I was continuously ill. There was nothing I wanted more than to be by Gio's side, but the longer I did that, the farther away Alessandro got. And that was not an option. Anger rose within me. It tapped into my spine and triggered energy that I was not sure I could handle.

"Okay, we'll just go on up and tell him we'll see him later then." Claire reached over the front seat to where I sat in the back and offered her hand. I gladly took it. Her touch immediately snapped me back into a calm state. I nodded my head in agreement, thankful she was near.

Another unfortunate side effect of hurtling back into myself, was my inability to control when my powers appeared and with how much force. Willem had been watching me carefully, helping me readjust to the influx of magick and find balance in the old ways, but there was something about me that I sensed he feared. He was always guarded against me, although subtly.

As if I couldn't feel it.

I wasn't sure what it was that bothered him, but as each day passed and my power became more apparent, Willem became more ... watchful, careful with both his words and his actions.

I reached for the door handle and pulled it back, pushing the door open with the side of my body. A warm breeze entered the car and ran its fingers through my hair. I inhaled deeply letting the thick scent of sage settle into my thoughts, and instantly I was swept back in time, lost in memory.

"KATARINA, you know better than to use your powers for your own gain. You can't take advantage of your gifts," my father had scolded me, the simple charm bag stuffed with sage and rose petals I'd made held firmly in his grip.

"I was just trying to ..." My voice trailed off. There was no use even attempting to explain myself. I knew what he'd say. I studied the ground, ashamed.

"Come." He placed his arm around me. "I know it is in your nature to try to lead the universe in your favor; Goddess knows that is how the Strega have done it for centuries, your mother included. But it doesn't have to be that way. You can use your gifts for good."

"But if what I cast won't be of any harm to anyone, what is the harm in it at all?"

"There is always a consequence to every action, Katarina. Never forget that. Always remember. For everything that is done, something must be undone," he said softly. "Your mother, Goddess rest her soul, found that out too late, but I know that she will be waiting for us in the spirit realm."

"Katarina? Katarina?"

Willem's voice broke through my thoughts and my gaze darted to his face. "Another memory?"

"Yeah." I said with a sigh, wishing I could go back.

His brow furrowed. "I know it's unfathomable, but as you spend more and more time in your original consciousness, the Goddess will find more ways of revealing your true abilities. These memories, the ones that pop up, keep them in your mind. There's a reason why you're remembering those specific ones. What do you think triggered it?"

I shrugged. "I'm not sure. Maybe the sage," I said, taking a deep breath, though I knew very well it was. I remembered the spell I had cast and held in the charm bag and shuddered. I was quite young, perhaps twelve or thirteen, when I'd done it. I had not yet understood what my father meant when he said that for every action taken, there is an equally powerful reaction.

It had been a simple love charm—to steal away the love interest of my good friend. It was the charm of an immature and spoiled child, one that thought too much of herself and not enough of others. At the time, there was no doubt in my mind that it would work, and I did not consider the consequences. I had wanted that boy, and I was going to get him. But as my father had reminded me, it would have eventually led to heartache and pain for others.

I cringed.

I was not that selfish, spoiled person anymore. I refused to believe it. I knew the difference between right and wrong. Besides, I was just a child when it had happened; I had since learned to control my instincts. I knew who I was … didn't I?

I know it is in your nature to try to lead the universe in your favor…

My nature. My father had suspected my instincts did not always play toward the good side of humanity. Even now, I could sense that part of me I was so afraid still existed.

"Well, it's gone now," I said feeling a bit uneasy. "Let's go. I want to see how he's doing today."

We entered the hospital from the south. The automatic doors slid open easily, allowing us to pass through without breaking stride. I could feel my heart racing as we approached the elevator.

"Claire, are the Watchers set up to cover him?" I asked, my nerves getting the better of me as we stood in the elevator. The ascent seemed to be taking longer than it usually did.

"Yes. A meeting was held last night and it all got sorted out. I believe Patrick is with him now."

The elevator bell dinged as we hit the third floor. My chest was tight as we made our way down the hall. The smell of hand sanitizer and plastic assaulted my senses.

I stood in the doorway for a moment before entering. Gio lay motionless, amid the continual beeping and clicking of the machines hooked up to him. I felt my heart strain against the grief that squeezed it. For a moment I couldn't breathe. I couldn't move. I just stood there, a statue of disbelief. It was Claire who broke the silence.

"Hey, Patrick, anything new?" Her voice came softly from

over my shoulder to the man who was sitting bedside. Funny, I hadn't noticed him before.

"Nah, Claire darlin', things are the same," he spoke to her with a familiarity that crossed over the line of mere friendship. I wasn't the only one who heard it. Willem tensed next to me.

I looked at the man that sat by my love's bedside. His wavy black hair was combed back off his face and a sly smile slipped across his lips as he ran his fingers through it. Who was this man with the missing eyes; the man who did not appear to need them because he saw everything? Claire had mentioned briefly that the ingestion of a poisonous plant when he was a teen had left him with a horrible infection that cost him his sight and it wasn't until after this tragic event that his gift had emerged. Though his eyes had been removed, it was as if he hadn't missed a beat. A slip of energy made me pause.

I studied him. As far as I knew, he had no need for eyes; all his visuals happened inside his head as accurately as if he were seeing them, maybe even more so. Since meeting Claire, and learning about what she was, I'd tried to think back, tried to remember if there had been others with similar talents when I was living in my original life. But it was still too far away. I couldn't recall. I had never heard of these people, these Watchers, or anyone else like them before this lifetime. And though I trusted Claire completely, I was not so confident about how I felt about the lot of them. But now, after hearing the comfortable tone of Patrick's voice, I also wondered just how much Claire had left out about how close they really were.

Willem seemed to hear my thoughts as he pushed gently past me into the room, making his presence apparent.

"Patrick, do you mind stepping out for a bit?" he said in a brisk tone. "Katarina would like some time alone with Gio before we leave."

Again, Patrick's sly smile peeked out from behind his short stubble.

"Of course. I'll just be heading down for some coffee, then," he responded as he stood up and put his sunglasses on with a fluid motion. As he walked past Claire he nodded slightly in her direction. Almost instantly she nodded back and then turned her attention to Willem.

"Willem, maybe we should step out as well," she suggested before turning to me. "We'll be right outside the door. Will you be okay?"

I nodded sharply.

She reached out for Willem's hand and led him to the door, stopping short to add, "Like literally right outside."

"I'm good. Thank you."

As I watched them leave, I reflected on how Claire had become such a close and important part of my life. She had helped Gio find me, given him refuge when he needed it. She had saved me from Alessandro, in more ways than one. I felt connected to her in so many ways, yet I hardly knew anything about her. But I firmly believed there was a purpose to Claire's path crossing mine. I just wasn't exactly sure of what that purpose was. I promised myself I'd think more on it once we headed out. Once we were in the car and driving, I'd have some time to reflect. Later. Now, I had to say goodbye.

I made my way over to the bed and carefully sat on its edge, gently taking Gio's hand in mine. It was so cold. I grounded myself and searched for the tie that had bound us lifetime after lifetime. There was nothing.

"Gio, where are you?" I whispered. "Please open your eyes. Please do *something*."

Tears began to stream down my face. I was surprised at how many there were; that they all hadn't dried out by now. As they fell from my cheek onto Gio's still body tucked under the hospital linens, I felt a surge of anger. It seemed to grow more intense with each falling tear. My magick grew, the power of my people, my inner Strega. I leaned in close to Gio's ear.

"Alessandro will die; I promise you that." The words came out clipped and walked the line between right and wrong. "I will find him and make him suffer slowly … painfully."

And I meant it. Getting rid of him would be a service to the universe. I affirmed my resolution with satisfaction. The heat of the energy I was calling rose up in me. It felt good and strong and powerful. It flowed thick through my veins, rising and rising, looking for someplace to go … at the ready.

I glanced at the hand I was holding and realized that if I did not control this energy, if I did not calm myself down, it could very well be sent into the one person I wished would live. At once, I began to control my breath. I grasped Gio's hand more firmly and remembered our time together. Even though brief, our connection was undeniable. He was mine. He always would be, just as I was his.

The hot energy began to subside as my thoughts steadied. Its ribbons curled back up in their spools, waiting to be called upon later.

"I'm so sorry, my love. I wish there was something I could do right now, some way to make things right again."

The words were empty. I was lost amid the grief that consumed me. I looked at his face, searching for some sign that inside his motionless body, the spirit of the man I loved was desperately trying to find a way to get out. A soft knock at the door caught my attention.

"If we're going to do this, then it's time," Willem said from the doorway, Claire tucked right behind him.

I looked over at him and nodded. Patrick had also returned and was standing behind them, waiting for my word.

"Okay. I'm ready," I said, though it was only a half-truth.

I squeezed Gio's hand once more and leaned forward for

one last kiss goodbye. No not goodbye. A kiss until later. My free hand rose to brush his cheek, my thumb rubbing gently along his strong jawline. As I brought my lips closer to his, I could feel his soft breath on my mouth. I remembered how he had felt as we kissed that night when it was just he and I alone together. I closed the gap between us. His lips were soft and as I held mine to them, as if I were being drawn into him, pulled into a dream, far away and deep into the soft blur of time.

Cimaruta.

The word flashed in my mind for a split second before I knew it was there. I sat up with a start and my eyes widened with surprise as I inspected Gio's face. Where had that come from? Was he sending a message? Was he trying to tell me something?

"What is it?" Claire approached me cautiously, a look of concern spread across her face.

"Nothing," I said, shaking my head. "Nothing." I probably should've shared what I'd seen—*Cimaruta*—but I wasn't sure if it was real or just a figment of my imagination. With a renewed energy, I stood to leave.

"Let's go."

"Katarina," Patrick called as I stormed down the hallway, "remember your roots. But also, remember who you are now. Don't forget."

I stopped and turned to look at him. What was that supposed to mean? Although Claire had more than vouched for him, I was getting a little fed up with his antics.

"Don't worry about me," I replied in a clipped tone. "Just worry about keeping Gio safe and out of harm's way. And call me the second anything changes."

"Of course," Patrick said. "That's what we Watchers do."

I hurried away and didn't look back. Something nagged at me, but I couldn't place it. It didn't feel right placing my trust in a stranger, and again I had to remind myself that the

Watchers were helping us. They didn't want Alessandro around anymore than I did. As I quickly made my way back outside, both Willem and Claire hurried to keep pace.

"What was that about?" Willem asked as we settled into the car and buckled our seatbelts. "Claire, are you sure about this? Is Patrick up for this?"

"He's one of the most competent Watchers in our group. He's my oldest friend … my closest … I'd trust him with my life," Claire said.

Her response was restrained, held back. There was something else she wanted to add but thought better of it. Interesting. I would ask what that was about later. Willem, on the other hand, had no such tact.

"Are you sure that's all?" he snapped.

It was impossible to ignore his harsh tone, and a long pause filled the car. What was wrong with him? In truth, I didn't know Willem all that well, but Gio had placed centuries of trust in him and that was all I needed. But now that Gio wasn't around … no. No, I couldn't let suspicions get the better of me. Damn Alessandro! He had me questioning everyone and everything around me.

Claire calmly turned to face him.

"Are you … jealous?"

Willem's cheeks flushed.

"Me? Jealous? Of what … No. I mean …" His voice trailed off in defeat. "Am I a fool?"

Claire reached over and placed her hand on his shoulder.

"No. Not at all. I get it, Willem, I do. You haven't felt love, or any related emotion, in centuries. Jealousy is a natural response. I don't think anyone blames you for feeling what you're feeling. But you don't need to worry about my feelings toward Patrick. I'm in love with you and I've been waiting for *you*. It's you I want." Her voice was steady, calm.

He shook his head. "My apologies. I don't know what's

gotten into me. I thought that when my soul returned, I would feel more ... more normal. But these feelings ... these emotions are too—"

"Human?" Claire said, smiling. "Average? It's okay. You've just forgotten how visceral feeling with a soul can be sometimes."

"Goddess help us all," he said as he started the car.

Slowly, we pulled out of the parking lot. My stomach clenched. This was it. Finally. We were on our way. The car bounced on the asphalt, and we rode in silence as we headed out of Freestone. The sun was still high in the afternoon and the sky was free of clouds. I leaned back in the seat and gazed out of the window.

Soon, you'll be a tiny speck on the horizon behind me.

I blinked. Given the circumstances of my arrival there, I had become surprisingly connected to the little town. I'm not sure what it was, but something about this small bit of northern California called to me. Despite the lie I had lived, it was my home ... for now.

As Willem approached the freeway entrance, he slowed.

"Where to? Does anyone have a suggestion?"

"South," I stated. "Head south and keep going until you get to San Francisco. I think it's time for us to pay a visit to Alessandro's office."

Chapter Five

GIO

"Well, I was wondering when you'd actually open your eyes."

I heard his voice before I saw his face. My thoughts were groggy, slowly moving in the direction of recognizing who it belonged to but not quite getting there. My eyelashes felt heavy and held my lids down, refusing to surrender to my desire to see.

A distant beeping echoed in my ears. Where was I? So close ... it was all just there ... My brain began to piece things together. A small town ... rolling hills ... vineyards ... a young girl ... pink hair ... Willem ...

My eyes flew open with a suddenness that demanded response.

"Katarina!" My voice was hoarse and barely a whisper, but the urgency was there. "Katarina! Run!"

I tried to move, but in vain; my body was too heavy. My legs were lead weights, anchors burrowing deep into the soft ocean sand keeping their ship steady. My mind sharpened and everything came back to me.

"Whoa, slow down there, Gio," Patrick said from his chair in the corner of my room.

"Patrick? Where's Katarina?"

"She's gone, mate."

The frankness of the statement knocked the wind from my chest.

"What do you mean, *she's gone*?"

"Well, it's exactly as I said. She's gone … as in not here."

The gaze I shot at him was so hot it could've bored holes in his eye sockets. As expected, Patrick picked up on it right away.

"Relax. It won't help getting yourself worked up. I promise, I'll explain everything. First, though, I suspect these doctors will want to have a conversation with you."

No sooner had the sentence left his mouth than the room began to fill with medical personnel, and I was bombarded with questions. By the sound of it, I'd been out for a while. My heart began to race. How long *had* I been here? The concept of time evaded me.

For the next two hours, I was prodded, poked, and questioned. After answering their queries and sitting through multiple examinations, the hospital staff conceded that I was healthy enough to be left alone. As the last nurse left, I laid back to catch my breath. I was no better off now than when I'd first arrived in Freestone. So much had happened and yet I had nothing to show of it.

"Are you ready to tell me where you were while your body was lyin' here?" Patrick's voice broke me from my trance.

"Tell me where Katarina is, and I'll consider it." My tone made it clear that I wasn't about to reveal any information until he told me what I wanted to know. "And while you're at it, Willem and Claire, too."

He didn't even try to evade it. "They left earlier today. The lot of them. Katarina, Willem, and Claire."

"Where did they go?"

Patrick took a steady breath before he spoke.

"I'm not entirely certain. They're tracking Alessandro, and they're—"

"*What?* What do you mean, they're tracking him?"

Patrick tilted his head to the side. "I meant what I said, mate. They've left to find Alessandro and kill him. I can say they started out south toward San Francisco, and that's the last I've heard ... or seen."

"What do you mean? You don't know where they are now? They haven't contacted you? Any of them?" It didn't make any sense. I had a hard time believing Rose would let Claire leave without some form of contact. Above all else, it was very unlike Willem to not check in.

A deep sense of dread loomed nearby. What had Katarina been thinking? It wasn't the first time she'd left me when I knew she shouldn't have. My mind flashed back to that night that had started the wheels turning centuries ago. Had she just stayed with me then, we could have lived one glorious lifetime together. No. No. I couldn't think like that. Yes, she was stubborn, set in her ways. But she wouldn't do anything to intentionally jeopardize our life together. Still, she was gone. She had left me again. Would history repeat itself? I took a deep breath.

"No, none of them. It's like they've vanished." Patrick's voice got serious. Shit. That wasn't a good sign. "We've been keeping our feelers out ... us Watchers ... but a few hours ago ... nothing. It's like they've gone completely off the grid. There's no indication that they exist ... anywhere."

"But where could they be?" I asked, stifling the panic clawing its way up my spine.

He rubbed the back of his neck. "We don't know. *I* don't know. And *that* is what bothers me most of all. What could be so strong as to hide the existence of three powerful magickal beings? And what in the hell could keep them hidden from an entire clan of Watchers?"

A cloud of doom loomed over my head. If Katarina, Willem, and Claire had gotten mixed up with some of the old ways, then there was no telling where they would be. Anger sparked to life inside me. It billowed up from my core at the thought of Katarina in danger with me so far away. It came alive and stretched its long arms, tapping into the energy of the earth, pulling its influence within my soul.

"Well, that's different," Patrick commented, his head tilting. "I mean, I was expecting many things to be different with you upon your return to us, mate, but I can tell you with one hundred percent certainty, I wasn't expecting you to be a witch."

His blunt words snapped me back to the present and I blinked. The anger slipped away and within seconds retreated to its depths.

"I think it's time you started talking," he said as he made himself comfortable in the bedside chair.

I looked at Patrick and rolled my lips. I'd have to explain how this happened to me, but I wasn't sure I'd be able to. I sighed. No time like the present and now was as good a time as any. Besides, the sooner I could get through this, the sooner I'd be out of here and on the road. I had to find Katarina. I hadn't existed for over four hundred years, watched her murdered over and over again, met death myself, *and* become a witch, just to give up now.

"All right, but let's get out of here first," I said as I began removing the last of the equipment that was still attached to me. "I have something in my apartment I think we both could use."

Sneaking out of the hospital was easier than I imagined thanks to Patrick's foresight and my newly acquired senses. It was as if my body finally understood how it was supposed to move. Before I was a shell. Now? I felt complete, more in tune with my surroundings ... alive. We exited through the front doors and I was hit by a warm breeze.

My entire body shuddered as the wind wound its way around my body. I could smell in its willowy fingers the light scent of lavender and sage. My ears twitched as a finch twittered in a nearby tree rustling its leaves as it hopped from branch to twig to branch, making its way from one side of the foliage to the other. My senses slammed into overdrive and emotion swelled within me. Everything was so ... real. How had I never noticed the living, breathing, pulsing of the earth before?

The answer was simple. I had never been what I was now.

I was a son of Aradia.

Just as Katarina was her daughter; I was her son. Willem was truly my brother. Blood did not relate us; it was spiritual. A connection that we were all bound to, just as the Watchers were bound with each other.

As Patrick and I made our way through downtown Freestone in silence, back to the small apartment above the thrift shop, I took advantage of the time to reflect on my new mission, my purpose in this life. Katarina's safety, by far, was of the utmost importance. That was top priority. We would be reunited, of that I was sure. It was just a matter of how. When. What I didn't like, and what created a huge amount of anxiety, was the fact that my friends had essentially disappeared into thin air. The uncomfortableness of that nagged at me.

Through the purple door, up the narrow staircase, Patrick followed. We entered the apartment, and I noticed everything was the same as I had left it. Funny how time had never really been my friend, though we'd been together for far too long. Always too quick when I needed more or too slow when there was more than enough. I scanned the apartment, now a bit dusty from neglect, and noticed how time had managed to stand still here.

Typical.

I walked into the kitchen and reached for two tumblers on the shelf. I grabbed my bottle of Glendronach fifteen-year single malt and poured out two generous glasses, handing one of them to Patrick.

"Take a seat," I said as I waved toward the living area. "You might as well get comfortable, because you're never going to believe this."

Chapter Six

KATARINA

We crossed the Golden Gate Bridge just as the sun was beginning to set. I looked out over the Pacific and wondered at how the dark-blue ocean managed to gleam with deep yellows and oranges as it reflected the sun's powerful rays. It truly was a sight to behold, an almost perfect sunset. The only thing missing was Gio.

"Now let me get this straight." Claire pulled up a map app on her phone. "We're heading downtown toward the financial district, right?" She craned her neck around to look at me.

"Alessandro's office has an address near Montgomery and Sutter," I said from my spot in the backseat. Even as I said it, it seemed too strange that I knew this. Alessandro had generally been so secretive about his office. What was even stranger was that I, as his wife, had never been there. Not even once. We had been married for nearly ten years, and he had never taken me there or anywhere associated with his job.

I thought back over the past decade and tried to recall what it was that Alessandro even did for a living. What had he disclosed? I had been told that his firm was involved in some sort of business consulting, but as I pulled our every recollection I could find, I had no clue as to what his job was.

I swiped through my recent life's memories until I found what I was looking for. My mind flicked back in time and pulled a specific memory to the forefront.

"Hey, babe, I found one of your business cards in the wash today," I had said, holding it out to him as I walked into the kitchen. I unfolded the loose card and been amazed at how it was still completely intact after being run through an entire cycle. I examined the white card with tiny black script on one side. *Estraggrine, Inc.* It was written in the middle of the card with an address and phone number underneath. *Alexander Martins* was written at the bottom. He had looked up, startled, from his place at the counter where he made a sandwich.

"What are you doing with that?" he snapped, then quickly collected himself and said, "Here, let me see."

"You know," I replied holding out the card, "Don't you think it's strange how I really don't know anything about what you do for a living? I mean, I know you're in business consulting ... and that you help out with environmental reports for new companies and things like that, but I've never actually been to your office or met any of your colleagues. I've never actually *seen* what you do."

He had carefully placed the knife down on the cutting board and approached me. He had plucked the card from my fingers and slid it into his pocket almost at the exact same time he gracefully wrapped his free arm around my waist and pulled me close into him.

Our faces were just millimeters apart. The scent of his skin left me intoxicated. His lips had been so close to mine, yet miles away. How had he done that?

"Now why, my love, would I bore you with the details of my work?" he had whispered, our lips nearly touching.

"Certainly, I would never forgive myself for taking one moment of your time visiting my office when I'm sure there are other things we could find much more pleasure in doing."

The words had been barely audible but didn't need to be. He had closed the already miniscule space between us, fully crushing the last of my curiosities with his hard, muscular frame.

I closed my eyes tight and swallowed hard as I returned to the present moment, trying to forget what had happened next. Claire turned around in her seat to face me.

"Katarina?"

"Just bad memories," I replied quickly waving her off. I was both horrified and ashamed about my past. Horrified that I had been taken advantage of in every way imaginable. Ashamed because a big part of me kept feeling that somehow, I should have known, and sensing that perhaps, somehow, I *had known*, and I let it happen anyway. It sickened and terrified me.

No. That wasn't true. It *wasn't*. What Alex had done to me was not my fault. He had taken every advantage of me. I shook my head, trying to clear out the thoughts of guilt. Alessandro was pure evil, a master sorcerer, manipulator, sexual predator, and cold-blooded murderer. This was his fault, *his* fault, and I'd be damned ... *again* ... if I was going to let him escape this lifetime.

"You want to talk about it?" Claire offered.

"Maybe some time," I conceded. "Just not now. I'm still trying to sort it out with myself, you know?"

Claire appeared to know exactly what I meant. She offered a friendly smile, then turned back around and focused on the road. Willem drove in silence.

We turned right onto Van Ness and made it only about a quarter of a mile before I saw an old woman pushing a shopping cart on the sidewalk. Something about her drew my gaze and I realized I knew this woman. I'd recognize her anywhere. It was the same woman who had sold me the necklace with the tree weeks ago on the sidewalk in Freestone. My stomach lurched. It couldn't be a coincidence.

"Stop the car," I said loudly.

"What? What do you—" Willem stuttered. Claire gave me a confused look.

"Stop. The. Car," I replied, this time with more urgency. "Hurry! She's going down that alley!"

Willem was still trying to pull over but had slowed down enough for me to hop out safely. Leaving the car door open and bolted down the street in the opposite direction to catch the woman who quickly disappeared around a corner.

"Wait! Wait!" I called after her, "Ma'am! Please, stop!" I turned the corner of a tall building and entered the narrow alleyway determined to catch her.

"Katarina! Wait!" I heard Claire call after me, but I couldn't risk losing the woman

I ignored her. I had to find the woman. Something about her pulled me toward her. I slowed down and stopped about halfway down the alley to look around.

Nothing.

Other than a couple of dumpsters, the alley was a dead end. A tall chain-link fence with barbed wire at the top stood at the end, closing it off. And there was certainly no woman. I shook my head. That couldn't be right. I'd seen her go this way. Where had she disappeared to? I jumped as a hand touched my shoulder.

"Jesus!"

"You know, this would be a lot easier if you would just tell us what's going on," Claire said through her panting. Both she and Willem looked winded but relieved.

"I'm sorry. It's just that I saw this woman come down here … I'm sure of it … and, now she's …" My voice trailed off.

"What woman? From where? Do you know her?" Willem was trying to be patient, though I sensed a frustration in his tone.

"She sold me a necklace a few weeks back ... in Freestone. Just a street vendor. I didn't even talk with her that long." I began to hear my own words and understood Willem's frustration. I began to pace along the width of the alley. "But there's a reason I saw her here, right? I mean, it felt different. Like she wanted me to see her again, to follow her. It just can't be a coincidence ... can it?"

The alley was narrow, merely a back access to the two buildings it separated. Other than the couple dumpsters along its sides, a few doors that appeared all looked well-worn and securely locked, and some trash littering the corners, there appeared to be nothing there. My gaze traveled across the buildings. Graffiti lined the brick walls. Claire and Willem watched me carefully. My eyes scanned for something, anything that might lead me to the woman.

"Well, since we're here, we might as well look around," Claire offered.

I nodded my thanks. We spread out and began investigating the area, though we had no idea what we were looking for. I walked a few feet deeper into the alley and closed my eyes. I envisioned the necklace purchased from the woman. It was a simple pendant, plain silver, a tree of life with a star superimposed on it. And yet ...

I thought about the many symbols of the Strega I had adorned as a young woman when I lived with my people centuries ago. The tree of life had always been one of the simplest symbols we could wear without completely outing ourselves to the rest of society. It was the most accepted. It was the one I had been wearing the day Gio and I had crossed paths the very first time.

I opened my eyes, letting the pain of not knowing if he

would wake wash throughout my body, leaving chills behind. No, he would wake up. There had to be a greater plan. The Goddess would not let it end this way. My vision blurred with tears. I walked over to a corner and tried to privately dry them with my sleeve.

Once the grief passed and I collected myself, I continued to search. I looked up at the wall where I stood. Graffiti of every color painted the brick. It was pretty. And unique. Messy, yet not. With every second that passed, it drew me in farther and farther, through the layers upon layers of old paint, one on top of the other, until a larger, darker tag emerged from the chaos.

"Willem," I said carefully, "come here, please."

Willem appeared next to me in seconds.

"Do you see it?" I asked, nodding toward the wall.

"It's a cimaruta," he said amazed. "Goddess above."

"What's a cimaruta?" Claire had joined us now in our corner of the alley, now studying the wall alongside us.

Willem turned to her. "A cimaruta is an old charm dating as far back as when Stregheria practiced La Vecchia Religione, the Old Ways. I haven't seen one since I left the Onesta." Willem paused as his explanation sank in. When he continued, his voice was quiet, serious. "After I decided to leave my parents, I was filled with bitterness. I was so ashamed of the pain that I'd caused. I wanted nothing to do with who I was or my so-called powers. I thought I could start over, be a new person ... forget." Willem looked down at his hands, which were now trembling.

"I became Willem." He gave a sad smile, then shook his head, turning his attention to the cimaruta. "This symbol, the cimaruta, was kept and worn secretly by those who practiced The Ways of the Strega. It was an identifier, of sorts. If someone wore this symbol, either in jewelry or on their clothing, then others in the clan would know they could trust them."

I cleared my throat and gestured towards the wall.

"See here?" I took a step forward. "The cimaruta is a sprig of rue split into three branches. Rue is the sacred herb of our Goddess, our queen, and each branch signifies one of her three forms." My hand traced the graffiti's lines to reveal its shape to Claire. "At the end of each branch are symbols that represent her forms and tie back to the Old Ways.

"The moon at the end of the first branch represents the Heavens, our Goddess in her maiden form. The moon also symbolizes the beyond, the beginning and ending of all. At the end of the second branch is the key. The key is a symbol of the earth because it is here where we hold the key to opening and closing power. In this branch, our Goddess is in her mother form, for it is here that she provides for her children." I spoke with ease, remembering the lessons and stories I had as a child with ease.

"At the end of the third branch you see a serpent," I continued. "The serpent is the most misunderstood portion of the cimaruta, as most associate it with evil. However, for the Strega, the serpent is a symbol of our Goddess in her witch or crone form, for just as the serpent is continually shedding its skin and renewing itself, the Goddess is in her last form and will certainly be reborn again."

My fingers traced the lines of graffiti as I spoke.

"What are these other symbols here?" Claire broke my trance with her question. Willem stepped forward.

"Other symbols have been added on or taken away, depending upon the Strega. It's personal," he said as he pointed to other pictures. "But, the rooster generally represents vigilance, this dagger"—he pointed to a crude drawing of a knife—"is for secrecy, and this here ..." he outlined the entire shape of a small blossom.

"It's vervain," I finished. "It's a very old symbol of our Goddess ... from the Old Ways. Vervain itself is a very small and subtle blossom. Most would miss it if they walked past it in nature. Because of this quality, vervain has always been associated with faeries and magick. Some ancient lore has also described our Goddess as Queen of the Faeries."

"Well, that explains a lot about the cimaruta," Claire replied. "What it *doesn't* do is explain why it's here, on this wall."

It was a good question. My mind flashed to our hospital visit earlier that day. The word cimaruta had flashed in my mind's eye. This wasn't a coincidence. I was sure of it now. I turned to Willem and Claire and explained what had happened earlier at Gio's bedside.

"Well then, let's focus our attention here," Willem suggested.

We stood in a circle, our hands held tight, closing us in to each other. We focused our energy and searched for a sign, a clue, to tell us if we were near anything that would help us on our journey.

As I gathered my center, I could feel Willem tap into his Strega magick. It felt familiar to me, like home. Claire's magick, though different—newer—still felt good. It was like a warm bath after a long day of work.

My focus shifted and centered. The vibrations I called from the earth itself were a combination of my mother's and father's magick, two sides of a coin. Though I tried to balance them, the more visceral, raw line, my mother's energy, seemed stronger ... no, *hungrier*, like a wild animal starved of prey.

I felt something at the edges of my magick. I couldn't quite make it out, but it was strong and growing stronger by the second. Would it give us a clue to where we should head next? I doubled down on my focus. Willem resisted and tried to pull his hand away, but I held onto him tightly and wouldn't let go. I didn't want to break the circle. Not when I felt we were so close to an answer.

"It's here," Claire gasped. "Do you see it?"

I had been so focused on trying to balance my power that I had forgotten I'd closed my eyes. When I opened them, I saw what Claire referred to. My jaw dropped and my gaze landed on the graffitied cimaruta glowing brightly on the old brick. Stronger and brighter than any star, the symbol blazed until the edges of its shape blurred and faded and revealed an opening in the wall beyond.

"Let's go," I said pulling the other two in the direction of the entrance.

"What about the car?" Claire said. "We can go back and—"

"There's no time, leave it," I interrupted. "Come on, we have to go." Urgency breathed down my neck and again, I pulled her toward the opening.

"Wait. Where does it go?" Claire asked resisting my tug, and I realized that for the first time since I met her, she was scared.

"It'll be okay," Willem comforted. "If it were dark magick, it wouldn't have opened for us."

She seemed to accept this small comfort and took a deep breath. Giving her one last squeeze, I dropped her and Willem's hands and entered the opening where the cimaruta had been, hoping that in its depths beyond we'd find the answers to our questions and come one step closer to catching Alessandro.

Chapter Seven

GIO

It didn't take long for Patrick to settle in.

"Well, go on, then," he prompted.

I wasn't sure what this would sound like. I wasn't even sure what I thought of it, and I'd experienced it firsthand. Would Patrick think I'd lost my mind? That Alessandro's blade had done more damage to my brain than to my body? Probably. But what choice did I have?

I took a steady drink of the scotch that filled my glass and gathered my thoughts. I was still unsure whether I could trust what I saw, or trust Aurelia, but Jack had been there. I let my mind drift back to the council of ancestors. Patrick sat and waited for me to begin. I opened my mouth and wondered if anything was real anymore.

"LONG AGO, WE WERE ALL HUMANS," Aurelia had said as she stood up and made her way toward the fire. She bent down and picked up some ashes that had scattered from the blaze. Rolling them in the palm of her hand, she took one more step closer until it appeared she was standing amidst the flames themselves. She opened her hand and blew the ash into their center.

The long tongues of fire rose up and danced like lithe ballerinas floating across a stage before settling down and opening to reveal the story of which she spoke.

"Legend passed down from generation to generation tells us of the goddess, Diana. Now, Diana has been known by many names: the mighty huntress, Goddess of the Moon, but to us, most importantly, she is Queen of the Witches."

My eyes widened as the pictures moved within the flames and gave Aurelia my full attention.

"During the twelfth century, Christianity began to take over the old ways. The Church was a heavy influence on the people, and those who did not conform to its ideas were dealt with immediately."

I remembered my life as a boy growing up near Florence. By the time I was born, Christianity was well established. My parents were firm believers in a Christian God and I, as their obedient son, did not question those beliefs. It wasn't until I was a young man, until Katarina, that I began to understand those beliefs were a far cry from reality.

"The stories passed down told of benevolent creatures; young, spritely women, faeries, if you will, that visited households at night, asking for food and wine. These faeries were thought to be creatures sent by Diana as tests of a person's goodwill. The households that took in these women and blessed them with their desires were rewarded with good fortune. Those that did not were left in struggle. And as consequence, the Fae were both revered and feared.

"It was around this time that Christian rule felt that to gain more supporters for its cause, the legends of the Faerie should be eradicated. It deemed that anyone who spoke of them, who believed these stories to be true, who participated in honoring them, was in league with the devil. The line between Christianity and La Vecchia Religione, the Old Religion, had been drawn, and those who did not move toward Christianity were persecuted and destroyed."

Aurelia spoke solemnly while I watched the scene play out in the flames before me. My stomach turned as I watched woman after woman executed in the name of God.

"What you have to understand, Gio, is that the Christianity of our time was evolving. It was taking over Italia and had more to do with power and control than it did with spreading its word.

"For a little more than one hundred years, our people lived in secrecy and fear. Many of us converted to Christianity, leaving behind our core beliefs to avoid execution. But there were those of us who refused to be led astray. We held tightly to our stories and shared them through the generations, constantly looking over our shoulders. But regardless of those who stayed the path, our numbers dwindled. It appeared that La Vecchia Religione would indeed die out."

Aurelia took a heavy breath. I sensed a deep sorrow fill her and permeate the circle. I glanced over at Jack. He had a somber expression. Looking back at the circle of fire, I waited for her to continue.

"Almost two hundred years had passed, and it was almost assured that the ways of our people would die out. But still, there were some who held on. I was only a small girl at the time, but my mother was already sharing the stories with me. My father would keep watch outside our home while my mother whispered the stories in my ear as she tucked me in each night. And each night, in my dreams, I would be visited by the faeries my mother told me about.

"Then, one day, *she* arrived." Aurelia paused and gazed into the fire.

I followed her gaze and saw an image of a beautiful

woman, with smooth olive skin and a sharp jawline. She was strong in build with long, curly hair and hazel eyes. Who was she?

"It is said that Aradia is the daughter of Diana, sent down from the heavens to keep the Old Ways alive. I knew when I saw her," she continued, "that this woman was there to bring back what was lost. That this daughter of Diana would save us all. However, La Vecchia Religione was too far gone. The few families that remained did not have the power to keep it alive.

"That is when Aradia taught us what is now known as Stregheria. Though we still had to keep secrecy, speak of nothing but Christianity in public, in private we were taught these new ways. We, the people of my time, became the first witches."

Aurelia spoke this last sentence with pride, and the circle's heat became more intense. Each ancestor that sat at the circle appeared to glow from the inside, emitting auras of bright yellow and orange. I looked down at my own hands, I could see a faint blue color emanating from my palms. I looked over at Jack in confusion. What was I seeing? Panic seized my thoughts.

"Don't worry," he said quietly. "Blue is a good sign ... you're a survivor, after all."

"But I don't understand. What's wrong with my hands?"

"Relax," Aurelia spoke calmly. "Everything is good. All will be explained ... just give me a moment more of your attention."

"So, what you're sayin', mate," Patrick blurted out yanking me back to the present. I blinked and turned my attention to him. "is that Aradia, one of the first witches, gave you the Holy Powers of the Strega?"

I lifted a shoulder. "It's not quite that simple," I replied.

"Alrighty then," he said. "Proceed."

I raised an eyebrow. When it appeared he wouldn't interrupt, I continued with Aurelia's tale.

AURELIA HAD REACHED out and touched the tips of the flames with her fingers. She took a deep breath and looked at each ancestor before continuing.

"Over the next hundred years, the New Ways that Aradia brought to Earth were studied and passed down. Whispers of our existence were alive in the shadows of our societies," Aurelia said. "Our name was Stregheria, and we lived true to the teachings of our beloved Aradia. Life was, once again, as it should be. We were in balance with nature and again in the good graces of our queen, Diana.

"But then, one day, some strangers appeared among our clan. I had long since moved on into the spirit realm at the time, but I continued to watch over *mia famiglia*. The strangers came into our society, into our culture, with their own ideas, their own influences."

Aurelia paused. "At the time, the Ilmalo were a little-known people. The Strega had heard of the Ilmalo, but mostly that was because they had fled their homeland and come to Italia to avoid persecution. Persecution was something the Strega understood, so when the Ilmalo came seeking protection, we provided it unconditionally."

I looked into the fire and watched the Ilmalo be welcomed into the Strega fold and waited for Aurelia to continue.

"It was not long before the Ilmalo's magick became entwined with Stregheria and together that new brand of magick grew rooted deep, challenging many of the original ideas. One of the influences of the Ilmalo was the use of sorcery. Before then, the art of sorcery was not used among the Strega.

"Some of the Strega elders began to question the motives

of those who wanted to use sorcery in Strega magick. However, many Stregheria sought to learn more about this new power, wanting it for themselves. It wasn't long before the rift between those who supported sorcery and those who didn't was beyond repair."

Aurelia paused a moment before continuing.

"The teachings of Aradia were becoming lost with the introduction of sorcery. Lines were becoming drawn and blurred and drawn again. It was at that time that the ancestors stepped in to guide the situation and lend counsel on what should be done.

"Shortly after, our word was put into action as ordered by the elders. The Stregheria would be split into two. Each branch would live as they were- two branches of Stregheria, each left alone to practice their way accordingly without interference from the other. Those who held true to the path and beliefs of Aradia would be known as Strega Onesta.

"Many, many years went by and each branch of Stregheria minded their own business. That lasted until our dear friend here"—Aurelia nodded in Jack's direction— "fell in love with the daughter of one of the most powerful Ilmalo. She, in turn, became equally enamored with him. Knowing that a direct descendant of the Ilmalo line would never be accepted into the Strega Onesta, he joined their camp.

"From them was born your lovely Katarina—a Stregheria of most unique and terrible power. A young woman descended from a lineage of sorcery *and* the pure magickal teachings of Aradia."

As Aurelia's story came to a close, I let the significance of it settle in my bones. I was not surprised at the anger building within me.

"Why tell me this now?" I snapped. "What difference does it make to me? Who am I in all this? I'm just a human. And apparently, a dead one."

Aurelia looked at Jack and nodded. Jack turned to me and smiled.

"Gio, I know this may be difficult to understand, especially after all you've just been through, but you're one of us now."

My head reeled. What the hell was he talking about? "I don't understand. What do you mean, *one of you?*"

"We all knew it was a possibility, but when Katarina drank the potion her powers were ... suspended, in a way ... until after you expressed your love. You see, love is and will always be one of the most powerful conduits of magickal expression. It is born of the highest vibration. When you both reached the apex of passion, her powers were returned to her. And since at that moment the two of you were connected both spiritually and physically, some of her power was directed into you."

I listened to Jack as he tried to explain how it came to be that I now possessed the gifts of the Strega. He had to be joking. This had to be just some wild fantasy my brain concocted to process my untimely death, right? I mean, how could it be possible? The idea that the craft of Stregheria was somehow sexually siphoned into my existence seemed ludicrous. There was no way. I had to get to the truth.

"If what you say is true, what difference does it make to me now? I'm dead. I saw Alessandro run his sword straight through my body."

"You are not dead, Gio," Aurelia said. "You are between worlds. The power of this realm is possessed by the Stregheria, both Onesta and Ilmalo. It is an in-between realm. One where we can contact our relatives and monitor the magick on earth though our energies. Soon, we will send you back. You will return to the body you inhabited before you came here but with the ability to practice witchcraft. It will be up to you whether you follow the Onesta or the ways of the Ilmalo. The choice will be yours."

My heart raced. Holy shit. I wasn't dead.

My darling, lovely, Katarina. I'll be with you soon!

There was no time to lose. "How do I get back?" I asked.

"Once we leave you, you will know the way," Aurelia said.

I looked around at the ancestors that circled the fire. Nodding their heads in agreement, one by one, they stood and walked back into the flames until it was just Jack and me.

"Don't you go with them?" I asked.

"It is not my time to live permanently in the spirit realm. I have other things to do before I go there," he said as he stood. "But before I leave you, I want you to have this."

He took his hand and placed it, palm down, against my forehead. It seared my skin. I screamed in pain as an image was branded in my brain.

Cimaruta.

He let go, and instantly the pain was gone, though the image was permanently fixed in my mind.

"Cimaruta?" I said. "What am I supposed to do with that?

"It will help you find your way," he said as he walked back into the forest from which we entered. "*La Vecchia Religione* ... it will tell you who you can trust ..." His voice faded as his image faded in the dense thicket of trees. "Don't forget ..." And then, just as he appeared, he was gone. When I finished retelling what had happened, Patrick's face was shook. He sat in the old chair stock still, jaw slack. He hadn't moved for some time.

"And that's all I remember," I said, getting up to refill my glass. "The next thing I knew I was in the hospital, you were there, and Katarina was gone. Again."

"Holy shit, mate," Patrick said as he shook his head. He knocked back his entire glass of scotch in one swallow and held it out for another. "There's only one thing we can do now. We gotta take this to Rose."

Chapter Eight

KATARINA

We had walked just past the threshold of the opening in the wall when a flash of light seared through the small space and the gaping hole was sealed. The cimaruta glowed in the stone where the hole had been, fading slowly until we were left standing in the blackness.

I could feel Willem standing directly behind me, and I could hear Claire's soft breathing quicken in the darkness. We stood still, the three of us, close together, afraid, unsure of what to do next.

"Willem," I whispered, scared to awaken whatever might be sleeping in the dark. A feeling of dread washed over me. Everything was too quiet. I needed to hear his voice.

"I'm here," he replied. I jumped a bit as I felt his hand upon my shoulder. "Remember, dark cannot exist without the light."

In some way, the sentiment was comforting. Without light, dark does not exist. I focused my energy on that thought. There is no dark without light. I called on the Goddess to help us.

"Lasciare i miei occhi vedono il percorso davanti a me." My lips moved, though barely a whisper came out.

Slowly my vision adjusted to the surroundings. In the distance, a small purple light appeared. It grew and grew until we could make out the cavern around us. The purple light stretched its beams along the cavern walls, illuminating the small space. I tried to listen to the outside world. In my mind, I knew the alley was just beyond the thick rock where the cimaruta had disappeared, but I couldn't see any evidence of it, let alone hear it.

Now that our surroundings were visible to us, I noticed that we stood in what appeared to be the beginning of a long tunnel that sloped downward. My heart sank. Always downward. Reason insisted, based on the alleyway entrance, that we should be standing in a building right now, but there was no indication we were in a place where outside reality held true. We were now in a world bound by magick.

The walls themselves were covered with tiny flecks of crystals, the clear gems sprinkled heavily in the face of the grey rock. I glanced back at Willem and Claire. Both were inspecting our surroundings, seemingly trying to figure out where we could be.

"There are many stories about places like this," Willem said suddenly. "But until this moment, I've never been in one."

"*Where* is this place?" Claire asked.

"A Strega Underground," Willem answered.

"It's been too long," I said under my breath. "Four hundred years later ... we're still in hiding ..." My voice trailed off.

Willem gave me a sympathetic nod.

"C'mon," he said after a moment. "Let's go."

We walked down into the tunnel toward a pathway that led us somewhere below the city into an area that appeared to be protected by time and space. There was very little talking among us as we trekked. The excitement emanating from Willem, and in contrast, the apprehension from Claire confused me.

When I was a girl, Strega kept to themselves. That was a fact. There was little interaction between those who practiced Christianity and those of the Old Ways. We were private and inconspicuous, but we lived above the ground. We were able to practice in our camps, out in the open, under the sun and stars, free to use the natural magick of the earth and the gifts of the Goddess in their most pure form. Was it possible that the basic freedoms we'd had centuries ago were so limited in the modern age that we had to go underground altogether? Like burrowing animals?

Curving this way and that, the path led deeper into an unknown until it came to an end. Emerging from the tunnel, we found ourselves standing on a ledge overlooking what appeared to be an underground city. My breath caught in my throat as I looked down at the bustle below. It was not a city of today, with modern roads and architecture, but one that mirrored those of long ago.

At first glance, it looked crowded and chaotic. However, upon further inspection, I could see that the chaos was quite organized. Booths and tents lined the two sides, creating a walkway down the center. Though I couldn't gauge what was happening within the tents, the booths appeared to be selling various goods from foods to herbs to magickal items of every variety. Each booth backed up to a larger, more solid structure that appeared to be housing or another business. The windows in those structures were adorned with planter boxes of brightly painted colors, all overflowing with various botanicals. But it was the bustling of the marketplace down below, the interactions of the people I witnessed as they bought and sold goods, that really caught my eye.

My heart ached with an echoed longing for home. Not my home in the current time, but my home of long ago, on the outskirts of Rome; the place where my life both ended and began and ended again. A flash of the past hit me full force and I steeled myself. They were happening more and more frequently. Small explosions of memory. I closed my eyes and let it consume me, opening my mind to the vision.

"Amore," Alessandro purred as he pulled me aside into the privacy of the shadows, "I cannot wait until we are united." His lips tickled my neck like tiny raindrops on an early spring morning.

"Are you sure it's me you want?" I replied. "You can have any girl in our camp. There are many families, if not all, that would support a union with their daughter."

"Katarina," he said as a smile formed on his lips, "why do I get the feeling that you're trying to convince me that I want someone else? What do I have to do to convince you that it's you I want. And if you don't know by now, you should know that I always have ways of getting what I most desire."

I let his hands find their way to my waist as I arched into him. It was true. Alessandro did have a way of getting what he wanted. His entire family did. Their understanding of our magick flowed deep in their veins and their talents were greatly revered, sometimes feared, by less-gifted Strega.

When I had made the deal to become Alessandro's bride, it was out of desperation to save my father from the beatings of the council. Had I known it was already too late, that he would die just weeks later, I would never have given my blood oath to marry him.

That he was handsome was unarguable. I would have been lying if I said I hadn't been attracted to him. I wholeheartedly was. I had often stolen glances of him during our rites and rituals. There was something about him that commanded attention. An energy that drew me in. He had both power and the confidence to wield it. A deadly duo.

But I did not love him. Not truly. I knew it in the deepest parts of my heart. Perhaps it was my father's influence after all; perhaps it was my own volition, but whatever it was, I was unable to give my love completely and freely to Alessandro. There was something *too* dark about him. Something that scared me. Something that reminded me of myself.

"It's no secret that you can and will have anything you desire," I whispered. His hands ran up the length of my torso. It felt good. *So good.* Matched with his lips that found the line of my collarbone, I was falling under his spell. "But you know how I feel. It's not unknown."

"Of course, I know." His voice took on an edge, and his body tightened. "There is not much that escapes my attention." His fingers tightened around my ribcage.

I held my breath.

"But I also know that while you may not be in love with me, you do not hate me. And that, *topolina,* is enough, because I shall love you enough for both of us until the end of our lives. And I know that eventually you will, one day, accept our joining as fate, you will see ..." His tension eased a bit as his hands continued to explore my body, making their way down my backside. "I can feel your desire for me. I would not pursue you if there were no desire." His thick, dark hair nudged my cheek as his face nestled in the crook of my neck.

I released a shaking breath, my insides quivering at his touch. Though I did not love him, I did desire him. How could I not? Other women in our camp looked at me and wished they could incite Alessandro's affections the way I could, and that sense of power engulfed me. Having control over his desire, his want, was intoxicating. I craved it.

I closed my eyes. I knew I should put a stop to what was happening, but feeling his need, his desire for me, took control of my senses. More. I wanted more. And I began to reciprocate.

"Desiring you has never been the issue," I whispered in his ear.

I arched my back, pressing my bosom into his chest. I could feel him harden against my thigh, a groan escaping from his lips. Tilting my head all the way back, I exposed the entirety of my neck, allowing him to feast on its fragility.

I could feel the power of taunting him with my body, leaving him surrendered to my whims. I wrapped my left leg around his hip and lifted my pelvis up to him, crushing his manhood between our bodies.

I felt him give his will up to me, and adrenaline whooshed through me as this strong and talented Strega fell under my spell. He, whose family had direct lineage to our makers, the powerful Ilmalo, was succumbing to *my* will. I was becoming drunk with the power of having him under my control.

"Katarina," he begged. "I know you feel it. Somewhere there is love for me inside you. Our fate could be sealed tonight, if you allow it to be." He kissed my ear lobe and tugged it with his teeth and paused. "But I also sense that you're hesitant. Afraid." His voice was barely audible. "Don't be afraid of what we could be. Together, we could rule. You would live like a goddess, and I, your consort." His mouth made a trail down to my chest. Tugging at the already loose fabric, he exposed my breast to the cool air. He quickly covered my taut nipple with his mouth hungrily, biting and sucking it with expertise.

"Perhaps," I said dreamily. "Perhaps I will grow to love you."

As the words escaped my mouth, I could feel his response to them. His energy grew excited, more powerful, as it leached from his skin, seeping into my pores. My body tingled in anticipation and my back arched even farther, pressing my breast farther into his mouth.

My eyelids fluttered in my desire and a thick strand of magick winding itself around our bodies. Powerful. Strong. Binding us together. The magick was pleased with our union, and it thrilled me, from my core, knowing that I would be able to control its power.

Suddenly, I heard my father's voice.

Katarina, be careful. Do not fall into the temptation of power. Follow your heart. Cara mia, stay true to your heart and love will provide. Then you will truly be powerful.

I snapped back from my trance. What was I doing? How could I have let things go so far? My father was right. I could not be lured into a life that was not true to my heart. It was not my path. It was not the way. I relaxed my body, creating space between Alessandro and myself.

"We must stop," I said. "There are rules to our joining. We mustn't keep going."

"You didn't seem so concerned about those rules moments ago," he responded as he continued to nibble my breast. I cupped his face in my hands and lifted him up until our gaze met.

"Don't worry," I said. "There will be plenty of time for that." I brought his face close to mine and gently rubbed our cheeks together, then, dragging my lips across the landscape of his features, I paused when our mouths lined up.

Our lips barely touched. With care, I slipped my tongue out just into the opening of his lips, slowly sliding it across the edge of his top teeth. I could feel him losing himself in my control.

"Soon," I said, "the hand-fasting ceremony will be done. We must wait until then."

I could feel his acknowledgment of what I had said, and I knew that what we had started was coming to a close.

"Yes," he conceded. "Soon you'll be mine. I'll be yours. And I promise you, I'll show you that I'm not so difficult to love."

~

THE MEMORY FADED like a cloud on the wind, and I inhaled deeply. My history with Alessandro was just one of the many histories seeping back into my consciousness now that Gio had released me from my prison. I opened my eyes and looked over at Claire and Willem, only to find them staring at the marketplace below. They hadn't noticed my lapse at all.

"Do you think there'll be someone down there willing to help us?" Claire asked.

"I do," Willem spoke confidently. "There's bound to be someone who can tell us something. Someone who knows more about what Alessandro has called up, and what we can do to stop it. That sort of energy doesn't just manifest itself."

"Then what are we waiting for?" I asked.

Guilt from my recent memory hung over me. But there's a point in every woman's life when she must stop blaming others and stop lying to herself. A moment in which she must admit that she is responsible for more than she has alluded to. A defining moment when she must admit who she was, or perhaps, who she really is.

As I stood on the ledge overlooking the Strega underground, the recent recall of my life with Alessandro clinging to me like an oil slick, I knew that for me, that time was now. I may not have been responsible for Alessandro's actions, but I was responsible for my own. I had flirted with darkness, let him touch and caress my body, even *enjoyed* it. And it was those very actions that could cost me the respect of the only friends I had. I had to tell them. They had to know. I refused to continue until they knew what my real part was in this story. They had to know who it was they were helping.

"Before we head down there," I said turning to look at them. "There's something I need to tell you."

They looked at each other with nervous eyes. Claire reached out and took Willem's fingers into her own.

"It's time you knew," I said.

"Knew what?" Claire choked out.

"Know who I really am ... what I'm capable of."

Chapter Nine

GIO

We entered the tavern. It was the same as the last time I was here with Claire, though instead of just Patrick sitting at the bar, there were several others that I could only assume were Watchers, given the setting, scattered throughout. Their chatter ceased as we walked up to the bar.

"We need to see Rose," Patrick said to the bartender. "It's urgent."

A couple of women sitting at a table nearby whispered to each other. Though they spoke in hushed tones far below the level any human ear could detect, their words appeared in my head as clear as if they had been spoken directly to me.

"That's him," the blonde one said. "The one assigned to Claire."

"*He's* the one," the other responded. "Whoa, if I was Claire, I'd be all over that ... forget the assignment."

"Right? He's gorgeous. But seriously, you better be careful of what you say," the blonde one continued. "I heard that the Strega he saved is part of the Ilmalo line. They're known for their revenge magick, you know."

"What a waste," her friend said. "He could have any woman he wanted, and he's with that abomination."

Anger flared white hot. Who the hell were they to judge? But this wasn't the time or place. Still a quick retort couldn't hurt, a little something to warn them. I called the energy of the earth below me to ground myself. I took a deep breath and turned, planning to confront them, when Patrick grabbed my arm.

"We don't have time for that. Let's go."

Patrick's firm grip brought me back to reason. With haste, we headed to the rear of the bar where Rose's quarters were located. My skin crawled. I didn't like being back here. It reminded me of how far I'd come, and how far I still had to go. I shifted from side to side, my body incapable of being still.

"We're wasting time," I snapped; my patience running thin. "Every moment we stand here, Katarina is slipping further and further away."

"I know," Patrick's expression was serious. "Don't think for one minute that I don't understand what's on the line. You're not the only person who's got someone to lose."

My breath hitched and my mind reeled. Claire. I pursed my lips. I knew there was something more between the two of them. There was something in his aura that told me a part of his soul was missing. How could I have been unsure before? I pushed out energetically toward him and gasped when his emotions consumed me.

"Hey, mind your own business," he said as he quickly shut me out.

"I—I'm sorry," I said, a ball lodged in my throat. I didn't mean to."

"Maybe not," he replied. "But we can't have you in places you don't belong, now can we? So why don't you worry about controlling those newfound powers."

I shook my head, releasing the last bits of his residual

emotion. Holy shit. Patrick was completely in love with Claire. So much so that my heart ached for him. I felt his sorrow, his regret, and understood every bit of it. My soul had been incomplete for lifetimes, how could I not? But there was also a sadness to it, and an acceptance, that went deep.

During the time Willem, Claire, and I spent together before breaking the curse, I had watched as the two had become closer and closer. I had hoped Willem would be able to overcome his stigmas and let himself love again. Because all those feelings Claire had felt had been so real and true ... and obvious. Even in my human form, I had known. Claire was in love with Willem.

And Patrick knew it, too.

As I stood there looking at Patrick, an intense amount of emotion for this man welled within me. He loved her, and he had let her go. He had put her happiness ahead of his own. His love was unconditional. Every bit of me ached. We had more in common than I thought.

"Don't, mate," Patrick said coldly, as if reading my mind. "Just ... don't. The only thing I've ever wanted is for her to be happy. If that means your friend Willem, then I won't try to stop it. If he can love her like she deserves to be loved, so be it. I'll step into the background."

He turned his face so that he was looking directly at me, though I knew there was no physical way he could see me.

"But in matters of her physical safety," he continued, his voice ominous, "well, I don't know him well enough to trust him capable with that."

"As you should, Patrick. Watchers always look after each other."

The sound of a familiar voice filled the room. Startled, I swung around to where Rose stood beyond the small doorway.

"I hope you have a plan for bringing my granddaughter back safely." I flinched at the intensity of her piercing eyes.

"Lady Rose," Patrick spoke steadily. "We will find and bring Claire back safely. I promise you that."

"The question wasn't for you. Of your intentions, there are no doubts."

I met Rose's gaze and held it with my own. "We will find her, Rose. And bring her home. You can trust me."

A heavy silence filled the room until Rose gave me a curt nod.

"Very well. I hope you will be to keep your word." She paused. "Be careful, Patrick," Rose said. "There are things at play you cannot control."

"That may be true," he replied, "but I believe that Gio may be the game changer no one was expecting."

"I'm listening." Rose's voice held the same intense tone. It charged the air in the room, electricity crackling with every word.

Patrick gestured to me to explain what had happened when my body was lying in the hospital bed. I nodded, relaying the events clearly and accurately as I was certain she was in no mood for misunderstandings. When I had finished, her expression had changed. It was softer. Less like she wanted to throw a dagger at me.

"It seems," she said, "that you have fallen into the good graces of the Goddess. The reasons why, I cannot say, but it is not my duty to explain the decisions of our Mother. However, I will say this." She took three large strides toward me, positioning herself just inches from me. "Just as Claire was charged to watch over you in your time of need, you are to her. I am tasking her life into your hands. Do not disappoint. Are we clear?"

Whether it was my newly-gained powers or the fact that Rose wanted to impress her abilities upon me, I'm not sure.

But I could see the magick emanating from her body. It radiated in hot waves of red and orange and sparked as it dissipated to the edges of the room.

"Patrick"—her voice was harsh— "you are to go with him. Take Rowan. She will guide you in matters unknown and can help *him* get control over his *gifts*." And then, just as abruptly as she came, she turned to leave. She stopped as she reached the small doorway but didn't turn around.

"Claire's mission is over." Her voice was steady, strong. "She did what she was supposed to do. I don't care about anything else. Bring back my granddaughter." She shot a look at both of us. "Make sure it happens."

She disappeared past the threshold into the darkness, the door closing behind her. The silence in the room extended for what felt like eternity.

"What you have to understand is that Claire is not only Rose's granddaughter, Gio. She's the Chosen One. As much as she'll deny it, Claire is the one that will lead us into the next phase of our existence."

"I'm sorry, the Chosen—"

"Not here," Patrick interrupted. "I'll explain in more detail, but first, let's go find Rowan. We've got a long journey ahead of us, and there's no time to waste."

I couldn't argue with him there. I was ready to get out of there A.S.A.P. We left the tavern, and I headed back to the apartment to gather a few things while Patrick went to track down Rowan. As I entered the apartment, I wavered. I stood in the empty space, letting the keys fall from my hand. They clattered onto the wooden side table.

My heart ached. I brought my hands to my chest and pressed down. It was the first time that I'd been alone since I had awakened in the hospital. I had hoped that I would've opened my eyes and she would've been sitting there, waiting for me. She would have been holding my hand as my blurred vision came into focus; her voice would have been the first thing I'd heard.

I walked over to my trunk and flipped open the lid. I searched through the stacks of journals until I came across the one with the faded blue binding, a thick strand of leather wrapped around it, holding it closed.

As I unwound the strap, I knew it had been decades since I last dared open this one. How could I? That lifetime had haunted my dreams for years. My fingers trembled as I carefully opened to the first entry.

December 20, 1927

The time that I have spent with her is more than I can bear, yet not near what I crave. She is my everything. She is my forever.

Today, we met at Carlo's for a drink. Goddess above, she is as beautiful as I remember. Even more so, if that is possible. My heart aches for her, but we must be careful. I am not sure if Alessandro is near ....

I sat on the dusty floor of my apartment and read the entry. It was the only other time I had almost saved her ... almost. My mind fell into the past.

The year was 1927. I knew Katarina lived somewhere in the middle of America. I had been tracking her for some time. I could feel her presence. The invisible thread that bound us together held strong and guided me through the varied landscapes, closer and closer to her.

At that time, Willem and I had traveled together. Times were different then. It was more difficult to be separated for weeks and months without any communication. The risk of finding her and keeping her safe before Alessandro got his hands on her was much higher than it had ever been.

I arrived in St. Louis on a warm afternoon in early July. Independence Day celebrations had been over nearly a week, but the town was still festive, with flags and ribbons hanging from store windows.

Being unfamiliar with the area, Willem had asked a stodgy store clerk where we could be accommodated. He pointed us in the direction of the Buckingham Hotel. The place had been around for many years and was accustomed to keeping long-term residents. It would gladly take in two weary travelers. As we made our way through the warm summer streets, I became more and more excited.

"This is it, Willem," I said. "I can feel it. My Katarina is here."

My eyes darted from person to person expecting to find my love in their faces.

"Calm yourself," Willem whispered. "Even if she is here, you must not forget that Alessandro is also most likely nearby. It worries me that he always seems to be one step ahead of us. Something's not right about that..." he rubbed his chin in thought, "I just don't know what. In any case, try to remain calm. And keep your voice down. You can't risk anyone hearing you."

We checked into our rooms and dined in the hotel restaurant. The Victorian-style curtains were a deep maroon and trimmed in gold. The art deco tables and chairs highlighted the popular architectural style of the time.

Prohibition was well into its reign in America at that time, but there were always those who fought against it. And it was those types of people who were of value to my cause. They were the people who knew things and could make things happen. People who lived on the outskirts of polite society. Over the years, they were becoming increasingly easy to spot. It had been my experience that becoming friends with these types of people was not only beneficial but imperative in my quest.

Over the next several weeks, I made friends with a small

group of gentlemen who partook in activities the rest of society pretended didn't exist. The speakeasy, though publicly deplored by the average citizen, was the not-so-secret haven where everyone gathered. All the while, I kept my eyes open for my dearest Katarina. Though the feeling that she was near grew stronger every day, I was unable to catch a glimpse of her.

Five months had passed and still there was no sign. If it had not been for our connection, I would've doubted she was there at all. But I had to remain patient. The Goddess had a plan for everything. Willem kept himself busy by focusing on collecting the ingredients needed to make the serum. This was always challenging since we never knew the exact location we were headed to, but I was thankful that Willem's brand of magick was focused on herbalism and potions. There was no plant substitution he couldn't figure out.

It was a cold evening in early December before I even stole my first glance at her. By that time, I had made a well-established speakeasy, run by my friend Carlo, my regular haunt.

That night I was sitting in my regular booth in the corner of the dark room. It was both farthest from and facing the entrance. A small bench set against the wall with an old wooden table was the extent of it, but it was comfortable, nonetheless. A rusted metal chair sat on the other side of the table opposite me. The faint smell of kerosene from the many lanterns dimly lighting the place flitted through the air. A couple of old wooden casks with chairs around each one had been set up to create tables throughout the darkened basement.

The bar itself was makeshift as well, but by far the nicest piece of furniture in the space. A carpenter by trade, Carlo had spent several hours constructing the solid piece that separated the bartender from the customers. Several mirrors were placed on the wall behind, of all different sizes and shapes, creating a reflective mural of secret drinkers.

In 1927, the speakeasy was not a place where you'd find your everyday, God-fearing man or woman, but as prohibition trudged along, it was becoming increasingly popular to sneak away to these underground watering holes. I had no intention of seeing Katarina there.

Yet, suddenly, one night, there she was. As soon as she took off her coat, I knew it was her. She looked exactly as I remembered. Possibly more beautiful. Her long dark hair was cropped in a short bob that framed her face. From my spot in the corner, I could see how the green and gold flecks sparkled in her eyes like a hidden treasure. She wore a low waist dress and fashionable French heels. Her red lips were a perfect bow.

My breath caught as she confidently walked up to the bar.

"What's a gal gotta do to get a Manhattan around here?" She smiled teasing Carlo, whose attention had been with some gentlemen at the other end of the bar. Carlo turned around and looked at Katarina, his eyes widened in surprise.

"Kathleen! What are you doing in here?" He jumped the bar and ran over to her, swooping her up in a big hug. "Do your parents know you're here? Oh, my God! How's New York? How's school? Are you back for good? Hey, everybody! My cousin's back from the big city!"

Carlo gave her another big hug before finally allowing her to answer the questions that he'd asked.

"Goodness, Carlo," she exclaimed, "let me catch my breath! How about you get me that drink and we can find a place to catch up?"

Katarina, now Kathleen, backed up against the bar and began looking around. I couldn't take my eyes off her. As her gaze made its way around the room, it found mine in the corner. Our eyes locked, and in that instant, there were only two people in that bar—she and I.

Carlo brought Kathleen her drink and led her away to the back. Immediately my body became anxious. Where had he taken her? When would they return? I tried to be patient, but now that I had seen her, I didn't want to let her out of my sight. I forced myself to remain in my seat and tried to look casual.

"Gio, I'd like to introduce you to my cousin," Carlo said from above my shoulder. "Kathleen, come here. I want you to meet a friend of mine."

I looked up and saw them both standing behind me. I stood.

"It's a pleasure to meet you, Kathleen." The name felt strange coming out of my mouth, but there was no mistaking that the woman who stood in front of me was my one true love.

And we hit it off famously. Just as I knew we would. Over the next two weeks we became closer. I was amazed at the ease of how comfortable it was to be with her. Carlo, though protective, appeared to approve of our time spent together and was helpful in setting up moments when we could sneak away from the prying eyes of nosy patrons.

It was Christmas Eve when I heard a panicked knock on my door at the hotel. I opened it to find Kathleen, hair disheveled, eyes red and puffy. Tear stains streaked down her cheeks.

"What's wrong? What's happened?" Instinctively, I drew her into my room, closing the door firmly behind her and locking the deadbolt.

"I'm sorry," she whispered as she stood near the bed. "I thought I had left him behind." Her voice was distant.

"Who? Who are you talking about?" I asked, urgency rising in my tone, though I certainly knew who she meant. There was only one person she could mean.

"Alexander," she said, "my ex-boyfriend from New York."

She looked down, unable to meet my eyes. "I— I should've mentioned him before. I'm so sorry." Tears began to stream down her face. "He, um, he ... wanted things from me. He was very assertive. Persuasive. I ... um, I became *involved* with him, but it was too much, it wasn't right. He wanted more. I was trapped. One night, after dinner, I slipped some laudanum in his wine. After he passed out, I snuck out. I had some money hidden and was able to escape and come here. I'd never mentioned my home before. How could he know? I'd thought he'd forget about me. I never thought he'd come searching."

Rage boiled up in my heart at the thought of Alessandro having his way with her ... again. It was too bad she hadn't thought to overdose him with the opiate. Like it would have made any difference; he was cursed just like me. He would live for as long as life continued and beyond.

"Kathleen," I said, cupping her face in my hands and tilting it up toward mine, "you have nothing to be ashamed of. None of this changes my opinion of you. I— I love you."

I brought her lips to mine, kissing them fully. Her response was immediate. She brought her hands to the back of my head, her fingers running through my hair.

"I love you too," she said in between kisses. "I know we've only just met, but I feel as if I've known you my whole life."

Our kisses became stronger, more intense, as passion grew within our bodies. I could feel her breasts through her thin blouse, and as she pressed against me, I felt myself harden in response. My lips found her neck as she offered it to me, my tongue tasting her sweet skin with every caress.

Slowly her hands found the front of my shirt. She unbuttoned each button until she was able to slip it off my body. I quickly removed the white undershirt and stood there, half-naked, quivering on the inside as her hands rubbed my chest, exploring every part of my torso.

There was nothing more that I wanted than to be with

her, but the serum wasn't complete. I knew that if there was any chance to break the spell Katarina was under, I couldn't take it any farther than it was now.

"Come away with me," I blurted.

She blinked. "Come away with you? Where?"

"Does it matter? We could leave St. Louis tonight. Go west. Head to California and start a new life together. I'll get a job there. Why not? Leave Aless—ander behind and never look back. What do you say?"

The silence ticked on for what seemed like an eternity. Finally, she nodded.

"Yes," she said kissing me again. "Yes!"

Just then an alarm blared. We stood frozen, our bodies pressed against each other, and waited as the loud, tinny sound echoed around us.

"What's that for?" she asked.

"You stay here," I told her. "I'm going to go find out what's going on." I threw on my shirt and went to the door. "You make sure you lock this behind me, okay?"

Kathleen nodded.

I left the room and headed down the hallway. As other residents of the hotel were coming out of their rooms, the corridor became more and more crowded. Suddenly, I felt it. At first, it was just a small tug on the line that bound me to my love. Quickly, the small tug grew stronger and stronger letting me know I needed to get back to her at once. My heart lurched and I turned around. As I fought my way back to my room through the crowds of people, I smelled smoke. Panic flashed through me. This was all wrong.

When I got back to my room, my stomach roiled. The door had been kicked in.

"Kathleen!" I yelled, searching the room.

"Now, don't you mean Katarina?" The voice from behind slithered up my spine into my ears.

I knew whose it was. With a deliberate motion, I turned around to see Alessandro standing in the hall, just outside the room. He leaned against the opposite wall, a knife in one hand and a handkerchief in the other. My stomach clenched.

"Now, don't get all mopey on me, Gio," he mused. "I haven't killed her … yet." His head tilted as a sick smile tugged at his mouth. "I'll let you see her once more. For old times' sake. Follow me."

He turned and walked down the hall.

I hated him. For a moment, I considered what would happen if I just came at him from behind, tackled him, took his knife and slit his throat. As much satisfaction I knew it would give me in that moment, I couldn't even bear to imagine the feeling that would consume me if Katarina died because of it, not if there was still a chance that I could save her.

And he *knew* it. He knew I wouldn't do anything to harm him if she was still alive. The halls were clearing out as he led me to a small utility closet just beyond the housekeeping room.

"I'll give you one minute to say your goodbyes. Then, I suppose, I'll see you the next time around. I must admit, Gio, I've been growing quite fond of our little game here. You make things so … lively." He clicked his tongue.

"Unfortunately, in this life, the bitch got the jump on me. She's getting craftier, that's for sure. You almost had her," he growled as his eyes grew dark. "Almost."

He swung open the small door. Katarina lay on the floor, hands and feet tied with strips of sheets. A thick piece of burlap was shoved in her mouth. She was dripping wet. My mind raced. Something about the room reminded me of the speakeasy, though I couldn't quite place it.

"Katarina!" I cried as I took a step forward. Alessandro put up his hand.

"Uh, uh, uh," he cooed. "I never said you could get close to her. I just said you could say your goodbyes."

I looked at Katarina. Her chest was heaving, eyes wide. A calf for the slaughter, she was terrified.

"My love, I'm here," I said, my voice cracking at the edges. I wanted to reassure her that everything would be okay, but I knew that would be a lie.

"Very good, Gio, very good," Alessandro said, a smug look on his face as he pulled a cigar from his pocket and lit it. "There's no reason to lie to the poor girl. She's been through enough ... don't you think?"

"You *will* pay for this," I spat at him.

"My friend, that's a bit played out now, don't you think? You know that the only person who will pay for this is Katarina. Unless, of course, you concede and let me have her. I mean, if you truly love her ..."

"The only way she will be with you is if she chooses to be. And I think you know by now that she would rather die than be with you."

Alessandro's eyes flashed red. For an instant, they stormed, his evil fully in control.

"So be it," he said as he flicked his cigar at Katarina.

Instantly, she caught fire.

"No!" I screamed as I finally recognized what was familiar. Kerosene. He had doused her with it, waiting for his opportunity to ignite it. I rushed toward her, but Alessandro held up his hand and an energy force held me still. I couldn't move. He held me captive as I watched her burn, her screams clawing at my heart.

"I know, I know," Alessandro continued, "it's quite cliché ... burning a witch and all. But there's something about fire overpowering even the most powerful ... so romantic. Serves her right for thinking she could escape."

Katarina's body writhed and twisted. Her screams rang in my ears as her body burned. I smelled her flesh as it charred, her entire form turning black and crusty like a piece of coal. My stomach hurled. It didn't take long for her to stop moving. I watched with blurred vision until she twitched one last time.

"You better give yourself some time to get out of here," Alessandro said as he released me from his energy and casually walked past me. "You know, before the whole place goes up. Not that it would make a difference."

I fell on all fours and heaved. No. No, not again. Frantically, I searched for something to cover her body with a sheet, a blanket, anything, but the whole room was in flames now. I knew that although I could not die in the fire, it would hurt like hell. And Katarina was already dead. There was nothing I could do. As the flames spread out, I thought about letting them consume me. If only they would, but I knew better. I had to get out. It couldn't end like this.

I TOSSED my head back and closed the journal, returning to the present. I sat quietly in the apartment, my eyes closed and let the horror fade away. I took a deep breath. Fire. I wasn't sure how, exactly, but there was something about fire that could beat Alessandro. What was it he had said?

There's something about fire overpowering even the most powerful...

I wrapped the strip of leather tightly around the memories binding them inside the worn book. I checked the time. I had to get moving.

I stood and collected a few more of my belongings before heading downstairs. Patrick would be ready to go, and I didn't want any more holdups. It was time to leave. I locked up the apartment and headed downstairs to the street. The sun was just beginning to set, and I shuddered as I looked up at the streaks of red painting the sky like blood on the horizon.

Chapter Ten

KATARINA

"Katarina," Claire began, "you can't blame yourself for Alessandro's actions. It isn't your fault that he's a murderous bastard."

I wasn't sure I believed her, but it was still nice to hear. I was barely able to get through the story; the embarrassment and shame were still clearly present. Still, after so many years. Of course, somewhere deep inside me I knew I was not responsible for Alessandro's actions, but somewhere deeper told me that I should have known better.

"Claire's right," Willem chimed in. "I may not be the best person to get advice from in matters concerning love, but I do know this: we all make our own choices. Just as you made a choice to believe in love, to sacrifice your world for love, Alessandro made a choice when he realized you had left him. He's the one who decided to use love as revenge.

"We all make choices, and we all have to live with the consequences." Willem looked me straight in the eye at these last words. "This is not your fault."

I was unsure if it was intentional or not, but the way his gaze penetrated my soul sent chills down my spine. Knowing what Willem had lost to help Gio through the centuries, I felt compelled to respect that feeling. Even if I knew he didn't still trust me completely.

He was, after all, one of the Onesta. It was no secret that the Strega Onesta and Strega Ilmalo bore a deep-rooted animosity toward each other. It was a rift that had begun well before my time. From my brief understanding of Willem's past, his family were among the Onesta elders. There was no mistaking his foundational beliefs of my people. We were, by ancestral allegiance, somewhat enemies.

I was a descendant of the Strega Ilmalo. And powerful blood line mixing magick and sorcery. Just as Willem had been taught about us, I had been taught about the Onesta ... with one exception.

My father was an Onesta defector. And while Onesta rarely accepted those of the Ilmalo back into their fold, the Ilmalo took every opportunity to acquire more followers. And turn them. Knowing that my father had publicly renounced the very clan that formed and shaped him, all in the name of love for my mother, was evidence for me that love, indeed, was the strongest power in the world.

So, when my elders spoke with disdain of the Onesta, I just couldn't accept it. I could never really accept that the Onesta's ways were detrimental to all Strega, that their desire to use their powers to help all of society would one day lead to the eradication of our kind. Though my father denounced the ways of the Onesta, I had always suspected it was only because his desire to be with my mother was far greater than his desire to uphold traditions that did not make sense to the love that he held deep in his heart.

I was destined to be caught between belief systems. However, my mother's passing at childbirth, left my father to raise me and become one of my most influential teachers. I remember the day I had questioned his loyalty to the Ilmalo.

"Father, how can you do nothing?" I had yelled when I entered our tent one night. Peiro, the father of one of my friends, had been taken by the church and accused of practicing witchcraft. "You have to do something!"

"Katarina," he calmly replied, "there is nothing that can be done. To help him would expose the rest of us and go against the natural law. Have you thought that Piero should not have been practicing like he was?"

"How can you even say that? He is one of our own!"

My father approached and sat me down on my bed. He situated himself next to me, his voice steady. Energy radiated from him, each word a tight bundle of white light.

"My dear girl," he began in hushed tones, "there are some things that are difficult to explain, but I want you to hear my words with an open heart ... with a heart that I know is half of mine. The fundamental teachings of our Goddess, our queen, are based in nature. We must abide by the rules of natural law. We must use our power to better the world. To help each other, that is one of our most sacred vows." He took a deep breath. "I know this is hard to understand. Piero is a friend. But he used his power for no good deed. His magick went against nature. He was careless and caused much pain to the humans he met."

I listened in silence.

"Yes, we have it in our power to manipulate that which is around us, to create our own fate, if you will, but just because we *can* do such things doesn't mean we *should*. The intentions we send out will come back to us many times over. This was the true way of the Strega before Onesta and Ilmalo existed. This is La Vecchia Religione. The Old Way, the way it is supposed to be."

Piero's capture had hurt, but I knew what my father told me was truth. I took a deep breath and nodded.

"You are special, mia cara. You are different. You hold both the old ways and a new line in your veins. The moment I held you in my arms, I felt your life energy pulse stronger than anyone I had ever met. That is what makes you special. That is what makes you powerful. You have abilities that are beyond most Strega. You also have the blood of balance and truth to keep you grounded."

~

I BLINKED and brought myself out of my reverie. The blood of truth. I was still trying to figure out what that meant. Perhaps if Gio and I had been able to run away together centuries ago, I would have figured it out. The thought of Gio deflated my heart in my chest and left a void in my soul. I looked from Claire to Willem.

"Regardless of the choices Alessandro or I made, Gio was an innocent in this. He was not, *is not*, one of us. The Goddess should have spared him. She just ... has to."

The words hung in the air. At least there was one thing we all agreed on. Gio should not have been mixed up in this. He should have been free of this hell a long time ago.

Claire looked over the underground city, an overwhelmed expression on her face.

"It's so dense down there. I wouldn't even know where to begin," she said quietly.

I looked out over the expanse. It was stuffed to capacity, people squeezing past each other along the thick primitive buildings. A thin layer of smoke hung just above the make-shift city, lending it mystery.

I dove back into the depths of my memory and tried to connect with my past. My mind swam past hundreds of years of information till it found the origins of my existence. I concentrated. If I were a revenge-stricken Strega, where would I go if I wanted to learn more about the dark? I opened myself up energetically. A small jolt hit a nerve as I realized that thought hit a little too close to the truth. My eyes scanned the perimeter of the city below until my gaze found a section of small marketplace tucked into the corner of the expanse.

"There," I said as I pointed to where my gazed stopped. "We start there."

"How do you know?" Claire asked.

"I don't," I answered back. "Not for sure. But there's something about that area that calls to me."

In truth, I had no idea why, I was still getting used to my capabilities, but there was a reason my eyes were drawn to that corner. It was like my gaze was led to that spot by an invisible ribbon tugging gently to its destination. And I had to start trusting my intuition.

My answer seemed to be enough for Claire and Willem to accept.

"Let's go," Willem replied as he started on the trail down the side of the mountain that led directly into the center of the underworld.

THE JOURNEY down the mountain was longer than any of us had anticipated. The narrow path was uneven, leaving little room for error in our steps. Claire followed Willem closely while I trailed behind. Focused on the road ahead, nobody spoke.

I was thankful for the silence. It gave me time with my thoughts. Though I had only shown anger and hate toward Alessandro, another emotion kept peering out more over the past few days. Now, it pained me to admit it.

Grief.

Unlike anger and hate, with their many grasping arms like black, sticky tentacles, grief left me with nothing to hold onto.

It was the misty air on a bright, sunny morning, confusing and frustrating to accept.

After the night Gio was stabbed, everything began coming back. When the intimate memories of Alessandro and I began to resurface, anger was the emotion that held me together. Anger, like hate, was easy ... simple. It made sense. It was the anger that kept me from dissolving. And it propelled me to its partner, hate. Together they kept me from crumbling into myself, from falling apart, from the realization that I had been abused on such an intimate level, in such a manipulative way.

Perhaps, that is where the grief had come from. Slowly emerging from the ruins of my soul, revealing itself only when I accepted that Alessandro had used me in the worst possible betrayal, a sick and twisted planned obsolescence.

It would have been easier to reconcile the abuse if he had only shown me violence and cruelty. But as the days passed by since I returned to myself, I could see past my anger and hate, into the memories that I did not want to admit; the ones of Alex and Kate Martins as husband and wife ... happy.

I remembered the long walks, running through the rain hand in hand, cooking together on Sunday afternoons, backpacking through Costa Rica ... laughing. There were so many moments of laughter. The sheer happiness of those moments cut my heart into pieces.

Those feelings had been real. As much as I refused to admit it, they still were.

Because in this lifetime, he had shown me love. In more than one lifetime, he had shown me that he cared for me. Why would he do that? Why would he hide his control and hate in soft moments that had made me happy? What was the point? Tears stung my eyes as I relived the emotions. I blinked them back.

I shook my head hard, hoping the memories would fall out permanently.

I hated it. I hated that all I could see in Alessandro was the many layers of his deceit, and beneath all the hatred that bound me, there was true sadness. Betrayal. How could he have done that to me? How could he have led me to believe I loved him? Played on my emotions and tricked me into feeling things that still echoed truth. He *knew* who I was, he *knew* I did not want him, and still he made me believe that I loved him, that he loved me, that he was the other half of my soul. He had stolen a piece of who I was and made it his. It was a piece I would never get back.

If he had just simply hated me, if he had just made me suffer, it would have made so much more sense. I could understand that. But to make me believe we belonged together? To show me kindness? To reveal his own vulnerabilities? It was an abuse far worse than any evil he could conjure, a calculated exploitation. And a grotesque truth hit me square in the face. I had given myself willingly to him for all those years.

And enjoyed it.

It was too much to fathom. My heart rate increased, and my throat constricted until air was barely passing through. I brought my hands up to my neck, my fingers clawing at its base trying to open the airway from the outside while my soul scraped and scratched from the inside, desperate to escape the horrific nightmare I would now carry with me forever.

It made no difference that a part of my sadness felt sorry for him. I would never forgive what he had taken from me. And for it, he would suffer ten times what I had.

At that passing thought, I felt my throat open, my heart slowed down, and a familiar burning stirred. I was grateful that anger and hate were there to offer their hand again. I pushed the grief away to make room for my old friends. I'd deal with the tears later.

"Katarina, we're here." Claire's voice broke through my thoughts bringing me back to the trail. Thank God.

I looked around. A black iron gate stood at the entrance of the city. I reached for the latch and lifted it without reservation.

"Let's go," I said as I led the way, not wanting to spend any more time in my head, not when Claire and Willem were close behind.

We wound around the many stalls that housed vendors selling their goods. Had this been above ground with the sunlight streaming down, a cool breeze the only savior to break the heat, it would've very much resembled the Farmer's Market that popped up every Sunday in Freestone from Spring to Fall. However, upon closer inspection, I noticed that along with the various fruits and vegetables, many stalls also had an assortment of dried herbs and oils, amulets and charms. The scent of frankincense and bay laurel wafted from the low window, talismans hung from their window boxes.

As I walked, I was pulled along by an invisible rope that was tied around my waist. It was automatic, I didn't have to think. My feet, guided by a greater power, stepped one after the other for about a half mile as we twisted and turned through the street until they stopped in front of a hut with a small door and a thatched roof.

"Here," I whispered. "We need to go in here."

Willem looked concerned.

"I think you're right about this one," he conceded. "I feel it too."

Claire stepped up behind me and placed her hand on my shoulder.

"I feel it too," she said, scarcely audible. "Though I didn't notice it until you pointed it out."

The hut was pulsing with power. Someone either very old or very influential was inside. To me, the power felt like a cold drink on a hot afternoon. My body instinctively wanted to guzzle it down. Willem and Claire, on the other hand, appeared to feel differently. I could tell by the rigidity of Willem's body and the stiffness in Claire's stance.

Though they both acknowledged and respected the power's existence, they were uncomfortable where they stood. It took me a second to realize the reason behind it. The power came from a Strega Ilmalo.

"Do you think you'll be able to go in?" I asked.

"Well, if you think we're letting you go in alone, you're crazy." Willem looked at me in disbelief.

I gave him a smile.

"Of course," I said.

I walked up to the door of the hut and knocked.

The wooden door at the hut's entrance was old and splintered. There was a small ornate window near the top, which I could only assume was used as a peephole of sorts. We waited in silence for someone to answer.

Nothing.

"Maybe, we missed—" Claire began but was interrupted by male voice from the other side.

"Who are you? What do you want?" the voice called through the door.

I looked from Willem to Claire.

"You better answer him, Katarina," Willem spoke in hushed tones. "I have a feeling that your Ilmalo blood is worth more than gold here."

I nodded. If there was one thing the Strega Ilmalo valued, it was bloodline. I just hoped that my blood was still strong enough to get our questions answered.

"My name is Katarina, daughter of Antonia, granddaughter of the Ilmalo elder Dante, leader of the Second Clan." I spoke my original title loudly through the door. I had no idea if this man would accept my name as value, would even know who I was, but I had to try. I steadied my voice and threw as much strength into it as I could before finishing. "And what I want is quite simple. I am here for answers."

The window at the top of the door opened and a set of green eyes peered through.

"It can't be … impossible …" The man's voice trailed off when we made eye contact. His breath hitched.

The window in the door slammed shut and the sound of several locks and latches being undone was heard through the wooded barrier. I glanced back at Willem and Claire.

"That's the first time I've heard you speak your full name," Claire said quietly.

"It appears to have had some effect," I replied, nodding to the sound behind the door.

"It was powerful," Willem commented. "Your name meant something … at least it did to him."

The wooden door opened wide. Standing in the archway was a man, mid-fifties, dressed in a pair of contemporary khakis and a baby blue polo. My brow furrowed.

"What?" he said as he studied my face. "Not what you were expecting? Well, let me assure you that you were the last person I was expecting today. Come in, please. And hurry! Before anyone sees you." He stepped aside and gestured into the hut.

We scrambled in at the invitation. As dilapidated as the hut was on the outside, the inside was the exact opposite. The interior was clean, the walls painted a pristine white. The furniture, quite modern with its sharp lines and sleek design, was covered in black leather and accented with red throw pillows and tablecloths. An industrial chandelier hung from a vaulted ceiling in the center of the room. In one corner stood a glossy black grand piano. In the other, a quiet Zen-like fountain.

Willem and Claire slowly took in the surroundings. It was

clear, by the shape of their wide eyes, that they were also anticipating something much different. I smiled. I had forgotten about the Ilmalo's love for beautiful objects. Of course, there would be magick cast to raise this home up to their opulent standards.

"Please sit, make yourselves comfortable," the well-groomed Ilmalo motioned to the couch. "My name is Matteo. This is my home."

"Thank you for seeing us."

"I'm sorry for my rudeness at the door, you just never know ... To be fair, I had no idea that you were an actual real person. I thought you were just a story my parents told me to warn me against falling in love with a *human*," Matteo said.

He said the word human as if it had spikes on it, shredding his tongue as it left his mouth. Out of the corner of my eye, I noticed Willem lean forward to shield Claire. Claire instinctively placed her hand on his leg, signaling to him that she was fine. Matteo also noticed.

"Speaking of human, isn't this interesting. But not a typical human, are you?" He directed his attention over to the couple who now both sat up in attention. Matteo sniffed at them. "I cannot imagine what the three of you have come here for."

"Like I said, we've come for answers," I said again as I caught and held his gaze.

"And what makes you think I have any for you?" he replied.

I decided that this would be an excellent opportunity to test my power of persuasion. If it was a pissing contest he wanted, a pissing contest he'd get. I stared directly at Matteo and continued to lock his eyes with mine. Reaching back into the depths of my brain I found the spark of influence I was looking for. Putting all my intention into my gaze, I willed him to think and to feel what I wanted him to. I willed him to submit to my dominance.

It was surprising how easy it was to access that part of me. Like riding a bicycle. I smiled. There was no way to compare such a whimsical activity to what was essentially mind control.

As I continued to force my thoughts, Matteo strained against the suggestions I was planting. He tried to resist, but he was no match for me. Enough was enough. That should teach him. I eased my thoughts out slowly. It was just a little taste of what I could do, and he knew it. Matteo broke eye contact first, giving me a small personal victory.

"Fine," he stammered as he took a handkerchief from his pocket and dabbed the sweat beading along his brow, "I'll tell you whatever you want."

"And the truth of it too," Willem added.

I'd almost forgotten he and Claire were there with me. I wasn't even sure that they knew what I'd done. I blinked and tried to cover how startled I was at his voice. I made a mental note to not let myself fall that deep again.

"Fine, whatever you want. Let's just get this over with."

"Someone has been accessing old magick and I want to know how it's being done," I said matter-of-factly.

I could tell by the tic in his jaw that he knew something, but I sat patiently as he worked up the nerve to say it. He let out a low sigh.

"You're right. Someone is tapping into something old and dark, but I don't know who it is." He paused and took the moment to once more pat his brow. When he spoke again, it was with caution. "About a year ago, my brother, Josh, was in an ... *accident*. He was attacked, his body looked as if it had been beaten with a large hammer, severely bludgeoned. The internal injuries were serious. Human doctors couldn't do anything; the trauma was too great. The Strega couldn't do anything ..." His voice trailed off into the memory before snapping back to the present. "There are some injuries no magick can heal."

"That's horrible. I'm so sorry," I offered when he paused again. My heart ached for his loss. I let the feeling ripple out into the room.

Matteo nodded his head and continued.

"The day before Josh died, he asked to speak to me privately. I was nervous because he was so frail ... I didn't want him to waste any energy he had left speaking to me, but he insisted. I didn't know how, but I knew that those would be his last moments." Matteo scrubbed the back of his neck.

"He told me he was sorry. He said he didn't understand the magnitude, the consequences, of what he had done. On and on, he kept apologizing. I asked him what he was talking about ... what was he apologizing for. He said he thought it was made up ... the old lore. That another Strega, with great power, came to him and asked for help ... Alec, or something like that. This other man had told Josh he knew of a way to grow more powerful than any Strega had imagined. I didn't really understand what he was saying, Josh was already quite accomplished. What did he mean?"

I stiffened at the mention of Alessandro. What had he wanted from Josh? It was all so confusing, a puzzle with too many pieces and not enough of them fitting together.

"Go on," I nudged gently. "What else did he say?"

"There wasn't much more. He was too weak. The last thing he told me was that he and this other Strega cast magick, that they were searching to gain power, but at the last minute, things changed, thrown back on him. He said he tried to stop it, but he couldn't."

"Stop what?" I asked, chills running up my spine.

"He said that Rau was returned." Matteo's voice was shaking as he said this last bit of information.

"Rau?" Willem interjected. "But that's ... that's ..."

"Impossible? Just old lore?" Matteo finished. "Well, I thought so too. Until just about the time she knocked on my door." He nodded in my direction. "You see, she's also supposed to be old lore."

"I hate to be the one to ask the obvious," Claire said suddenly. "But would someone please explain to me who the hell this Rau is?"

Chapter Eleven

GIO

Rowan drove a silver Prius Prime, though I suppose it made sense. Watchers didn't only look out for people; they were also charged with the health and safety of nature. It somehow seemed *right* when the hybrid wagon pulled up to the curb outside of Claire's store. Patrick was already in the passenger seat, so I tossed my bag in the backseat and climbed in after it.

Rowan looked at me from the rearview mirror.

"So, you're the immortal human turned witch?" she commented off-handedly.

From my seat in the back, I had a limited view of her face, but I could see her eyes looking at me in the reflection. Though their color was typical, plain brown like many people have, their shape was intriguing. The almond shape was delicate, becoming thinner toward the outer edge. Her deep copper hair was curly, and long enough to be pulled back into a loose bun. It was the color of the setting sun in October. Thin tendrils fell out and brushed against her tawny-beige skin. She adjusted the mirror, and I caught a quick glimpse of her mouth. She wore a pinkish lipstick that matched her fingernail polish.

"And you're the one who's supposed to help me, right?" I answered back.

My curt reply let her know that I was in no mood for niceties. I'd been waiting a long time for this moment. Too long.

Rowan turned around to look me in the face.

"Okay, let's start over," she said, her tone calm, steady. "Hi Gio, I'm Rowan. It's nice to meet you. I believe you and I will be spending some time together."

The genuineness in her tone struck a chord in my heart and I knew I couldn't hold on to my rudeness.

"Thank you, Rowan, for coming with us," I replied. "I know that since my arrival, the Watchers have been working overtime. And you have my deepest gratitude. I just hope we can find Katarina and Claire and get back as soon as possible."

Patrick shifted in his seat impatiently.

"Well, now that introductions are out of the way, let's get a move on, shall we? The longer we sit here idle, the farther they get from us." His voice was strained, edged.

I glanced at the man in the passenger seat. My stomach tightened. How would it feel to love someone so much knowing they were in love with another? Would I be able to willingly step aside, allowing love to grow without me, if I were in Patrick's shoes? I shook my head and prayed I would never have to find out. His devotion to Claire was beyond what I had initially assumed. And I respected it greatly.

Still, part of me wondered if there wasn't an ulterior motive hiding behind his gallantry. One thing I knew well was that good intentions are the downfall of desires of the heart, especially when magick is in the mix.

"You're right, Patrick," Rowan replied. "Let's get out of

here. One question first. Do we have any idea where we're headed?"

They both turned and glanced at me, with expectant expressions. I blanched when I realized they were waiting for me to make the call. The problem? I had no idea what to do, or where to go.

"What?" I said under their stare.

"Gio," Patrick said, his voice calm, "for centuries, you and Katarina have been connected. You've been able to find her time and time again by following your intuition."

"Yeah, so? I mean, yes, that's true. But we've always been connected by a thread, some sort of magickal energy that pulled me toward her. But when we were together in the clearing and I became mortal again, that connection was lost. I felt it disappear. I guess it wasn't needed anymore. We were finally ... it was supposed to be ..."

My voice stopped, stuck in the back of my throat, refusing to continue. This was supposed to be over. Done. I had found her. We were together. All of this was supposed to be finished.

Instead, I found myself sitting in the backseat of a car with two strangers waiting for my direction, not knowing the extent of danger Willem and Claire were putting themselves into on my behalf, and Katarina farther away than I had ever known. Oh, and it was a minor miracle I was still living. I laughed. Sure, I was living, but I was barely alive. Barely living alive— the story of my life. None of this was fair. Anger flickered in my core. I could feel it grow inside me.

Rowan sensed a change in me and reached over the seat, her hand touching my shoulder.

"Gio," she said in a measured tone, "I know that what has happened makes little, if any sense to you. It could be that the magickal connection you and Katarina had when you were human has been severed. But you've got to start trying to understand that you're no longer the person you used to be.

You're no longer human. You're a son of Aradia now. This isn't a gift that's bestowed upon many. If you can just let go of the anger, let go of the unknown, I can help you find your power. I can lead you to the magick."

I listened to her words. Could it be true? Ever since I'd awoken from my sleep, I had the *knowledge* that I was now gifted with Strega magick, but other than a few extra sensory perks, I didn't really *feel* that magickal. Since I opened my eyes, I had not performed any sort of bewitchment, conjuration, or spell. Not one ounce of divination. I wasn't even sure how I could even go about it. How does a Strega make anything happen? Hell, for that matter, how does *any* magickal being make the power happen?

What good was magick when I was still operating on human laws? But I had no idea how to access Stregheria. If Rowan could help me come to terms with my new gifts, then nothing could come between Katarina and me. Together, we would be unstoppable.

"All right," I admitted. "I'm willing to bite. Tell me what to do."

Rowan took a deep breath.

"For now, all I need you to do is try to think like Katarina. Hopefully that'll get us started in the right direction."

"What do you mean?" I asked.

"Well, for starters, if you were Katarina, where would you go to begin to look for Alessandro?"

"Are you serious? *This* is your plan? I thought you'd have something a little more mystical than 'imagine you're Katarina,'" My stomach twisted as the anger flickered again.

"Calm down," Patrick interrupted. "We just need to get started in the right direction. Sometimes a hunch and a little common sense is just as good as a spell."

"And takes a lot less energy," Rowan added.

"Fine," I conceded.

I stared out the window. What would I do if I were in Katarina's shoes? Where would I go to find Alessandro? That, after all, would be the one thing I would do—look for Alessandro, find him, and kill him.

Alessandro would be in hiding. He'd need a place to rest, to recoup. *Where* was the question. I thought back to the interactions Katarina and I had before everything went down in the clearing that night. Was there anything that she had said that would be a clue? Where else would there be ties?

"San Francisco," I said.

"What do you mean?" Rowan asked.

"Alessandro worked in San Francisco. Katarina mentioned it once. If I were Katarina, I'd go looking for him in places I knew he'd been. Places he spent a lot of time at, hoping there'd be some bit of information or clue or something to lead me closer to finding him."

It was a hunch, at best. I had nothing to prove this other than my intuition and common sense, but it felt right. I waited for Rowan and Patrick to respond.

"Good enough for me, mate," Patrick said after a beat as he turned around in his seat. "Rowan, you heard the man. San Francisco it is."

Rowan started up the car and pulled onto Main Street. I watched silently as the town became a blur against the sky. I rested my head against the glass and closed my eyes. I imagined walking down the streets of San Francisco and seeing Katarina through the crowd. In my daydream, she would turn and see me, a smile spreading across her face, her eyes lighting up with joy. Just like an old-time movie, when two lovers meet after a long absence, we would run toward each other, arms outstretched, each step bringing us to that moment when we could finally hold each other again. I would bring her close to me, one arm wrapped tightly around her waist, one around her back, and never let her go.

"We'll stop here for now."

I blinked and sat up, confused by the voice that brought me back to the car ride. How long had we been driving? I couldn't believe I had let myself lose track of time.

"Where are we? Why are we stopping?"

"We're in Sausalito," Rowan replied. "A pit stop."

I looked for Patrick, but his seat was empty.

"Patrick went ahead to open up the place," Rowan said, answering my question before I had the chance to ask it.

"Where?"

"A safe place."

She took the keys out of the ignition and grabbed a small messenger bag from the center console.

"But why are we stopping? Shouldn't we keep going?" I asked. "We're nearly there."

Rowan paused briefly before putting the strap of the bag over her shoulder.

"There's something we need to do first. Something *you* need to do, especially if there's a chance our paths may cross Alessandro's," she answered, opening the car door and stepping out. She stretched and looked at me through the tinted glass. "Well, come on."

I didn't know what we were stopping for, but asking questions was getting me nowhere. If there was one thing I learned over the centuries, it was that a witch never said more than what they were ready to reveal. Apparently, that went for Watchers, too. It was infuriating and frustrating, but experience had taught me that if I wanted answers, it was best to go with the flow and be ready for anything.

I got out of the car and looked around. We were at the docks. There was a bite to the air that wasn't in Freestone. The breeze had a chill to it, and I could smell the water. I looked past Rowan to where I assumed boats would be tied and was surprised to see a community of floating homes, moored with thick ropes, which bobbed and rocked ever so slightly at slips lining the dock.

I followed Rowan past the main entrance, through the gate, and down the wooden pier toward the back of the community. As I walked down the dock, I noticed a symbol carved into each of the slip railings. I ran my finger over the next one I passed, curious about the shape. The shape illuminated as my finger brushed over the metal. In the center was a perfect circle, a crescent moon facing out on either side. My hand jolted back as I saw the purple glow from beneath my fingers.

"It recognizes you," Rowan said, not looking back. "If you had any doubts about your power before, that right there is evidence that you do indeed possess a gift."

"What is this place?" I asked, though I knew full well a straight answer would be hard to come by.

"Come on," Rowan urged. "This is it."

She reached the third to last house on the dock and turned left, up the slip. The brown shingles on the house's exterior were neat and tidy, perfectly placed in tight rows. I followed her up the ramp and almost bumped into her when she abruptly stopped at the door.

I sensed a sort of energy field between the door and where we stood. It felt thick against my skin as it pushed out, pressing against us. I remembered a similar feeling when I had first stood outside the Watcher bar in Freestone with Claire. Goddess, that seemed so long ago. I leaned in closer to Rowan, listening carefully as she began to speak.

"Smoke of fire, water, earth, and air, watch over this space with vigilant care, drive away all evil and fear, for only good shall enter here."

I stood in silence, listening, as she repeated the chant three times. At the end of the third incantation, the energy field began to shift. It became softer, more flexible. It wrapped around me instead of pushing against me. Rowan reached forward and held the doorknob. Turning it to the left, she pushed inward. The door opened fluidly as she walked into the house.

I followed her closely.

The door closed abruptly after we entered, sealing shut. I looked around. To the right of the entry was a small den-like room. Directly ahead was a narrow staircase leading to a second level. We headed left and entered a room that under normal circumstances would have been a living room. Tonight, it was meant for something else.

The furniture had been pushed to the room's walls, leaving an open empty space in the center. I walked farther into the room. Hundreds of candles were lit around the perimeter, and I could clearly see a large circle drawn on the floor with a star filling it up, each point touching the circle's edge. The star seemed to radiate in the soft glow of the candlelit room. I drew a breath in. I had seen this before.

"In order to call your power to you, you must first dedicate yourself to your Goddess." Rowan's voice slid smoothly into the room. I looked at her, my eyes questioning.

"You must declare your allegiance through ritual," she continued.

"How am I supposed to do that?" I asked.

"That's why she's here." Patrick patted my back as he entered the room. I jumped at his presence. For a man with no eyesight, he sure did get around with ease. "Rowan's a scholar among us Watchers. She's dedicated her life to the study of the history of magick, nature, and the like. She'll help you claim your allegiance, and once that's done, you'll be able to access your power."

He walked over to Rowan and reached into his coat pocket.

"Here you go, just what you asked for," he spoke quickly

as he handed her a small bundle wrapped in a worn cloth. Rowan took the bag and gave Patrick a hug.

"Thank you, brother," she whispered in his ear. "I am indebted to you. May the Goddess protect you for now and always." She gave him a kiss on the cheek, and he bowed his head to her as he backed away to the edge of the space, eventually sitting on a chair that had been pushed into the corner.

Rowan turned her attention toward me.

"Well, shall we?" She nodded in the direction of the circle on the floor.

I followed her to the center of the pentacle where she knelt and took off the messenger bag she had brought from the car. She opened the flap and removed a sharp blade, a small vial of oil, a stick that looked to be a wand of some sort, and a chalice. Though the wand and the blade seemed mundane in appearance, the chalice looked like something from a different world, or maybe time, with ornate etchings carved into its gold cup.

"Sit," she directed as she made herself comfortable in the center of the pentacle.

I took a seat opposite her as she began to place various objects onto the floor. She unrolled a mat, setting it between us. The thick fabric was stained and torn at the edges. At its corners farthest from me, she placed two short white candles. In the center was a small gourd cut in half.

"This will be our spirit bowl," Rowan explained as she poured a dark, red wine in its cavity, adding a pinch of salt to the velvety liquid. She added the vial of oil to the mixture. It collected on the top of the liquid in a thick pool. She took a sprig of rue from the bag and placed it to the left of the bowl.

She continued to work quickly with minimal talking, mostly providing a quick explanation of a tool or artifact. After a few more minutes, she sat still. I looked at the mat before me. Just above the spirit bowl lay the blade, to the right was the wand, and below was the chalice. I sat in silence as I took it all in, memorizing it for future use.

"Take off your clothes," she said rather abruptly.

"Excuse me?" I responded. Had I heard her correctly?

"You'll need to remove your clothes." She smiled, adding, "For the dedication ritual. It's really old school, offering yourself to the Goddess in your most natural state, and since that's what was practiced in your original timeline, it'll be more effective if—"

"Don't worry, Gio," Patrick interrupted, a sly smile tugged at the corners of his mouth. "I'll be right here to make sure there's no funny business. No need to be shy now."

The laughter in his voice irritated me. I shot him a look of disdain, knowing that even though he had no eyes, he'd somehow see it clearly. I turned back to Rowan. Her face held a look of seriousness, and I realized she was waiting for me.

There really wasn't a decision to be made. I knew what needed to be done. I was a son of Aradia now, and Diana was my Goddess.

I stood up and began to disrobe. Kicking off my shoes, I removed each sock, setting it just outside the circle. My hands found their way to my belt, where I quickly loosened the buckle and unfastened the buttons on my jeans. They fell to the ground, and I stepped out of them. Removing my shirt was more difficult as I became conscious of the scar left behind by Alessandro's blade. It was still raised and red, jutting across the front of my chest. I knew a twin of it could be found on my back, though I couldn't see it.

I looked at Rowan, who waited for me in the circle. She sat cross-legged, her hands quietly in her lap, her eyes looking straight into mine, urging me to hurry up. With a deep breath, I took down my boxers and stood in the room completely naked.

"Come sit here and we'll begin," Rowan said.

I felt exposed as I walked back to the center of the pentagram and sat down. It was not just my nakedness that left me feeling vulnerable. My hand touched the thick scar across my chest.

"Gio," Rowan said gently placing her hand over mine, "Your scars don't make you less—they prove you survived. Beauty isn't in what's unbroken, but in what still chooses to shine. Don't let the bad memories overcome what you are fighting for, what you are."

She held my hand firmly and removed it from my chest, revealing the scar.

"You're astonishing. Truly. Let your scar be a testament— not just to what you've endured, but to what you've become. It carries the strength of our Goddess, the love you share with Katarina, and the proof that even in the darkest of battles, you are still here, still fighting."

I swallowed hard, choking back the emotion that collected in the back of my throat. I nodded.

"Tell me what I need to do," I asked, her words giving my voice strength.

"Tonight is the full moon," she began. "It's found in the histories, that on a full moon a new devotee, *un 'offerta*, shall give himself up to the Goddess, and if favored upon, shall be granted the powers of the Strega. So, for starters, you'll need to follow all that I say so we can get through the ritual. Understand?" Her voice was firm now, unwavering with authority. I nodded in agreement. "Good. Let's do this."

She took the sprig of rue and dipped it into the spirit bowl, making sure it was coated with the oil. Bringing it up to my chest, she anointed me with it in the shape of a pentacle touching my forehead first, then my right breast, my left shoulder, my right shoulder, my left breast, then back to my forehead.

"Hold out your hands," she directed, "palms up."

I held out my hands in front of me. Rowan delicately placed the wet rue in my palms and nudged them above my head. She took out a piece of paper and opened it up, holding it in my line of sight.

"Read this out loud," she ordered.

I looked at the discolored piece of paper. The fine script was written in dark ink; a glint of candlelight revealed a purplish twinge. I steadied my hands above my head as I said the words.

"Goddess above, I kneel beneath the moon, the same moon that all Strega have knelt before, and I feel their power. On this night, I am one with them. Hear me now, Diana, hear my plea to you on this night, O Goddess of the Moon, Strega Queen, ruler of witches, for I come to you with symbols of the Old Ways. Hear me now and look upon my humble soul."

Rowan nodded, encouraging me to continue.

"I have heard the words of your daughter. I believe in the truth of your Word. Just as the moon shines down upon the earth, receive me. Let me walk beside you, in your name, a son of Aradia, and grant me the powers and gifts of the most divine."

As I finished the last sentence, Rowan took the rue from my palms and dipped it again in the bowl of wine. She anointed me once more, dragging the sprig across my torso in the shape of a pentacle. When she finished, she placed the rue back in the palms of my hand and pulled a second slip of paper from her pocket. She opened it and again signaled for me to read.

"Most sweet Diana, bearer of light, faithful Aradia, Daughter of the Queen, rulers of starlight and nature, in homage to you, I offer my soul. As you will it, so may it be."

For a third time, the rue anointed my body in the familiar pattern. However, this time when Rowan finished, she carefully placed the sprig back on the mat just to the left of the bowl. She took the bowl and poured the remaining liquid into the chalice. She lifted the chalice and held it out to me.

"Now, to finish the ritual you must read the inscription on the chalice before you drink it." She added, "Finish the wine completely."

I gave the contents of the chalice a look.

Rowan shrugged. "It won't taste great, but it won't kill you."

I nodded. "Okay, then what?"

"Then we wait for a sign and see if your Goddess has bestowed access to the power of the Strega gifted to you."

I pursed my lips. *Oh well. Here goes nothing.* I took the cup in my hands and looked carefully at the inscription.

"By the light of the full moon, of all that is unseen and seen, I ask you, Diana, Queen of the Holy Strega, I ask you, faithful Aradia, daughter of the Goddess, to give me a token sign of your approbation. In your name, so may it be."

I brought the chalice to my lips. The metal was warm. I could feel the liquid grow warmer as it passed up the cup wall and into my mouth. My tongue became full as the pungent, oily liquid covered it like a warm coat. My body radiated its heat. I could feel the red nectar seep into my blood as I finished every last drop.

When I had drained the cup, I placed it down and waited. As Rowan sat there watching me from across the mat, I became aware of my nakedness. Not in the physical sense, but in the spiritual. My soul felt completely exposed. Rowan's eyes were authoritative. Her stare penetrated my soul. Slowly, she reached over, took my hand, and smiled.

"O Goddess, surrounded by your pure, white light, guide this man toward the truth. Nothing but good shall come to him. Nothing but good shall go from him. So mote it be." Her voice was barely audible as she spoke the words bringing my hand to her lips. A soft breeze lifted her hair as she placed a full kiss on my fingertips, inhaling deeply. "It worked, Gio. Do you feel it?"

I froze. I closed my eyes, and succumbed to the moment, feeling the wind blow through me, in me, like cool silk against my warm skin.

"What is it?" I replied, my voice hazy from the breeze.

"Your request has been granted. The powers of the Strega have been bestowed upon you, and now you have been given access to them." She gently let go of my hand and took out the small cloth that Patrick had given to her earlier.

Slowly, she unfolded the cloth and took out a small bronze charm. I knew what it was before she had the chance to speak.

"Cimaruta," I whispered.

"Yes," Rowan answered. "And now it is yours."

She lifted the thin strap of leather the cimaruta hung from and rose to her knees. Carefully she leaned forward across the mat and tied the charm around my neck. The minute the charm touched my skin; I felt the line between Katarina and myself ignite in a rush. I gasped at the intensity of the connection.

The vision became clear, and I saw her, my love, as she drove into the city. Her and Willem and Claire. I saw her run into an alley, Willem and Claire not far behind, and enter a porthole through a wall of graffiti. The three made their way down a cavern to an overlook that revealed an underground city. They entered the house of a man—older, blue shirt—the door closing firmly behind them. The wind sucked out of my lungs and the vision dissipated.

"I know where to find them," I struggled to breathe as I spat out the words.

"Well, it's about time." Patrick, silent through the ritual, made his presence known again. "Now hurry. Put your clothes on and let's get out of here."

Chapter Twelve

KATARINA

Matteo had offered to put us up. It was a kindness that all three of us were wary of but grateful for. Not sure how much we could trust him, we opted to take refuge in the same room for the evening. Though in all honesty, I don't think that Willem or Claire would have let me out of their sight, even if it had been an option.

Matteo's house was well-equipped for unexpected company. The room he showed us was beautiful, decorated in black and white, with two queen beds, a bedside table positioned between them and an en suite bathroom just to the right as you entered. An oversized window was located on the far wall with a heavy black curtain drawn over it, shutting out any opportunistic beam of light, or prying eye, that tried to push its way in. The modern-style dresser, a sleek piece of furniture with glass knobs, sat against the wall opposite the beds with a large flat screen mounted above it on the wall. A plush black chair sat in the corner with a standing lamp behind it, its neck craned downward.

We entered the room and stood just inside the space,

taking it all in. Matteo looked us up and down, his expression hinting at the extent of our worn state.

"There are clean towels in the bathroom and some extra clothes in the drawers ... for sleeping, if you need," he said in a careful tone. "Help yourself to anything you find. This is my main guest suite, so I like to keep it prepared for whoever may drop by."

"You have many unexpected visitors?" Willem asked.

"No, not really. But you just never know who will show up," Matteo replied as he stepped out the room. "I'm just down the hallway if you need anything. Goodnight. I'll see you in the morning." He turned to leave, then thinking twice, turned back to us. "Breakfast will be at eight. Sharp."

He left the room. His footsteps receded down the hallway, and after a heavy door opened, all sound faded as it shut with a loud click. Exhaustion suddenly hung over me and all I wanted to do was sleep. Feeling confident that we were as safe as we could be under the circumstances, even if it was in the home of the brother of the Strega who had helped Alessandro raise the demon Rau, I was ready to turn in. A few more minutes passed and after I was certain Matteo had settled in for the night, I turned to Willem and Claire.

"I'm feeling we need to protect this place," Claire whispered in the silence of the room. "I'm gonna throw up a few wards."

"Need any help?" Willem offered.

Claire shook her head. "Nah. It'll just take a minute. I've been doing these since I was an eight-year-old hiding from my grandmother in my treehouse."

Willem nodded and sat on the chair in the corner. He scrubbed his face with his hands and leaned back as she walked to the southeast corner of the room.

"Protect this space from evil, keep harm at bay, by the moon

and stars let all that is here be guarded, shield us from darkness, in her name."

She walked the room in a clockwise position, stopping at each corner to repeat the spell. She also spent time at the window, inspecting underneath the curtain, and at the door. When she had finished, she flopped down on the bed.

"Do you think we can trust him?" Claire asked.

"I think we can trust him for tonight." I replied. "His brother is dead, and Alessandro is responsible. Doesn't seem like there'd much love lost between them by helping us."

"Grief makes loyalty unpredictable." Willem responded.

I shot him a look. "What is that supposed to mean?"

Willem held up his hands. "Only that desperation makes strange allies. Let's hope Matteo stays on our side of strange."

I was overreacting. Willem wasn't questioning me—only Matteo. But doubt had a way of seeping in, twisting even the safest words into something sharp. It's exactly what Alessandro would want. "Man, I'm exhausted," Claire breathed in an obvious attempt to decrease the tension that had somehow filled the room "I think today is starting to catch up with me."

Willem walked over and sat next to where she was laid out and ran his hand through her hair. Needing some space, I rummaged through the dresser and was surprised to find a pair of light-weight drawstring pajama pants and a T-shirt.

"I'm gonna go clean up," I said, pulling out the clothes and heading to the bathroom.

Looking around, I was cautiously impressed by our host. It could've been in a five-star hotel. Fresh towels were hanging on the wall racks and anything else I could've desired was in little travel-sized packs that were spread out among the bathroom drawers, medicine cabinet, and under the sink.

I nearly cried when I found a tiny bottle of bath salts. Running a warm bath, I took a few deep breaths as the steam began to fog up the mirror. I sat on the edge of the tub and looked down in the rising water. When the tub had reached capacity, I opened the salts, and slowly poured them in.

"*Sale della terra salire fino al cielo. Mi mostra il demone che cerca di distruggere me,*" I whispered, not wanting my friends to hear. I sat in anxious silence as I waited for the spell to deliver.

Though it had been some time since I had cast a seer spell, I was quite sure I could do it. It was, after all, one of the first spells any young Strega learns as she begins her study of the craft, and it was one I had been quite adept at.

I sat at the edge of the bathtub, my knee bouncing up and down in anticipation. I exhaled deeply as the tub's water slowly began to bubble. The salts rose to the top of the water, swirling at the surface, steam rising from their trails. I knelt on the floor facing the water and extended my arms over the tub, my hands just inches from the water's surface.

I leaned farther over the basin, my hands now anchoring myself on the wall, and watched as a white film collected on the surface of the water, then slowly dissipated to the edges, leaving the center crystal clear. I looked into the water, as crisp as a mirror, except instead of a reflection, it was a window; a window that opened into the sky on a clear night when you can count every star in the heavens.

I took another deep breath and held it for a moment. I knew what would happen next. From the depths of the water, I could see the outline of a dark figure take shape. It rose to the top with deliberation, materializing as it got closer and closer to the water's surface. I clenched my teeth together.

Slowly the form appeared in the water. A monstrous figure of a man with a wide chest and shoulders took shape before my eyes. His torso was well-muscled and strong. The short, stubby horns that just protruded through the surface of his scalp were barely visible save for the blood they left dripping down his face. His skin, thick and rough, was darkened, most likely from the pits I sent him to centuries ago. But it was his eyes that made me heave in anxiousness. His eyes were nearly black.

Demons don't age. In fact, they can quite easily take any form they want to. But this one—this one held onto the form I remembered, the form I had sent from this earth before.

It had been a while since I had seen Rau, but if Matteo was telling the truth and Rau had somehow made it to the earthly plane again, the demon would surely remember me. Now, as I sat in front of the tub, in the Strega Underworld, I shuddered at the image before me. There was no mistaking it. It was him.

I watched, hovering frozen above the water, as the reflection of Rau opened his mouth in a silent scream, spit flying out and catching on his sharp, pointed incisor. He looked over his shoulder and turned as a second figure began to take shape in the water's mirror. I knew this figure before it was formed, the outline of his body was one I knew well. My stomach twisted in a knot as Alessandro appeared next to the demon, placing his hand on its leathery shoulder.

It was then that one of my core memories slithered its way out from the center of my consciousness and into the present day. I pushed myself back from the bathtub wall and sat back on my heels, letting the memory come back to me.

I was fifteen years old—just a kid, but back then, it was different. I was a woman, for all intents and purposes. Well, at least I thought I was. We all did. *Il destinata a sette*, the destined seven. There were seven of us who had been born within the same year, over the course of the seven full moons.

The entire camp was abuzz when the births happened. We were the chosen ones, the seven of us. The first four births were males: Vittorio, Alessandro, Genovio, and Santario. The last three were females: Novenia, myself, and Carmelita. I was the sixth birth in the string. Carmelita was the youngest, and even though I only held one month seniority over her, I was extremely protective of her. She was the closest I'd ever have to a younger sister, and I loved her as such.

The elders had foreseen that together we would rise to a power never before seen. Looking back on it now, I realize that it was for this reason that they had beaten my father mercilessly. They had planned I would step in and offer myself to one of the males in exchange for mercy. A voluntary union would make for a powerful one. The fact that it was Alessandro was a bonus; he had proven to be the most gifted out of all the males. The most powerful. Little did the elders know that the bond we all shared had begun to fray years before, when the brutal act against Carmelita had pushed us farther magickly than any of us had wanted to go.

"Are you sure about this?" I whispered, my breath curling in the cold night air.

Carmelita stood in the center of our circle; her fists clenched at her sides. "He didn't hesitate when he took from me," she said, her voice steady. "Why should I hesitate now?"

I nodded and looked around. Every single one of us was prepared. There wasn't one ounce of apprehension in our circle.

It had only taken one full moon and seven nights after Carmelita was assaulted by a brutish human before we decided to take matters into our own hands. Back then, it seemed so simple. One of ours was wronged, so in return, the wrong must be given back.

It was midnight when we gathered in the forest, miles outside the camp. We moved in silence, casting the circle, offering gifts to the Goddess and God. Together, we formed the five points of a pentacle, Carmelita in the center,

Alessandro just outside, holding the offering—a small rabbit —waiting to greet the demon we were about to summon.

Rau, the demon of death.

The plan was simple: summon him, command him to destroy the man responsible for Carmelita's suffering in the most inhumane way possible, and send him back.

Stories from the Ilmalo told of Rau, how he would be called on to extract vengeance upon those who asked for it. It made perfect sense at the time. If ever there were a time for vengeance, it was now. There was not one of us who disagreed with the summoning.

"*Rau, malingno, scuro un o onnipotente, ascolta il nostro grido. Alzati e vendicare,*" we spoke in unison, repeating the phrase seven times. Our collective magick gathered in a dense storm of power. The air became so dark we could barely see each other across the circle. I remember how my chest felt heavy as the pressure from the air became too much for me to breathe easily. I struggled to maintain my composure. I wasn't the only one.

Vittorio was the first to double over.

"Stand up!" Alessandro ordered when he noticed our brother bent over in pain. "Stand up!"

"I can't," Vittorio sputtered. "Something's wrong ... I can't ... I can't ..."

"What's happening?" Novenia screamed. "What is it?"

I stood there in horror, unable to think, unable to move. If Vittorio fell, our circle would be broken, and the demon could very well be released into the earthly plane.

"Alessandro," I yelled over the growing roar of white noise that was now collecting above our heads. "Alessandro, take Vittorio's place before it's too late!"

Vittorio screamed in pain. We all looked at him, afraid for his life, and we could see that he was barely holding on.

Suddenly, his body began to convulse. He was lifted slightly up into the air just a few inches above the forest floor.

"It's too late," Alessandro said, his face white as reality set in. The six of us stood frozen in our spots, our eyes unable to pull away from Vittorio's body. "Rau has him. He's taking the offering he wants." His hand loosened, the rabbit falling from his hands and landing at his feet with a small thud on the soft earth.

The rest of us continued to stand in terror as we watched the demon take our friend. We knew instinctively what had to happen next. Someone had to put Vittorio out of his misery. We looked around at each other in panic, our wide eyes begging in silence for each other to do what none of us wanted to do ourselves. No one wanted to accept the responsibility of killing Vittorio before Rau was finished with him. And yet, it couldn't go on. I wouldn't let it.

I tilted my head back, looked up at the moon and extended my thoughts to the Goddess, asking her guidance. In my mind I saw what needed to be done. I wasn't sure where the thoughts had come from, I just knew that they were sent to me: a divine message.

My head snapped forward. It was too late for Vittorio, but if we acted quickly, we would be able to stop this. We could banish Rau back to the hellish dimension from which he had come.

"Alessandro, you must do it! You must end his suffering before Rau is able to take him. Do it, please!" I yelled, my eyes demanded his compliance. He heard the Goddess in my voice and did not question my words. He nodded his head, and I knew he would do my bidding. My body jerked in revulsion, sweat collecting on my brow, as I knew that Vittorio was to die soon.

Alessandro walked over to the circle and stood behind Vittorio. "Katarina, are you sure?" He looked every bit the man who would get things done. I looked at him and firmly nodded.

"Then I will do this," he spoke clearly; confidently adding, "I do this because you are telling me it must be so." He stepped forward and pulled his knife from his belt. He stood behind Vittorio and brought the blade to his throat. He screamed as he pulled the blade through the soft part of our friend's—our brother's—neck. I remember looking into Alessandro's eyes the moment he'd done it and saw the momentary satisfaction gleam from his dark irises.

I didn't have time to think about that split second when Alessandro appeared more demon than human himself because in that moment, Rau seeped out of Vittorio's physical body and materialized in the forest. With no body to feed from and the summoning still incomplete, he was too weak to take a true physical form but stood among the trees, a shadow of a man.

"*Una dannata*, I cast you back to the world from which you come!" I yelled.

"You can't stop me, little witch." The demon directed his gaze toward me. "I am Rau, demon of death!"

I continued my chant, raising my arms, my forefingers and thumbs touching, creating a triangle above my head. "Rau, Demon of Death, I cast you back to the depths of the darkest dimension, deep into the realm of death, hidden from all, lost among the souls of those who are banished from above and below. I send you there with the power of Diana, Goddess of the Moon, Queen of all witches!"

A knock on the door jolted me back to the bathroom floor.

"Katarina"—Claire's voice was hesitant—"is everything all right? May I come in?"

I looked back at the tub, taking one last glance at the images on the water's surface, cementing the face of Rau in my soul. Not that I needed to; his face was something not easily forgotten. I quickly waved my hand over the water and the image faded away, turning back to the thick salty water that it had begun with. The fragrant smell of ylang ylang rose to my nostrils and I knew the spell had been displaced.

"Yeah, everything's fine," I answered in a measured tone, not wanting to tip Claire off to the fact that I had just moments ago been casting. I dipped my hands into the steamy bath water and rubbed my face with the liquid, past my forehead and through my hair. I stood up and turned the lock.

"Come on in," I said as I opened the door.

Claire stood in the threshold and looked past me into the inconspicuous bathroom. Her eyes quickly darted to look at the tub, her gaze holding there for just a moment before she looked back at me.

"I'm not even going to ask," she muttered as she walked into the bathroom leaving the door open behind her.

I stood there in silence as she turned on the faucet and leaned over the sink. She splashed her face a few times, then turned off the tap, and grabbed the perfectly folded hand towel that lay just to the right of the sink.

"How did you know?" I whispered, hoping that Willem couldn't hear.

"You don't have to whisper," Claire said. "Willem went to the kitchen. He's hoping to find some useful ingredients we can take with us. Oh, the spell left residual energy ... there." Claire pointed to the inside edge of the tub. "It usually takes at least five minutes after dispelling before I can't sense the after effects."

Claire made a face of disgust.

"Believe me, it's nothing I'm thankful for. My life would be so much easier if I couldn't detect these things ... but I guess it's just another one of my so-called gifts. Oh, and just in case you're wondering, you don't have to worry, Katarina, I'm not planning on telling Willem you were casting in here. Unless, of course, there's something you'd like to share?"

Claire looked straight at me and for a moment I felt ashamed. If I had been more practiced, there was no way she would have ever detected that I had been casting. As it was, I was still dusting myself off, so to speak. I made a mental note to practice my dissipation skills.

"I wanted to see if it really was Rau," I said. "We have a ... history, of sorts, and if Rau is the demon we are dealing with, if he is the one helping Alessandro, then we have quite a bit to prepare for."

Claire closed the lid on the toilet and sat down.

"I know I'm not ready to hear this," she replied, her voice raspy.

"I just needed to see for myself ..." My voice trailed off.

I looked at Claire. She sat patiently and waited for me to continue. I knew I owed her an explanation, both her and Willem. They were willingly following me into this mess, and they deserved to know everything. I knew they were dedicated to defeating Alessandro, if not for me, then for Gio. I had to trust them. I had to tell them everything.

"And is it him?"

"Yeah, it's Rau," I said definitively. "I saw him, clear as day."

"Okay," Claire spoke slowly, waiting for the rest of the information. "Um ..."

"There's something you need to understand before I tell you the rest." I took a deep breath. "I've told you a lot about my past, but not everything—not the important parts, the ones that might change how you see me." I held out my hand to her.

Claire met my gaze. "I don't know how to prove to you that you can trust me, but I do. And I don't know how many times I have to tell you—we're in this together. There's not much you could say that would change that. I've said it before and I'll say it again, my opinion of you is based on who you are now."

"But do you want to know it all?"

Claire didn't hesitate. "I already know what I need to. And that's what matters."

"You didn't answer my question," I responded. "Now is just a moment in time that I'm living in. But me, the person who lives in all the moments across time, all the Katarinas or Kathleens or Kates or whatevers, we all have the same beginning." I held out my hand farther toward her, praying that she would take it and accept me for me, terrified that what I offered her now, this glimpse into my soul, could very well shake her to the core.

"What I'm offering you, Claire, is an opportunity that I have never offered anyone before." My voice began shaking. I took a short breath to steady it. "I'll ask once more. Do you want to know everything?"

"No secrets?" Claire asked.

"No secrets."

"You don't frighten me." She reached out her hand and placed it in mine. "I believe in you. I believe in Gio. I believe in love. I want to know everything."

"So may it be," I whispered as I felt her skin touch mine.

As soon as our hands met, my fingers wrapped around hers and held them fast.

"*Dea sopra, le nostre anime intrecciate, come prendo, do il mio, per sempre, per sempre.*" I spoke the words quickly, not allowing her to change her mind.

Though Claire was a magickal talent, a rare find amid all the watered-down practitioners of modern times, she was young. She was new. She was nothing compared to what was out there.

She was nothing compared to me.

I took hold of her hand and spoke the words again, this time with the intention of a true Strega. Our souls were instantly pulled together, completely melded into one energy form.

Claire's eyes widened as she was sucked into my memories, every past life that I had. I could feel her energy within mine and was able to guide her through, past the nineteenth century, past the seventeenth century, all the way back, deeper and deeper, until she was firmly with me that night Rau was summoned.

Though she was not there in physical body, she was there in my memory, like a spirit watching a dream. I opened my mind to her, let her see what had happened that night in the forest, then let the rest of the memory unfold for us both.

Rau had tried to charge me, but I held out my hand, stopping him in his tracks.

"You are not welcome here, demon," I spat at him. "You are banished to the realm in-between. May you never find your way here again."

He screamed, a ghastly, awful sound that tore the night into two as the ground opened underneath him and a red glow emanated from the split. The light looked like flames as it broke into tendrils and licked at his flesh, wrapping around his legs and torso. It pulled him into the void of the earth slowly, his screams filling the air with a suffocating heat.

"I will not forget this, witch." His words were blades slicing my ears. "I will come back for you. A demon never forgets."

My heart raced as I held my ground and continued to extend my energy toward him, pushing him farther into the void, sending him deeper into the realm of the banished.

The earth groaned as he passed through its opening, weary of the entity it was carrying to the next plane. Then, just as suddenly as it began, the ground creaked shut and everything was quiet. Everything was still.

Six of us stood, one fallen. Vittorio's body lay in a heap at Alessandro's feet. Alessandro stood in Vittorio's spot, blood smeared on his hand and the front of his shirt. He was breathing hard, but not for the reasons the others had thought.

I knew better. I could see past what the others did not want to look around. Alessandro looked directly at me, bloodied and exhilarated.

He was excited.

The taste of death, the act of killing, is the most powerful drug for those who are walking the thin line between good and evil, and Alessandro was hooked instantly. I could tell by his expression. I could tell by the way the corners of his lips wanted to tilt up in a smile. While the others closed the circle and gathered around our slain friend, Alessandro just stood there and looked at the world through blood-tinted lenses.

I knew this because I felt it too. I felt the power of what we had done. I felt the energy of the Goddess flow through me as I banished Rau. I felt the power of ordering Vittorio's death. Of watching Alessandro murder our friend and knowing that he did it only because I had told him to.

It was both intoxicating and terrifying. Alessandro's eyes met mine and held my gaze for a moment before bowing his head in acquiescence, submitting to my bidding. He knew how it felt. I returned the nod, then joined my friends to care for Vittorio's body.

Though the bond the seven of us had shared had been stripped of one member physically, it was nothing to what was stripped from us psychologically as we tried to make peace with what had happened. Genovio, Santario, Novenia, and Carmelita were eventually able to find peace with Vittorio's death, though they did not forget. They continued the path of the Strega Ilmalo, but with caution, never willing to give too much into the power.

Alessandro became the opposite. He had tasted what could be. I was his goddess, and he was a god. I didn't realize it then, but my actions that night, the power I held as I asked him to kill Vittorio, sealed his fate. From that moment on, Alessandro was changed. I was his maker ... and he wanted only me.

Perhaps, if I had accepted my actions, if I had given in to a darker power, Alessandro and I would have controlled it all, together. The heavens, the earth, the underworld ... everything.

But I didn't. I couldn't.

My father's blood ran through me too. Though I was quick to betray Vittorio, I just couldn't betray the part of me that knew what I had done was wrong. And I would never be able to forgive what I had done that night, not just to Vittorio but to Alessandro as well.

I would never forgive, and I certainly would never forget.

I let my mind open further for Claire to explore, not only the memories, but the emotions behind them. I opened my heart and all the secrets it held, for the first time in my existence, and willingly gave them to her. With certainty and assurance, I showed her that it was I who had created Alessandro. That for all the torture and pain and heartache that everyone had suffered over the course of four hundred years, there was nothing more to its beginning than a fifteen-year-old girl who had made a tragic choice. A girl who had gotten drunk off power.

As I took her through the years of my original existence, I showed her everything about me. Just as she had wanted, there would be no secrets between us. No more.

When there was nothing more to share, I led her slowly back through the centuries, through the memories of my more recent lives, always ending in the same fate—except this one. In this life, there was still a chance for me to right all the wrongs I had committed, if I could.

As the spell finished, my grip on Claire's hand loosened. When I felt the pressure release from between our palms, I knew it was safe to let go.

Claire didn't speak. She swallowed hard; her breath was shallow. Her features were pale grey and worn. All except her eyes. Her eyes were bloodshot. With a gentle touch, I wrapped my arm around her waist and led her to the bathtub where I sat her on the edge. I knew the spell would be much harder on her than me, but I knew she had been strong enough to handle its effects.

I tested the bath water. It was still warm. I helped her out of her clothes and into the tub. The salts would help her shed the residual magick from her body. When she was settled, I stood and went to the sink. I searched through the medicine cabinet and found a small vial of lemon oil. I filled the small glass on the counter with cold water and placed two drops of the oil in it. Turning back around, I sat on the floor next to the tub, glass in hand.

"Claire? Can you hear me?" I asked, though I knew she could.

Claire sunk into the warm bath, submerging her head in the water. When she finally re-emerged, she wiped the water from her eyes and stared directly at me.

I handed her the glass of lemon water. She took the offering and drank it down quickly. She handed the glass back to me and took a deep breath.

"Katarina," she spoke softly, "It was you."

I dropped my eyes, ashamed that what she said was true. She continued.

"You and Alessandro. The two of you ... shared that power. Shared that experience. It's why he can't let go. It's why he's summoned Rau. It's always been about you. Don't you see, the two of you were ... are ... what every myth and legend speak of ... the physical embodiment of the Goddess and God above ... the chosen ones ..." Her voice trailed off.

"I know that ... now," I answered. "But you have to understand that the moment I knew I could choose differently, that I could choose my own fate, I did. You think I don't know how fortunate I am to have my father's influence? It was what saved me ... saved us all, from me."

"But it was too late for Alessandro," Claire interrupted. "I saw the thirst for blood in his soul, his innate ability to do whatever it took, with pleasure, to please you. For him, there was never a choice to be made. Just time to wait until he could fulfill his destiny."

"And I took it from him," I finished. "As swiftly as I showed him the possibility, I took it away." I covered my face with my hands, too ashamed by my actions of the past. After a minute, I looked up. "I knew he could never let go of the power that he was promised. And now, after all this time, after centuries have passed, he has gone back to the beginning ... with the summoning of Rau."

Claire was silent as she took in my words. She sank deeper into the bath and let out a shaky breath. I realized that though she was able to converse, she was still recovering from the soul-bonding spell.

Worried, I asked, "Are you all right? How are you feeling?"

She shot me a pointed look. I cringed at its sharpness, and I wondered if since she now knew the whole truth, would we ever be as close as we once were?

"I'll be fine," she spoke after a brief silence. "I won't fault you for how I'm feeling right now, since I did say no secrets between us and it's my own fault for participating in a spell I didn't fully understand. But damn, Katarina, maybe next time a little warning, huh?" She shook her head in disbelief, adding with a slight smile, "I mean, you Italians are either all or nothing."

"I suppose you're not far off with that statement." I smiled, holding back my true feelings of relief.

Claire rose from the tub and grabbed a towel from the hook on the wall. She wrapped her hair up with it, then slipped into the robe that was hanging on the hook next to it. She was silent a moment before speaking again. This time, her words were chosen with care.

"Now that I know where all this is coming from, now that I know what we're up against, I still choose to stand by you. Not only for Gio, but for you too. You had a choice. You could have gone with Alessandro ... but you didn't. Knowing that accepting the power you were offered would have led you to be worshipped by all, and not only *not* choosing it, but choosing to pave a road quite the opposite ... well, that tells me more about you than any of your memories could. I say let us all choose our own fate. Let us walk the path that we create in life ... in love. I won't back down from whatever we cross. Just always know I'm on your side, our side, the side of good. No matter what."

I didn't realize I'd been crying until a tear dropped from my chin and landed on my leg with a soft splat. I wiped the salty tracks from my cheeks and swallowed.

"Thank you," I whispered. "Thank you for believing in me. I promise I won't let you down. I won't let Gio down."

"You could never let me down." His voice was smooth like caramel as his words glided into the bathroom.

My breath hitched, my heart both stopping and hammering at once. For an instant, I was paralyzed. I had to be imagining it. It couldn't be real. I didn't dare turn around.

I search Claire's face, seeking confirmation—proof that this was just some auditory hallucination. But she stood frozen, wide-eyed, staring past me toward the bathroom door. Her mouth hung open, jaw slack in utter shock.

Chapter Thirteen

GIO

As we crossed the Golden Gate Bridge into the heart of San Francisco later that night, I couldn't believe how my eyes saw everything differently. I'd always suspected that Katarina, or even Willem or Claire for that matter, saw things in the environment that I could never detect, but I had no idea.

I could now see the vibrations of the objects around me. I looked down toward the water. A thick, heavy blanket of fog covered the strait, completely obscuring the view. As a human, I would have been weary of the sight. Humans, by design, have terrible eyesight. Perhaps that is one of the reasons why they have always gathered during the day, working during daylight hours, leaving the night for the creatures of the otherworld ... and witches. When you can't properly see your enemy, why would you risk an encounter?

But I was no longer a mere human. Diana herself had presented me with the gifts of the Holy Strega. I was now one of her sons. I could see deep into the fog and sense the cold, dark water below, its surface a mass of tiny rough waves bouncing off each other.

The bridge itself was lit by large industrial lamps positioned along the deck, each one holding an oversized bulb that emitted a fuzzy yellow glow. The round red suspension cables burst forth from the deck's railings, shooting their way up to the main cables.

I rolled down the window and leaned my head out a bit. The crisp bay air filled my lungs as I inhaled. I felt intoxicated by the scent of the ocean and the city as we approached the tolls. I closed my eyes to take it all in.

"Gio," Rowan said from the front seat, "the first few weeks will be the hardest ... you know, sensory-wise, but just take it slow and it'll pass."

"Everything's so different," I replied, my eyes still closed as the wind ran over my face.

"On the contrary," Rowan responded, "everything's quite the same. It's *you* who's different."

I brought my head back into the car and thought about that for a moment. She was right; everything was the same. I was the one who had changed. I was not the same Gio that I was when I had found Katarina, in this life or in any other. I was Strega now. I looked up at the moon and silently thanked Diana for granting me her favor. I wondered if Katarina looked up at the same moon tonight. It was Patrick that brought me back to the conversation.

"How about you test out your new power and put some feelers out for anything happening, mate?" he said as we passed through the tolls.

My look must have been one of pure confusion because Rowan continued.

"Witches, in general, are pretty good at activities that require intuition. If you study any sect of the craft, you will learn how to trust the rhythms and signs of nature and how they impact you. It taps into the aspect of listening to the spirit ... Watchers do this too."

I waited for her to go on.

"But Strega, especially those of the Old Religion, those who have been blessed by the Goddess herself, have what I call extended intuition. It's kind of like a magickal GPS. And like calls to like. From what I've read, Strega who have an unbreakable connection will always be able to find each other, especially in times of need. It's a survival mechanism of sorts. And from what I hear, you and Katarina have an unbreakable connection."

Her last sentence left me deflated.

"*Used to*, Rowan. We *used* to have an unbreakable connection. That was before Alessandro severed it the night I went into a coma."

"Mate," Patrick chimed in, "weren't you listening? That was before. You're Strega now. You have a connection to all Strega. Just try ... you owe Katarina that much. Hell, you owe Claire that much."

Though his words were brusque, his speech held truth.

"Okay," I said. "How do I do this?"

Rowan was silent. She looked at Patrick, then back to me.

"Umm, well, I'm not quite sure." Her voice sounded embarrassed by the fact that the highest level of Watcher scholar didn't know how to use the magick she studied. "But from what I've read, it doesn't seem that hard. All you really need to do is set your intention. If you want to find Katarina, think of Katarina. Picture every detail of how she looks, how she smells, how she sounds ... everything you can remember and just concentrate on that. The magick will take care of the rest."

I sat back against the seat and placed my hands on my thighs. I closed my eyes and took a deep breath, letting every image of Katarina that I could recall flood my memory as I set my intention. There were so many images over the centuries that at first it was hard to focus. But as I calmed my center, as I pushed through to set my focus, forcing each memory of her to move in my mind in slow motion, I began to feel a small shift in my being.

It was as if a thin piece of string gently tugged at my heart. In my mind's eye, I could see a long, red, velvety rope extending from my body and reach out into the space before me. It stretched out far beyond where I could see, but I knew that if I followed it, Katarina would be at the other end.

"Head downtown," I directed Rowan, who did not question my words. "Toward Van Ness."

As Rowan drove with precision through the trafficked streets of San Francisco, I kept blurting out directions. Even at this hour, the city was bustling with activity. Suddenly, the rope led off to the side of the street, leading down a narrow and dark alley.

"Stop here!" I yelled from the back seat. "We have to go down that alley!"

Rowan screeched the car over to the side of the road and threw on the brake. We jumped out of the car, Rowan grabbing the few bags we had with us, and quickly we made our way down the alley. The narrow passageway led to a dead end, but in my mind's eye, the rope that connected Katarina and I did not.

"Where to now?" Rowan asked as she examined the graffiti that lined the concrete walls. "It doesn't look like there's much here."

I could feel that my connection to Katarina led me to somewhere beyond the wall, but I was unsure of how to get through,

"There must be something here," I commented. "Through this wall ... that's where we need to go."

Patrick walked down the length of the alley, around the dumpsters, his hand dragging against the brick wall of the building. I knew his vision extended far beyond the physical plane.

"Patrick," I called. "Come on over here and look at this graffiti. This is the way in, but I just can't figure out how."

"Way in to where?" Rowan asked.

"I'm not entirely sure, but it's the way to Katarina," I said; then added, "And where we find Katarina, we find Willem and Claire."

Patrick studied the wall. He raised his palms and placed them against the wall's surface, his gaze directed at the barrier. With one eye white from blindness, the other missing completely, I knew that he was using some other sense to see beyond the rough exterior.

"It's an entrance," he said. "I can see past the wall, it's not real ... an illusion. Beyond this there's an opening, a tunnel, that goes deep beyond the ground we're standing on now." He paused, then added, "That's as far as my vision goes."

"But how do we get past the illusion?" Rowan asked.

He shrugged his shoulders, and we stood in silence. There had to be a way in. What was I missing? I looked up at the moon.

"Goddess guide me," I whispered.

The image of the cimaruta flashed in my head. I took a few steps back from the wall and studied the graffiti for a moment. My eyes followed the thick black lines of spray paint as they crisscrossed around the space, overlapping and jumbling in various spots. It didn't seem like much of a tag. I looked around at other parts of the alley where the walls had been covered by various gang signs and names.

The lines in front of me looked different than the more iconic-looking tags found near the entrance of the alley. It was undisturbed. Specific. I watched closely as I tried to make sense of the mess in front of me. Again, a picture of a cimaruta flashed in my mind.

"Cimaruta," I whispered to no one as my hand went instinctively to the charm around my neck.

"What was that?" Rowan asked, her attention focused on the wall.

"The cimaruta," I repeated. "The charm on my neck. I'm not sure why it keeps popping up in my head. It just seems ... important ... a sign."

I stared at the wall. I felt like I should know something but had no actual idea of what I was to know. Again, I looked up at the moon.

"I don't know what it is I'm supposed to do. I need help. Guide me ... help me find Katarina."

For a third time, the cimaruta flashed in my mind. This time, before it went away, I grasped it with my intention and held it firm in my grip. Perhaps, there was a reason why I kept thinking about it.

Let me in.

As I held onto the image of the symbol, the graffiti on the wall in front of me began changing shape, sliding and slithering on the wall, taking a form that I was becoming quite familiar with: a sprig of rue, a moon, a snake, and a key.

My heart hammered in my chest.

"Look," I called to the others. "We can enter here."

I placed my hand on the cimaruta symbol on the wall and felt a pulse from beyond the cement.

Let me in.

It wasn't a request. In answer to my demand, a small light appeared in the center of the wall and continued to grow until it was the size of a doorway. When it was large enough for the three of us to pass through, the light faded, and a tunnel revealed itself in the beyond.

Without hesitation, we stepped through the threshold, following the tug of the invisible binding that connected me to Katarina. We followed the narrow path down, deep into the underground until we emerged at an overlook that opened into a vast cavern.

Below, I saw what I knew to be a Strega colony of sorts. I could feel the connection with the people that bustled about. I could sense their magick; it felt like mine. It was familiar in a way that a home is after many months of travel.

"This way," I said as I headed down into the world below. The tug on the rope that connected me to Katarina pulled with more force and urgency as we trekked down to the city and weaved through the marketplace, in and around stalls, past herbal stands and food vendors alike. My path was quick and decisive; I had no doubts. I didn't slow for Patrick and Rowan; I only hoped that they could keep my pace. The urgency was too great.

We walked and walked until we found ourselves at the doorstep of an older looking home. Suddenly the tugging stopped. My body thrummed with energy, but I didn't move.

"Are you sure this is the place?" Rowan asked. Patrick's impatience got the best of him.

"Jesus Christ what are you waiting for? Knock on the damn door!"

We didn't need to. The door was opened by a well-dressed middle-aged man.

"Why am I not surprised to see you here?" he said in a resigned tone, looking me straight in the eye. He looked at my companions. "Not sure about you two, but hurry up, get in before anyone sees you. It was bad enough taking in the other three, but now ..." His voice trailed off.

"Well, hurry." He gestured to us to come in. "I'm sure you're anxious to see your friends."

Chapter Fourteen

KATARINA

I slowly turned, following Claire's gaze, knowing whose voice had spoken but not yet ready to believe it was true. As my eyes found the doorway, my vision instantly blurred with tears. It couldn't be. How? I opened my mouth to speak, but nothing came out.

"You're here," Gio spoke softly as he entered the bathroom and knelt by my side.

Again, I tried to speak, but only a soft cry came out.

"It's okay. I'm here," he spoke with caution. "Katarina, I'm here."

"Is ... is this real?" I asked not trusting my senses. I wanted to touch his face, kiss him, and hold him close, but I was afraid he would disappear. "Claire, is this real?"

Gio smiled and took my wrist. He lifted my hand and placed it against his cheek.

"Does this feel real to you?" he asked.

I nodded and began shaking.

He leaned in and rubbed his cheek against mine, our skin crackling against each other's with the intensity of our connection.

"How about that, my love? Does that feel real?" Again, I nodded.

He pulled away and stared deep into my eyes. The crystalline blue of his irises searched deep into my soul. Slowly, he leaned in, stopping just as our lips brushed together.

"How about this? What does this feel like?" he whispered, holding still. His breath was hot and sweet against my lips.

My heart hammered double time, and my breathing grew shallow, excited, as shivers played up and down my spine, leaving my stomach wide open to the thousands of butterflies that flew about in it.

"How can this be? How did you find us?" I whispered, our lips dangerously close to each other. My free hand found its way to his cheek and stopped just short of touching it. I was still afraid the tips of my fingers would pop the image in front of me.

I took a deep breath and carefully brought them to his cheek. When he did not disappear, I pushed them farther back, running them through his dark, curly hair. He closed his eyes as my fingers tangled into his soft curls.

"This. Is. Real." Each word was its own sentence as he spoke it to me. "I'm here."

I closed my eyes and let myself fall into the moment, our lips finally touching in a soft kiss.

"I hate to be the one to interrupt." Willem's voice cut through the kiss. I kept my eyes closed just a second longer before opening them again.

"We've got a lot of catching up to do," Willem said. "But it can wait. Tonight, we rest. C'mon Claire, Katarina and Gio will stay here. We'll be staying next door. Patrick and Rowan will stay in the room at the end of the hall."

The moment Gio's lips had touched mine, I had forgotten about everyone else. My cheeks flushed in embarrassment, and still, I didn't take my eyes off him. I couldn't. What if when I did, he'd disappear again?

"Rowan and Patrick? What are they doing here?" Claire asked.

"C'mon, I'll explain when we're settled." He nodded his head in the direction of the door, hinting that she needed to make herself scarce.

"Of course," she said quickly as she darted out of the bathroom. "Katarina, we'll talk tomorrow."

I heard the two of them whispering frantically to each other as they made their way out of the room, closing the door firmly behind them.

Finally alone, it began to sink in that Gio was really here. I couldn't stop my heart from thundering. He helped me up off the floor and led me to the bedroom. I sat on the bed and watched him as he walked to the other side of the room.

He looked healthy. Strong. Nothing like the person I'd left in the hospital bed hours ago. But there was something different about him as he walked to the bedroom door ... something more. I couldn't quite pin it down until he lifted his hand just above the lock and held it there for a second before the bolt clicked into place.

My breath caught in my throat. How could that be?

He turned around and looked at me. It was the first time we had been alone since that horrible night in the forest. There was nothing more I wanted to do than run up to him and crush my body against his, wrap my legs around his waist, feel his hands prop me up and squeeze me tight, feel him deep inside me and fall into each other ... forever.

But how had he locked the bolt on the door?

"Katarina"—his voice sang to me like an angel chorus—"there's something I need to tell you."

Chapter Fifteen

GIO

I was grateful when Willem and Claire left the room. In all honesty, I wasn't sure that they'd leave us alone, but Katarina and I needed this time together. She looked as if she was in shock, though it couldn't have been half as shocking as it was for me to see her ... glowing ... beautiful ... and still as vibrant as the first time I laid eyes on her. No, more so now. My eyes saw much more than they ever did.

I led her to the bed and sat her down, then walked over to the door and stood in front of the lock for a moment. I hesitated. Just as I opened the portal to this underworld, I knew I could lock it simply by willing it. But should I? I wanted nothing more than to be alone with Katarina. I wanted nothing more than to feel her touch and hold her and melt into her being. I had waited too long for this moment ... again.

Alessandro had done his best to make sure that the short amount of time Katarina and I had together would be our last. I shuddered as I thought about how close he had come to succeeding. In truth, he technically did win.

I had died. In true mortal form, no less. If it hadn't been

for Claire ... if she hadn't healed me, made me strong enough to meet Katarina's father, Jack, before my soul left my physical form completely, well, that would've been the end of the story.

But she *had* saved me. I had done nothing but make requests of her and take refuge among her people, and I gave her nothing in return. Yet she kept my spirit, and my body connected just enough to pass through to the realm of the Goddess. Claire, whom I owed more than I could ever pay back, more than anyone should ever owe another, asked for nothing in return. She had acted to honor love. To honor her Goddess. To honor herself as a Watcher.

All the sacrifices and tough choices that Claire had made were for me. For me ... and for my Katarina, who now waited on the bed. All of the sacrifices and struggles seemed like nothing as I thought of the woman who had suffered what felt like an infinitely greater amount than I could ever endure.

As I stood in front of the door, I thought back to the moment when Katarina had agreed to run away with me. She had fallen for Gio, the human. I smiled at the word ... human. That Gio was someone I knew well. He was affectionate and kind, smart and skillful, trusting and truly honorable. He was also weak and afraid, timid and unsure. A liability. Satisfaction welled in me as I realized that Gio, the human Gio, was long gone.

I was not that person anymore. And Katarina, my beloved Katarina, deserved to know who I now was before we could be together once more.

I raised my hand just above the lock, angling my body so that she was sure to see. I didn't have to turn around to know that she watched my every move; my energy was so focused on hers. Now that I had been given my powers, directing my energy was coming along. I made a mental note to thank Rowan for all her guidance.

Lock.

I envisioned the lock turning, the cylinder rotating the deadbolt cleanly.

Lock.

I ordered it to happen. With a quick movement, the lock snapped shut. I heard her catch her breath, then hold it, leaving the room in eerie silence.

"Love," I said as I turned and made eye contact with her, "there's something I need to tell you."

She looked at me, eyes wide, and I saw the recognition of what I was in hers.

"But ... how?" she asked breathlessly.

"Do you remember that night in the forest? The night that Alessandro"—I chose my words carefully— "ran his blade through me?"

She looked at me as though I had lost my mind.

"Of course I do."

"Well, so do I. Except that my memories include a visit to the realm of the ancestors where I met ..." My voice trailed off. This was harder than I thought.

"Who, Gio? Who did you meet?"

"Your father, Jack." I blurted. "He was there to greet me when I crossed over."

"My father? How do you know it was him?"

"I know it was him because it wasn't the first time we'd met," I said, my eyes darting away from her for the first time since I had laid eyes on her that evening.

It was time to tell her everything.

Time to tell her about the boy who once carved figurines from scraps of stone, selling them in a desperate bid for freedom. Time to confess that it was her father who had given me my first taste of wealth—the gift that finally allowed me to escape my cage.

Time to reveal that the very figurines she had received for her birthday had set off a chain of events leading to her father's torture, and ultimately, her forced marriage to Alessandro.

Our fates had been entangled long before we ever knew each other. And I—I had been the unwitting architect of so much of her suffering.

She sat beside me on the bed, silent, listening. Tears welled in her eyes as I unraveled the truth—our truth.

It killed me to watch the different levels of anguish as they moved through her expressions, but I continued speaking until there was no more to say. When I finished, I sat and waited for her to reply. After what felt like forever, she spoke.

"I can tell by the way you're looking at me, you're afraid," she began. She brought her hand up to my cheek and brushed her thumb against my lips. "Don't be," she whispered. "I'm not sure what I can say other than I don't blame you. None of this is your doing. There's a reason why the Goddess has chosen our path. What that exact reason is, I'm not sure ... yet. What I *am* sure about is that my love for you has not changed. It never will."

She leaned in and placed a gentle kiss on my lips, like roses covered in dew. The moment her lips pressed into me; my world spun. It shifted off its axis and turned around as I tried to maintain control of myself. I couldn't get lost, not yet. I still had one more confession. Though every muscle in my body fought to do the opposite, I pulled back from her advance.

"There's still one more thing that you should know," I whispered.

"I know what you are," she responded, collecting herself from the moment. "I could see the difference in you. I'm ... I'm just not sure how it happened."

As I recounted my meeting with the ancestors in full, she listened intently, absorbing every detail. She didn't interrupt or ask questions—just sat in quiet acknowledgment, her eyes confirming that she believed every word.

I told her how Patrick and Rowan had been sent with me, how Rowan had helped me earn Diana's favor, guiding me through the dedication, and how, in the end, we had worked together to wield the magick I had now been blessed with.

When I finished, she had tears in her eyes.

"What is it?" I asked, my heart aching. Had my words upset her? I couldn't let this go on. How would I end this cycle of torment? My fears were squelched as I looked deeper and saw the slight glimmer of hope sparkling behind the tears.

Hope. I had always thought of it as a uniquely human emotion, but I understood now—it was something that transcended all beings.

Looking into her eyes, I saw it clearly. Hope was what kept her holding on to our love so fiercely. It was the quiet belief that, one day, we would be free to share it—openly, without restraint.

"Gio," she said, her voice cracking under the emotion, "everything you've just told me I know has been done because the Goddess has willed it to be. We were meant to be together and together we will destroy Alessandro. Love will conquer. We are on the path of righteousness, the path that will rid the world of the evil that threatens the delicate balance and the very existence of the Strega."

She moved in closer to me. I could feel her body's heat as she crossed over into my space. We sat there on the bed facing each other, both silent, anticipating what would happen next, knowing it had been too long.

She reached out and took my hands in hers. Our fingers laced together, and I could feel her pulse beating to escape. I pulled her close and she tilted her head, her lips ready for mine to take them.

I gently pushed against them, my mouth opening to nibble on her bottom lip. She tasted delicate and sweet, like wild orange blossoms dipped in honeysuckle. Her response was immediate and uninhibited.

Her tongue slipped through the opening of my mouth and teased me, licking the line of my lips and teeth. I could feel her need, her urgency. I was right there with her, but I gained control over my physical need. I wanted to savor the moment.

Hands still clasped; I lifted her arms above her head. I slid my hands back down her arms and along the sides of her body, memorizing every curve along the way. When I found the bottom of her shirt, I lifted it up and over her head, tossing it to the floor.

I pulled away and looked at her. She had always been the most radiant creature I'd ever laid my eyes on, but now, looking at her through Strega eyes, I was able to see how she truly glowed from the inside out. She sat and watched me as I took it all in.

"It's amazing, isn't it?" she said with a smile. "The way you can see things now, huh."

"*You* are absolutely amazing," I repeated, never taking my eyes from her body, lust filling me up and sending chills throughout my torso.

"I wasn't talking about me," she laughed. "I meant the colors, Gio! The clarity of what you can see, the vibrations, the intensity ... *everything*."

I was only half listening to her. I brought my hands up to her waist and massaged her midsection in slow strokes, my thumbs gently pushing into the soft part of her stomach, my fingers stretching as far as they could around the curve of her waist and up her back.

She let her head fall back as she leaned into my touch; her eyes fluttered as she felt me explore her. I placed her back on the bed and leaned over her stomach, my lips tracing the line from her navel to just below her bra. Feeling frustrated by the barrier, I quickly snapped it off and tossed it aside. Katarina gasped at the suddenness of the exposure but did not stop it. Instead, she arched her body, inviting my lips to her.

My throat burned with passion; I could barely breathe, the air escaping it was so hot. I brought my mouth to her breasts, taking my time to ensure each one was attended to properly. Katarina's hands danced through my hair. When my mouth found her nipple, her hands tugged at the curls, making my hunger grow.

I eagerly suckled each one, pulling and nibbling the rough tissue carefully with my teeth. Katarina wiggled under the pleasure.

"Gio, come here." Her voice was breathless as she pulled me up to her, our eyes meeting once again. "I need you closer."

We froze for a moment, staring at each other, my fully clothed body now atop her half-naked one. Then, like an unexpected storm, we erupted. Our lips came together with force, our tongues exploring the other's mouth with need.

Her hands made quick work of my belt and pant buttons as she struggled to push them down, off my thighs. I pulled off my shirt in one movement, then lifted my body off hers just enough for her to use her foot to push my pants and boxers off my legs.

She pressed against my chest with her hands, and we rolled over. She sat up, straddling me, her hands on my torso as I undid her pants and lowered them to her hips, exposing black lace underwear.

As I was trying to figure out how I would get her pants completely off her, she gingerly pushed herself up. My jaw dropped as she stood up on the bed above me and slid her pants all the way down to her ankles. Kicking them to the side, she slowly lowered herself onto me, never breaking eye contact.

My hands found the thin fabric that was the last barrier between our bodies. I let my thumbs play just at the edges of the lace. Katarina pulled the hair tie from her locks, her hair spilling down in thick raven waves.

"You're so beautiful," I whispered. "I've been waiting for you, wanting you for so long, that this doesn't feel like it's real."

"Does this feel real?" she teased, using my earlier words as she ground her hips down, her hot center leaving a wet spot on my torso.

I saw the fire in her eyes and knew that it matched mine. I gripped her panties and ripped them off in one movement, tossing them aside, and bringing my hands back to her waist. She fell forward onto me, our mouths hungrily meeting again as I lifted her hips just enough and carefully slid myself into her.

She gasped in pleasure. My head spun. Her rhythms were tuned to mine as we rose steadily together, rocking in time to our beating hearts. Faster and faster, harder and harder, I could barely hear her moans over mine.

Higher and higher. More and more. Our bodies pressed and thrusted and slapped together until I felt her tighten around me and knew that she would soon release. I drove into her deep, and steady, wanting her drunk with ecstasy, hoping that she was as pleased as I.

She angled herself up, hands on my chest, and looked into my eyes. I could feel her rising, coming close to the edge, and I knew I wasn't far behind. She pushed her hips forward once more and in that small movement, the world exploded. Our eyes were locked together as our bodies melted into one, pulsing and squeezing and throbbing, as waves of pleasure rolled over us.

When the earth had finally ceased moving, she lay down on top of me and I could feel the satisfaction radiating from her body. Her hair spilled down over us. I could feel her chest return to a steady rise and fall as she caught her breath.

Neither of us was in a hurry to move; we didn't dare. Though we knew it to be reality, after four hundred years, we still didn't trust the moment to be truly ours.

"Siamo finalmente insieme," I whispered, daring to test the dream, "Finally together. I still can't believe it."

She rolled off me to the side and rested her head on my shoulder, her fingers tracing patterns on my chest. I tensed as she grazed over my scar. She closed her eyes and inhaled gently before she spoke.

"Believe it, my love," she said. "Finally, and forever. We are meant to be. I knew the Goddess would bring us together, that I would finally be yours and you mine." She lifted her head and looked at me, adding, "And know this, Gio. Now that I have you, there is nothing that will keep you from me. I will do whatever it takes ... we will never be apart again."

I held her gaze and looked deep into her eyes. I knew every word she said was a promise. I could see it in her depths of her gaze. Those eyes, that pulled me in deeper, with a strength that left me no choice but to submit. Those eyes that were sprinkled with little gold flecks that burst like stars when she was happy. And just beyond that, deep within her soul, tiny glints of red swirling about in the darkest center of her irises.

<h1 style="text-align:center">Chapter Sixteen</h1>

KATARINA

I could hear him breathing next to me. I could feel the warmth radiating from his body. I couldn't stop the smile that spread across my face as the last several hours tumbled across my memory. I opened my eyes and glanced at him. He lay sleeping peacefully. His face was smooth, flawless. He looked like an angel. His curls were tousled, spilling over his ears. I watched him closely, not quite believing he was here with me. I memorized the heavy rise and fall of his chest as he slept.

Light from the marketplace beamed into the room from the edges of the curtains indicating it was morning. The underground must've spelled an illusion to replicate the patterns of day and night. Made sense. How else would those who lived down here tolerate it?

A far away sound in the house told me that others were up and about. Soon, we'd have to join them. My heart tightened in protest that it would willingly stay in this room forever with Gio if it meant we could be together, alone. My mind argued that we would never be able to truly be together, to be free to live our life, while Alessandro was alive. Now that he had Rau to command, his destruction would be ... a bit more complicated. Not impossible, but a challenge still. I resigned to the thought. We'd have to leave the cocoon of our room.

Not wanting to wake Gio, I slipped out of bed and tiptoed into the bathroom. I closed the door behind me as I turned on the light and looked at myself in the mirror. Though many lives I had lived, there was never one in which I looked quite as much like my original self. I smiled at the image in the mirror. I pulled my hair away from my face and looked into my eyes.

"You can do this, Katarina," I said to my reflection. "Goddess, help me choose the right path." I looked deeper into my eyes which now housed the green and gold flecks of my father. As I had become more comfortable with my powers, the flecks had begun to become more apparent. I didn't realize how much I'd missed those flecks until I thought back to the countless lifetimes in which they were lost. Unfortunately, they weren't the only things to return.

"Come on ... please don't be there ..." I said to myself as I leaned forward, examining my eyes farther. Disappointment swelled as I saw the one thing I didn't want to find. Tears blurred the mirror image as I saw the tiniest bit of red in the center of my irises.

"Shit," I said, as I sank back away from the mirror when the telltale sign of the Strega Ilmalo appeared, evidence that darkness still dwelled inside me.

I tried to compose myself. It didn't mean anything, did it? My heart knew different as I remembered the first time I had noticed them. Shortly after the incident with Vittorio, the elders had called each of us that had participated in the ritual, one at a time, into the council tent.

"Child," said Dahnya, the eldest. "Explain to us what you were thinking when you thought so foolishly to summon the demon."

Though I knew what we'd done was wrong, my mother's

blood flowed through my veins just as much as my father's. My mother would never have let anyone speak to her in such a manner. Being just as stubborn and self-indignant, I held my ground.

"Those men in town hurt one of ours. Carmelita will never be the same after what they did to her. You know it as well as I, and I would rather die than see them go unpunished." I lifted my chin, challenging them to argue. The council looked among themselves, not knowing what to make of my boldness. Convinced that no one would refute me, I continued, "That's why we called upon Rau. He was to avenge the wrong that Carmelita was given. The only mistake we made was not realizing that he wanted a human sacrifice. If we had known that, then we would have gotten one of the men that hurt her and given him willingly."

Every member of the council looked startled, frightened at seeing a young version of a woman they thought had passed long ago.

"Do you mean to tell us that you actually saw Rau?"

"Yes. We saw him, and then ..." My voice had cracked. I gathered it quickly, shifting my weight and planting my feet deeper into the ground. The council whispered among each other, their shock evident in the way their words bounced and hissed in the stale tent. "When we realized what he wanted, what he was taking, and we knew that nothing could be done about it, we had to stop him. If Rau had fully taken Vittorio, he would have done more destruction than we imagined. So, we sent him away."

"Do you mean to tell us that the six of you, six *children*, banished him?" one of the council members spat. Agnolo was a despicable man, even for Strega Ilmalo standards. I could hear the bitterness in his words.

"No," I answered back. My anger had been piqued, and I directed my energy toward him. "The *six* of us did not.

Alessandro and I did it ourselves." As soon as the words left my mouth, a wind swept through the tent, swirling around me and lifting the edges of my skirt off the ground.

Some of the council looked shaken while others appeared excited, their faces a mixture of fear and eagerness. I was dismissed from questioning and ran directly back to my tent. Throwing myself on my bed, I sobbed. Hearing my father approach, I frantically dried my eyes and searched for a tiny mirror to fix my hair.

I froze the moment I brought the mirror up to my face. Dark eyes, flecked with green and gold, looked back at me as always. But something was different, something strange. Amid the green and gold was red. Red, the color of passion. Red, the color of anger and rage. Red, the color of love and hate. Red ... the color of blood.

I had the blood of Vittorio on my hands, and it was written in my eyes, a marker for everyone to see.

I spent the next years of my life trying to atone for my past mistakes, trying to fade the red. I remembered what the old Stregheria had said: the darker the red, the more presence in the eye, the further into the darkness you will be drawn.

Now, standing in Matteo's bathroom, I again looked in the mirror. It wasn't much, just the tiniest bit. Still, I'd have to be careful. There was no telling how much, or how little, influence it would take to affect me.

No. I shook my head. I did not suffer to take a long fall into the darkness now. I was strong enough to hold my own. And now, with Gio at my side, I would not fail. Love would prevail.

I yawned and stretched my neck and shoulders. Though I needed sleep last night, it didn't happen. Remembering the reason why dreams had eluded me, I smiled again. I thought about joining Gio in the bed once more, then thought a shower would be beneficial for both of us.

I turned the water on and let it run until steam rose from the faucet. I lifted the shower lever, letting the water flow as I began opening the cabinets in search of a towel. As expected, Matteo had an abundant stock of freshly laundered linens stacked high on the shelf. I reached to grab one, then jumped when a set of hands wrapped around my waist from behind, though I could tell who it was by his touch.

"I didn't mean to startle you." Gio's voice was velvet as it wove around my neck and into my ear. He pressed his body against mine, his lips brushing against my upper back.

I closed my eyes, forgetting the towel, and melted into him.

"I didn't want to wake you." My voice was breathless.

"I know, but I'm awake anyhow," he said between the kisses he trailed across my shoulders.

His hands slid over my belly and up my torso, cupping my breasts and gently massaging them. I let out a soft moan and pressed up against him. I could feel his nakedness against my back, his entire body ready for me. I turned around to face him and found his lips immediately, my mouth hungry for him again. Always hungry. We stood there and held each other tight as the bathroom filled with steam.

I led him to the shower, being careful not to break our kiss. He pushed the curtain aside and helped me in, quickly following. Our need was still intense as we stood in the tub.

Finally breaking the kiss, I looked at him as I took the soap from the shelf. I held it tight in my grip as I ran my hands over his body, working up a thick lather. He stood still and let me touch him, cleansing him of any residual guilt he was holding onto. When I had finished, he took the soap from my hands and did the same. We moved under the water stream and stood in the shower, letting the hot water flow over our bodies, washing the hurt and mistakes of centuries past down the drain. We were clean now.

I pulled my fingers through my hair, rinsing it completely, and looked at him. He watched me with pure desire in his eyes. I could wear it like a coat, it was so thick in the steam. Last night had been our night, a night to take our time, to savor our reunion. I could see in his eyes that this time would be different. I clenched my jaw in anticipation and hoped that it wouldn't be much longer.

He grabbed my waist with both hands and pulled me toward him until our bodies were pressed hard against each other. I brought my arms around his neck and lifted myself up, my mouth to his, my legs wrapping around his body. A low growl escaped his lips as he turned and pressed me against the shower wall, his hands holding me up by my backside.

I could feel his energy, hot and raw, as it crawled from his skin to mine. I shuddered in ecstasy, my need growing with every kiss. I could feel him ready, waiting for me. I shifted my hips up, angling my body for him. He did not hesitate. A cry escaped my lips as he swiftly entered me.

He was so hard as he pierced me over and over. His movements were rough, urgent. I met his eagerness with enthusiasm. A soft moan rolled off my tongue, sending him into a greater frenzy, his hands firmly grasping me and rocking me back and forth. His lips ceased kissing me and just stayed locked on the crook of my neck as his hair nudged my cheek.

I tried to focus on the moment, to be with him entirely, but he took me to places I had only dreamt existed. I felt myself quickly rising. I could hear his breathing, ragged against my ear, and knew he was close behind me.

I closed my eyes and let all inhibition fall away. I released fully onto him and gave him everything I had of myself. I heard him catch his breath, then felt him resign to pleasure, a hard pulse lost in my contractions. His body trembled as we experienced each other fully and completely until the waves slowed and ebbed, each of us satiated ... for the moment.

He held me against the wall as we caught our breath, our chests rising and falling in a contented rhythm. He gently stood me up, careful to make sure that I had my footing before loosening his grip, though I did not loosen mine.

I would never let go of him again.

"I will never leave you," I whispered through the steam.

"My love," he spoke, tilting my chin up so that his eyes met mine, "you will never have to. Ever again. I promise." He placed a tender kiss on my lips.

I held him for a few minutes longer. Poisoned thoughts of Alessandro slithered into my consciousness like slick black snakes. They were impossible to avoid, even in my happiest times. What Alessandro had done to me, what he had done to Gio, was difficult to reconcile. I silently gagged as I remembered the last time I had been with Alessandro. Hatred sparked, threatening to burn whatever was left of my conscience. With effort, I snuffed it out. I couldn't let it consume me. If it did, Alessandro would win.

Sensing my discomfort, Gio wrapped his arms around me and hugged me.

"I only hope one day, we will be free to live our life together in peace. With nothing but a future ahead." His voice was sad, as if he knew that day might never happen. "Leave everything else in the past."

"It will happen," I responded. "Look at what's already happened. Just yesterday I didn't even know if you were alive. And today, here we are. Never in another four hundred years would I have guessed that I'd be standing here with you right now. We will have our day, love," I continued. "Now that we are together, nothing can stop us."

~

GETTING DRESSED WAS BITTERSWEET. We clothed ourselves in silence, neither one of us wanting our time together to end. We knew that we needed to meet with our friends and coordinate our next move, but we had had less than twelve hours together, not nearly enough time to move forward. I would've willingly stayed another twelve *years* locked in that room with him and it still would not have been enough time.

When there was nothing left to do, I looked at him and waited for him to go.

"Come here," he said, his hand beckoning me forth.

I walked over and fell into his arms, my sadness quickly rising to the surface. I looked up at his face. Tears were already beginning to collect in his eyes. He didn't even try to hide it.

"I'm not ready to leave this room," I said.

"Me neither," he replied. "But we must."

He was silent for a few moments before continuing.

"I want you to know that I'm here to fight beside you. I've been given these gifts for a purpose, and I intend to use them. I know that you're an extraordinary and powerful Strega, but I think the Goddess intends for us to fight together. And if we're going to beat Alessandro, that's how it must be. I need you to know, to truly understand, I'm not just a human anymore, I no longer need you to protect me. We can do this together."

I listened as he spoke, a myriad of emotions flashing across my heart. I was not sure I believed them, but I wasn't going to argue. We would fight together, but if it came down to his life or mine, I would do everything I could to preserve his.

He just didn't need to know it.

"I know," I responded. "And I understand. I knew the moment you locked the door last night that the Goddess has special plans for you. It's not common for Strega magick to be given to humans, and it's not to be taken lightly. Only those worthy, those with a purpose, are given such gifts."

"Not that I mind finally being able to stand my ground against you witches"—I could hear the playfulness in his voice turn serious— "I do wonder how my true path will unfold."

"One thing is for certain," I added. "Alessandro will never in a million years see this coming."

"Alessandro thinks I'm dead. He ran his sword straight through me." His voice was cold. "I cannot wait to return the favor."

I squeezed him tight as I remembered just how close Alessandro had come to killing him. I also knew that there was no way I was letting Gio get that close to Alessandro ever again. That was my job to finish. My hand traced over the spot on his chest where the scar was still raised like a bumpy caterpillar. He stiffened at the touch. Gently, I pulled my hand away.

"Come on," I urged. "It's time. I'm sure Claire and Willem are dying to see you."

We walked down the long corridor and entered the living room. Everyone was already awake. Claire and Willem sat together on the smaller couch. Patrick, and this new Watcher — Rowan—were sitting across from them. Matteo sat alone in a black leather chair. A coffee cart had been rolled in and rested near the fireplace. The smell incited my hunger, and I brought my hand to my stomach in reaction.

"I suppose a cup of coffee is in order before we get things started here," Gio announced as we walked into the room.

Everyone grew silent. Claire stared at Gio, her face still white with shock. He walked up to her, leaving about a foot of space between them.

"Claire ..." he began.

He didn't get to finish. She flew forward, throwing her arms around him. He returned her embrace equally.

"Don't you ever do that to me again," she sobbed, her words spilling out frantically, "I thought you were dead. I did what I could in the forest, but I thought it was too late, it wasn't enough. I can't believe you're here. I tried to stop Alessandro. I tried to kill him, I did, but he isn't dead and now you're here and alive and you and Katarina are together and—"

"Claire," Gio interrupted gently, "slow down." He took hold of her shoulders and pulled her back, looking her in the eye. "Slow down."

She nodded.

"I need you to hear this," he said. "There is nothing I can ever ... *ever* do that would come even remotely close to repaying you. You saved me, Claire. *You.* Not just in the forest, but from the moment you took me in.

"It's because of you that this time we have a chance to destroy Alessandro. It's because of you that Katarina and I are together. *You* are the difference this time. I'm not sure what the Goddess has in store for you, but I know I have nothing but gratitude toward you. I owe you my life ... on so many levels." He reached back and held out his hand to me.

I took it as I watched Claire hear his words. Her lips trembled as she listened.

"Because of you"—he brought my hand to his mouth and inhaled deeply— "I am no longer barely living. Claire, I'm fully alive now, stronger than I've ever been. With more understanding of life than I've ever had. You have to understand that. Please, don't hold on to the guilt any longer."

Claire looked at Gio and wiped her tears away. The rest of the room was silent as we all waited for her to respond. I wanted to hug her, tell her that Gio was right, but I was still unsure about how she was dealing with our soul-sharing the night before.

I did not want to push my limit with her ... just yet.

"I'm just … I just can't believe you're standing here," she finally said, breaking the silence.

"There's so much I have to tell you," Gio eagerly said. "I'm sure Patrick and Rowan have caught you up on some of the more … surprising updates, but there are some things that only I can tell you."

Claire nodded in understanding. "Later," she said. "Right now, Matteo was about to tell us more about his brother, Joshua."

For the first time, Gio looked around the room. Everyone was staring at us. Matteo, always the host, albeit reluctantly, broke the ice.

"May I get you some coffee?" His voice was formal, polite. I didn't trust it. Looking at Gio, I could tell that he didn't either.

"I'll get it," Gio offered, walking over to the cart. He shot a questioning look at Claire. I could sense it was about Matteo. Claire nodded in reassurance. I sat down next to Patrick on the couch.

"How're you holding up?" he asked quietly as I got comfortable. He was wearing his signature black Electric sunglasses, though we were indoors. I remembered a brief conversation we had about them in the hospital, shortly after Gio had been admitted.

"Do you always wear sunglasses indoors?" I'd asked, taking the seat he offered me one morning when the hospital was unusually quiet.

"It helps people not to judge me by what they think are limitations," he responded making himself comfortable in the plastic chair next to me.

"People will judge you anyway," I said.

"That's true," he had replied, "but I'd rather have control about what they are judging. That way, they'll never really know what to expect."

I thought about that conversation now as I answered him.

"I'm holding up quite well, thank you," I responded, smiling. He smiled back.

Patrick was a mystery, but I was beginning to trust him. That, and the fact that even though he had no actual vision, he watched Claire like a hawk. There was just something about that level of protectiveness I could relate to.

Gio handed me a coffee and I made room for him next to me. It was Willem who spoke up next.

"Now that we're finally all together, we need to figure out what were up against. I mean, is it even possible that Alessandro has summoned a demon?"

The room grew silent at the mention of Rau. The others began to discuss the possibilities of Rau's ascension and what it would mean if it were real.

I shot a careful glance in Claire's direction, curious to see her reaction to the conversation. She sat next to Willem and remained silent, though I knew she was thinking about what she'd learned last night.

There were too many secrets among us, but this was not one that could be divulged. Claire's gaze met mine and held it for the briefest of moments. I took that opportunity to test out a side effect of the spell.

Are you listening? I sent the thought across the room. *Can you hear me?*

Claire's eyes widened as her gaze shot in my direction, then looked down, trying to remain inconspicuous.

"How are you doing this?" she sent back. I smiled at the connection. It was something I knew could very well happen, but only when the two involved were loyal to each other. I knew for certain now that Claire would never betray me.

"Don't freak out, okay? It's a side effect of the spell we did last night—"

"The spell you did!" Claire corrected.

"C'mon, don't be mad. It's too late for that now. Besides, you have to admit, this could be quite an advantage."

"Shit. Can you hear my thoughts?"

"Only the ones you send to me ... most of the time," I answered. *"It's the same from this side. But just think about the possibilities."* I could tell that she was thinking about it.

"Fine. We should tell them about you and Alessandro, the whole story, how the two of you were taking shape to be the Goddess and God incarnate." Claire looked around the room and pretended to listen to the others.

"I can't. Not yet. Besides, it doesn't change what's happening now. I also don't entirely trust Matteo, either." I nodded my head at what Rowan was saying about Rau and what her studies had told her.

"Listen," I said, *"I just need to know if Matteo is someone to trust."*

"Okay." She responded. *"I'll see what I can do to find out. In the meantime, now that Gio's back, let's just try to keep him alive."*

I nodded in agreement, then added, *"Oh, and Claire, last night you weren't the only one who got a good look into a soul. Funny thing about that incantation ... I guess I should have warned you ... Strega spells are tricky like that. Anyway, I want you to know...,"* I paused and thought before adding, *"I know about you and Patrick."*

Claire's face turned white as she tried her best to act as if nothing was wrong.

Chapter Seventeen

GIO

Even based on the limited information that Matteo provided; we were all in agreement that Alessandro had indeed successfully summoned Rau. Just the thought of going up against such a powerful force left us concerned about what our plan of attack should be.

Collectively, we were an eclectic mishmash of magick, each bringing his or her unique power to the table. I was relieved to now be an equal to them. Though I was far from having mastered my abilities, I had always been a quick study. Under the guidance of my friends, I was sure to learn to use my powers with ease.

Matteo was turning out to be a valuable asset and a good guy. He kept us fed and comfortable. There was reason to believe that he wanted to see Alessandro dead just as much as any of us, but I was still leery of his motives. He told us about the Strega Underworld and gave us a basic understanding of how things worked. Now that we were in the Underground, Willem thought it best if we shared as much about Strega culture as possible. It took some time to explain the intricacies of revenge-casting to our Watcher friends. Though common among Strega, Claire, Patrick, and Rowan had been unfamiliar with the term. However, it took only a short while before they seemed to understand how deep the idea of revenge ran in Strega blood. It solidified the danger we were walking into.

Our respite at Matteo's also gave us time to figure out possible places Alessandro was hiding. On the third morning, we all met in the dining room. We sat around Matteo's table, still at odds with what our next move would be.

"I still think we should be sure of Alessandro's location before we make our move," Willem said.

"The longer we wait here, the less chance we have at finding him at all!" Katarina's frustration flared. "I know you think we're being cautious, but we're wasting precious time."

"But Katarina, we don't have any place to *go*. Where do we even start?"

"I think we should continue where we started a few days ago. Head to his office, or its vicinity, look around, see if there's anything there that may give us a hint of where to go next."

"Maybe we could poke around down here and see if anything unusual has been traded lately," Rowan suggested. "Who knows? We may just find out that we're not the only enemies Alessandro has made."

"If we did that, we'd have to use extra care to not arouse any suspicion. We don't know if Alessandro has made any friends, either," Willem commented.

"I'll help," Matteo said. "I could do it."

You didn't need to be a witch to feel the tension in the silence that followed. No one spoke; they didn't have to. The silence said everything we all thought. Was Matteo really someone we could trust? I sensed Katarina was on edge when the man was around, and I knew where I stood. But the lack of response from the group told me that we were not the only ones who had reservations about the man. It was not lost on our host.

"Look, I know that you don't completely trust me. That's fine," he began. "But I did not ask you to come here. *You* found *me*. You showed up at my doorstep. Whether you want to believe it or not, I'm in just as deep as you are now. Strega can be … unforgiving. If Alessandro has made friends, it's just a matter of time before word gets out that I'm harboring you, and that is something that I'd like to avoid."

He looked at Katarina, giving her a slight nod, then continued, "If you're going to do something, whatever it is, you need to do it already, because I don't know how long my wards will keep out prying eyes."

Matteo's speech might not have convinced everyone, but one thing was certain: we needed to act, and it had to be soon. Willem, resigned to the unavoidable, opened his hands palms up to the sky.

"Well, it appears that there's no more room for discussion. One group will go to Alessandro's office to see what they can dig up. Another group can poke around the Underworld here and see what emerges," he suggested.

"I'm going to Alessandro's office," Katarina stated. It was not a question.

"*We're* going," I corrected.

Katarina smiled as she reached over and squeezed my hand, though I could sense a tightness in her lips. I knew it would take time for her to adjust to the fact that I was no longer human, and to accept that I'd been given the gift of magick for the sole purpose of protecting her and defeating Alessandro. I had to give her time. She would come around, and soon she would understand that we were equals.

The conversation continued and after some debate, it was decided that Katarina, Claire, Patrick, and I would head above ground and see what we could find at Alessandro's office.

Matteo, Rowan, and Willem would stay back and dig around the Strega Underworld for information. It took some convincing, but Willem finally relented, understanding that between his and Matteo's Strega blood and Matteo's familiarity of the city layout, they would be able to navigate the Underground virtually unnoticed. Rowan's knowledge of Strega and its customs would also make her less conspicuous than if Claire or Patrick went.

With everything settled, Katarina and I retired to our room to pack a few things to take with us. Katarina gathered a few charms from her belongings Willem had eventually collected from their car. She changed her shoes to boots before grabbing her coat. She pulled her thick, dark hair back into a ponytail before slipping a large pocketknife into an inside sleeve in the garment.

I raised an eyebrow at her.

"Just in case the magick isn't enough," she replied. "There are few things that will drain evil's power faster than a spelled silver blade."

"And Alessandro?" I questioned.

"I'm talking about Alessandro," she responded coldly. "He's as close to pure evil as any Strega can be at this point. That's what happens when you sell yourself to Rau."

There was something in her eyes that told me there was more to Rau than everyone thought, something only she could tell. What did she know that she wasn't admitting?

She held my gaze and challenged me to ask with her stare, to question her statement. I opened my mouth but thought otherwise. There was no need. I trusted her completely. Katarina would tell me when she was ready.

As if in gratitude for that unspoken acknowledgment, she ran into my arms and squeezed me tight. She held me close as she buried her face into my shoulder.

"Thank you." Her words were muffled against my arms,

but I felt their enormity. After a minute, she pulled back. "I will tell you. I promise," she said, confirming my suspicions. "There's nothing that's more important than our bond. Our trust. Our love. Whatever happens, we must keep that in the forefront. We must not forget our bond to each other, especially when things may appear different than they are."

I pulled her close and held her into my chest, taking in her scent.

"I could never forget," I replied. "I don't know how many different ways I can tell you that there is not enough time that could pass to make me forget who we are, how much I love you, but I will continue to say it until you hear it for good. I will never give up on us. I will never forget our love. *Ever.*"

As if my words finally began to sink in, she nodded. I could feel her chest expand in my arms as she took a deep breath and looked up at me.

"Alessandro will be a distant memory, and all this will pass," she murmured. "I know it will. I can feel it."

A soft knock on the door interrupted our conversation.

"Gio? Katarina?" Claire called through the door. "We're ready."

I nodded at Katarina and took her hands in mine, squeezing them briefly. She gripped mine in return, then let them go as her own hands dropped to her sides. It was going to be a long night. Time to get down to business.

It took twice as much time making our way up to the surface than it had coming down. Claire, Patrick, Katarina, and I emerged into the alley where the cimaruta had opened the Underground up to us.

It was night. A thin layer of cloud cover in the sky hid the stars, only letting the moon peek out every now and then. I could feel a soft mist in the air as it landed on my face, moistening my skin.

"Typical," Katarina muttered as she pulled her coat tight. "I'll take that as a good sign."

I started at the comment, abruptly remembering that Katarina had lived a life in and around this city for thirty years. With him. It was hard to imagine, trying to reconcile the memories of past lives with the consciousness of who you truly are. I thought about all the time I had spent on this earth, and though at times it was unbearable, I was comforted by the fact that I was always myself. Katarina, on the other hand, had lived numerous lives, always someone different, never remembering who she was until now.

The thought weighed me down like a sandbag.

"So which way?" I said, shoving my feelings aside.

"It's not far to downtown, I say we walk," Claire said as she led us out of the alley and onto the surface streets. "Come on, this way."

By the look of traffic, the night appeared to be just getting started, but Claire was right—it was probably best not to try to park downtown. And after days of underground, a walk under the open sky seemed like just the medicine needed. With Claire and Patrick in front of Katarina and me, we walked up the block in silence. After several minutes, it was Patrick who spoke.

"So, Katarina, tell me about Alex. I know quite a bit about Alessandro, but I don't think I know much about the man you were married to." His voice was even. Calculated.

Though we were not touching, I felt Katarina tense beside me. Wanting to jump into the conversation but knowing that it was her choice on how to proceed, I waited for her to respond.

A wave of peace rippled over our group, and I knew she was centering herself. By the way Claire and Patrick responded to the energy, I knew they'd felt it too. Claire looked back at Katarina and they exchanged a look that seemed to carry more information than a mere glance could. It lasted for just a split second before it faded, and Claire looked forward again as we continued walking.

"Well," Katarina said, knowing that sharing her intimate knowledge of Alex might help in the long run, "with others, he was charismatic ... you know the saying: *Every woman wanted him; every man wanted to be him*? Well, that was Alex." She swallowed hard but pushed through the uncomfortableness. "He commanded a room, but it never seemed like it was driven by him. Others demanded his attention, craved it, and he always gave them exactly what they wanted." She paused. "I remember wondering how someone who shone like that could ever be interested in a person like me. At least, that's what he influenced me to think.

"Of course, now that I think about it, he charmed himself up the ass, but still, the way people looked at him, our neighbors, his colleagues, strangers at the grocery store, anyone ... they admired him."

"So, he used his magick to make himself seem godly," Patrick said. "I get that. But how was he at home? What did he do for fun, what were most of your interactions like with him? Was there anything that sticks with you *now* that might help us find him?"

Katarina was silent. After a few moments, she continued.

"He was always active, always moving," she said quietly. "He'd wake up early and take off for hours, riding his bike, surfing, diving for abalone ... always outdoors. He'd come home and I'd still be sleeping, and he'd tease me for being so lazy, knowing full well that he was the one that spelled me to sleep so long ... to keep me ... contained."

My stomach lurched as Katarina reminisced. I forced my anger to stay buried as I listened to her describe the abuse she had to endure.

"When we were together, it was all about him, what he

wanted to do, what he wanted to eat. If I argued, he'd put a stop to it."

"Stop it?" Patrick persisted. "Like with a spell?"

"I wish that was all it was ..." Katarina's voice trailed off in memory. "Patrick, how much do you know about the Old Ways of the Strega?"

"Not that much," he replied. "Just what I've learned from Rowan the past couple of days."

"There are some things that can't be found in books," Katarina said quietly. "Stregheria is a powerful and old religion, but as with any religion, certain branches practiced in different ways. The Ilmalo found early on that if a spell is cast with intense energy behind it, then the strength of the spell is greater and the chances of success are almost ensured." She paused. "Do you know what the Ilmalo found to be the strongest type of energy to cast with?"

Patrick shook his head. "No, I don't."

"Sexual energy. The Ilmalo discovered that when you cast with the intensity of sexual energy behind it, almost nothing would stop the spell. So, to answer your question, Alex, my doting husband, would throw up a haze spell, then proceed to cement his intentions with sex. And all I wanted to do was please him." A sour laugh escaped her throat before she added, "We were married for nine years. You figure out what type of *man* he was."

She stopped walking, letting the statement sink in. She closed herself off to the group and let the energy of her experiences with Alex dissipate into the night. Patrick, Claire, and I froze where we stood as we felt it roll past our beings. Even in the darkness, I could see Claire's horrified expression, and again, it looked as if she had heard something more than we had. Patrick removed his Electrics and rubbed his eyes. He looked like he was trying to erase an image, with no success, from his brain.

I stood next to Katarina, hardened by her words, but not shocked. I'd witnessed the descent of Alessandro throughout the centuries, each confrontation more sadistic than the last. Though his actions disgusted me to the core, this was not about me. It was Katarina who had endured an abuse far worse than I would ever know. It was my job to hear her words, to stand next to her, to wait with an open heart for her to return to me.

Slowly, I felt her open again. She looked over at me and shrugged her shoulders, not knowing what to say. It was Claire who spoke next.

"Katarina," Claire said, "what about that necklace he gave you? The red one? It was already loaded before he gave it to you. How did he set it? Someone had to have helped him."

Katarina's eyes flashed as she realized that what Claire said was true. The necklace he had given her was already loaded with magick. If sexual energy was what he had been using, who could have helped him?

"Oh, my Goddess," Katarina whispered. "I don't know why I didn't see it before. Claire, you're right. I can't believe I missed it. That necklace was chock full of magick well before he gave it to me. So how did he set the spell?"

"But who would he have gone to?" I asked. "There's no way he would have chanced sleeping with just anyone."

"You're right," Katarina replied. "He wouldn't have. It would've been someone he trusted, someone who needed him as much as he needed her."

Katarina's eyes widened as she realized exactly whom Alessandro had been in bed with. "I'm so stupid. I can't believe I didn't think of it before."

"What? What is it?" I asked.

"Celia. It was Celia."

"Who's that?" Patrick asked.

"The only other woman Alex ever talked about. The only

other woman in his life. He said they were childhood friends ... distant cousins. Whenever I wanted to go out with my girlfriends, Alex encouraged me to take Celia along. He said it was important to him for me to accept her. Practically threw us together every chance he got. Over time, I started losing my own friends, one by one. Pretty soon there was only one friend left ... Celia. She was even my maid of honor."

She laughed sarcastically and shook her head.

"In the early years of marriage, I had trouble ... adjusting. Celia was always there for me. She even moved to Freestone the first few months we lived there. She'd help me through whatever it was, and I'd go back to Alex, happier than ever. When she moved back to here, I was devastated ... then Dave and I clicked, and you all know the rest." She paused. "Son of a bitch! Fucking Celia! I should've known."

Claire stepped forward and offered her hand. Katarina took it and again they exchanged a knowing look. After several minutes, I sensed her returning to a calmer state.

"Well now we're getting somewhere," Patrick added when things calmed down. "First, we'll hit the office, then we can focus our efforts on finding Celia. Katarina, please tell me you know where she stays in the city."

"She's gonna wish I didn't," Katarina replied. "Let's go."

We reached downtown and headed to the address Katarina had remembered from Alessandro's business card. We ended up in front of an abandoned building in the middle of renovations. Ripped brown tarps hung from the risers that were set against the boarded-up facade. The windows were covered from the inside with newspaper.

"Lovely," Patrick commented as we surveyed the scene. "If this doesn't scream *Caution: Masochistic Strega at Work*, I don't know what does."

"Looks pretty empty," Claire stated. "I'm not picking up

on anything residual, either. Gio, let's head around the back. Katarina and Patrick, you try that way."

I wasn't entirely set on separating from Katarina, but I knew that there was no one here. I could sense it. Besides, it would give me some time alone with Claire and there were a few things I wanted to ask her.

Claire and I walked around the side of the building. The gate was an old, cast-iron piece, rusted through. There was a padlock on the handle.

"Stand back," I said, motioning for Claire to move.

I held my hands in front of me, palms out, directing my focus to the padlock. I could feel the energy collecting in my hands. When it felt as if it would burst out, I released it toward the padlock. *Open.* The rusted lock exploded with such force that it sent three pieces into the air. Claire stood there in shock.

"I'm still learning to rein it in a bit," I admitted, though secretly I loved the rush of power as it flowed through my system.

"That's pretty impressive," Claire replied as she picked up a piece of lock, then dropped it quickly. "Ooh, still hot. And, to think not too long ago, you walked into my store a mere human."

She pushed open the gate, and we stepped through, over the threshold.

The back of the building was overgrown with weeds and tall shrubbery. It seemed odd that a place so dilapidated would be found smack dab in the middle of downtown; I was expecting a space with more concrete and angles, not the rounded, messy tangles of nature.

"Things have changed, haven't they?" I said as I followed Claire, working up the courage to ask her what I really wanted to know.

"Not that much," she replied cautiously.

"Enough, though ... or so I've noticed," I responded.

"What do you mean?"

"Something's different between you and Katarina," I began. "I don't know what it is, but it's hard not to notice. At least, it is for me now."

Claire turned to look at me and took a deep breath.

"I'm not going to even try to lie to you," she started as she began climbing over a thick hedge. "But I am asking you, as a friend, to please not talk about this right now. It's complicated and I—ah!"

"Claire!" I cried as I watched her fall over the hedge into the dense thicket on the other side. I ran to the spot where she fell and leaned over to find her.

She was nowhere to be seen.

"Claire!" I yelled, panic rising in my voice. Where in the hell had she gone?

"Gio? What's happened?" Patrick came up from behind me. I turned to see him and Katarina running through the open gate.

"She's gone!" I called back. "Claire's gone. She was climbing over this hedge and fell back. I went to help her up and she had van—"

"I'm here." Claire's voice came from the opposite direction. "You guys have to check this out." She ran over to the hedge where I was standing.

I grabbed her arm.

"Don't. Do that. Again," I warned, releasing the stress from the moment before.

Patrick, also visibly shaken, was able to control his emotions better than I.

"You guys," Claire said, "check this out. It's an *orbis onerariis*."

Claire pulled back the mess of overgrowth. Below it was a

small circular disc. The faintest black light emanated from its edge.

"Patrick, do you remember? When we were younger?" Claire asked, then turned to explain. "When I was like fifteen, I was all into the whole rebellious phase, you know, sneaking out of the house and stuff. But it's pretty hard to be sneaky when your grandmother is like in charge of everything and your mom is potentially just as powerful. So, Patrick helped me create an *orbis onerariis* for my room. It would allow me to enter one place and exit another."

"Did it work?" I asked.

"A little too well," Claire replied in a strange voice. "Typically, you set it up for one direction of travel, then you set another for the trip back. I guess, I should have known back then that my power was much stronger than I thought. My *orbis* could go both ways."

"Claire," Patrick warned.

Claire stopped speaking. When she continued, she left her rebellious teen years in the past.

"This one here, like mine, can travel both ways. Not only that, but there's a pit stop in the middle. And *that* is somewhere you're gonna want to see."

Claire hopped over the hedge, landing on the disc and crossing her arms over her chest. I felt her release her guard and within an instant, she was gone.

"Katarina, you're next," Patrick called, helping her over the hedge.

"No," I stopped Katarina from climbing onto the disc. "I'm next."

Before any argument could be made, I hopped over the hedge and stood on the disc. Just as I saw Claire release her guard, I let mine drop. The moment I did, I felt as if the air was squeezing my body tight, pushing my ribs into my lungs. Before I could panic, it was over, and I was standing in a room that resembled an early 20th-century apothecary. Tall cabinets were stuffed with curios of all sorts. Various bottles stacked above a set of drawers that lined the walls were full of herbs and powders. Claire was standing near a long wooden counter with a large brass scale at the end of it.

A few seconds later, Katarina stood next to me, followed by Patrick.

"What is this place?" I asked.

"Welcome to The Lost Apothecary," a strange voice boomed from a doorway that had until now gone unnoticed.

Startled, we all jumped, moving closer to each other. I saw Katarina instinctively bring her hand to her coat where she had hidden the knife. The man put his hands up in a peaceful gesture.

"I did not mean to startle you. It's just been a while since I've had new visitors down here. Strange that the only ones who come to visit me anymore are you Italian folks," he said as he eyed Katarina and me.

Instinctively, I put my body between Katarina's and his.

"I can see that you're in no mood for chitchat," the man said. "So, I suppose we should just get down to business. What can I help you with?"

As he walked into the room, I was able to take a good look at him. Smooth, flawless skin with a deep, warm tone gave him an undeniable presence. His aura shone bright, making him seem otherworldly. Or more otherworldly, that is. He wore a traditional Jodhpuri-style suit made of silk, the trousers a smooth, maroon color, and the coat a deep navy lined with hand embroidery along the collar and at the buttons. He wore matching embroidered flats. Rectangular spectacles sat low on his nose. When he reached his place behind the counter, he waited patiently for one of us to speak.

"Is there something I can help you find?" the man asked again in a polite voice when none of us answered.

"We're just passing through the city and happened upon your place," Katarina said casually.

"My dear girl," the man said, sounding chafed, "one does not simply 'stumble upon' my shop. It is only here for those who are seeking it. Please do not insult me with half-truths."

He looked around at our party with deliberation. "So, let's start at the beginning, shall we? What, my friends, can I help you with?"

"We're looking for a man," I began, not wanting to tell him too much, but just enough for him to sense the truth. "He's Strega, like us," I said, gesturing to Katarina and myself.

The man looked us up and down, then over at Claire and Patrick, who had thought it best to fade into the background.

"And them?" he asked, nodding in their direction.

"Friends," I replied. Then, changing the subject back to what we wanted, I pushed on. "The man we seek has something that he shouldn't, and we wish to relieve him of it."

The man eyed us carefully before speaking again.

"I know whom you are referring to." His voice was flippant. "However, information such as this is the most expensive thing in my shop. It will come with a price."

"How much do you want?" I asked.

"I do not require money," the man spoke carefully. "What I seek is something of far greater value ... something that is not easily obtained. Let me first introduce myself. After all, it would not be proper to make deals with total strangers."

I eyed him carefully.

"My name is Akshay," he said and bowed slightly, never lowering his gaze from us.

The hairs on the back of my neck stood as chills traveled up my spine. I was sure that I didn't want to know what the man sought, but heard the words come out of my mouth before I could stop them. I took a step forward.

"Akshay, my name is Gio. And I'm sure we could go into

further pleasantries, but I'm afraid we are short on time. So please tell us what it is that you want."

Akshay smiled. I could tell from his demeanor that he knew we'd pay nearly anything for the information that he held.

"What I seek ... is a kidney."

"What the hell?" I said as disbelief spread across my face. Even after four hundred years, I was shocked by what people desired. I looked at the faces of my companions. It was apparent that they felt the same. "Why do you need a kidney?"

"That is none of your concern."

"We don't have a kidney," Katarina said.

"Ah, but I'm afraid you do. There are several standing in front of me."

I tensed. "Forget it. We'll find another way."

"Fine, then," Akshay said. "You may see your way out. There is no need for you to be here. I hope that you find the man you are looking for. If you do find him, please be kind to the lady he's with. We had such a lovely chat the last time they visited."

I could feel energy ripple from Katarina's body.

"Celia," she whispered.

I knew Akshay had slipped that little bit of information out on purpose to help motivate our willingness to produce a kidney for him.

Katarina stepped forward and said, "You can have mine."

Patrick, Claire, and I all stepped forward to stop her. Claire got to her first.

"Like hell, Katarina. There's no way you are giving him your kidney," she said. Then, stepping just a bit closer to her, she looked directly at her. I could see the exchange of information being discussed through their eyes but didn't know quite how it was happening.

"Very well," Akshay said. Then, looking to Claire and

Katarina, he continued, "While you two finish your discussion, I'm going to close down for the night."

So they were communicating. But how?

"Wait," Patrick called out as the man turned to leave. "You can take mine."

Claire snapped out of her conversation with Katarina and looked at Patrick.

"Patrick, no, you can't," Claire said.

"Yes, Claire, I can," he replied taking off his jacket. "The way I see it is that there's no way any of us is going to let Katarina give up hers. We need Gio whole too, and if you think I'm returning to your grandmother's place with *you* one kidney short, then you're absolutely mad. Besides, I'm already two eyes out and it rarely slows me down, so what's one more organ?"

Before any of us could stop him, Patrick tossed his coat down on the floor and bounded up to the counter.

"You can have one of mine."

"Very well," the man replied looking pleased. They shook hands, sealing the deal "The deal has been made. First, I will take what is mine; then, I will give you what it is you seek." Turning back to Patrick, he added, "Take off your shirt and lie on the counter ... face down."

Patrick swallowed hard but did not hesitate to remove his shirt. He handed it to Claire, who was now by his side. Claire's eyes were red with worry as she watched Patrick climb up onto the counter and lay face down on the smooth wooden surface.

Akshay brought his hands over the lower part of Patrick's back and held them over each side for a moment as if deciding which one he would take.

"Claire," I whispered as Katarina and I joined her next to Patrick, "be ready to get him out of here when this is finished. Take him to the surface and heal him as much as you can. Katarina and I will stay and get what we came for."

Claire wiped her tears with the back of her hand and nodded. She held Patrick's shirt close to her body. I could see her hands shaking.

After going back and forth for several minutes across Patrick's lower back, Akshay appeared to decide on the right kidney. His hands lowered to just an inch above Patrick's skin and hovered there.

"*Take what is mine, the flesh before me. Obtulit semper, never taken,*" Akshay repeated to himself as a small red light began to burn bright from his palms. "*Take what is mine, the flesh before me. Obtulit semper, never taken.*"

The ball of red light seemed to grow thicker and denser with each repetition of the incantation. Akshay's hands began to vibrate from the energy. Suddenly, the red light turned black. Akshay let out a roar as he shoved his hands through Patrick's body. Patrick screamed in agonizing pain before passing out.

Katarina embraced Claire as she tried to lunge for Patrick. Instinctively, I stepped forward and pulled them both close into my arms. Claire's eyes were glazed over in tears as we all watched in horror as Akshay's hands rummaged around the inside of Patrick's lower torso.

When they had found what they were looking for, Akshay pulled both hands out with a sharp tug, Patrick's limp body lifting, then falling back down on the wooden counter with a sickening thud.

I watched how Akshay held the dark brownish-red organ in his hands, his eyes alight in excitement. He placed the kidney in a clear glass jar on the counter, screwing the lid on top with care and went back to Patrick's still body.

We were silent, save for Claire's sniffles, as we waited for what would happen next.

With a quick movement, Akshay waved his palms above the jagged opening that was left. The wound sealed instantly.

He went back to his fresh harvest and began cleaning up the area. Patrick moaned and moved slightly.

"Let's get him out of here," I said as I moved to turn Patrick over on the counter.

"Patrick," Claire whispered, "can you hear me?"

Patrick moaned softly but was only half conscious.

With care, we sat the eyeless Watcher up, pulled him off the counter and stood him up on his feet against Claire. She brought his arm around her shoulders and grabbed the waistband of his pants.

"I've got this, Gio," she said through gritted teeth. "Don't let his sacrifice be for nothing. Get the information we need to find Alessandro."

Katarina and I watched as she carried the man to the *orbis onerariis* disc. They stood on it for a second before vanishing.

I looked over and saw Katarina watching the spot where they were just a moment ago.

"And now I assume you will be wanting the information you came for." Akshay's voice still excited from his latest acquisition.

I looked to Katarina and saw her body stiffen.

"Tell us what you know," she demanded. "Tell us everything about the man and his female companion."

Chapter Eighteen

KATARINA

"The last time the came in was a couple weeks ago. Over the years, they've been frequent visitors, but something was different this time," Akshay spoke evenly and unhurried. "At first glance they looked like every other magick-addled couple, looking for their next fix."

I looked over at Gio. He was focused on Akshay's words, as if trying to decipher hidden meaning between them.

"*Magick-addled*?" Gio said.

"What I mean was that they looked ... drunk. Like they had gotten greedy and taken in too much outside power. It's not uncommon to see many young practitioners these days who cannot hold their magick. It becomes an addiction, something they cannot live without. Before they know it, they do not practice magick anymore; it is the magick that is practicing them. In the past, the man had proven to be a powerful sorcerer and the woman not far behind. I sensed something was not right."

I rolled my shoulders back at his words. I knew what he meant by magick-addled, and it hit a bit too close to home. My mind flashed to a moment of my youth when I was first beginning to practice the art of Strega.

"I bet I can lift that larger stone," I had boasted to my father one afternoon during lessons.

"Really, mia bella?" My father replied, raising his eyebrows in amusement.

Extending my arm, palm up, I pushed my energy toward the stone. It wobbled but did not rise. Not wanting to be wrong, I took a deep breath and refocused my energy. This time I could feel the magick sear through my body and the stone wobbled a bit more. Knowing that I needed just a bit more energy, I searched for a life force to steal from.

A small bird had been pecking at the mud in the shallow creek bed. I reached out with my energy and wrapped it around the little bird. I could feel the bird's quick heart as it tried to fight against me, to get away, but I held fast to it.

Slowly, I sucked the life force from its body until I thought I had just enough to move the stone. Pulling it through my system, I expelled it from my hand toward the large stone. It rose up with ease.

I laughed, delighted at myself. I could feel the magick flow through me. I was invincible.

My father sat up from where he sat against the tree startled, a look of concern on his face.

"Katarina, what did you do?" He stood and rushed over to where the bird was now lying in the small puddle.

I was too pleased with myself, felt too good, to notice the little bird. I was already looking for my next energy fix.

"Katarina!" My father yelled. "Look! Look at what you have done."

His voice crushed my high. I looked to where he knelt, the little bird lay still in his hand.

"With every action you take, there is a consequence you must be prepared for. Taking energy from others is a very dangerous hobby, my dear. Take too much and you may find that nothing will ever be enough until you take it all," he said in a serious tone. "Are you prepared to live with that in order to accomplish your goals?"

I stood stunned in front of him. I was torn over how to feel. Taking the bird's life force had felt so good, but as I looked at the lifeless creature, its eyes empty and black, I knew that I could not let my desire ever again get the best of me.

I shivered at the memory.

"You know what I speak of. I can see it in your face." Akshay's voice was knowing. I blinked slowly, acknowledging his words.

"I know that magick can be addictive," I replied. "It can hurt just as much as it can heal. And I know that if you take too much of another's life force, you will never be whole until you are always filled with another's energy."

I kept my eyes on Akshay, refusing to look at Gio. I was not prepared for him to see the Ilmalo side of me yet. How could I tell him that I knew exactly what Akshay spoke of? The moment the energy from that tiny little bird left my body, I felt the emptiness in my soul. My first instinct was to immediately search for ways to fill it.

At first, I had struggled daily with not refueling the void with another bit of energy, but it was my father who had helped me, led me to understand what the feeling meant, to learn how to manage the craving.

I could feel Gio reach out to me. His hand slid along my lower back, and he gently pulled me closer to him as if sensing my vulnerability.

"What does this information tell us?" Gio asked moving the conversation along.

Akshay huffed, shifting his eyes to Gio.

"The woman was holding up the man as they staggered in. Like I said, *at first,* I thought they were intoxicated. But then I realized that it wasn't that at all. He was seriously injured, his energy sucked dry. And I could feel something dark about him as they came farther into the shop. Something stronger than I have felt in a long time. It stuffed up my shop with its oppressiveness."

Akshay leaned closer to us.

"The woman, she had it too. It sloughed off her with every step. Pure blackness ... demons, if you ask me."

"Are you sure?" Gio inquired.

Akshay looked at him seriously.

"I don't speak lightly about demons, young man, and I cannot tell you for sure. But I can tell you that they asked for a reishi tonic."

"Reishi? The immortality drink?" I questioned shocked. "And you gave it to them?"

"My dear," Akshay chided, "a pure immortality tonic would cost more than anyone could imagine. Even for the two of them, and their pockets seemed to be well-lined. No, the woman specifically asked for a lesser variety of the plant, something that could keep the man alive for a bit longer, so that they could reach their destination. As I said before, the man was in a grave state."

Akshay paused.

I took the moment to steal a glance at Gio. If Alessandro was that seriously injured, then perhaps he was still in the city. I wasn't sure what Gio thought, but this wasn't the time to bring it up.

"What else did the woman say?" I pursued.

Akshay looked at me and smiled.

"After I made the tonic, she gave it to him. I helped her move him to the back area to lie down until it took effect. We came up to the front here and had tea while we waited," Akshay relayed, drawing out his story for pure amusement.

I could tell Gio was losing his patience with this

storyteller. Sensing a change in the energy as well, Akshay continued.

"I asked the woman what had happened. She told me there had been a misunderstanding; that her lover had been injured by a colleague when a contract was not upheld. She told me that it was always that way with the real Strega. Too much passion ... or something along those lines."

Akshay held my gaze. I felt a bit of vomit creep into my mouth at the mention of Alessandro. Why hadn't I seen it before? Why had I been so blind to Alessandro and his ways? I cursed myself again for the incompetence I had so wholeheartedly shown. How could I have let him control me like he did? Was I not more powerful than he?

"Did they say where they were headed?" Gio's voice broke me out of my self-deprecating spiral.

I looked up at Akshay, eagerly awaiting his response.

"I asked the woman if they were also requiring accommodations, I will occasionally board those who are passing through, but she told me that their plans were to remain in the city. She would've said more, *my tea* would have ensured it, but the man awoke and interrupted us. He reeked of the darkness he came with. The woman, startled into silence, hurried over to his side."

"Did they say anything else?" I asked. "Anything at all?"

Akshay took a moment to reflect. I could almost see the scene he relived in his mind.

"I'm sorry to say no, there was nothing else," he eventually said, though I was not sure I believed him. "They paid for the tonic with coin I have not seen in many, many years. Italian in origin, but I will accept almost any currency ... as you well know."

I grunted in disgust. I'd heard everything Akshay had to say and was ready to go above ground. I had not forgotten about Claire and Patrick and thought that Gio and I had been pushing our time in the shop. Anxious to get back to our friends, I moved to make our departure.

"Thank you, Akshay," I said. "You have given us much to think about. But for now, we must take our leave. Our friends will be awaiting our arrival above ground."

Akshay brought his palms together in front of his chest and gave a slight bow.

I turned to head back to the *orbis onerariis*. Gio was right behind me. My heart warmed. It felt good to have him so close. I reached out to take his hand which he immediately received. It seemed normal. Natural. As we approached the disc, I saw a slight quiver in the air above the bookshelf just to its right.

"Oh, shit," I whispered to myself as I threw my body against Gio, pushing him behind a thick curio cabinet filled with brightly colored tapestries. We fell to the floor just as a bolt of energy sliced through the air where we had been only a second ago.

"What the hell was that?" Gio gasped.

"Rau ... maybe," I answered.

I could feel my eyes turning red as I spoke. The anger in me was so great there was nothing I could do to stop them. I turned my head away from Gio, hoping that he did not see the change in color.

"You are not welcome!" Akshay's voice carried throughout the store. I tried to see what was happening from where we hid, but there were too many obstacles in our path. "I send thee out with all the power of the gods and goddesses behind me. This is a place of respite. This is a place of refuge. You will not bring your kind in here, demon!"

I heard a monstrous roar. It was so vile, so blood-curdling, I felt it in every cell in my body. I tried to get up. There was no way I was going down without a fight. Gio pulled me into him and held me down.

"Don't," he whispered. "Look!"

He pointed to the narrow space between two shelves. From that vantage point, we could see Akshay's feet as they came around the counter and walked methodically toward where Rau had thrown the energy.

"This is my shop, demon. It is neutral ground," Akshay continued with each step. "There are rules even you must abide by."

As Akshay got closer and closer to where we hid, we were able to see him emerge from behind the shelves. He held his hands out on each side of his body, his palms facing up. In each palm, a bright, blue light crackled and popped as it grew. For a moment, it looked like he was holding lightning.

"I did not call your name. I do not let you in, demon. By the power of the gods I hold in my hands, be gone!"

Akshay released a deep bellow as he brought both hands above his head and with a massive lunge forward, threw the blue lightning toward where the demon had been.

An explosion erupted when the lightning hit its target. Silence.

Gio and I lay on the floor of the quiet shop.

"Are you all right?" he asked after a minute.

"Yes. You?"

"To be honest, there's a lot more to having Strega power than I know what to do with yet," he replied.

"Hey, you two!" Akshay hissed from the end of the aisle. "The demon is gone for now, but I have a feeling the only reason I was able to rid us of him was due to the element of surprise—that and the fact that he did not have a pure physical form. But I don't know if he'll be gone long. It depends on if the witch binding him will gain control."

"Did you see him?" Gio asked, brushing off his pants as he stood up.

Akshay shook his head.

"No, I could just sense his presence. Then I saw the attack," he added. "But this is my shop. It has always been a place of neutrality. In the three hundred and forty-three years I have been in business; I have never had a demon set foot on the premises. I do not intend to let them start now. "Akshay shook his head.

"No, this is not right. I don't like this one bit. And I think this has something to do with the Strega you were asking about."

"Look, Akshay, I'm going to be blunt," I said, straightening my shirt. "The man we are looking for is quite dangerous. He is into something that has allowed him to use very old Strega magic ... from the Old Ways. Please believe us when we tell you we only have one mission in life—to hunt this man down and destroy him. You've seen firsthand how reckless he has been to resurrect a demon. So if there is anything else you can tell us about where he may be, now would be the time to say something."

Akshay reached into his pocket, pulled out a small business card, and handed it to me.

"This fell out of the woman's coat when they first arrived. I saw it fall and waited until they left to pick it up."

I took the card and read it.

"Club Shadow?"

"It's a private club for big players in the underworld. If he's not there, I can assure you that someone there knows him, knows where he's been staying. Now hurry. Go!" Akshay urged.

I grasped the card firmly in my hand before slipping it deep into my pants pocket. I reached out and held Akshay's hand.

"Thank you. We won't forget this," I replied, heading toward the *orbis onerariis*.

"I hope you don't. I may need your help one day.

Especially if your friend finds out that I am the one who helped you find him."

"He is not our friend," I called back as Gio and I stepped on the disc. "And if we find him, he won't have time to figure it out because he'll be dead."

The next moment, I was outside of the building in the unkempt backyard space of the abandoned office building.

"Claire!" Gio cried as we became accustomed to the change in light.

Claire and Patrick sat side by side against a brown fence on the East end of the space.

I sent a message to Claire the minute it appeared in my brain.

"Please tell me that Patrick is okay."

"Yes, he's fine ... for now. But we really need to get him back to Matteo's house. He needs rest."

Gio made it to the two before I did. He crouched down next to Patrick.

"Well, who would have thought that I'd outlast you in this mission?" he teased the injured man.

Patrick smiled. "Now, don't get too cocky, mate. I may be a bit slow now, but maybe this was the only way to level the playing field. I mean, I have to give you some chance of being as cool as me." He winced in pain.

Claire let out a frustrated breath, but the tension in her shoulders eased and a faint smile tugged at her lips. I could tell that she was overwhelmed with relief that Patrick had the energy to be sarcastic.

"Okay guys, enough," she scolded. "I think it's time to get back to Matteo's before anything else can go wrong."

Gio and I glanced nervously at each other. It was so obvious that even Patrick was able to catch it.

"What?" Claire began, "Wait! Do I even want to know?"

"Let's get back to Matteo's first. Hopefully Willem and

Rowan will be back. Then we'll fill you in," I said calmly, blocking my thoughts.

I could feel Claire poking around in my head, looking for answers.

"Tell me, Katarina."

"Later. I promise."

Claire shook her head in resignation, knowing that I wasn't going to budge on this matter. Then she and Gio got on either side of Patrick and lifted him up into a supported standing position.

When we got to the street, I hailed a cab. We awkwardly climbed in and headed back to the entrance of the Underworld. It felt like an entire year had passed, when in reality it had been only a couple of hours. I leaned my head against Gio's shoulder, relaxing against the rise and fall of his chest while I looked at the stars. I was surprised at how many were visible. Typically, you had to be out on Twin Peaks with clear skies to see any stars in this city.

Gio pressed his lips to my hair and kissed my head. He stroked the top of my hand with his thumb. I knew that if I let myself, I could fall asleep just as I was. I could let everything else go and just fade away with Gio.

But that wasn't going to happen. It couldn't. As much as I wanted to pretend that we could live together in peace without ever having to look over our shoulders, I knew it was a lie. I had to stay awake, stay sharp. I couldn't let myself relax too much, no matter how tired I felt. Because our night was just getting started.

Chapter Nineteen

GIO

Willem and Rowan had already returned by the time we stumbled into Matteo's house. Patrick was still too weak to hold himself up alone, so Claire and I supported each of his sides, our arms wrapping around his lower back. Considering he had just lost a vital organ; he was doing much better than I had anticipated. I marveled at how Claire had been able to get him back this far.

However, to Willem, Rowan, and Matteo, he must have looked the worse for wear, because as soon as we entered the living room, all hell broke loose.

"Patrick! What happened, Claire?" Rowan shot out. Willem jumped up from where he had been sitting on the couch, tossing the book on his lap aside.

"Rowan, dear," Patrick said managing to sound playful, though I knew he was in a great deal of discomfort. "Nothing to worry about, girl. Just something that needed to be done."

Rowan's eyes widened as Patrick's head slumped forward onto his chest. He had passed out from exhaustion.

"We need to get him to a bed," Claire ordered.

Claire and I hauled Patrick into the small guest room. I was glad that Matteo had taken care to have queen-sized beds in all his guest rooms; it made getting Patrick in it that much easier.

The room itself was decorated in the same black-and-white motif that styled the rest of the home. Though there were no windows, the room appeared light and airy. A small circular onyx writing desk sat in the corner of this room with two pristine white upholstered chairs on each side.

Claire turned off the main light as I switched the bedside lamp on. Patrick was barely conscious.

"Claire"—his voice was raspy as he reached out to grab her arm as she covered him with the blankets—"just lie down with me for a minute ... please."

"Of course," she responded without hesitation, positioning herself next to him above the covers.

"Claire, if things don't go well, if this is the end—"

"Stop right there," Claire interrupted. "This is not the end, and you know it. So don't even try to say what you're about to."

I stood next to the bed in silence, watching the two exchange what I feared were last words.

"You know, I told myself when I took this job that I would do anything I needed to in order to keep you alive and safe. I wanted to prove to you that I'm still a man of my word, that I would do anything for you ... you know, ever since ..."

Patrick winced in pain. Claire turned on her side and gently placed her arm across his chest.

"Don't," she whispered. "None of that matters. It never did ... at least, not to me. You can't keep beating yourself up over something that wasn't your fault. I was just as much a part of it as you were. Truth be told, it was *my* fault. Your sacrifice was far greater than mine."

Claire brought her fingers up to Patrick's eyes. Removing

his sunglasses, she revealed the two scarred-closed sockets. She brought her fingers to each one and softly caressed the rough skin.

I watched as her fingertips began to softly glow a pale white light as she brushed her fingertips over the old wound. Patrick seemed to relax under her touch. I remembered all too well how gifted Claire was in the healing arts.

Patrick took a deep breath and let go of any remaining efforts to stay awake. He slumped back into the bed.

"There," Claire said, looking up at me for the first time since we entered the room. "He should be resting for a while now. He'll never recover if he continues to think of old wounds that won't change anything."

She slowly got up from where she lay and walked over to the small table. Taking a seat in one of the chairs, she placed both elbows on its surface and buried her face in her hands.

"Claire, you did good," I said as I walked over to join her. Although I had questions about what I had just heard, I wanted to check in with her first. "Quite amazing, in fact. But how are you really holding up?"

Claire's wry, muffled laugh was a bitter release of air through her hands.

She lifted her face; she looked wrecked. Her eyes were red and puffy, her skin a pasty white. I could see that her lips were becoming dry and chapped, and I wondered if it was because of the amount of stress healing someone put on her body or if she was simply dehydrated.

I stood and went into the small bathroom attached to the room. I filled the water glass at the sink, grabbed a box of tissues and returned to the table before I dared to continue.

"Here," I offered, handing her the glass before taking a seat on the other chair.

Claire brought it to her lips and took a long, slow drink before setting it back onto the table.

"I don't know if I can do this," she said after a couple minutes. "I'm trying, please believe me, I am. But I don't know if I can do this."

"I know you can do this," I said as I reached across the table to cover her hand. "You are the reason we all are able to."

She let my statement set, then nodded.

"It's just that after I had taken Patrick up to the surface ... I sat there next to him ... and I ... I thought, this man, this person lying in front of me, was dying, and his only chance of surviving was me. It was up to *me* to heal him, to bring him back ... And it was *Patrick*, of all people. He *knew* what he was doing. He *knew* he was putting his life on the line. But *why*? Why did it have to be Patrick?"

If I was going to ask anything about the relationship between the two of them, it had to be now. I opened my mouth to ask, when a gentle knock on the door interrupted.

Quietly, the door opened. Willem was standing there, a steaming mug in his hand. Claire smiled at him as he entered the room, making no noise. He glanced over at the bed where Patrick lay.

"How is he?" Willem whispered.

"He'll be okay," Claire replied. "One kidney short, the jackass, but ... okay. He just needs some time to recover."

"Aye, Katarina filled us in. Here, this will help him along." Willem placed the mug on the table. "It still needs to cool completely, but I thought I'd get it here as soon as it was done."

I looked into the mug. An iridescent blue liquid filled it halfway.

"It's from my mother's book. It's one of the oldest cures for physical repair the Onesta have. You'd be surprised at how well-stocked Matteo's pantry is," he said adding as he nodded to the mug. "It won't grow a kidney, but it'll make him feel like brand new."

"Thank you," Claire said, leaning in to hug him.

The two embraced tightly and I realized I'd forgotten how strong their bond was. Willem pulled back first, taking Claire's face between his two hands.

"Please tell me that I don't have to worry about you doing something like this," he said seriously. "I cannot continue this mission if I believe all Watchers are as impulsive as he is."

Claire smiled but didn't answer. I found it oddly unnerving.

"So, is there anything in your mother's book for me?" she asked, changing the subject. "Cause my anxiety is through the roof."

Willem smiled, reached into his back pocket, and pulled out a small silver flask.

"It's not from my mother's book, but it'll do for your nerves just the same."

Claire took the flask and uncorked it. The thick, peaty smell of a highland whisky caught the air. She brought the vessel to her lips and took a long pull. Passing it over to me, I did the same. The heat burned as it traveled down my throat. I handed it back to Willem, who followed suit before placing it back in his pocket.

"Well, I'll be heading back to report to the rest," Willem said. "Claire, after he takes that drink, he'll go back to sleep for another few hours. We'll be in the great room. I think that you'll be surprised at what Rowan and I were able to uncover."

Willem turned and headed to the door. Claire followed. I stole a glance at them as they talked in hushed tones. Before he left, Willem pulled her close and kissed her full on the mouth and she melted into his embrace.

I shifted my eyes back to the potion, giving them their moment. One of the most precious, and often overlooked, treasures that life offered was human connection. Every moment, no matter how small or apparently insignificant, was important and deserved to be honored as such.

The truth of that statement stung.

When Willem left, Claire came back to the table and picked up the mug. She looked over at Patrick.

"You care about him deeply," I commented.

"He's very special to me."

"In what way?"

She had the mug between her two palms and brought it up to her face. She inhaled deeply, then turned back to me.

"What are you asking, Gio."

"It just seems like the two of you have a past that goes beyond friendship."

"I suppose sooner or later you'd find out anyway," she began, her face saddened. "I was hoping that I could leave the past behind me, but I can see now there's no way around it. I was just hoping that the Goddess would see fit to leave this discretion a secret."

She shook her head.

"But we all know the truth will find a way out. And so I guess I just have to trust that you ... will not judge me by my past actions, but for who I am now."

"Claire, we all have our secrets. We all have made past mistakes. There's nothing that you can tell me that I cannot forgive."

She didn't look convinced.

"I'm not so sure about that. But there's no use keeping it a secret any longer," she said. "Will you just hold off on telling Willem until all this is over? I don't need him distracted."

I held her gaze for a long moment before answering. "That's your secret to tell, not mine," I said. "If you want to wait, that's your choice. But once this is over, you owe him the truth."

Though I was torn about keeping something from

Willem, I would. Claire had never acted in any way but loyal and trustworthy in her interactions with me, despite the fact that I had put her life at risk. If she wanted to hold onto her secret until Alessandro was dead before telling Willem, then I would respect that.

"And I will tell him," she said. "I promise. Just later."

"I understand," I assured her.

Claire placed the mug back on the table and sat in the chair, this time, flopping down and stretching out her legs in front of her. She reached her arms above her head and stretched out her body. She was a waif of a girl, long and lean. I could see the muscles in her arms tighten as she stretched them out a bit farther before releasing with a big sigh.

"Do you remember that first day we met, and I told you that my mother was out of town, that I was the one who was there to run things?"

I smiled in acknowledgement. I had been so suspicious of her at our first meeting. I hadn't known at the time that she would be the key that helped Katarina and me get farther on this journey than we ever have before.

"Well, that wasn't entirely true," she continued. "The truth is that my mother has not been home for years. She left on my seventeenth birthday, and I doubt I will ever see her in person again. Every now and then I'll get a phone call or an email, but she keeps her distance. Because the truth of it, the hard truth that I don't want to admit is ... she's disgusted by me."

Claire paused as the words echoed in the room.

"What do you mean, she's disgusted by you?"

"You know, when I was younger, thirteen or fourteen years old, my powers were emerging. It was apparent early on that I would be my grandmother's replacement—that I would look over our people, lead them, help them to be the best they could be. My grandmother knew it, my mother knew it, and I suppose somewhere deep down, I knew it as well.

"They were so pleased ..." Her voice trailed off in the memory. She took a deep breath before continuing her story.

"My mother left after she found out what had happened with Patrick. I overheard her and my grandmother arguing over it. Then, on the morning of my seventeenth birthday, she was gone. Said she had some traveling to do. But I knew the truth."

Claire was silent, lost in her memories.

"What happened with Patrick?"

Claire swallowed hard. I could hear how her voice wavered as the knot in her throat returned as she tried to speak.

"Perhaps it would be best if I show you," she said as she slid her hands across the table for mine.

I didn't hesitate. I placed my hands in hers and was instantly drawn into her memory.

I looked around the room in Claire's mind and recognized a party. Teens were scattered about in groups playing various drinking games and smoking pot. Claire was standing in the middle of the room, looking at her phone. Only this Claire looked a bit younger, with less worry and time on her face. Her cheeks were smooth and pink. She looked ... innocent. She wore long blonde hair down to her waist. Half of it was pulled back in one thick braid. She was wearing leggings and a plain, light blue sweater that hung down to her knees.

Suddenly, a younger Patrick was by her side. Like Claire, he looked as if years were erased from his face, which was worry-free and nicely tanned. He wore a T-shirt and cargo shorts, but the most striking difference was his eyes. Not only were both of his eyes fully intact, they were the color of amethysts in the sun. They almost glowed.

"Claire," he said as he grabbed her around her waist and

kissed her quickly, "you're here! I knew it would work ... I just didn't know when."

"Well, your *orbis* did work ... and brilliantly, I might add. And there's no way my grandmother or mother will know I snuck out. It was like the best plan ever. You, my dear sir, are amazing."

"Well, it kinda helps when you can see most of the future." He winked at her.

Smiling, the younger Claire jumped up and wrapped her arms and legs around Patrick, who held her up around him. Their lips met passionately as if they were the only two in the room.

After a few minutes, Claire hopped down and took Patrick's hand. "Come on, let's get out of here."

His characteristic half-smile spread across his face. Patrick was more than happy to oblige. They left the main party in search of a more private space. Claire's memory took me with them to a smaller room at the end of the hall. The couple entered, slamming the door behind them, then fell onto the bed in a passionate embrace.

I knew that Claire was sharing this memory with me, but it felt like an intrusion. Not to mention I was shocked by what I was seeing. Though their relationship had always been somewhat of a mystery to me, I hadn't considered it to have ever been mutually intimate. To see the two of them like this, in love, was both shocking and confusing.

However, I didn't have to sit with the feeling for long. The door burst open and two bulky guys rushed into the room, closing and locking the door behind them.

"Well, look what we have here," the taller one sneered.

Claire and Patrick jumped off the bed and faced their aggressors. Patrick stood with his body in front of Claire's.

"What do you want, Blaine?" Claire yelled over Patrick's shoulder.

Blaine looked over at his buddy and smiled.

"It's quite simple, Claire." He laughed. "You stood me up last week for this douche." He nodded at Patrick. "As I see it, you owe me one night."

"That's not going to happen, mate," Patrick answered. "So, you might as well make this easy on yourself and just leave now."

"Oh, look here, Tommy," Blaine said to his buddy who was laughing. "The little guy has something to say."

"Stay out of this, dumb ass," Tommy snorted. "This is between Blaine and her highness."

"Blaine, you're drunk and high," Claire challenged, her eyes narrowed. "Go sleep it off and I promise I'll never talk to you ever again."

The two boys had different plans. I shuddered as a sinister gleam twinkled in Blaine's eye. The two charged the young couple. Tommy grabbed Patrick easily, while Blaine went for Claire.

"Don't fight me, Claire," Blaine said as he grabbed her wrists and pulled her close.

The moment that Blaine grabbed her, Claire stopped fighting and became very still. Her eyes turned grey and cloudy. I watched as her body began to glow all over. Blaine took a step back, his eyes widening in surprise. Tommy let go of Patrick.

"Claire, no!" Patrick yelled, but it was too late.

The three boys stood in the room as the glow around Claire became brighter and brighter. She raised her hands and sent the energy in Blaine's direction. Blaine was struck down by the impact and crumpled into a heap on the floor.

I watched as Tommy's expression turned to fear as he took a few steps back and tried to unlock the door with fumbling fingers. Claire quickly turned to the boy and with another surge of energy, Tommy staggered back a few steps before joining his friend on the floor.

The bodies were lifeless shadows on the carpet.

"Don't you ever touch me again," Claire said in a calm and eerie voice before her eyes cleared up and turned back to green.

After a silence, she shook her head.

"Oh, no. No, no, no. Goddess help me! What did I do, Patrick?" She said, panicked. "I mean, I know what I did, but I couldn't stop myself, I … I wanted them dead. It was self-defense, though. I mean, you knew what they were going to do to me, right? Oh, Goddess, what am I going to do?"

"Don't worry," Patrick said calmly. He lifted her chin gently and looked into her eyes. "We'll take care of this. I know what to do. No one has to know."

Suddenly, my eyes stung, forcing me to rub them with my fingers. When I reopened them, I was once again sitting in the room with Claire. Patrick was still sleeping.

"You killed them?" I whispered.

Claire nodded, ashamed.

"I did. And Patrick helped me cover it up … to protect me."

"But what happened next?"

"Patrick helped me move the bodies to the forest, where we buried them in the old pet cemetery. After we had placed the last stone on the mound, Nemesis, the goddess of revenge, appeared before us. She demanded an explanation. Before I could say anything, Patrick … so impulsive … stepped forward and took the blame.

"I tried to intervene … tried to tell the truth. I was sure that if we told Nemesis the truth behind our actions, *my* actions, the truth of what Blaine and Tommy were planning to do, she would understand.

"But Patrick didn't want to leave it to chance. He agreed to accept the consequences for both our deeds and in exchange, our secret would forever be concealed from our people. He ..."

Claire's voice broke. She looked over at Patrick, tears streaming down her cheeks.

"Is that what happened to his eyes?" I asked.

Claire nodded. She grabbed a tissue and blotted her tears away.

"First, Nemesis took his eyes, his gift of foresight. She left the rugged scars there as a mark for everyone to see that justice was administered. However, what she did next, neither one of us expected."

Claire cleared her throat before continuing.

"Nemesis forbade us to be with each other. She told us that if we pursued a relationship farther than friendship, the deal would be void, our secret would be set free, and we would no longer be under her protection. My heart broke when she handed down her final judgment, but there was nothing to be done. To go against her would just make a mockery of his sacrifice.

"I knew I had to distance myself. I had to make myself stop loving him. At first, I couldn't even see him, my heart would ache so. But after a while, our feelings for each other changed. We realized that we would rather have each other in our lives than not at all, because when it came down to it, we couldn't survive without the other.

"But Blaine and Tommy's disappearance quickly spread. When Patrick emerged with the mark of Nemesis, everyone knew that he knew what had happened, that he was somehow involved, but no one dared question it because justice had been served. Everyone knew that sometimes it's better not to meddle in others' business, especially if it involves a deity. Everyone, except my grandmother and mother. They both approached us and interrogated us thoroughly, but neither one of us would talk.

"It wasn't long after I overheard them arguing over it. Mom had seen what had happened in a dream. She demanded I be held accountable, but my grandmother refused, saying that she would denounce my mother from the clan if she said anything. Grandmother claimed that if Nemesis had dealt with it herself, then that should be the end of it.

"My mother couldn't even look at me. Not only had I gone against the golden rule of the Watchers, to protect and preserve human life, but I'd allowed someone else to take the fall.

"At least that's how she saw it. She left soon after ... on my seventeenth birthday. After that, I gave up all magick. I put no further study into my powers despite my grandmother's pressure. My mother eventually did come to an understanding about that night, but I know she still struggles with it."

When Claire had finished, she leaned back into the chair, exhausted.

"I know what I did was wrong. *At the time*, I knew it was wrong. That has never been the question. What I didn't know then was that magick comes with responsibility. I was so powerful ... reckless. My actions were something that I will always regret. I just didn't know how powerful I was. If I had known, if I hadn't been so impulsive, I would never have hit them full force."

I looked at the girl in front of me and realized that she and I were no different. Though her life was much younger, she lived with similar regrets, similar struggles. I realize that Claire wasn't who I thought she was at all, but just as quickly, understood that it really didn't change things.

"What you did was an accident. A horrible, terrible accident," I began. "But what Patrick did ... he knew what he was doing. He had already accepted the responsibility when he made the choice to help you cover up your mistake."

"He was just trying to protect me … as he always did … still does …" Claire defended.

"Always will." Patrick's voice was raspy as he finished Claire's sentence.

Startled, we turned our attention to the wounded man. Claire immediately got up and went to his side. Sitting on the bed, she brushed his dark hair off his forehead. Bringing the mug with Willem's potion, I joined them at the bed, sitting on the opposite side.

"I bet you never saw that coming," Claire said as she held his hand. "After all these years, finally telling someone about what really happened." She paused. "Patrick, you don't have to protect me anymore. You've already given up so much."

"Claire, I don't want to hear any more about it. You know, even more than I, that protecting others is what we do. It's in our blood. I had to give my kidney before you went and did something equally as stupid, like offer one of your own. Now, I may not have foresight like I used to, but I can still see some things." He turned to me. "Gio, please tell me there's a nice scotch in that mug you got there."

I smiled.

"I wish I could say it was, but perhaps, this once, it's something a bit better."

"Blasphemy," he said with a wan smile.

Claire took the mug from me and brought it to his lips.

"Here, drink this," she said, her voice was calm, steady.

Patrick drank without question. When he finished, she placed the mug on the bedside table and turned back to him.

"How do you feel?"

Patrick's face looked relaxed, peaceful.

"Wonderful," he said his speech slurred. Then, turning to me, he added, "Oh, I think you were right about the drink, mate. And that's saying a lot."

Within seconds, he passed out.

Claire rearranged the pillows and straightened the covers once more. She leaned over and kissed him chastely on the lips.

"Rest well, my dearest. Next time, I will try to protect you," she whispered in his ear. When she was satisfied he was comfortable, she stood and stretched.

"Gio, about what I told you ..." she began.

"Of course. I won't speak of it to anyone ... not even Katarina," I assured her. "I promise."

Claire looked at me with heavy eyes and gave me a half smile.

"Katarina ... um, she already knows," Claire admitted. "And, since we're on the that topic ... there's something else you should probably be aware of."

I sat back down and waited for Claire to tell me what I suspected I already knew.

Chapter Twenty

KATARINA

I knew that Claire and Gio would need some time to get Patrick situated, so I took the opportunity to pour myself a drink. Walking into the kitchen, I approached the refrigerator and searched for something to calm my frazzled nerves.

Matteo's refrigerator was fully stocked. It took a few minutes before I was able to find a dark bottle of craft beer hidden in the back. I eased it out and then began pulling cabinet drawers, in search of an opener. Matteo, Rowan, and Willem walked in with a thick book. The former two sat down at the farm table opposite the fridge and began flipping through the pages. Willem headed straight for the pantry.

"Please help yourself to anything that is there," Matteo called out after Willem.

I continued sifting through each drawer with more and more frustration as the bottle opener eluded me. Matteo, sensing my rising temper, stood and approached me. He held out his hand.

"May I?" he offered.

I handed him the bottle roughly. Waving his hand with a smooth movement over the bottleneck, the cap instantly popped off and landed in the open trashcan.

Of course. Magick.

I hadn't even thought to use it. I closed my eyes and took a breath to steady myself. I had spent too long out of my own consciousness. I was still thinking like a human and reacting like an inexperienced Strega. I needed to get things together before someone got seriously hurt. Who was I kidding? More than one person had already been seriously injured. I only prayed that I could get back to the old me before someone died.

Matteo handed the beer back to me before returning to the table where Rowan sat. I tipped the bottle back and took three large swigs. It was a thick, heavy stout that reminded me of a past lifetime spent in nineteenth-century London.

In that existence, I'd been a bartender. It seemed strange to me that I could pull up memories from other lives within the blink of an eye, but there they were, clear as the day they happened.

I leaned up against the kitchen counter as I fell into the memory of the life I had lived. Out of all the reincarnations, that one was my least favorite. I had worked out of a brothel, or bawdy house, as they were called, located in the Whitechapel district of London.

WHITECHAPEL, at that time, was steeped in poverty. Crime and disease were no strangers to the residents of the district. Violence was the norm. I had grown up in a large, crowded house, the sixth child, so it was no big surprise when I ran off to the brothel for a job at the age of fourteen.

Being young and pretty, Lady Pemberton took me in without question. However, instead of preparing me to work with the male callers, she trained me behind the bar. I looked well beyond my fourteen years and possessed a wit and a charm that lured men in. In those times, it was desirable to have a female serving the drinks, and Lady Pemberton recognized my persuasive ways and youthful beauty as an asset to her establishment.

The days were long, but the nights were longer. If ever there were a man with questionable morals, he could be found in Lady Pemberton's bawdy house. And she taught me to flirt properly with the men to get them to spend more money on alcohol.

I remember how pleased she was with how well I seemed to take to the job. Men were enamored with me, drawn to my every word, drunk off my voice; I could talk them into just about anything. At the time, I had no idea that my ability to coerce the men, to sweet-talk them, was just my subconscious tapping into my innate power of Strega persuasion. But it didn't matter to Lady Pemberton, and it didn't matter to me either, since I was making good money for a woman and growing my wealth substantially.

It wasn't until seven years into my tenure that I had accumulated enough wealth to purchase my own apartment. I was so proud to have my own place to live, to be independent and not require the assistance of a man to get by in life. Little did I know.

It was late September. I was getting ready to head home after a particularly chaotic night. As the custom, I was always sent home with an escort, but this night he had fallen unexpectedly ill and there was no one else available to see me home.

"Kitty, why don't you just stay the night here?" she had insisted.

"I do appreciate the offer, but I only live right around the corner. Surely, I can get myself home without any trouble," I had argued, fastening my thick wool overcoat tight around my body.

"Very well, dear. That's fine," she replied, convinced by my influential tone. "Just be careful, little dove."

"I'll see you tomorrow." I smiled as I left the house.

I tried to walk home quickly but was forced to take my time. The gas lamps that lined the street, in conjunction with the heavy fog, did not create easy travel. As I slowly meandered home, a chill crawled up my spine. I kept my head up and shoulders back, my hand gripping the small gun deep within my coat pocket.

The night was quiet; I was the only one on the street at that hour. The sound of my shoes made a hard clacking on the pavement with each step. It was unnerving. And felt different than nights past. I walked faster.

As I rounded the corner, something shifted in the air and I noticed my shoes were no longer alone. There were now two sets clacking shoes along the street. The first was mine, and the second came from a pair of shoes that seemed to be a little distance behind me. I tightened my grip on the pistol and pushed forward. I was only a half block from my house.

The shoes behind me picked up speed, their sound getting closer and closer as I approached my apartment building. I picked up my pace, self-preservation vaulting me forward, not caring if I couldn't see what lay ahead of me. I knew these streets well enough to know that I had only fifty more feet to reach the entrance of my building.

The shoes pick up their pace once more, this time running. They were almost upon me. I let go of the pistol in my coat pocket and lifted my skirts, with the intention of running the rest of the way home.

As I took a few more strides, I could see the door to my

building but was blindsided by a blow to my right side. I staggered as a hand was placed over my mouth, another around my waist, and I was yanked into the alley alongside my building.

The man turned me around and pushed me up against the brick wall. I looked into his eyes and gasped; they were red. Though I had no idea who it had been in that life, now I saw Alessandro staring at me in the memory.

"Good evening, Kitty," he breathed, his foul-smelling breath hot against my cheek. "Or should I say Catharine?"

He removed his hand from my mouth.

"How do you know that name?" I whispered back, confused. I had been born Catharine, but Lady Pemberton insisted that I take a new name for business purposes.

"Oh, I know a lot about you," he snarled. "More than you know, my love. Such as how you whore around in that old broad's house without shame!"

"I am no whore!" I yelled back. "And I do not appr—"

"Silence!" he interrupted, grabbing my face and holding it still.

He licked the entire side of my face. His tongue was rough and sticky. I fought the urge to vomit.

"Don't you touch me!" I hissed back as I tried to break from his grip.

"Why is it always the same with you!" he snapped. "Don't touch me; let me go; you're hurting me; I will never love you ... again and again and again. You really need to come up with something different. This conversation has become quite dull."

He reached into his pocket and removed a large butcher's knife. He brought the blade up to my face and held it there before swiping it against my cheek several times, cutting the flesh with long, deep slices.

I tried to scream, but the pain was too great. I fought to

stay conscious, but it was a losing battle. Sensing my fading alertness, Alessandro lifted my chin and brought his lips to mine. He kissed me roughly, forcing his tongue deep into my mouth.

"You disgust me." I gagged when he pulled away.

"Well, that's a new one," he replied. "See you in the next life, my love."

He lifted the knife horizontally and slit my throat several times with deep cuts. He took a step back to admire his handiwork, his hands covered in my blood. I brought my hands to my throat instinctively, though I could sense I had mere seconds to live.

Alessandro turned to walk away, then thought twice about it. He stood in front of me and plunged the knife several times into my stomach. The light of the gas lamp began to grow dim, and I could tell that my blurry vision had nothing to do with the fog.

I was dying.

I dropped to the cold ground. Turning onto my side, I remember the last sight of that life was a pair of shiny black shoes clacking on the pavement as they headed out back down the road. The sound of his whistling still echoed in my ears.

I blinked out of the memory. I poured the rest of the beer down the drain in revulsion and looked at the two on the table.

"Matteo, I'm going to need something a little stronger," I said as I tossed the empty bottle into the trash.

Matteo looked up from the book and pointed to the top cabinet just left of the refrigerator. I reached up and opened it, taking out an almost-full bottle of Clynelish. I found a glass and poured myself a healthy amount. I took it down in one long, throat-searing swallow, letting it warm my body. I hoped it would settle my stomach.

Willem finally emerged from the pantry, his arms full of

various roots and herbs. He set up a station and began mixing a concoction.

"I can make a revitalization potion for him," Willem said as he began sorting and preparing the ingredients. "Tell us exactly what happened, Katarina,"

Matteo and Rowan were now fully attentive and waited for me to speak. I went into detail about the events of the evening, leaving nothing to their imaginations. I told them of the *orbis onerariis*, Akshay's shop, how payment was made, and the information that he gave us. I told them of Rau's surprise visit and how Akshay had temporarily fended him off.

Willem continued to work on the potion throughout my story, but I could see him stiffen at the mention of the demon.

"Well, that makes sense," Rowan spoke as she slid the tome she'd been looking at toward me. "Look, it's right here in the book. If Alessandro had resurrected Rau, he would need to periodically offer him human life force as payment. It would be his way of keeping the demon bound to him. But with Alessandro injured, maybe he is unable to provide the demon with what he needs. Maybe his binding would be weak and Rau would be able to act of his own volition, even with no physical form."

"Hold that thought, Rowan," Willem said. "I'll be right back."

I watched as he poured an iridescent blue liquid into a mug and rushed off to the back rooms. Pouring myself another glass, I walked around the counter and joined them at the table.

"If there's one thing I know, it's that this particular demon is not one to be contained, no matter how many books tell you he can be bound," I replied. "Even if bound to a Strega as powerful as Alessandro, he will find a way to break free of the constraints. The only way to control him is to send him back to where he came from. There is no 'in-between' with that one. Especially if Alessandro is using the demon as a source of dark power ... he will be unable to control it."

"It was Josh, wasn't it?" Matteo spoke softly after a few minutes. "Josh was his first sacrifice to the demon, the one that enticed him, the one that lured the demon to bind himself to Alessandro."

Rowan and I dropped our eyes in acknowledgement of what Matteo was only now realizing.

"But ... but ... I don't understand. Alessandro's one of us! He's Strega Ilmalo, just as you and I are!"

Matteo's eyes shot an accusatory look at me from across the table.

"Matteo, Alessandro may have been born Strega but let me assure you that he is far from that now. His allegiance rests with one entity alone—himself. He does not stand for the true nature of the Strega, and that is why he must be stopped ... at all costs. Know that I will not rest until I hold his heart in my hand and watch as it stops beating."

Something in my expression must've shown him my words were more than the plain, simple truth; they were a solemn vow. I wouldn't rest until I had his heart in my clutches.

Willem rejoined us at the table.

"How is he?" Rowan asked, her mouth a thin line, her brow scrunched together.

"He'll live, but it was a close one," Willem replied. "We can all thank Claire for saving his life."

Rowan released a big breath and relaxed her shoulders. She looked pale and worn. I thought about how she must be feeling at this moment, thrust into a situation in which she could very well perish.

"Claire and Gio will be out in a bit. I gave them the potion, but it still needs to cool. So, what is our next move?"

I didn't hesitate to answer. "I want to go Club Shadow. Akshay suggested we start there."

"How do we know if we can trust him?" Rowan inquired. "He did take Patrick's kidney, after all. How do we know he's not leading us to some underground magickal organ removal facility?"

"We don't know if we can trust him," I responded plainly. "But consider this. Akshay didn't reveal the card to us at first. It was only after he was threatened that he gave it to us and told us that we could find what we were looking for there."

"That's a good point," Matteo agreed. "If he were trying to set you up, he would have sent you there to begin with. Information is valuable wherever you are. But information that pertains to Club Shadow holds a price four times that. Akshay wouldn't have handed information of that value over to you for just a kidney, that much I can say."

"You know Club Shadow?" Willem pressed Matteo.

"I know *of* Club Shadow," Matteo corrected. "Rumor has it that the business that happens there is questionable ... even for the Strega Ilmalo. I would never get myself mixed up in such a scene. I've heard stories of people's lives ruined simply from poor choices made during one of their events."

"If it's such a bad place, how is it still in business?" Rowan asked.

"Just because something *shouldn't* happen doesn't mean it doesn't," Matteo responded. "Club Shadow feeds off the ignorance of the human world. And the humans? They don't question club business."

Rowan's eyes showed understanding.

"Humans don't truly believe in magick," she spoke, saying what we were all thinking.

"Exactly," Matteo answered.

"If there's any chance that we'll find more information about where Alessandro and Celia are hiding, it's going to be there," I said. "But if we all go, we may attract more attention than we need."

"What do you suggest?" Willem asked.

I looked around the table at the three of them. I could tell by their resolute expressions that each one of them was committed to our mission. The problem was that I wasn't as committed to sending them to their deaths. I shifted in my chair, an uneasiness settling into my body. My stomach turned as a slight wave of nausea hit me. I slowly pushed my drink away, taking a cleansing breath before I continued.

"I suggest," I began in an even tone, "that Gio and I go to the club alone. We'll be less conspicuous as a couple than an entire group of seven would be. Besides, Patrick will still need to heal. Willem, you and Claire need to get him back to full health. Rowan, we need you to research possible spells that can send Rau back and Matteo, this is your world down here. You know it better than any of us. We'll need you to keep us informed of anything that may become a problem."

"I don't like this at all," Willem said as he stood up from the table and began pacing the kitchen. "It doesn't make any sense for you two to go in there by yourselves. Not when there are people here who can back you up."

"I'm with Katarina," Gio said as he and Claire entered the room. "There's no reason for us all to be there."

I stood and walked over to Claire, embracing her.

"How are you?" I asked telepathically.

"Katarina, I told Gio about everything. I had to. He's promised to keep my secret until all this is over. I don't want Willem distracted. Okay?"

I nodded into her shoulder, squeezing her one last time before releasing her. I looked at Gio. He gave me a knowing look. Good. Now there were a few less secrets between us.

Reaching out, Gio took my hand and gave it a squeeze. I looked into his blue eyes and wondered when all this would be over. When would we have a chance to simply live our life together?

As if hearing my question, he leaned over and gave me a quick, soft kiss. I closed my eyes to fight back the tears. The immense amount of emotion that rushed through my body in a wave took me off balance. I swayed a bit before I felt Gio's hands on my arms.

"You all right?" His voice was concerned.

Opening my eyes, I shook off the dizziness and realized that I was truly exhausted. I nodded.

"I'll be fine," I answered. "I'm just tired."

Gio placed his arm around me as we joined the others at the table.

"So, are we in agreement with what to do next?" I asked, looking around the table at each of them in turn. Since no one argued, I took that as a sign to go forward with the plan.

"Okay, then it's settled. For now, we rest. Tomorrow Gio and I will head out to Club Shadow and hopefully, find more information about Alessandro's location."

As I stood in the shower, steam rising around me, I let everything we had accomplished so far settle into my brain. I was surprised that there was room for anything new; my previous lives seemed to fill up most of my schema.

After taking my time letting the hot stream of water hit my aching body, I turned off the shower and dried off. I combed out my hair and wrapped the towel around me, then walked into the bedroom.

Gio was already asleep. Foregoing pajamas, I dropped the towel, flipped off the light, and crawled into bed next to him. Sensing my body near, he turned over and draped his arm around my waist, pulling me into him.

His chest was hot against my back. I could feel the energy

radiating from his torso as I spooned into him. It felt amazing as it penetrated my skin.

I closed my eyes and let all my worries go with my next exhalation.

"Good night, my sweet," he whispered in a sleepy voice.

I felt him lean forward, his lips kissing the back of my neck, and for the first time in a long time, sleep came easily.

Chapter Twenty-One

GIO

Club Shadow was everything I might've expected from a high-end secretive supernatural club scene. The building itself was a renovated warehouse located south of the Market District. Walking up to the building, one would never guess that inside would be one of the most illicit venues in the city.

Matteo had insisted that if we were going to have any chance of being let into the club, we had better adhere to their strict dress code policy. It was also a good thing Matteo had some friends in the fashion industry to lend us some clothes, because neither of us had anything that would have sufficed. As we stepped out of our rented limo, my eye caught a shimmer from Katarina's dress.

The deep purple micro-mini sequined garment was nearly black and clung to every one of her curves snugly. Spaghetti straps held up a plunging neckline in the front. A pair of heels completed her ensemble. Her hair was pulled back into a large, low bun that sat off to the right side of her head, a purple lily tucked into the top. A delicate arm cuff wrapped around her left bicep. She was stunning. I struggled to keep my eyes off her.

I, on the other hand, felt far less enticing, though I noticed a few head turns as I exited the vehicle. A tailored black shirt fit my body perfectly, leaving no room for the imagination. It was tucked into a pair of snug dark-grey Armani pants. A pair of black shoes and a belt finished the look. It felt a little bit constricting and a whole lot boring. At least, that was my opinion, though the way Katarina looked at me made me consider otherwise. It was a hungry look. I smiled to myself as I remembered what she whispered to me as we stepped into the limo.

You look good enough to eat.

I hoped we would be able to test out that theory later.

As we made our way to the entrance, a massive man in an all-black suit stood just to the left of the door.

"Card, please," he stated in a neutral tone.

I pulled the card Akshay had given us from my pocket and presented it to the guard.

He examined it carefully, then leaned toward the door handle and pulled it open. "Enjoy your night," he said as we walked over the threshold.

The heavy door closed slowly behind us. A loud click echoed in the entryway as it shut completely.

Katarina and I walked farther into the building. It was warded like nothing I had ever felt. From somewhere inside, we could hear the muted pulsing and thumping of music. We walked a bit more to a second door at the other end of the corridor. I stepped forward and pulled it open.

It took a moment for me to process what the interior of the club looked like; it appeared so chaotic. The large room was dimly lit with deep yellow backlights and decorated in black and gold. Waterfall chandeliers were suspended from the ceiling by thick golden cords. A wrap-around bar took up the entire length of both the south and east walls of the building.

The dance floor was located at the very far end of the club, where music was piped in from speakers positioned on a stage where workers hustled between sets. I took note of the throngs of people bustling about, though I wasn't at all surprised. Men and women from all corners of the underground intermingled with each other, drinking and participating in other displays of vice.

I scanned the seating area, trying to get my bearings. There were booths throughout, some on the floor level, others positioned on raised daises. Stairs along the west wall led to a second story balcony level complete with its own bar, though not as impressive as the main one down below.

"Do you see any other exit?" Katarina leaned in close to me so that I could hear her over the music.

I shook my head, still scanning the area.

"No, but my guess would be behind the stage."

"I thought that too. Let's keep it in mind ... just in case."

She reached over and stroked my back.

"You ready?"

"Almost," I replied.

I turned toward her and pulled her close to me. My hand pressed into the soft skin exposed on her back. I could feel every curve of her body through the thin material of her dress. I leaned in and kissed her hard.

She immediately responded. Her mouth opened as an offering for my tongue, which I accepted. She pressed her body toward me, and I could feel her breasts crush against my chest. The music faded and the crowd grew quiet. In that moment, there was just Katarina and me. It was the same as it had always been, but different ... more. I could feel her energy mixing with my energy as we kissed, but there was something else there, something I couldn't quite explain. There was an energy present that was a combination of both ours, yet entirely independent. I marveled at how becoming a Strega had impacted my ability to feel so much more than my human self. I didn't know if I would ever get used to it.

I had to force myself to pull away. Katarina's expression was proof positive that she had felt it too.

"I love you," I said. "I just wanted you to know that."

"I do know it," she replied. Still looking a bit thrown off, she added, "I love you, too. I know you know it. Promise me you'll always remember it."

A shadow flitted through her eyes. It was there for just an instant, then it disappeared as she continued, "We'll get through this. No matter what happens, we'll come out of this together." Taking my hand, she led me to the bar.

"Two Hibiki's, please. Neat," I ordered when the bartender came around.

The young man was immaculately kempt in his crisp black shirt rolled up to his elbows. I took our glasses and placed some cash on the bar, walking away. Handing one of the glasses to Katarina, we walked over to the first platform.

"Where should we start?" I asked, looking around for an idea.

"There," Katarina said, looking across the room.

My eyes followed her gaze to a VIP section on the second level. The balcony was roped off, giving a striking man and the three women at his table ample room to move around.

Katarina threw back her drink and headed toward the stairs. I followed her closely, my senses up, ready for anything.

As we approached the section, another bodyguard in a black suit stood in front of a thick black curtain blocked by a gold-colored rope.

"This room is for VIPs and their guests only," he said in the same neutral tone the one at the front door had used.

Katarina leaned into the guard. "Oh, I can assure you that I am a VIP."

I could feel the wave of influence as it rolled off her tongue and into the ears of the bodyguard. He stood there quietly for a moment, an internal struggle on his face.

"How are you doing this?" he choked out. "This place is supposed to be warded."

Fuck. She needed a bit more power behind her spell to overtake him fully. I took a step forward and placed my hand on his arm.

"You can trust the lady," I said. "She speaks the truth."

I pushed my influence toward him. The guard struggled a moment longer before he let the spell take him.

"Of course you are, ma'am," he said in a compliant voice. "Please, right this way."

He bent down and unhooked the rope. I looked at Katarina and smiled. She walked through the curtains and entered the private space beyond.

As we had seen from the ground floor, a man sat at the table nestled in a circular booth. The women were obviously his entertainment for the evening, and upon our arrival, they looked us up and down before standing, determining that whatever we were here for, was something they weren't invited to join.

"Should we come back in an hour?" the tall blonde one said in a sultry voice.

"That would be lovely," the man spoke with a British accent. A Londoner, if I was remembering correctly.

The women each gave him a lingering kiss, far too intimate for public, before leaving through a second exit in the curtain. He eyed them like the candy they were while Katarina and I patiently waited. When the second blonde had finally cleared the area, he turned his attention back to us.

I looked him over. Though he was sitting down, I could

tell he was a tall man, well over six foot, if I had to guess. He appeared to be on the leaner side, but not in a skinny way. He had the physique of an athlete. He wore a polished suit with all the right accessories. He spread his arms across the back of the booth bench as he leaned back and caught Katarina's eye.

"I must admit it was quite bold of you to use your influence on my guard. But frankly, I'm more impressed that you were able to succeed. Brilliant," he said in a smooth voice. "How ever were you able to disarm my wards? I must know."

"A lady never kisses and tells." Katarina smiled.

The man looked both disappointed and amused.

"Do tell me, to what do I owe the pleasure of this visit?"

"We are looking for someone who may frequent here," I said, trying to sound as casual as I could under the circumstances. "Someone ... like us."

The man smiled and crossed his arms behind his head.

"I see," he said patiently. "And why do you think I could possibly help you with that?"

"Are you not the person in charge? Do you not call the shots?" Katarina inquired. "I could see the moment I spotted you that only your power is able to reveal itself in this club. Surely, a person of such high ranking, a person who *knows* things and can make them happen, is allowed to flex magick like you do."

"Very perceptive, love." The man smiled at Katarina acknowledging her accuracy. "It's true, I do have a certain ... clout around here. But again, your request begs the question, *why* do you think I could help you with that? There are several thousand clients that frequent the club regularly. How am I to know who is who?"

"Do you honestly think that we believe you do not know each and every member who enters your door?" I countered.

The man raised his eyebrows.

"What can I say? You got me there," he replied as he

gestured for us to take a seat. "I do say, this is turning out to be quite an entertaining evening. Please join me."

Katarina hesitated, then took a seat to the left of the man. I slid into the booth next to her.

"How rude of me," the man spoke as he turned over two glasses and poured us each champagne. "We haven't been properly introduced. My name is Joseph, Joseph Poole."

He held out his hand. Katarina reached over with caution as she shook it.

"And you are?" he politely inquired.

"Katarina ... Rossi, and this is my husband, Gio," Katarina said.

My heart skipped when I heard Katarina refer to herself as my wife. Funny things, titles. They provide a legitimacy that's recognized only by the living. In my soul, and before the God and Goddess above, Katarina and I were already joined for all of time. We were more a part of each other than any other two creatures in existence ... much more so. But the thought of Katarina as my wife struck a nerve in my physiological existence. I hoped that I would be able to honor her in that way one day soon.

Joseph released Katarina's hand and reached over to shake mine.

"Now, that introductions are through, may I offer you something to eat? Beluga?" he asked reaching over to an iced tray.

"Joseph, we are simply here to acquire information about the individual we mentioned earlier. No niceties are required," I answered.

Joseph stopped and looked at us both.

"Very well," he said curtly. "I can see that this is purely a business venture for the both of you. But I must ask, why do you think I *would* help you? I don't know anything about you, other than you are quite rude, and as far as I can see, what you ask is for me to break the confidentiality of the clients that come to Club Shadow." He sniffed. "And unfortunately, that is something I simply cannot do. Besides, what am I to get out of it? You offer nothing in return.

"Name your price," I said bluntly.

"Oh, my dear fellow." Joseph laughed. "Do you think I am so easily won over as to be bought out? No, I'm sorry, there is no amount you can give me that I do not already have. Look around. Does it look like I am in financial need?"

"Perhaps," Katarina chimed in, "there is something else that you want? Something that money cannot provide? Perhaps, there is something that would be worth an exchange."

My eyes darted to Katarina, then back to Joseph. I wondered what it was that she was thinking. Joseph appeared amused.

"Well, now things are getting interesting," Joseph replied. He leaned back against the booth and relaxed. "What do you have in mind, my darling?"

Joseph and I waited to hear what Katarina had in mind. I knew that I could trust her, but I didn't like being in the dark. However, given our circumstances, I suppose we didn't really have much of a choice.

"I will show you how I broke through your wards," Katarina said.

Joseph was intrigued but tried to play it off.

"Surely you can't think that your little magick trick could be worth the information that you are requesting from me?" he said sarcastically.

"Suit yourself," Katarina responded. She then added, "Good luck with that. I wonder if club members will feel the same when they discover how easily I was able to break through your shoddy protections? Anyway, it was lovely to meet you."

She motioned for me to slide out of the booth. I could tell by her body posture that she knew he would take the bait, so I didn't hurry all that much.

"Wait," Joseph said, annoyed. "Perhaps we can work something out. Tell me again who it is you are looking for?"

Katarina slid back down in her seat and looked at Joseph.

"Two witches ... like us," she began. "The man has a bronze complexion with dark hair and red eyes, the woman is tall with a thin build. She has long, curly brown hair. The man may be behaving ... strangely. The woman never leaves his side."

"My dear," Joseph puffed, "you've just described most of my clientele."

I remembered what Katarina told me about the information Rowan had uncovered about how Alessandro and the demon were bonded.

"He carries the mark of a demon named Rau," I interrupted. "The letter R with a line running horizontally through the bottom half of it. It would be behind his left ear ... or possibly at the wrist."

Joseph grew silent, his body still. The polite, jovial British presence was gone. His face became grave ... serious at the mention of the mark. It was clear that he knew something about Alessandro.

"Have you seen him? Was he with the woman? Tell us what you know," Katarina implored.

"Yes, I have. Both of them. They were here not long ago," Joseph began. "The man called himself Alex, the woman, Celia. They were making nice with many of our patrons ... being quite friendly, if you know what I mean."

I knew exactly what he meant. I stole a glance at Katarina. She was able to mask her disgust.

"I was monitoring them from up here. After all, it is neither unusual nor a crime to combine sex with magick, especially in some of the older traditions. And, as long as everything is consensual, who am I to keep adults from their kinks? That is, after all, one of the benefits of coming to the club, to let off a little steam in a way natural to our origin."

Joseph's face grew dark.

"But these two ... there was something about them, something *off*. I couldn't quite place it from up here, so I went down to the floor to introduce myself."

He paused as he relived the night in his head.

"When I approached, I saw them with one of our newer regulars, a young woman. She had come alone, and they were on her like a lion after a gazelle. They were dancing, the man at her front, the woman at her back. I could tell that each of them was whispering in the woman's ears. She looked dazed ... fried ... magick-addled ... but I could see a resistance in her eyes. Like she knew something was happening to her, but she didn't know what it was or how to stop it. All she wanted was to be with them. It appeared they were somehow inducing her compliance, though I wasn't sure how."

Joseph looked at Katarina.

"Like you, they had somehow found a chink in my wards."

I reached over and placed a hand on Katarina's thigh. Her jaw had been clenched the moment Joseph hinted at the way Alessandro was luring people to go with him. After years and years of being abused by him, it was a miracle that she could remain so calm.

It terrified me.

"As I neared them, something off-stage caught Alex's attention. When he turned his head, I saw the mark, just as you described, behind his left ear. At first, I thought it was a tattoo, but when I was just feet from them, I saw it glow ... it looked like burning embers. That's when I knew he had a demon bond. The woman had the same on her wrist.

"I retreated to the guard station to inform them that they needed to be prepared for a removal. As much as we will let slide here, we draw the line at demons. Anyway, we went back, full force, but they were gone. All three of them. I don't know how it had happened so fast. I was out of the area for less than a minute, but there was no sight of them. Security footage revealed that they left through the secret exit behind the stage with the girl."

Joseph's face looked worn.

"Do you know where they were headed?" Katarina asked.

"I asked around the club that night. There were a few people that overheard them talking about a flat on the west side."

"Have you heard anything about the girl? Has she returned to the club?" I asked.

Joseph diverted his eyes to the table. "No," he said solemnly. "She hasn't returned. I fear she never will."

Katarina reached out and touched Joseph's sleeve. "It's not your fault," she reassured. "Alessandro is a monster. There are no lengths he wouldn't go to get what he wants."

"And now, I believe I owe you something," she continued.

Placing her other hand on Joseph's shoulder, Katarina closed her eyes and focused her life force, pushing her energy through him. Joseph's eyes widened as he received the information from Katarina.

"You may want to link the fifth, seventh, and ninth wards to close the third web. It only opens a centimeter, but it's enough for someone with the right amount of experience to find, if they are looking for it."

She turned to me and motioned that it was time for us to take our leave. With a quick farewell, we made our way down the stairs back to the main level. When we reached the dance floor, Katarina froze.

"Alessandro," she whispered.

I followed her gaze, but I couldn't sift through the crowd.

"Where?" I cried, leaning in as the music seemed to get louder.

Katarina brought her mouth to my ear. "Over there!" she cried. "There, next to the speaker!" She took off through the dance floor.

"Katarina! Wait!" I called after her, pushing my way through the crowd. I could see her just in front of me as she weaved in and out of the bodies. I was right behind her.

When we made it to the other end of the stage, she stopped suddenly. Alessandro was nowhere to be seen.

"Where'd he go?" she asked. "He was right here! I swear, Gio! I saw him."

Scanning the dance floor again, all I could see were bodies pressing up against each other. The music pumped a rhythmic beat. It reverberated across the dance floor. Then, out of the corner of my eye, I saw a flash of red. Turning in the direction from where it came, I saw the edge of Alessandro as he disappeared behind a couple. It was a flash and I was only able to catch a second's glimpse, but I knew in that instant it was him.

"There!" I said, taking Katarina's arm and turning her in the direction where I saw him.

We pushed our way to the other side of the dance floor, but there just seemed to be more and more people gathering there. The music was getting louder and louder, bumping over and over, forcing Katarina to cover our ears.

I stopped. No. Something wasn't right. This shouldn't be happening. I looked around and noticed how everyone seemed oblivious to the noise and the increasing crowd of people. How they just continued to jump and dance in a frenzy, mindlessly, as if they were unable to control what they were doing.

"We have to get out of here!" I yelled in Katarina's ear. "Something's not right. I can sense it."

Katarina grabbed my hand, fear in her eyes. "It's a trap."

I held her hand firmly in my grip and headed to the edge of the dance floor desperate to make it to safety. It was a near-impossible feat, but after several minutes, I could finally see the end.

We pushed our way through the final line of people, expecting to emerge into the seating area, only to find ourselves back at the opposite edge near the stage as if we had never left.

"Gio ..." She trembled.

"What's happening?" I asked over the now-louder music.

"Be alert, love," Katarina yelled in my ear. "Don't leave me!"

I opened my senses to the crowd, searching for Alessandro. I could feel Katarina's grip on my hand.

As my senses were opened, I felt a prick in my aura. It was just a tiny prick, but it got my attention. I took a step to the left to see where it had come from. There, lurking in the wings on the side of the stage, was Alessandro. He stood there staring at us, his smile exposing glistening white teeth.

"Do you see him?" I asked, anger building inside me.

"Yes," Katarina replied.

I could feel the weight of her hatred grow at an exponential rate. She let go of my hand. Not wanting to be separated while still in the crowd, I turned around to take it again.

She was gone.

"Katarina!" I called frantically. "Katarina! Where are you?"

Forgetting about our mission, forgetting Alessandro, I scanned the crowd in a panicked search for a glimpse of Katarina. Suddenly, he was there.

"Oh my, Gio." Alessandro smirked. "Here we are again. And to think I thought our fun was over."

I spun around to meet the monster's eyes.

"Where is she?" I demanded, grabbing his throat with my hands.

Alessandro gurgled under my grip, his eyes widening in surprise before a smile spread across his face.

I let go of him, tossing him to the floor.

"Well, looky who's got some power now." He laughed.

"Where is she?" I demanded again.

"Oh, you mean my *wife*," he said. "Well, I'm sure you understand that sometimes a husband needs to reprimand his wife in private. You know, to save face. I hope you don't mind, but I've taken her somewhere special. We have to clear a few things up."

I lunged to grab him.

He stood up and snaked out of my grasp.

"Uh, uh, uh," he chided. "Now, what would happen to Katarina if something happens to me? Have you asked yourself that question, Gio?"

I froze in place, every muscle in my body tense. Rage began to bubble inside my core. What good was having the power of the Strega if I didn't know how to use it against him?

"Now, first things first. I know all about you and your little gang of Watchers. And I know what you have been up to. Not cool, Gio. Not cool. I'd like to offer you a way out, you know, for old times' sake. This could all be over now. All I want is Katarina. It's all I ever wanted. Just give her to me and everyone else will live. Walk away, let me have her. Surely you don't think that her life is worth more than all the lives of your friends? What do you say? We gotta deal?"

"Go to hell, Alessandro," I spat. "You will never win."

Alessandro twisted his mouth. "Oooo, I'd thought you'd say that. In that case ..."

Alessandro snapped his fingers. The music blared through the speakers, louder and louder and louder, until there was nothing but feedback emanating out of them. I watched as he laughed. The music continued to build as I covered my ears.

The sound was so great that it threatened to burst my ear drums. I squinted my eyes in pain. The speakers started sparking and with a few bursts of flame and a loud flash, they exploded, sending a trail of embers sprinkling over the dance floor.

Silence.

I looked up in a panic and searched for Alessandro, but he was already gone. He was gone. Katarina was gone ... again. My heart beat heavy in my chest as I knew that there was nothing more I could do here. I looked around at the other clubbers. There was an overall sense of confusion and fear. I looked up to where Joseph was sitting. He looked just as confused as everyone else. Knowing that Alessandro had been able to spell the entire club was more than concerning. Though I wanted to break, to crumple right there on the floor of the club and scream in pain for my loss, I knew it wouldn't help anything.

As of right now, Katarina was alive. She was alive, but not for long. I had to warn the others. I pulled out my cell and dialed Willem's number. He picked it up on the first ring.

"Gio, what's wrong?"

"I need to speak with Claire, Willem," I demanded. "I need to know where Alessandro has taken Katarina and only she can tell me."

Chapter Twenty-Two

KATARINA

I opened my eyes. I was in the trunk of a car, and a small one at that. My head touched one side of the vehicle while my feet bumped up against the other. I tried to wipe my eyes and only then noticed that my hands were bound at the wrists with a thick, glowing red rope. It illuminated the cramped space just enough to reveal my grim situation. I struggled to wriggle my wrists around in the binding, only to quickly realize that the rope had been spelled with something much stronger than what I could break by myself.

My heart began racing. How could I have let this happen? I should have been more careful, but when I saw Alessandro in the club, rage had taken over and my judgment had been clouded. I thought only of getting revenge, and my attention was so focused on him I didn't think of anyone else that could have been working with him. I didn't think of the real danger I was in.

He had been counting on that.

The moment I let go of Gio's hand, the instant our physical connection was broken, I felt a set of hands around me. One arm around my upper torso, a hand covering my mouth. Then there was nothing. There was no time for me to fight back. I had been knocked out.

Now, lying in the trunk of the car, I could tell that a spell had been used to render me unconscious. My head ached and I could feel the residual effects of it with each bump in the road.

Alessandro's scheme had been planned out perfectly.

The only solace I found as the car went along was in the fact that Alessandro had taken great care to subdue me. Not kill me. Not yet, anyway. I quieted my mind and did a quick inventory. Other than being unable to use my magick, and a general sense of achiness, it appeared that I was physically okay. He wanted to keep me under control, not injured or worse. This led me to believe that whatever Alessandro had in store, he wanted me alive ... for now.

I listened carefully and tried to distinguish various noises and sounds from inside of my motorized casket. I could tell when the vehicle approached a stoplight as opposed to a stop sign by the length of its pause, and when it went over the muni tracks, but after a while I had lost count, not to mention that I had absolutely no idea in which direction we were heading.

After a while, I noticed that the muni tracks had become less frequent, and the stoplights had been entirely replaced by stop signs. I tried to think of areas in the city in which this traffic flow occurred. Most likely we were no longer in the city center—or any neighboring district, for that matter. Although I wasn't quite sure how long I'd been out, instinct told me that it hadn't been that long. My guess was that we were still somewhere within the city limits, just in one of the outer neighborhoods.

I scooted closer to the back of the trunk and tried to see if I could hear anything happening inside the car's interior. I could vaguely hear the melody of classical music from the radio. It sounded like a piano concerto. If I had to wager, I'd bet that Celia was driving the car. A concert pianist, she had played the day I married Alessandro. My eyes narrowed. I swore to the Goddess, that bitch was going to *pay*.

Suddenly, the car took a tight turn, slowing into it until it came to a stop. We were in a driveway. After a brief pause, the car slowly pulled forward just a few more feet before coming to a complete stop, then the engine shut off.

I heard the driver's side door open and close. The sound of shoes clacked on the cement, drawing near. I heard the click of the trunk and was blinded by fluorescent lights as the lid was flung open. I squinted, trying to get my bearings until my eyes adjusted.

"Well, long time no see, Katarina," Celia said as she stood, smiling, over me.

"Screw you, Celia," I replied. "Though I'm sure Alessandro has been taking care of that. Too bad it only happened because I was finished with him first."

It was petty, but I couldn't help it. And I was counting on it getting under her skin. An angry Strega is not always the smartest.

My comment unnerved her. I could see it in the way her lips tightened as her smile faded.

"You think you're so clever. Always the favored one … Alessandro's favorite. Well, let me assure you that your time to have him is over. You had your chance, Goddess knows why, and you blew it. The only reason you're not dead right now is because Alessandro likes to play with his food before he eats it. And he's not the only one. Rau will want to see you before sunup."

My throat tightened. Rau. I wasn't sure what Alessandro was planning, but if it included Rau, I was going to need more than my own power. My mind searched frantically for a plan that would help buy me time.

Celia grabbed the center knot of my wrist binding and pulled me out of the trunk with ease.

"Let's go," she commanded. "I've been given specific instructions on how to get you ready for tonight. You can't possibly see Rau looking like a hooker."

She pushed me forward, through the garage. I scanned my surroundings in hope of catching any information that might give me some idea of where I was, but it was empty. Other than the car, the only items in it were a workbench with some basic tools and few buckets of blue paint near the side door. For some reason, something on the floor near the buckets caught my attention.

Beach sand. Perhaps we were in a neighborhood near the beach. My mind flipped through the rolodex on San Francisco neighborhoods. The only one I could think of with access to sand was the Outer Sunset. It wasn't a lot to go on, but it was all that I had. If only I could get rid of the binding. With it gone, my line to Gio would be reestablished, and I'd be able to connect telepathically with Claire again. As it was, the binding covered everything like a wet blanket. I had nothing.

Celia continued to push me forward, up a flight of stairs to what I assumed would be the main level of the house. I was still trying to remember everything I saw as I walked, never knowing what would be the clue I needed to figure out my location. As we reached the top of the stairs, Celia reached from behind me and opened the white door.

"Hurry up," she demanded, giving me a hard push.

I stepped into the room and was astonished at how different this room was from the garage. As plain as the garage was, this room was very well-decorated. There were bookshelves, cabinets and end tables along the outside of the space, all intricately carved in the ornate folk style that gave the Strega their flair. In the center of the room was a set of large maroon couches surrounding a circular coffee table.

Underneath the furniture, the floor was covered by a thick Persian rug. There were candles everywhere, red and black. The combined soft glow of their light fully lit the room.

As Celia pushed me across the area toward a narrow hall, I was able to catch a glimpse through the bay window. Though it was dark, there was a streetlight outside directly across from where I stood in the living room. Quickly, my eyes zeroed onto that spot, hoping to recognize some sort of physical marker that could give me another clue.

Looking down the length of the streetlight's illumination, I saw a sign posted a few feet behind it in the landscape. *Beach Access.* Below the words was an arrow pointing to the left. My heart fluttered with excitement. Celia roughly pushed me from behind again.

"What's wrong, Katarina? Why are you dragging your feet?" she teased. "Don't worry, it'll all be over soon."

"Don't be so sure, Celia," I responded, trying to sound as cocky as possible. "Alessandro has spent the past four centuries trying to make me his. You think he's going to give me up so easily?"

I heard Celia's grunt before I felt the blow to my head.

I SENSED the argument before I opened my eyes. I could tell that I had been moved to a bed. The voices were no further than just outside the door.

"I gave you specific instructions not to hurt her," he demanded.

"I'm sorry. I don't know what happened," Celia pleaded.

"I do. You've always been jealous of her. Her power and her beauty." Alessandro's voice was curt.

"Alessandro, I—"

The sound of a slap echoed through the house.

"Shut up. I don't want to hear your stupid excuses. Not when everything is finally going as planned. We've been in this together for a long time, and I've told you that Katarina is the one. She will always be the one."

I heard a sniffle.

"Oh, love," Alessandro cooed, "don't let it get to you. You will always be my second choice."

The sound of kissing caused a wave of nausea to roll through my stomach.

"And you will be rewarded accordingly, mark my words," Alessandro assured.

"Of course. I'm sorry. I was stupid. It will never happen again. Please forgive me," Celia begged.

"Of course I forgive you," Alessandro purred. "I will always forgive my pet."

The back of my head was pounding harder now as another wave of nausea struck. With my wrists still bound, I was helpless to relieve my pain. Unable to control the sickness any longer, I thrust my body to the side and vomited off the end of the bed.

I felt his hands on me before I knew what was happening.

"Don't touch me," I gagged.

"Come now, don't be like that," he said. "You need help. Despite my very specific instructions, Celia really did knock you a good one. Still so jealous of you after all these years, it appears."

He lifted me up and rested my head on his lap. He wiped my mouth and forehead with a cold towel. My body shook at his touch.

"Calm down, love, calm down," he cooed. "It's no use fighting me, especially in your condition."

Tears welled up in my eyes. I fought them back with a ferocity that I had found deep in my core. I would never let him see me cry again. I would never give him that satisfaction.

"What am I going to do with you?" Alessandro said softly. "You know, despite your trying to kill me obsession, you will always hold a part of my heart. It's going to be so hard to get rid of you this time, you know, since you won't be coming back. But, alas, I promised you to Rau. You remember Rau, don't you, love? Yeah, well, he's back and he's still pretty pissed about what you did to him all those centuries ago.

"You know, I really did try to convince him of something else to exchange for the power I'm channeling, but you know how demons are. It's their way or ... death."

I listened to his insane rant while carefully planning my next move.

"Alessandro," I sputtered, trying to sound as pathetic as possible, "please undo my bindings, let me heal myself, then you can put them back on."

Alessandro clicked his tongue.

"So sorry, love, though it's a nice try," he said. "You're just going to have to tough through this the old-fashioned way."

"And Rau?" I questioned. If Alessandro wasn't moved by sympathy, then perhaps he would be moved by fear. "Will Rau be satisfied to receive me like this? Will he be pleased with your treatment of his sacrifice?"

I felt Alessandro tense. He was silent for a few moments before he spoke.

"I'll heal you," he said.

"It won't be as good as if I do it myself. You know as well as I that I have always been skilled at healing, far greater than you. Of course, it's your decision. Just please, do it quickly, I feel like I'm going to be sick again."

Alessandro contemplated his choices. As I had hoped, his fear of the demon spurred him to unfasten my bindings.

"Fine," he conceded. "I'll undo the rope, but I will only go as far as untying the knot and releasing one wrist. And you'll only have thirty seconds to do it. I hope your skills aren't still rusty, my love."

Alessandro sat me up before placing me back on the bed, my head propped up on the pillow. He muttered some words under his breath, and I could feel the knot at my wrists begin to loosen. I knew that I wouldn't have a lot of time; I just hoped that the release of one wrist would be enough for me to connect with Claire. Enough for Gio to feel my soul pulse for him. I felt Alessandro's hand reach into the binding as he gingerly removed one wrist and placed it across my chest.

"Your thirty seconds starts now," he said.

I began to focus my energy just enough to alleviate the pounding in my head. Though nowhere near an accomplished healer, there were a few tricks I had learned to help with superficial pains. As my energy radiated around the back of my skull, I frantically sent a message out to Claire.

"CLAIRE! HEAR ME! OUTER SUNSET ... NEAR OCEAN ... BLUE PAINT ... DIRECTLY ACROSS STREET LIGHT ... BEACH ACCESS SIGN!"

"Katarina! I hear you! Are you okay? Are you—"

"Time's up," Alessandro said as he grabbed my wrist and placed it back into the binding. He secured the knot, then fiddled the rope with his fingers. A smile spread across his face.

"Do you remember that one night in New Orleans?" he asked. His expression mirrored a cat just after fattening up on milk.

My stomach whirled. I should have spent some energy on my stomach. If he was going to keep bringing up the past, I would surely retch.

"I remember how you violated me, if that's what you're referring to," I spat. The only chance I had to get him to stop strolling down memory lane would be if I angered him enough. It was a risk, but with Rau hanging in the balance, I felt confident that no serious harm would come to me ... well, until then.

His face tightened.

"Oh, my apologies, Alessandro. I suppose 'violate' is pretty harsh, considering how unimpressive it all was ... how unimpressive *you* were." I let my lips settle in a smug half-smile, hoping to twist the blade a bit more.

His jaw clenched at the insult. If there was one thing Alessandro could never handle, it was a ding against his ego. I smiled inwardly in satisfaction.

"You're making it really easy to kill you now, bitch," he said as his eyes flashed. "It won't be much longer. You know how Rau is ... always at three thirty-three."

He took out his phone, checking the time.

"I see that you have him back under your bidding?" I said, trying to get him to talk more. "Didn't seem like you did a couple nights ago, when he ventured out on his own into Akshay's shop."

Alessandro looked thoughtful.

"Yes, that was a misunderstanding on my part. Apparently, if you don't keep *exactly* to your word, then you lose some of your pull. Trust me, I learned my lesson from that one. How was I to know that dyed blonde hair wasn't the same as blonde hair? If you ask me, he just wanted a twofer."

My mind jumped back to the club. That poor girl.

"Doesn't matter now," Alessandro continued. "You, my dear, are the final request, the one to seal the deal, so to speak. Once Rau takes you, I will be given the full strength of the power below."

I looked at the man who sat next to me on the bed. He was nowhere near the level of insanity I had thought. No, he was further gone. His eyes were now almost fully red. The irises were swirling storms of torment. His skin, though still bronze in color, held a sallow, yellow hue. He had lost any sort of human resemblance. His aura was black and his soul was gone.

I shuddered as he turned his gaze to me.

"You better get changed, my love. The summoning will start soon," he said. "I'll send Celia in to help you get ready. Though I have to say, you do look ravishing in this," he traced his finger along the plunging neckline of my dress while his other hand ran the length of my thigh.

He leaned down to kiss me. I tried to turn my head, tried to avoid his touch, but he brought his hand to my chin and held it in place. He pressed his lips onto mine. I clamped my lips together, refusing to allow him to enter with his tongue. Frustrated, he licked the outside of my mouth, lapping it like a feral animal. I clenched my teeth together, my jaws tight.

He pulled back.

"Celia!" he called. "Come help my Katie here get ready. I need to prepare."

Celia appeared in the doorway and waited for Alessandro to leave before entering. Walking over to the armoire, she opened the doors. The closet was empty save for one dress. My heart stopped as I recognized what it was; she had helped me put it on nearly ten years ago.

She took it out, and holding it up by the hanger, my wedding dress draped down to the floor.

"I hope it still fits," Celia said. "You *are* looking a bit heavier than the last time you wore this."

My face paled as I realized I was going to have to put on the dress again. It was just a symbol, but it stood for the beginning of my life with Alex—a life that I had chosen to live.

I remembered the day he had asked me to marry him. We had taken a trip down to Monterey for the weekend and stayed at the Oceanfront Beach Resort. I remember being blown away by the rolling beachy hills of the property and the golf cart each guestroom was assigned to get around the resort.

I was just twenty-one, and my previous weekend getaways consisted of camping overnight at a festival and staying at a Travelodge on my way to visit friends. But he had insisted that we spend some alone time with each other, outside of our normal life.

That day he had taken me to the aquarium and shopping on Cannery Row. We'd even gone for a romantic walk on the beach. That night we dined at the resort restaurant. I had the salmon, he ordered the steak. It was all still so clear. After dinner, we took our golf cart back to the room. Dessert and champagne were waiting for us as we walked into the suite.

"Katie," he'd said, "did you have fun today?"

"Oh, my God, Alex, today was unbelievable!" I cried. "I don't think that I've ever had such an amazing day."

"Well, I'm glad, because you deserve it," he replied.

"Deserve it? How?" I asked.

"You've just been through so much in your life, so many ... obstacles," he said. "It's nice to know that I can at least pay you back for my part in any troubles you may have had."

"What are you talking about? Since the moment I met you, my life has only gotten better. With you around, I have yet to have a problem."

"I'm so glad you think so," he had teased. "Because it's going to make this a whole lot easier."

He reached into his pocket and took out a small velvet box. Getting down on one knee, he looked up into my eyes. I remember thinking about how mesmerizing his eyes were.

"Katie, you are the love of my life," he began. "You are my past, my present, and my future. My heart has been yours for four hundred years, and it will continue to be yours for eternity. Will you do me the honor of being my wife?"

At the time, I had thought it romantic. I remember thinking how poetic it was, his use of hyperbole. I hadn't thought he literally meant four hundred years. My response felt like a betrayal to myself, though I know that I couldn't truly be faulted.

"Oh, Alex," I glowed, overwhelmed by his gesture. My whole body had trembled in excitement. "Yes! Yes! Of course I will be your wife."

I pulled myself out of the memory before I fell too deeply into it. I did not want to remember any more.

Celia came over and helped me stand. With a small knife, she slit the sides of my dress and removed what was left of my clothing. Then she helped me into the dress. The front bodice had been altered to allow her to button it at my shoulders while leaving my wrists bound. Adding insult to injury, Celia had been right; the dress was a bit snug.

"One last thing," she said as she ran over to the desk. Rolling up the cover, she removed a simple wreath.

Standing next to me, in front of the mirror, she arranged the wreath on my head. She pulled the bun on my head loose with a rough tug, my hair falling past my shoulders in dark waves.

"Isn't this familiar?" she remarked, staring at our reflection.

I swallowed hard.

"Let's go," Celia prodded. "It's time. Don't be nervous. I'm sure your second marriage will turn out better than the first. Though, your groom ... I hear he's got quite the temper," she purred.

We walked out into the living room. The black and red pillar candles were nearly half burned. Alessandro had cleared out the table and couches and removed the rug. Drawing the curtains closed, he stood in the center of the floor where a large circle had been traced out, a pentagram filling its space.

He turned to us as we entered the room. He froze when he saw me.

"My Goddess," he whispered. "You have never looked more beautiful. Rau will be most pleased."

I simply stood, silent. There was nothing else I could do. The bonds around my wrists had rendered me powerless. Unable to use any sort of magick with them secured, I would be defenseless against Rau when he was summoned. I suppose there was a bit of romantic irony to the whole situation somewhere. I just couldn't seem to make peace with it.

Alessandro motioned for Celia to place me at the fifth point. He and Celia took their place at the two points opposite me, leaving the two points to my left and right vacant.

"There are not enough people here to perform the summoning," I said.

Both Alessandro and Celia laughed.

"Katarina"—he chuckled— "I would think you'd know by now that tapping into dark power does have some benefits. We don't need five. Three will suffice."

My breath grew ragged as I felt true fear creep in on me for the first time.

Alessandro began the incantation to cast the circle. I thought quickly. Waiting for their attention to be focused elsewhere, I carefully smudged an edge of the circle, breaking its line. When the circle had been cast, Alessandro went into the summoning.

"Rau, *signore oscuro, demone degli inferi, che io chiamo te per unirsi a noi sul piano terreno di accettare il mio ultimo dono, un'offerta per sigillare il nostro accordo ... Katarina Liberati, figlia scelta della Strega Ilmalo.*"

I felt the wooden floor beneath my feet tremble as Alessandro said the incantation. Celia began to laugh in excitement.

"Now, to expedite his return ..." Alessandro said, unbuttoning his shirt.

Removing it, he let it fall to the floor. He reached around his back and pulled a hunting knife from a sheath attached to his belt. Its handle was black, and its silver blade glinted in the candlelight. He looked at Celia and nodded.

She carefully walked the inside perimeter of the circle to his side. Rolling her sleeve up, she offered her arm. Alessandro made a quick slice. The thin red line took a second to appear. Kissing her wound gently, blood lingering on his lips, he shook her arm, the red liquid flung its way to the center of the pentagram. I watched in horror as each drop sizzled when it hit the floor.

Rau was coming.

Celia made her way back to her point before Alessandro continued. I had to stall.

"Alessandro, wait," I pleaded. "You don't have to do this. Bringing Rau back to earth permanently will ensure the death of life as the world knows it. If you have ever truly loved me, please reconsider. You don't have to do this."

Something flashed in Alessandro's eyes. For an instant, the red had vanished.

"You cannot trust her," Celia chimed in. "She has done nothing but betray you. From her first life to her last, she has done nothing but cause you pain."

Alessandro shook his head. The red returned.

"You know nothing of our past lives. You don't know Alessandro as I do," I yelled at Celia. Then, turning to Alessandro, I pleaded, "Alessandro, look at me. Look into my eyes. This is no spell. Look! I am still bound!"

I held up my wrists to show that I was still under his control. Alessandro looked at me. He did not speak.

"If you choose to not go through with this ... if you choose to keep Rau at bay," I continued. "I will concede. You win, Alessandro. I will be yours ... just as you have always wanted."

I knew what I offered was more than I could give, but I

could not allow Alessandro to continue. I wouldn't be with him for long anyway. I would sacrifice myself to the cliffs the first moment I could sneak away.

I only hoped that Gio would understand, though I knew he would never forgive me.

Alessandro's eyes grew calm. The red faded as the storm within settled, and for an instant, I believed he would accept my offer.

"My sweet, sweet Katarina," he said sadly. "Don't you see? It's too late for that."

The red flashed anew in his eyes. The storm rose again, a violent tumult of color.

"After all these years, you finally want to offer the only thing I have ever wanted," he hissed.

I could feel his anger rise with each word. I flinched at its intensity.

"But you see, the problem now is that you are no longer for me. You are now Rau's. Once he arrives, you will be his to do with as he pleases."

I heard Celia cackle over his speech.

"Ah, the price of love," he continued. "I hope your few moments with Gio were worth the eternity of torture you are about to endure."

He held the blade in his right hand and cut his left wrist, the red horizontal line emerging on his skin. With a flick of his arm, he sent drops of blood toward the center of the circle. Like Celia's, each drop sizzled as it hit the floor.

The ground rumbled and I heard a roar from the otherworld as Rau grew closer. The candles flickered but did not go out. I tried to remember exactly what I had done to send the demon back to the underworld the first time. Not that it mattered, my bindings made it a moot point.

I thought about Alessandro's final words to me.

I hope your few moments with Gio were worth the eternity of torture you are about to endure.

I thought back to the stolen moments we had during this life before the curse had been lifted—the coffee shop, the bookstore, the clearing. I remembered how it felt when I saw him again at Matteo's. How our time together, though short, was the most precious of my whole existence.

I opened my mind to past lives as well. I saw the brief glances, the knowing smiles, the shared stolen moments, and I realized that in all my lives, I would never exchange one moment with Gio for a lifetime with Alessandro.

I took a deep breath as the truth settled my soul. I had lived an eternity, and those memories would get me through another one.

The boards on the floor now threatened to break under the force of the shaking.

"Well, my love," Alessandro said smugly, "any last words? If you have anything else to say to me, this is your last chance."

I looked him straight in the eyes, courage funded by my new resolve.

"I'll take my chances with the demon," I said as I smiled.

Alessandro recoiled as though I'd actually slapped him, just as I intended.

Suddenly, the shaking stopped. Everything went calm. The candles flickered, then blew out. The room went dark. A second later they burst back into flame with a flash.

There standing in the center of the circle, was Rau. His skin was a bit darker from what I remembered, his features contorted by the candlelight.

"Well, hello there, little one," Rau goaded as he caught my eye. "I believe we have some catching up to do."

"Shit," I whispered, my heart racing as I looked the demon dead in the face.

Chapter Twenty-Three

GIO

Matteo greeted me at the door.

"Follow me," he demanded. "They're in the den."

I didn't question his command. I followed him through the house and down a spiral staircase located off the hallway that led to the kitchen. We descended with speed, each step a bit faster than the last. When we reached the bottom, Matteo led me down another short hallway. He stopped before a set of heavy wooden double doors.

Grabbing the handles, he thrust them open. The room looked like a cross between a library and an arsenal. Though the lighting was dim, I could see built-in bookshelves lining the walls from floor to ceiling, each one crammed with tomes of all sizes and thickness.

As I walked farther into the room, I noticed several low tables adorned with a wide variety of blades and various other weapons. It took a moment for my brain to comprehend what my eyes were seeing. Swords of all types, with their matching sheaths, were displayed on the velvet tops of waist-high tables.

Willem, Claire, and Patrick were at the far end of the

room, picking up various weapons and strapping them onto their bodies. Matteo cleared his throat, and they all looked up.

Immediately, I was approached by all three.

"Tell me exactly what happened," Willem demanded.

"I can't hear her, Gio! It's like she's completely out of my head ... just gone!" Claire panicked.

"Just tell me what to do," Patrick instructed.

I could barely understand their words as they spoke over each other in a frenzy. I took a step back and motioned for them to be silent.

Someone was missing.

I looked around the room and noticed Rowan, deep in the volume of a thick book. It had a faded and torn binding. Thick, dark letters in archaic script were written on the front.

Un'indagine Dettagliata in Demonologia, A Detailed Investigation of Demonology.

I walked over and stood in front of her.

"Tell me how to banish the demon," I commanded.

Rowan looked up from the book, her eyes red and puffy from reading through the night.

"I ... I ... can't," she whispered. "I haven't found anything."

"Gio," Willem interrupted. "Was Rau there? Did Rau take Katarina?"

I shook my head.

"No," I responded. "It was Alessandro. That's certain. But he was able to influence the entire club, Willem. He was able to control every aspect of it, everybody in it. That's power that no witch, no matter what tradition, can do without the assistance of something with serious weight.

"You can be sure that whatever Alessandro is turning into, we are no longer dealing with Strega Ilmalo. He's now something more, something I don't recognize. He has given himself fully to the darkness, I could see it in his eyes. There's nothing to stop him from completing his part of the bargain with Rau. And instinct tells me somehow Katarina plays a role in this deal. The only thing I'm certain of is that we don't have much time."

I turned and looked back at Rowan.

"So, Rowan, if we have any chance, any chance at all, you need to find a way for us to remove Rau from this world. I need something ... anything within the next fifteen minutes, then we have to go. Any longer and we can almost guarantee that Katarina is dead. This time, I fear it will be forever."

Rowan nodded and dove back into the book. Willem placed his hand on my shoulder. He led me to the table where he, Claire, and Patrick had been arming up.

"We have no idea what we're really getting into," he began. "So, we need to be prepared for any circumstance."

"I still don't understand why there's not one gun in the place," Claire muttered. "It'd be nice to have some actual firepower backing us."

Rowan spoke up. "One thing I have found is that if Alessandro is invoking Rau tonight, no amount of firepower will be of any effect. If anything, demons feed off the energy released from a firearm. The beast would grow stronger with each bullet shot. It is believed that a demon must be slain by a sword forged of steel, but it doesn't say exactly how."

I watched as Claire reluctantly agreed while she continued to attach a small but fierce-looking blade to each wrist. She rolled down her sleeves to conceal them. Willem had already holstered a larger blade around his waist and Patrick strapped an ankle blade on his lower leg above his boots along with a hearty sword at his side.

"It's good to see you up," I said as I walked over to him. "But are you well enough to come with us?"

"Don't even try to have all the fun without me, mate,"

Patrick replied, then nodded at Claire. "I've already heard it enough from this one. I don't need you after me as well."

"I was just going to say that it's good to have you back."

"Gio, I think I have something over here that you'll want to see."

Matteo beckoned me over to a longer table closer to the entrance that was covered with a navy-blue cloth. I walked over to the table as he pulled the covering off.

Underneath lay a silver blade, approximately two feet in length and three inches wide. The hilt was bronze with one large red stone embedded in the pommel and one on each side of the quillons. The grip was black as night.

"I have been collecting these weapons as a hobby for many years," Matteo explained. "I did not think that one day, they would actually be put to use."

He picked up the sword with both hands and offered it to me hilt first. Carefully, I took the piece. It was heavy, but not so much so that I was unable to wield it. I placed the sword back on the table and attached its belt around my waist. Picking the blade up, I slid it into its sheath.

"Meet me upstairs in five minutes," I told the group as I headed toward the thick double doors that led back to the staircase. "Rowan, bring every book you think may have a clue as how to defeat Rau. We don't have much time."

I stormed out of the room. Heading up to the quarters where Katarina and I had stayed, I had to try to connect with her before the others were ready to leave. I needed to see if there was any indication she was still alive.

Inside, my heart was holding on by a thread, but I refused to let it snap. All I needed was five minutes. Five minutes to test my newfound powers—to challenge this gift the Goddess had bestowed upon me.

I burst into the bedroom, slamming the door behind me. I took off the belt that held my weapon and stripped the shirt off my back. Taking a razor from the bathroom, I made a slice across the tip of my right middle finger. Pressing my thumb against it, I squeezed the blood out. I bent down and drew a circle on the white tile floor.

I lit the white candles on the counter near the sink and hit the lights. Sitting in the center of the circle, I closed it for protection, using the invocation just as Rowan had the night the Goddess had granted me her favor. When I felt the rush of power flow from the crown of my head through to the tips of my toes, I began my search for Katarina.

The moment I was brought back to life—sent back to Earth—the connection between Katarina and me had been there. It always had. True, it had taken Rowan and heightened senses to point it out, but it had always been there. The delicate magickal thread that bound us only grew stronger the closer I got to her.

I had felt it tugging me forward as I made my way through San Francisco the night we arrived. It led me to the alleyway where the entrance to the Strega Underworld was hidden. It guided us through the twisting maze of stalls and vendors to Matteo's door—where I would find my love waiting.

But this felt different. The second she let go of my hand, the connection dulled, and then became undetectable. Gone, just like that. I was still trying to figure out what it meant.

Deep down, I knew Katarina was still alive. Alessandro wouldn't have gone through all that trouble just to kill her immediately. No—if Alessandro was anything, he was predictable. He'd want to torture her one last time.

A cold chill traveled down my spine as I thought about what Alessandro might do, might *be doing* to Katarina at that moment. I cut off the thoughts before they took control. I had to focus. Thinking about what might be happening would do me no good. I took a deep breath and focused.

I imagined the thread that once connected Katarina and I

together in my mind. It was bright red, thick and satiny. I stretched it out and sent it into the atmosphere. It snaked through the universe searching for my love. It flew past the Underground, out into the busy city. It weaved downtown, to the east, to the south ... nothing. It made its way through the crowded neighborhoods ... nothing. I sent it far, far out to the west ... nothing.

Suddenly, I remembered what Joseph had said just before we'd been ambushed by Alessandro's spell. West of the city. Club guests had referenced the neighborhoods on the west of the city. I was not terribly familiar with San Francisco, but I knew there were neighborhoods that were located out toward the coast.

I sent the ribbon back to the west, this time focusing on the area closest to the ocean, hoping ... praying to the Goddess whilst I worked her magick, to find my Katarina.

Nothing.

Whatever magick Alessandro had employed, it was powerful. Pulling my focus back to the bathroom, I opened my eyes. I remembered the visions I had when I was in the worlds between and focused my energy on my newfound power. Could I feel her? Could I be led to her once more? A sharp wind blew through the bathroom. The candles flickered. Then, nothing. Dammit. After a few more minutes of nothing, I heard a knock on the bedroom door. It was Willem.

"Gio, we're ready."

"I'm coming now," I answered as I blew out the candles and flipped on the bathroom light. I threw water onto my face and looked in the mirror.

"Katarina, I know you're out there," I said to my reflection. "Just hang on, love. I'm coming. We all are."

I quickly returned to the bedroom where I threw on a shirt and refastened the sword to my waist. Grabbing my jacket, I headed to the main living area where everyone was waiting for me.

~

"It must be some sort of binding spell," Rowan said. "They're not used very often any more these days; most witches can work things out without going there, but I've read that back in the day, they were pretty handy when you wanted to incapacitate your enemy both physically and psychically."

"I've never experienced this," Matteo said. "It doesn't make sense that I can't even sense the tiniest bit of it, that I, Strega Ilmalo by true bloodline, cannot even pick up on the spell? To think all that time Joshua had been messing with it, and I had no idea … It's not right. How could someone do something this egregious against their own kind?"

Rowan looked at him with sympathetic eyes and shook her head.

"I'm so sorry, Matteo, I wish I had answers for you, but I don't know," she answered. "We're talking about very old magick here so there's a lot we don't understand." She paused. "And I doubt if there's anything left of the Ilmalo in Alessandro."

"What does that matter, how old it is?" he asked. "Ilmalo is Ilmalo."

"I've been reading in your books that it matters because over time, like everything on this earth, an evolution will take place. Spellwork is no different. As it travels through time, a little change here, a line there. Practitioners of all traditions add their own footprint to a spell. It's like the natural selection of magick. The best spells adapt while the weaker ones get left behind … lost to time … forgotten. Everything evolves together.

"But Alessandro is not a modern-day Strega. He's one of

the first who just also happens to be alive in modern time, which means he remembers the original spells from the beginning of Ilmalo existence, the ones that were never supposed to survive. Add a little dark power into the mix, and ...” Rowan let her voice trail as if she was lost in thought.

"She's battled him once before." Claire said quietly.

We all looked at her.

"What did you say?" I asked, stunned.

Claire swallowed; her face drained of color.

"I ... I saw ... I mean, she showed me ..." she stuttered. Willem reached over and took her hand.

"It's okay, tell us."

She drew a deep breath. "When she was a girl, there was a group of them. Seven, altogether. One of them had been attacked and in revenge, they tried to summon Rau. Alessandro was there. But it didn't work right. There was a problem with their summoning. One of the seven was taken as a sacrifice. Katarina broke the circle. She took the power offered to Rau and used it against him. Alessandro was by her side. Together, they sent him back to his realm, but I'm not sure exactly how."

Willem closed his eyes.

"I heard this story as a young boy. The Onesta would warn their children to stay away from Ilmalo clan members. They spoke of how their children would summon demons, how they would sacrifice their friends' lives for power.

"I thought it was all a tale. Bedtime stories to frighten the children into being good. I had no idea that it had been real. That Katarina had been a part of that nightmare."

Claire pulled her hand from his.

"No, Willem. You don't understand. Katarina *stopped* it. She knew it was wrong. Alessandro wanted to continue, wanted more of the power they had harnessed. None of their friends could stop him, but Katarina did. She stopped it. If we can find her, then we can stop Alessandro from allowing Rau to walk the face of the earth."

"That only gives us another reason we need to find her now. If she was able to stop him before, she can do it again. I know she can."

When no response was made, I continued.

"The club owner Joseph said he witnessed Alessandro and Celia luring a blonde client out of the club. Before he could interfere with their plans, they'd already gone. But he also said that other guests that night mentioned they'd been talking about their flat on the west side of the city.

"I tried to reach out there with my senses; I tried to make the connection with Katarina, but I couldn't do it. There was nothing ... just static."

"It's the same with me. I can't connect with her, either," Claire chimed in. Seeing my warning look, she added, "It's fine. Everyone knows I'm telepathically connected with her. I told them. I was so panicked when I felt it disappear suddenly that I came clean."

I nodded.

"What I don't understand is how they're able to prevent her from sending a message at all," she continued. "It's like you said, Gio. All I hear is static."

"So, what's the plan?" Patrick asked when the room fell silent. "I know I've got no eyes, but as I see it, the longer we wait around, the more likely Katarina will be lost to us forever. Alessandro may be keeping her alive now, but I suspect he has plans for her."

Patrick was right. We had to get moving. The problem was where to begin.

"I say let's just head out toward the ocean," Patrick continued. "It seems as good a chance as any at this point, and who knows, you just may be on to something, mate."

I nodded.

"I agree," I said. Then looking around at the faces that looked back at me, I had a sudden urge to protect them. "But I don't think we should all go."

"Well, I'm coming with you," Claire spoke up. "If Katarina suddenly connects with me, you're gonna want to know. She may lead us to where they're keeping her."

"And there's no way ... *no way* you're leaving me behind. After all these years, I wouldn't know what to do with myself if I wasn't in some sort of danger," Willem added.

He stood up and patted my back.

"Then it's settled," I said. "Willem, Claire, and I will go out and start looking. The rest of you will wait here."

Matteo, Rowan, and Patrick erupted in an argument.

"Listen," I demanded. "We don't have time for this. Rowan, I need you here with the books. If you find something that could be valuable, that could give us an advantage, call us immediately. I'm counting on you to be here."

I could tell by the look in her eyes she wasn't going to fight it. She sat back down on the couch.

"The same goes for you, Matteo," I said next. "You have an amazing resource here at your house. Stay with Rowan, help her find what we need. You know where everything is. You can make it happen faster. My friend, coming here, finding you, it makes me believe more in divine intervention. I cannot thank you enough for your kindness and generosity. There is nothing I can do to truly repay you."

"There actually is," Matteo spoke solemnly, his voice took a low tone. "Avenge my brother's death. Kill Alessandro."

We shook hands and locked eyes. It was understood that I would do everything in my power to do just that.

"Well, since I won't be reading any books any time soon, I suppose I'll just be joining you then, mate," Patrick said.

"No, Patrick," Claire interrupted. "You're not strong enough. You should stay here and rest."

Patrick smiled. "Claire, stop. I think we both know that's never going to happen. There's no scenario in which that version of the story gets back to Rose. Besides, even though my gift of foresight has been taken, my intuition is stronger than all of yours combined. And an extra set of hands never hurt in combat."

I had to admit, he had a point. I was also tired of arguing. We needed to leave. "Patrick, I'm not even going to try to talk you out of it," I said. "If you want to join us, we'd be lucky to have you."

"Then it's settled," Willem said. "Let's get moving."

Rowan handed over her keys and we started the journey out of the Underground. When we reached the surface, we found the parking garage had housed the car. Clicking the sensor, the headlights flashed a few vehicles down.

We made our way to the car and got in. I sat in the driver's seat and started it up. The car gently purred. Throwing it into gear, I sped out of the garage and into the dark city.

I headed west. I drove through streets well above the speed limit, but I didn't care. That wasn't even a concern. My only objective was to get as close to the beach as I could in as little time as possible. Goddess help any cop who tried to pull me over tonight.

It made sense, his choosing that neighborhood. As much as sense could be made with him. He'd want to be close to the last place where he had Katarina. My thoughts flew back to that night a few weeks ago when he had had fallen to his death ... well, his apparent death, from the cliff to the beach below.

Everything about Alessandro made my skin crawl. I shuddered at the fact that I knew him so well. Well, at least I thought I had, until he started going deep into dark power. For centuries we had played a sick and twisted game, neither of us ever winning. Katarina was the only loser. Now the game had changed. The stakes were higher. This time there would be a victor. The loss would be greater than it had ever been. This time the game would be over.

I pressed my foot down on the pedal and the car engine purred louder as it flew up and down the hills. The rest of the passengers were silent. There wasn't much to say. We all understood the gravity of the situation. One mistake, one mistimed step, could mean the end of it all. The city lights blurred in my peripheral vision as I drove with conviction. The flickering took me back to a life just prior to this one.

NEW YORK CITY, 1985.

Willem and I had just tracked her down after losing her once as she hitchhiked across the country. She'd left her house late in the night in Dayton, Ohio as we watched from afar. We'd followed her to the interstate where she caught a ride with a trucker heading east. She was still in school at the time, living with her parents.

We stayed with her through the night, but somehow in the confusion of a truck stop, we had lost her. It was a good thing that our bond had been as strong as ever at that time. I'd been able to direct Willem where to drive easily enough until she was in our sights once more.

We caught her trail just past Philadelphia. Alessandro was close as well. I felt him. As always. I didn't know where, but the urgency pecked at me like a vulture. I could feel his evilness. I knew we had to hurry. We had to find her first, before he could get his hands on her.

Into Manhattan, we traced her path through the night. It was close to ten o'clock when she got out of the last car, her oversized purse slung over her shoulder and headed into a nearby diner. When she emerged, she looked nowhere near the eighteen years of age I knew her to be.

She wore a long-sleeved metallic gold wrap dress, slit up

the side with matching heels. A thick belt was wrapped around her waist and her hair was covered on top with a gold-sequined scarf. Tight, frizzy curls pushed out past her shoulders. Big hoop earrings hung from her ears. Gold eye shadow and lips finished the look.

She was a golden goddess. We watched as she caught a cab, then followed her to her destination.

When the cab stopped at 254 West Fifty-fourth Street. I wasn't surprised. Studio 54 was famous. Whether you were into the club scene or not, the business was a name known well by pretty much everyone at the time. She'd gotten out of the cab and headed into the building. She walked past the long line outside, and straight up to the bouncer, who just bowed and let her pass. Had she done this before? Was there some connection we had missed?

Willem and I had to sneak our way around back. As we entered the club, we split up. I scanned the crowd for Katarina. It didn't take long to spot her in the center of the dance floor. My heart stopped when I saw who she danced with. Alessandro.

Of course.

His arms wrapped around her body and pulled her close, kissing her neck. I seethed as I watched him violate her. He lifted his gaze to meet mine, giving a crooked smile. Whispering something in her ear, she laughed and nodded. He reached into his pocket and pulled out a small silver vial. Unscrewing the top, he pulled it off, revealing a little spoon at the end. It was filled with white powder. Holding it up to her nose, she quickly inhaled. Blinking her eyes, she exhaled, letting the drug take effect.

Alessandro whispered again and the two headed backstage.

I pushed my way through the crowd, following them to the secluded area. When I approached them behind the stage, he had her backed up against the wall, her leg lifted around his waist, his head buried in her breasts.

"Get away from her."

Alessandro laughed.

"Man, you really know how to kill a good time, don't you?" he said without turning to face me. "Get off it, Gio. It's over."

"Who's that?" she had said behind him; then, meeting my stare, let her leg drop to the floor and pushed him away.

"I know you. Don't I? You ... you look so familiar."

"Ugh, just when the fun was about to start. You two are killing me," Alessandro said under his breath. He looked at Katarina, switching up the tone in his voice. "I don't know, baby. Do you like the way he looks? You know, sweetheart, he could always join us, if you'd like."

She stiffened at his tone. She tried to push him farther away, but he had a vicelock grip on her. I took a step forward, but he pulled a knife from his pocket.

"Don't move."

I froze.

He turned Katarina around and held her in front of him, his eternal shield.

"Now, I know you know how this goes," he began. "But let's see if she does, shall we?" He leaned in closer to her ear. "Let's play a little game, baby, okay?"

Katarina's eyes widened where tears began to pool.

"What're you doing, Alesso? What's happening?"

"It's called Choose Your Death: Drug or Blade. Here's how the game goes. You take that little fun vial out of my pocket and start snorting until it's gone. And if you stop, I'll stab you. Get it?"

"But ... but ... it's too much ... I can't do it all. I'll OD," she whimpered.

"Oh, well, that's the game. And the price you pay for

being such a rotten whore," Alessandro said in a mocking tone. He jabbed her with the knife, just enough to hurt. "Let's go, kitten ... don't be shy. You know where it is. Unless you want this knife in your side right, that is. In which case, I'm happy to accommodate."

Katarina, trembling, reached into his front pocket. Alessandro purred as her hand searched the cavity.

"Always a tease." He smiled wickedly. She pulled out the silver vial and held it in her trembling hand.

"Don't be shy, baby," Alessandro cooed. "You weren't a second ago." His free hand squeezed her breast.

She unscrewed the top and began taking small bits of drug. Tears were streaming now, her mascara running down her cheeks.

"Alessandro, stop!" I yelled. "It's me you want to punish. Let her go!"

Alessandro smiled. "Oh, I believe I am punishing you." He laughed. "And doing a fucking fine job of it."

And then, without warning, he slit her throat.

I'D BEEN TOO LATE THEN, but not tonight. We hit a straightaway that headed directly toward the beach, and I slammed my foot on the accelerator. We were just inside the Outer Sunset, but I kept going. Instinct pulled me straight ahead to the ocean. Golden Gate Park was just a blur to the right.

Suddenly, without warning, my throat closed. My lungs seized mid-breath, my heart stopped beating. My mind clouded and I felt dizzy. I was unable to control my body; my body was in control of me. It demanded I pay attention. It flooded my existence and completely filled me up.

It was the ribbon. The thick, satiny ribbon from my mind,

the one I had sent out looking for my connection to Katarina. It swirled around in my head and snapped me awake. Breaking out of the constraints of my aura, it immediately reached out and searched for the connection.

"Stop!" Claire screamed.

Even in the confusion and pain, I was able to slam my foot on the brakes, skidding to a complete halt in the middle of the road. The few cars that were out managed to narrowly avoid us, honking and cursing at us as they passed.

"What's wrong?" Willem asked. "What's happening?"

I would've looked at Claire except I was struggling with my own psychic distractions. It was Katarina. I knew it was. I could feel her pull as my heart started beating again. It called to my very soul.

I could hear Claire gasping for air. She wheezed in and out, fighting to take a full breath. I could hear Willem and Patrick calling out to her, trying to get her to respond.

"Claire," Patrick pleaded. "Claire, what is it?"

"She's alive," I said, looking at Claire for the first time. "I felt her. She's still alive."

"She is," Claire said, gasping for air. "I heard her just now ... in my head, she spoke to me."

"What did she say?" I asked. "All I felt was an urgent pull to the southwest."

"It was just a string of words ... I think they were clues," Claire said. "And there was something else ... like a red glowing rope ... around her wrists."

"A binding," Willem offered. "The Strega Ilmalo used to use them as punishment within their own camp. For them, there was nothing worse than a Strega without power. Tricky little spell, if you ask me, and when pumped with the magick Alessandro now appears to possess, it's no wonder why we can't pick up on Katarina's signal."

"It doesn't make sense, Willem," Gio said. "If the binding

prevents us from picking up her energy, then how was she able to send it out?"

"And why such a short burst?" added Patrick.

The moment he asked the question, I knew. Something had shifted. Something in her captivity had changed—just enough for her to seize a fleeting chance and reach out.

Dread coiled in my gut, tight and unrelenting. My mind lurched through the worst possibilities, each one springing open like a rusted jack-in-the-box, its twisted melody of fear rattling through me. Why had Katarina been cut off? What had changed? And more importantly—was it already too late?

"Tell us exactly what you heard, Claire," I demanded.

Claire sat in the passenger seat and stared back at me.

"She's near the beach. Close enough to be near the sand. We have to look for a streetlight with a beach access sign posted next to it. She's in a flat there ... across the street, possibly light blue in color. That's all I got."

I put the car in gear and accelerated. We were so close now. If we could just get there before anything else happened.

When we finally ran out of the road, I threw the car in park and got out. Standing on the driver's side of the car, I looked south down the street. Miles of road lay out before us. To the right, I could barely make out the sandy dunes that led to the water, but I could hear the rhythmic sound of the waves as they crashed on the beach. To the left, across the street, was a line of homes. One after the other, they lined the street, each too close to the other.

"Remember, we're looking for a streetlight with a beach access sign next to it," Claire said as she began walking down the street.

"Or a light blue house," she sighed in resignation realizing that a quarter of these homes were light blue. "I wish I had more information."

"It's enough to get us to where we need to be," Willem comforted.

We half walked, half ran down the street, our eyes feverishly scanning for the clues that Katarina had given us. I was frantic, though I knew it would do me no good. I had to stay focused, but my subconscious took over.

"Over here!" Willem called.

We ran to the streetlight where he was standing. The beach access sign was located just behind it in the landscape. Looking across the street, I saw a three-story Victorian-style flat. Even in the yellow hue of the streetlight, I could tell it was light blue.

"Katarina," I whispered, "we're here. We're coming."

I only prayed that it wasn't too late.

Chapter Twenty-Four

KATARINA

"You have no idea how long I've waited to meet with you again," the demon spat. I could feel his hot, sour breath on my throat.

"I can assure you the sentiment is not returned," I replied tartly.

Rau laughed deep from his belly.

"Rau," Alessandro interrupted, "I stand before you with my final payment, evidence of my loyalty to you. I offer you one of my own in exchange for the power you have promised."

Rau snapped his head around. Celia winced and diverted her eyes as he shot a quick glance at her before gazing upon the speaker.

"Very well," Rau said. "Our bargain has been met. I release the power from the otherworld. It is yours to use as you see fit."

He snapped his long fingers. There was a sudden flash of light from above and a low rumble from below. Alessandro raised his hands above his head to accept the gift.

His body began shaking as he accepted the full power the

demon bestowed. I watched in horror as his eyes grew a deep, dark red. I shuddered at what the power would really do to him. Would he even be able to harness such a monstrosity?

The demon turned his attention back to me.

"And, now my sweet child," he drooled. "It is time for us to have a little fun."

Rau flicked his tongue out and licked my chin. The rough, sandpaper touch of the organ burned my skin in its track. I could hear Celia laugh in delight as she watched the demon prepare to have his way with me.

There was nothing I could do. My wrists strained as I tried to pull them free from the binding, but it was no use. It was too ironic. Of all the ways in both the earthly plane and beyond that I could have perished, I would have never suspected that I was going to die, completely incapacitated, at the hands of Rau.

I calmed my body and accepted the fate that awaited me at the end of a journey that had lasted too long. I took a deep breath and focused my essence on the Goddess. I closed my eyes and prayed, in vain, that Rau would end it soon, though I knew he had not even begun.

"What's the matter, Katarina?" he asked. "Does my face scare you? Can you not look upon the one you so willingly sent back hundreds of years ago?"

I ignored his words.

"Open your eyes!" Rau commanded in a booming voice, slapping me in the face. "Look upon your new mate! I want to see the fear in your face when you understand what that really means!"

I squeezed my eyes tight. The binding may have controlled my ability to use magick, but it did not control my free will. My physical body was still mine. If Rau wanted to see my eyes, he would have to rip them from my skull. I suppressed a shudder as I realized that could very well happen.

"I will never bow down to you! And I will never do as you command!" I spat back; eyes still shut. "Though, you're right about one thing. I *am* sorry I sent you back. I should have killed you when I had the chance!"

Rau laughed.

"We will see who is truly sorry," he said in a calm voice.

I could feel his fingertips as they grazed up each arm. Refusing to open my eyes, I could only imagine the demon residue they left behind as they traveled up both sides of my neck, past my ears, stopping at my temples.

I could feel the excruciating heat from his fingers as they rested at my brow. It felt like ten white hot needles. I struggled to remain silent. I feared I would pass out from the pain.

My mind began to lose its grip on my will, and I fought the urge to open my eyes, to see what it was that was causing so much pain. Then the images began. Rau sent them with fervent hatred.

I saw Willem and Claire. They were sitting on a park bench somewhere in the city. Quietly sharing a moment, whispering to each other, stealing kisses, laughing. They looked happy, content.

A man approached them wearing a long coat. He asked them a question. I knew that the man was not good, that he wished them harm. The man turned and I saw his face. It was Alessandro ... but not. He had masked himself, hid his true being.

I knew it was a vision. I knew that Rau had only sent me the images, that they were not the truth, but it felt so real, like a glimpse into a shred of the future.

I wanted to yell to them, warn them, but I couldn't. Alessandro pulled a gun from under his coat and shot Claire in the head, her brain splashing out onto Willem's lap. Willem, shocked into silence, just sat there paralyzed as Alessandro took out a knife and stabbed him twice in the side before making a long slice across his stomach, his intestines spilling out.

My heart screamed. A long, bellow of sorrow. And then, suddenly, the image changed. Like a television, it flipped to another station.

Gio was walking in the woods.

Oh, Goddess, I thought to myself, *please don't let me watch Gio die again!*

The searing pain on my brow burrowed deeper as Rau sent the image further into my being, making it clearer and stronger than real life itself.

It had recently rained. I could smell the clean, fresh scent of the trees and shrubs as Gio walked along the path. I could feel my throat start to close as I watched him casually strolling, completely unaware of the evil I knew lurked close by.

I waited anxiously, bracing myself for something tragic to occur—for Alessandro to emerge from behind a rock and to run a blade through Gio like he had before—but nothing happened. The vision was unusually calm ... uneventful. A pretty woman ran up to him and took his hand. He held it and smiled as they continued to walk together down the trail.

Then it hit me. And my heart crushed under the truth.

I would've preferred a punch to the face, to be dragged across rusty nails, to be buried alive for eternity—anything but this.

Gio was happy. Worse, he looked relieved. As if my absence had lifted a weight he had carried for four hundred years.

The realization shattered something deep inside me. Had I been wrong this whole time? After everything—after all the years he spent searching for me, fighting to save me—was he truly better off without me? Was it me who was holding him back from a life of love?

. . .

THE FUNNY THING about doubt is that you don't need that much of it at all for it to blossom, for it to take over your mind like a weed. For it to germinate and spread through your entire existence before it soon becomes what you are, before it becomes your truth.

No, I had to stay strong. Rau knew exactly what he was doing, taking my most vulnerable part and extorting it to fit his mold of twisted retribution. No, I couldn't believe the images he spoon-fed me. Could I?

No, Gio loved me. We were two parts to a whole, each half completing the other. His love was as unwavering as mine. But would he be happier if he were released from this nightmare? Would his life have more meaning if there were less of me in it?

The answer was simple. Of course he would. And, if that meant a life without me, then that's how it must be.

Rau laughed.

"So predictable," he tsked. "So easy to manipulate. For as much trouble as you have given Alessandro over the centuries, I'm surprised at how easy it is to get into your mind."

"You will never get into my mind."

He already had.

"Then why are you doubting?" he scoffed. "Why are you questioning your entire existence? Perhaps, it is because deep down, you know he truly is better off without you. That you have caused him nothing but pain and grief and sorrow. That you have lured others into your nest of deceit and struggle. That you are no better than the evil you pretend to fight."

I pursed my lips as they began to quiver. Rau continued, this time in a more soothing tone.

"Where are your friends now? Where is your lover? They are nowhere, Katarina. They are happy to be rid of you, relieved that they can now live their lives free of the fighting, free from the suffering, free from the demands and the selfishness you bring."

I was silent. I tried to push out his words. I tried to pretend that I couldn't hear them, that they were just random sounds that meant nothing, but I couldn't. They did mean something. The fact that they bothered me so much told me, at the very least, they held a tiny bit of truth.

My resolve stumbled a fraction, and that was enough for my heart to surrender to the doubt. Like a house of cards, it all started to tumble down around me like a contorted emotional Rube Goldberg device.

I wanted to scream at the demon, to curse him, to spit in his face, but I didn't trust myself enough to speak. I was breaking at my very core. Doubt had planted its seed, and it was already sprouting.

Now I feared that even if I weren't bound, I wouldn't be able to fend off the demon. He'd taken a part of my spirit away and replaced it with the idea that if I truly loved Gio, if I truly felt the love that I said I did, then I would let him go. I would let him live his life without me, free of the torture that I had caused.

If given the chance, would I allow Gio to be free of this nightmare? Or would I be so selfish as to commit him to another lifetime of misery? Would I submit to Rau if it meant giving Gio a chance at peace? The questions rattled around my head, but I knew the answer.

I *would* let him go.

If it meant that he could live a happy life, I would let him go. I would submit to Rau. It wasn't even a question.

Tears escape my eyelids as I dropped my head in defeat. I opened my eyes and met the demon's eyes.

"Make a deal with me to give Gio the life you showed me, a life unharmed and I will do as you wish," I said in a quiet voice, knowing that if demons had any sort of weakness, it was the desire to make a deal.

Rau breathed heavily, the thick twang of his vocal chords,

vibrating with each rise and fall of his chest. He dropped his hands, and I could see him contemplating my offer. It was but a brief glimmer of hope.

"It is too late for deals, Katarina," he replied. "You will do as I wish, or I will force it from you."

"Never—" I began, but Rau flicked his hand.

My bound wrists raised up high above my head. The rope affixed itself to something I could not see. I felt like I was being hung on an imaginary hook. I dangled from it, my tiptoes barely touching the floor below.

I looked over to where Alessandro had been. He stood there still, completely occupied by his new-found power. His aura was black. Celia rolled her hands over his body, drunk from the power, caressing his torso. They were consumed by it, oblivious to what was happening just across the circle.

My eyes darted back to Rau. He was staring at me ... waiting.

He brought his hand to my cheek, stroking it gently before sliding it behind my neck and gripping my hair in his gnarled hand.

"Now I will have you all to myself."

My body betrayed me. I started to tremble in fear as he spoke.

"Get your hands off of her."

My head snapped in the direction of Gio's voice, hoping that he was truly there to save me and also praying that he wasn't. He entered the room without hesitation. Claire, Willem, and Patrick followed close behind. With a sharp movement, he threw a silver blade and hit the demon in the shoulder.

Rau roared in aggravation as he grabbed the hilt and pulled the knife from the wound. Thick black blood oozed from the opening.

"How?" he roared, grabbing staring at the blade. He threw

the knife on the floor and staggered to the edge of the circle. "How did you break through?"

I started laughing. It was a deep laugh that started from the depths of my belly and rose steadily until it erupted out of my mouth. Rau looked at me with rage. I looked down at the spot where I had smudged and broken the circle. It had been just a small opening, but it had been enough.

"You will not win again, little witch," he spat. "I will kill your love and come back to claim my prize." He backhanded me, my stomach heaving at the slap's intensity, and I was sick on the floor.

"Katarina!" Claire called, stepping forward, but Willem held her back. I was glad that he had. There was no telling what Rau would do.

Rau tried to disappear. He couldn't. Just as I had hoped, the tiny break in the circle trapped him between two worlds and until the circle was closed, then reopened, he would be stuck in this realm without the mobility to retreat to safety.

"Damn you!" he bellowed as he approached Alessandro and Celia.

"You let her break the circle," he accused them, taking a step back and touching the entry point of his shoulder wound. "You tricked me. You let her tie me to this realm."

Alessandro looked smug. The power had filled up more than his aura.

"I did no such thing. I have kept my end of the bargain. Our deal has been made," he said. "Now leave me, demon. We have no more business."

Alessandro turned and looked toward the rest of the group who had arranged themselves strategically along the outside of the circle. Claire had kept an eye on where Gio's knife had fallen and was making her way to it with caution.

"You are no match for me." Alessandro said to them. "Not

anymore. Get out of way or die." He stepped out of the circle and grabbed a sword that had been mounted on the wall. Celia followed suit. Grabbing the small knife from where Alessandro had laid it, she stood by his side.

In the circle, Rau roared in anger. I hung from my invisible hook, hands still bound. With a wave of his hand, a sword appeared in his grasp. He swung it around a few times before speaking.

"If you think you can defeat me, then I welcome the challenge. Step into the circle. Come and get me," he said, saliva dripping from his mouth. "Alessandro may possess dark power now, but I am Rau, Demon of Death, and I assure you that I will not be easily slain."

The room grew eerily quiet. There was not a sound to be heard. There was no movement. Everyone was frozen. If only I could access my power. I would push it through a sword, fortify it with my intention, and run it through Alessandro.

The anger inside me continued to build until I felt it in every cell of my body. But maybe there was a way. It was dangerous, but maybe, just this once, I could release the good that had been holding my true nature at bay. Maybe, I could fall into the dark. I stilled my body and steadied thoughts. I welcomed the Ilmalo part of my soul, my mother's soul, into me fully and completely.

I looked down at the floor. My vision was still blurry from the combination of Rau's slap and my throwing up. I waited while my sight cleared before speaking.

"Be careful, Rau," I chided. "Or you just might be facing me, and we both know how that ended last time."

My voice had taken on a rough quality, the kind of roughness that is acquired after a woman has been scorned past the point of forgiveness. It startled me as it filled the room. It was alien as it moved around in the void.

And then the chaos erupted.

Shouts and screams came from every direction. If the silence was unnerving, the noise was even more so.

I scanned the room but wasn't prepared for what I saw. Willem and Patrick had gone after Alessandro and Celia. Gio, new blade in hand, had charged the demon while Claire was on the floor near my feet. She had picked up the discarded blade from Rau's shoulder.

"Hold on, Katarina," she said. "Just give me one more second ..."

"No!" Rau yelled as he threw a wall of power at Claire.

She ducked out of the way, but the wall had been so wide that it clipped her left side, knocking her to the floor. The knife fell from her grip and slid under a chair, far out of reach.

Gio attacked the demon over and over, never relenting. Their swords hit each other with a sharp metallic sound, sparks flying from them with each impact.

"Claire, hurry!" I called to her.

I could feel the energy shift inside me, and I wanted nothing more than to be freed from the binding. Claire abandoned the lost blade and pulled a smaller one from a wrist sheath. She pulled a chair over and stood upon it. Taking the knife, she tried to cut through the rope around my wrists. It didn't budge. The small tool made no mark on the rope, let alone slice it.

"It's not working," she said, panicked.

"You need to neutralize the spell," I yelled. "You'll never be able to cut through the magick with a regular blade. You either need to remove the binding spell or spell the blade!"

She hopped down from the chair and stood in front of me, her back facing the fighting. Behind her I could see the others in combat. Alessandro was able to deflect Willem's blade with ease, almost as if he were toying with the man.

Celia appeared quite trained in combat; her skill was

surprising. But she had her hands full with Patrick. Eyes or no eyes, he was proving himself to be quite adept at countering her every move. Still, he did not seem to be gaining any sort of advantage against her.

I forced myself to glance back at Gio. He was quick and aggressive, but Rau was better. He was able to maneuver away from any attack that Gio unleashed.

"Claire," I spoke as calmly as I could. "You need to get me out of here now."

She nodded. Holding the knife in both hands, she offered it up to the Goddess.

"*Blade of fire, blade of rage,*" she began chanting. "*I ask you, turn a page, increase your power tenfold, on this night in the moon of gold, guide it strong, guide it true, bring power to thee, so may it be.*"

I watched intently as Claire said the invocation. After the third time, the knife glowed a bluish white, then faded back to silver.

"Done," she said to herself as she stood back onto the chair and got ready to cut the rope.

I could feel rage twirling inside my stomach. Claire held the knife in her hand and closed her eyes. With one quick swipe, she easily pulled the blade through the rope.

I fell to the ground. The moment I hit the floor I felt the rage within me ignite. The power that had been contained within me by that piece of red rope was a storm inside my body. I stayed on the ground for a second longer, just enough time to get my bearings. I could feel the blood of the Strega Ilmalo rise within me. It pushed any reservations I had about tapping into it aside like a ragdoll. It pushed my father's blood, the blood of the Strega Onesta, far into the background.

I closed my eyes and let it wash over me, handing myself over to it with pleasure. A second later, Claire was by my side.

"Katarina, are you okay?" she asked, as she placed her hand on my shoulder.

Slowly, I looked up, opened my eyes, and met her gaze. Her mouth dropped open. I knew what she saw. I could see the reflection of my red eyes in the glare of hers.

"Katarina," she whispered.

"Don't get in my way, Claire," I warned. "Just let it be. Tonight, I take care of something that I should have been taken care of a long time ago."

I stood and held out my hand for the blade that she had used. She placed it in my palm.

"Rau!" I called.

Rau stopped fighting and turned to face me. Gio froze in place.

"This ends here. Now."

"Katarina," Gio pleaded. "Katarina, you don't have to give in to it. You don't have to do it that way."

"There is no other way," I replied. "I tried sending him back before and look where that ended up. I won't make that mistake twice. This is the only way. Tonight, he dies."

I threw the blade in my hand at the demon, and it pierced his thick skin, embedding itself deep into the center of his chest.

Rau roared.

Stumbling, he dropped his sword and tried to regain his balance. I slowly approached him with measured steps, ready to consume every bit of his existence. Gio intercepted me and grabbed my shoulders.

"Katarina! Stay with me. Please, stay with me!" He shook me firmly.

My mind clouded. The only thing I held onto was anger and hate and revenge. I looked toward Rau and felt his energy there for the taking. I felt his force ready to be siphoned.

Gio turned my face toward his. "Look at me, Katarina," he

said calmly. "Please, look into my eyes. See me. See who I am. Through my eyes, see who you truly are."

Through anger and guilt and revenge, I heard his voice. I heard his words, I sensed the goodness in them, the trust that followed them, the belief that I did not have to follow a path into darkness, that I could be good.

I blinked once. Twice. I could feel my connection to the dark fading slowly. The desire to consume an energy that was not mine, retreating. In its place, a golden light rose up. Inside, the storm began to calm. Gio took my hand and held it gently.

"Claire," he called quickly, "if we close the circle, we can send him back for good."

Claire pulled a knife from a sheath on her other wrist and sliced her palm. She ran to the spot where I had broken the circle and completed it with her blood. Then she ran up to us and grasped our hands.

"Gio, hurry!" I urged as Rau began to recover.

I looked over to where Alessandro and Celia were fighting our friends. My eyes widened. Alessandro had the upper hand on Willem, who was simply fighting to keep him contained. Patrick looked no different than before, but then neither did Celia.

Claire was distracted by the fight that continued while we began to close the circle.

"Claire, you need to focus," I said. "If Rau is able to recover before we can do this, then we will all suffer for it."

Claire nodded.

The three of us closed our eyes. Gio said the words and the circle closed.

"*Oh, Diana, Queen of the Witches, hear our call to you now,*" I began. "*Give us the power to banish the evil, the Dark Lord Rau, to his place in Tartarus for all eternity, never to set foot in this earthly realm ever again.*"

"NO!" Rau roared.

"Again, Katarina," Gio cried over the monstrous howl. "Say it again!"

I repeated the invocation. Claire squeezed my hand tight as the walls shook, the floor rumbled with each word. The candles flickered and went out.

The room flashed bright, then went black. We could hear the fighting continue on the other side of the room, but we couldn't see what was happening. Suddenly the candles burst into flame, and the room was bright with their light.

Rau was gone.

The stillness passed and time continued. Willem and Patrick still battled across the room. Claire tried to let go of my hand to help them. I held on to it firmly.

"Wait. We can't let go until the spell is complete. Gio, complete the cast," I said, my heart racing in my chest.

Gio went through the steps as quickly as he could. When the circle was opened, and the spell was complete, we turned to deal with Alessandro and Celia. Alessandro looked up from his duel with Willem and smiled as he looked from me to Gio.

I watched in horror as Alessandro easily disarmed Willem and ran the blade through his middle with ease. He'd just been toying with him. Toying with us.

"No!" Claire screamed as she ran toward them. Alessandro looked at her and pulled the sword out of Willem's body once more, before plunging it back in, piercing his heart.

Taking advantage of the distraction, Celia quickly moved and sliced Patrick's throat in one swipe. He fell to the floor instantly, blood spilling from the mortal wound.

The three of us stood there in shock, unable to think, unable to move.

"Well, I suppose this is where we end for the night," Alessandro said in a sadistic tone. "But don't worry, Katie, we'll be seeing each other again real soon."

He pulled the sword out of Willem's chest. The large man

fell to the floor like a crumpled rag doll. He looked at Claire, who stood frozen mid-step.

"Oh, my. Whatever will you do?" Alessandro said clicking his tongue. "Which one to heal first? Or at least try to heal, though I don't think you'll have any luck. But it's more than just a question of healing, isn't it, little girl? I suppose the real question is which one do you love more?"

He swiped his hand across the room and the candles went out. When they came back on a half second later, he and Celia had vanished. The only sight before us were the bodies of our friends lying on the floor. Claire was the first to move.

"Gio, pull Patrick over next to Willem side by side," she ordered as she knelt in a puddle of blood. She straightened out Willem's body, placing his arms at his sides.

Gio didn't move. He watched Claire as she continued to work.

"Gio! Hurry! There's no time!" she yelled unbuttoning Willem's shirt.

Gio and I moved to Patrick and lifted the Watcher's body with care. We placed him next to Willem. Gio made sure that his legs were straightened out.

I knelt on the other side of him.

"Katarina," Claire said in an unnaturally calm voice, "loosen Patrick's shirt collar. I need to have access to the wound if I'm going to seal it."

"Claire—" I started.

"Do it!" she interrupted sharply.

The tears welled in my eyes as I followed her request. Gently, I unbuttoned Patrick's shirt collar, revealing the deep neck wound. Celia had sliced it from ear to ear. There was no blood flowing now, he had bled out. His skin felt cool under my touch. I closed his mouth and wiped the blood spots from his face with my dress.

Claire had opened Willem's shirt and put her head to his chest.

"I just need to find the slightest beat," she began.

"Claire—" I tried again.

"Not now, Katarina! I'm trying to find his heartbeat," she shot back.

She placed her head on his chest.

"Come on, Willem," she said to herself. "Don't leave me now. Just hang on a little longer … just give me something I can hold onto."

I looked at Gio in desperation. His eyes were red and swollen. Tears collected in the corners. His lips trembled.

"Claire," he said in a soft tone, moving to kneel behind her and placing his hand on her back. "What do you want me to do?"

Claire sat up.

"Here, listen for his heartbeat, I can't seem to find it," she said scooting over to the side.

He placed his head on his friend's bloodied chest. The wound was wide open. He lay there for a few minutes before sitting back up.

"I can't find it, Claire," he said, his voice cracking.

Claire looked confused at the statement, then shifted her eyes over to where Patrick lay still. She stared at him, her mouth barely open. She reached out and lifted his arm, her fingers searching for a pulse at his wrist.

"I don't understand," she said. "Gio, I don't understand. Why doesn't he have a heartbeat? Why isn't Patrick moving?"

Her hands started to shake; her face grew grey in color. Patrick's wrist fell from her grip.

"What's happening, Katarina? I don't … I don't understand," she yelled, her voice rising with each word. "Why is he just lying there? Why are they both just lying there?"

I choked on the sob that lodged itself in my throat.

"Wake up, Willem!" she screamed. "Wake up!"

She pushed Gio aside and pounded Willem's chest. His body lay unmoved. She frantically pushed him away as she stood up. Slipping on the blood, she fell hard on the floor.

Gio rushed over to her and gathered her in his arms. His face was contorted and pained. Pulling her close, she broke down into sobs.

"It's not real. This can't be real."

Gio held her tight in his embrace.

"I didn't save them. I didn't save them. I didn't save them."

Her voice was a scratched record. It reeked of rotted realizations and foul memories. My ears burned to hear the words. Gio held her tight and rocked her back and forth on the floor trying to comfort her. But how could he, when he felt the pain, as well? When he had lost not just a friend, a fellow comrade-in-arms, but a man who had saved his life, a brother through time? How do you comfort incomprehensible loss?

I sat on the floor in a blended pool of the blood of two men who gave their lives to save mine. My chest hurt. My ribs tighten against my lungs, making it impossible to take a full breath.

My brain denied what my eyes saw, even though my soul knew the truth. Sound disappeared as I watched Gio hold Claire like characters in a sick silent movie as they clutched each other in desperation.

My gaze drifted back to the two men who had given all of themselves, trusted their beliefs and followed their hearts for the greater good. I sat still and felt the stickiness of their blood as it congealed on my fingers. My heart sobbed, filling up with grief and hanging in my chest like a sponge that refused to wring out.

And though I knew they would do it again if they could,

without question or reservation, all in the name of love, my world shifted harshly. My body tossed, wrenched with the turmoil, my stomach sickening again as I sat there, motionless, in the surreal bubble of consciousness that was closing in on my very existence. I released my grief and felt the immense, overwhelming emptiness for the two men who had selflessly given their hearts and ultimately, their lives, for me.

Chapter Twenty-Five

GIO

Rowan led the way as we entered the bar. Katarina held Claire's hand as she dragged the younger woman along. Claire had been in a semi-comatose state since the night Willem and Patrick were murdered. I barely remember it myself; everything was still broken into bits and pieces, fragmented shards of memories that when put together still didn't make a complete picture.

I remember Katarina calling Matteo and Rowan.

"We ... need you," she had said. "Something ... horrible ... it's Patrick ... Willem."

Her voice had broken. I was still sitting with Claire on the floor, covered in blood.

When Rowan and Matteo had arrived, the bodies had already paled to grey. I remember how the absence of color made looking at them more bearable. It looked less real, more like wax figures made to resemble our friends. It somehow made it better, and much worse.

Rowan had gotten sick. She ran from the room down the hall, and I could hear her strained retching as it echoed through the silence.

"Oh, Goddess," Matteo had whispered, losing his balance and falling to one knee. He brought his hand to his mouth and coughed into it. "Goddess, please bring these souls, the souls of our friends, allies in your name, close to you in the afterlife. Know that they are men of honor and give them peace in their next journey into your realm."

His other knee had given out and he fell backwards until he was sitting there, unable to move.

I remember how we sat there while the sun rose and fell again. It wasn't until that night that Matteo and Rowan were able to convince us to go back to the Strega Underground. Matteo had insisted that Rowan take Claire and me back to his home. He would take care of the house.

And the bodies.

Though he didn't say it at the time, I knew what needed to be done. The bodies needed to be disposed of. I suppose I should've been grateful he knew what to do. I was in such shock, I didn't even question when Katarina stayed behind to help.

Let the Strega Ilmalo handle this, Gio. It will be done right. This is not for you. Take Claire and care for her. Keep her safe. I had blinked twice when the words came through in my thoughts sounding a little too close to Willem's accent. But it was enough for me to comply.

Rowan had driven in silence. The city was a blur to our left and right. Claire sat in my embrace, unmoving, as we made it back to the alley. Walking through the underground seemed both too quick and endless. Claire sat at the kitchen table in her soiled clothes and didn't speak.

Eventually, Rowan had taken her to the bedroom and helped her shower and change. After a while, I walked to my room and did the same. I stood in the bathroom and looked at myself in the mirror. My reflection horrified me.

The blood of my friends had covered my clothes. It was

stiff in my hair. It was dried in the folds of my knuckles, in the cracks in my skin. The dark circles under my eyes only accentuated the paleness that haunted me.

I peeled off my clothes, heavy, sticky layers of cloth I no longer recognized. I turned on the water and watched steam fill the room. I stepped in the shower and let the water hit my skin. Were it not for the steam I wouldn't have been able to tell if it was cold or hot; I was numb far beyond temperature. Water ran down the drain, brown, dark crimson, then red, finally fading to pink, and then clear. Would my memory of that night fade the same way? I couldn't imagine it ever would.

I dressed and made my way back to the living area before Katarina and Matteo returned. An hour later Rowan joined me, having spelled Claire to sleep.

We sat in silence.

Rowan didn't press for information, and I didn't offer it. When Katarina and Matteo returned, there was even less talk. They didn't have to speak. The sounds made by their movements, the heavy footfalls and hard swallows, stuffed the house to capacity, and were reminders that two of us were missing. They cleaned up and we all went to bed.

That was days ago.

Now, as we dragged Claire through Watcher headquarters, we knew that we'd all have to relive those moments again. I just didn't know if any of us could handle it.

Rowan walked in first, Matteo and I followed. Katarina and Claire brought up the rear.

The bar went silent.

The Watchers stopped what they were doing and turned to look at us. Their stares hit me straight on. I took a step back as their collective force flexed their power.

Rowan was silent. She walked straight to the back of the bar, through the door and down the narrow hallway that led to the small waiting room. We followed her. We took a seat and waited for Rose to emerge. Katarina helped Claire sit on one of the big leather chairs, positioning her arms across her lap.

Claire hadn't spoken since she awoke from Rowan's spell. Hell, she barely responded at all. Only occasionally did she make eye contact with any one of us, and when she did, it resulted in sobs.

We didn't know what to do. Katarina, seemed more in tune with her than Rowan, Matteo, or I. And I wondered if there was something the two women were keeping from the rest of us, something they shared telepathically.

Katarina stayed close to Claire, opting to stand behind the chair she was sitting in, her hand gently resting on her friend's shoulder. Rose did not keep us waiting long. She stormed into the room, her power hanging around her like a shroud.

"Rowan!" she yelled. "You were supposed to be the voice of reason! Now you come to me to say what? How do you reason that one of our own is dead?"

Rowan had braced herself for the accusations that Rose threw at her.

"You're forgetting yourself, Rose," she challenged. "We did not just lose one of our own. Willem fell, as well. With him, a part of Claire was slain. How can you stand there and accuse me when your granddaughter is clearly in need of deep healing?"

She gestured to Claire, who sat in the chair, unresponsive.

"My granddaughter," Rose whispered. "My dearest granddaughter."

She ran over to Claire and knelt before the chair. Taking both of Claire's hands into hers, she brought them to her mouth for a kiss.

"Claire," she begged. "Claire, do not go to the other side. Do not give in. Do not give up."

Rose placed both of Claire's palms against her cheeks.

"Feel my energy, Claire," she begged. "Feel it as it travels through me to you. Feel my aura, my life essence. It is yours, my darling girl. It is yours to take."

I sat and watched as Claire was unresponsive to Rose's pleas. After some time, Rose carefully placed Claire's hands back on her lap and stood. She turned to face me, her wrath barely contained within her body.

"You, Gio, have forsaken our family," she began. "You brought this upon us all."

I didn't even try to defend myself. In the wake of Willem's and Patrick's death, I had found myself thinking the same thoughts that Rose now spoke. It was Matteo who stood.

"I'm just a stranger. I won't even begin to pretend to know about what has happened here before their paths crossed mine. What I *can* tell you is that the person who killed your Watcher, who slew the Onesta, the one who stole your granddaughter's love, is not Gio. The monster responsible is Alessandro."

"Do not waste my time with your twisted story," Rose spat at Matteo. "I know about your kind. I know about Strega Ilmalo. I know all about the half-breed, as well."

She turned to Katarina for the first time since she entered the room.

"I have no words for you, witch," Rose said, her eyes glowing purple. "Except that I wish you had taken your mess with you into your next life."

Katarina stiffened. Now furious, I stood and stepped between the two women.

"*This* does not continue," I commanded. "This will not happen, Rose. You don't get to say whatever you want with no consequence."

It was the first time since the night in the flat that my voice had held any sort of authority to it.

"Rose," Rowan interrupted, "you have been our leader

since I was born. You were the leader of my parents, since they can remember. For decades you have been the one who has guided us through our toughest times. You have led us to believe that it is our duty to help the lost souls that wander this earth, those who need our help.

"Do you now stand here and so easily dismiss the same morals and principles that define our very existence? That *you* have taught us? Are you willing to lose sight of your teachings because it is now *you* who must learn the lesson?"

Rose took a deep breath and calmed herself. Her eyes returned to her normal shade. She closed them and let her body relax, letting go of the anger that, just minutes prior, had taken over.

"What you say, Rowan, is true," she responded after a minute. "My apologies. I lost myself in anger and grief. Forgive me."

Rose looked at Rowan and nodded, then back to Claire. Her face was saddened.

"I cannot possibly imagine the loss she must feel. To lose not one, but *two* close to you is more than anyone should have to bear. But she is my granddaughter, she has my blood, and we are not weak people. We are strong ... leaders. She will come around. I know it."

"If I may speak candidly," Matteo interrupted. "This atrocity was the doing of Alessandro and his follower, Celia. It was the two of them who caused this, and they must pay for it. They must pay for what they have done—for Willem, for Patrick, for the countless bodies they sacrificed in order to gain more power ... for my brother, Josh. Their deaths will be avenged."

"And when do we take time to mourn our loss? To honor our dead?" Rose asked. "Is it always this way with the Strega? To immediately seek revenge without first laying to rest those who have fallen?"

There was a silence in the room. I held my breath. It was Rowan who broke the tension.

"I think we all agree that we must honor those who have sacrificed themselves for the greater good. But, right now, you must listen to our story. You must know what happened in all its details. Then you will understand why action, *revenge*, if you wish to so characterize it, is so quick on our minds."

"Very well," Rose said. She took another glance at Claire before sitting on the couch in the center of the room, her face stoic. "Tell me everything."

The story wound itself around the tongues of Matteo, Rowan, Katarina, and me. We added our parts as we remembered, filling in the gaps for each other. When we'd gotten to the end of the tale, Rose's face still held the same stoic expression, though it appeared to have paled a few shades.

She looked over at Claire with a deep sadness in her eyes.

"And what of the bodies?" she asked. "What happened to their bodies?"

"There was no other choice," Matteo choked out. "There was too much darkness left behind on them, too much residual evil. When Alessandro had run his blade through ... when Celia had dealt Patrick his fatal blow, they sealed it with evil. There was no other alternative, Rose. We had to dispose of the bodies in the cleanest way possible."

"Fire," Rose whispered.

Matteo, hanging his head in shame, nodded. His pain radiated to all of us. I looked down, unable to even chance a look at Rose. To burn a witch was to say goodbye for all time. Forever. For centuries, non-magickal people had used fire to cleanse the body from the evil they felt it harbored. It was a gesture of finality that surpassed all things eternal.

Even though I knew that Willem was not coming back, the thought of him burning brought a horrible feeling from deep inside my stomach. It made not seeing him ever again real. I heard Katarina inhale sharply behind me. I turned to look at her. Her hand was covering her mouth and nose.

I listened as Matteo continued to relay the details to Rose while I heard Katarina's breathing become shallow. I took a few steps to be near to her, to be at her side, but it was too late. Her eyes rolled back in her head as she passed out. She hit the wall twice before landing on the floor in a heap.

"Katarina!" I cried as I rushed to her side.

I turned her over and stroked her face. She was breathing.

"Here," Rowan said, taking a small vial out of her pocket and handing it to me. "Put this under her nose."

I took the vial and uncorked it. Waving it under her nose a few times, I cringed at the scent. Katarina's eyes fluttered. As she slowly came around, the panic in my heart subsided.

It was all too much for her to handle. It was finally catching up. I'd been so wrapped up in my own loss, my own grief, that I thought about what it was like for her. To have to continually relive the abuse at the hands of Alessandro, to have to dispose of our friends' bodies, to burn a Strega, to know that Alessandro had yet another day to live. I should have been more aware of her needs.

"Katarina," I said softly, "are you all right?"

"What happened?" she asked, confused.

"You fainted," I replied. "Matteo was talking about ... you fainted, love."

She looked around the room, collecting her bearings. With care, I helped her up. Rowan had backed up to give her space. Claire still hadn't moved.

I walked her out from behind the chair and offered her my seat. She refused it, instead opting to sit on the arm of where Claire sat. Placing her hand on the soft leather of the chair arm, she looked down at the young woman's face, tears in her eyes. Claire sat unmoving for a moment, then suddenly looked up at Katarina.

Their eyes met for an instant before Claire lifted her hand and placed it on Katarina's. She squeezed it tight, her eyes filled with tears. I knew that they were communicating, but I had no idea what they exchanged. I fought the urge to question it. There would be another time. But for now, Claire had responded, and that was all that mattered.

"I can see that the alliance with my granddaughter goes far beyond your relationship," Rose directed to me.

"We have all been deeply affected by what has happened," I replied steadily.

Rose was silent for several minutes. I could tell that she was thinking carefully about what to say next.

"In three nights, it will be the new moon," she began. "On that night, that we will hold a ceremony to celebrate the life and sacrifice of one of our beloved Patrick. We shall also honor the Strega named Willem. My granddaughter's affections toward him are no secret, and I cannot imagine why the Goddess would allow such tragedy to befall her not once, but twice."

She turned to Claire and addressed her directly.

"Claire, I know you can hear my words. I also know that you will return to us when you are ready. But think hard before you ally yourself further. You have completed your duty. You have brought Gio into the present day. You have reunited him with Katarina. Your mission has been completed. You are released from your duty.

"A Watcher's sole purpose is to help those who are lost. Once the job has been done, you are free to move on. Choose to move on, my dearest. If you choose otherwise, I see nothing but hardship for you in the future. I see your pain. I see your struggle. Please, my granddaughter, my blood, please hear me now and heed my words."

With that, Rose turned to address the rest of us.

"I invite you to join our ceremony to say goodbye to your friend. It will be held at moonrise at our farmstead. Rowan will bring you there."

Rose stood. With one final glance at Claire, she turned and left the room from the same door she had come through.

"It's time to go," Rowan spoke in a matter-of-fact tone. "There is nothing more for us here."

THE SUN WAS JUST ABOUT to set as we passed through the gate of the Watcher farmstead. The winding road leading up to the main house was thick with blackberry bushes. Vintage advertisements from the nineteen-fifties were posted randomly along the fenced path. To an outsider, there was nothing to draw extra attention to the road; it looked like a typical driveway in these parts.

We drove a mile or so deep into the property until the bushes were accompanied by trees and other dense foliage. At the end of the road was a circular parking area. Rowan stopped the car and sat in the driver's seat.

"We have to walk from here." Her voice was neutral. She said it as if she were merely relaying facts, not informing us of where we would attend our friends' funeral.

"I don't want to be late," Claire said.

Since our visit with Rose, Claire had slowly begun coming out of her shell state, or at least that's what I called it. Specifically, from the moment she and Katarina had their private exchange at the bar, she began to rouse from her depths of grief.

I still had no idea of what they'd said to each other. Though I wanted to know, there just didn't seem like a good time to bring it up, and if I were being honest, I was purely satisfied to have Claire beginning to interact with the world again. I really didn't care that much what had been said, as long as it worked.

And it had.

Claire unlocked the door and opened it wide. The night had taken a brisk chill to it. She wore black leggings and a black silk top that hung down mid-thigh. Her black high-tops were tied with black laces. She wore a long black sweater. She walked to the edge of the circle drive and looked out toward the west, the setting sun making the pink streaks in her hair seem even brighter.

I got out and walked around the other side of the car where Katarina had already opened the door. I offered my hand, and her fingers gripped mine tightly as I helped her out. Over the past few days, she'd been more sensitive than usual. We'd talked about what had happened after I'd left Alessandro's apartment, but it had only seemed to make things worse.

I was afraid she was shouldering too much of the blame, and it was beginning to bleed into her day-to-day life. If I knew anything about Katarina, it was that she wouldn't be completely well again until Alessandro was dead.

Though I agreed Alessandro would pay, I was, at the moment, not in a hurry to find him. Right now, it was time to lay our friends to rest. I needed to say goodbye.

We all did.

Katarina took my hand as we followed Rowan and Claire through the bushes to a clearing where the Watchers were gathered in a semicircle, Rose at the forefront, facing them. In the center were two mounds of dirt, symbolic graves covered with bright orange chrysanthemums, lilies, and lavender. Sage and frankincense burned in censers hanging from nearby trees.

We walked to the gathering and took our place up at the front. Rose nodded when she saw us. She looked toward the

Watchers and began the ritual by casting a circle. When the four elementals had been addressed, she closed the circle.

"Goddess," she began, "we ask you, wise mother, to take these souls into your embrace and release them from the pain and suffering they endured while defending the purity of true love. We ask that you call them by name, that Willem, eldest son of the Strega Onesta, seventh clan, and Patrick Michael Ryan, beloved Watcher and guardian, be taken into your fold and protected in the afterlife from this moment until the end of days on Earth and beyond."

Rose lit an herbal incense stick and smudged the two mounds until the earthy smell of pine, mint, and lemon hung in the space. She knelt on the ground between the mounds where a clay bowl, a small knife, a cup of wine, and a pomegranate lay.

Picking up the pomegranate, she cut it open with the knife and holding one half upside down, she hit it several times with the blade's hilt. Dozens of red seeds came tumbling out into the clay bowl. She then dug a small hole in the earth. Picking up the bowl with both hands and offering it to the heavens above, she poured the seeds into the earth, followed by the wine.

The Watchers were silent as we all watched Rose cover the hole with the displaced earth. She took her time completing the ritual, allowing the Watchers to pay respects to their brother. It took hours for the entire ritual to be completed. A fire was lit and illuminated the space as Rose led the Watchers through song and chant, through tears of grief and mourning.

When the moon was more than halfway through the night sky, the Watchers slowly began to disperse. One by one, the crowd thinned out until it was just Rowan, Claire, Katarina, and me. We stood in silence. There was nothing to say.

Rowan stepped forward first and approached the mounds. Kneeling in front of them she spoke. "Patrick, my dear friend, you were everything I thought a Watcher should be. You were kind and considerate; responsible and playful. You showed me what it meant to persevere. I will miss you dearly. Please come visit me in my dreams, friend.

"Willem, I did not know you long or well, but what I did know is that you were truly an honorable man. Blessed be in the afterlife, good Strega."

She stood and turned to face the rest of us.

"You need some time to yourselves. I can wait in the car. Please take all the time you need."

Claire nodded and thanked her. Rowan left the clearing and headed back to the car through the brush. Katarina, Claire, and I stood motionless in the night. After a few minutes, it was Katarina spoke up.

"I don't know what to say. Guilt hides my grief," she admitted. "Here are two men who gave their lives for a battle that was never theirs to begin with. They sacrificed the ultimate sacrifice ... for what? Alessandro is still free."

Claire took her hand and drew it to mine. She entwined our fingers until we were holding hands.

"For that, Katarina," Claire said. "They gave up their lives for that."

She paused before she continued.

"Patrick was the most loyal person I have ever known. He stood by my side; he protected me when I should have protected us both. He was a man of integrity and virtue. He was my first love, my oldest love ... my truest friend. I don't know ..." her voice cracked. "I don't know how to live without him because I never have." She paused.

"He fought because he knew, like we all know, that if Alessandro wins ... love loses. He fought because he knew what it feels like when love loses. We both did."

Tears began to roll down her cheeks freely. She looked from one mound to the other. Her quiet tears grew louder.

"And Willem … my Willem," she gasped between sobs. "I … I don't even know what to say to him, Gio … I … I don't know how I'm going to be able to continue …"

Claire choked and hiccupped through the sentence, barely able to speak the words. She began to sway, and I made it to her side just as she collapsed. Catching her in my arms, I placed her on the ground.

"You don't have to say anything now," I said. "Right now, is your time to let the emotions out. Cry into the dirt, scream into the sky, let everything fall out into the universe, release it from your body, let it be free."

"I can't …" Claire sobbed. "I can't, Gio. I can't do it."

"Of course you can. Just take a deep breath and let it all go," I said softly.

Claire's voice was barely intelligible, her sobs were so strong. She shook her head vehemently.

"No, Gio," she said adamantly. "I. Can't. If I do, then that means that Willem is actually gone and he's never coming back. I don't know what that will do to me."

I held her tight. My arms wrapped completely around her as we sat in the dirt. Katarina stood near and watched us with tears in her eyes. I knew she continued to hold blame for the death we honored today.

We all did.

In a way, we each felt that if we had said something a little different, or acted in a minutely different way, then we would be standing here planning our next move with them, not saying our final goodbyes.

My eyes glazed over the two mounds of dirt. One for Patrick, a man I had not known long, but whom I knew to be an exceptional being. And one for Willem, a man whom I had known for centuries. A man who was not just my friend, but my brother.

There are no words one can say when it is time to bid

farewell to someone who has touched your life on such a deep level. There are no words that can soothe the pain of that loss. There are no words that can fill the gaping hole in your soul that person once occupied.

I closed my eyes and let my mind wander through the thousands of memories of the man who had stood by my side, fighting a battle that continued still. It didn't seem real that he would not live to see us win.

Willem had saved my life more than once. His death didn't make sense. I tried to wrap my brain around it, but it seemed incomprehensible. It still seemed unreal. My heart cried heavy, bloody tears for the loss. I only hope was that I'd be able to avenge his death, sooner rather than later.

Katarina approached and wrapped her arms around us both. She sent healing energy through the touch. It pulsed in waves, immediately soothing as it hit my skin. She gave us the strength to grieve fully without inhibition. Claire felt it too. As soon as the first wave hit, she burst into louder gaping sobs. She reached over and wrapped an arm around Katarina's waist, holding her closer still.

It must've been nearly an hour before anyone spoke. I was the one who broke the silence. Though I didn't know what words to say, I knew that anything would be a step in the right direction.

"It's okay, Claire, let it out. Everything ... everything will be all right. Not today, not anytime soon, but someday, it will be all right," I whispered in her ear. "I promise."

I'm not sure why I added that last part. If I knew anything about life by now, it was that you shouldn't make promises you can't keep, especially in matters of revenge. I don't know why I said it, but I did. I prayed to the Goddess I wasn't lying.

Chapter Twenty-Six

KATARINA

"Is she asleep?" Gio whispered as I entered the studio and approached the small kitchen area. He was going through the motions himself. Reaching up to the cabinet, he pulled two glasses down from the shelves, a bottle of twenty-one-year-old single malt sat on the counter. He poured the two tumblers half full and passed one to me.

I took it and held it close to my chest.

"I was able to convince her to take the tincture, though I'm not sure how much she understood of what I was saying, she was so ... out of it, just someplace else," I said in a low tone. "I'm worried. One minute I can see a small slice of the old Claire in her eyes, the next ... nothing. Just emptiness. I fear she'll never recover. Not really."

Gio walked around the counter and leaned up against it. He held the glass to his lips but didn't drink. He just let it rest there, his thoughts somewhere far away. I put my glass down and stood in front of him. Wrapping my arms around his waist, I looked up at his face.

"Hey," I said softly. "Where are you?"

He looked down at me and smiled. His blue eyes were

glistening behind tears. He put his glass down on the counter and returned the embrace.

"I was just thinking about Willem," he said. "You know, I never really considered his death as a possibility in all this. I thought that if anyone was going to die, it would be me."

"Or me."

He nodded.

"And now where are we?" he continued. "We're no closer to getting rid of Alessandro than we were when all this started centuries ago. What are we doing here? You are the love of my soul, my very essence. Here we are, together at last in the same place and time, and still, we cannot be together peacefully." He released a long breath. "I just want it all to end. No more fighting, no more death. Haven't we all suffered enough? Haven't enough people been hurt?"

I took a deep breath and let the raw truth of that sink in.

"I don't know" I admitted. "Since that night, I've been going over everything in my mind again and again and again. Could something have been done differently? Why does this cycle of destruction follow us wherever we are?

"And you know what keeps coming up? The Strega Ilmalo. It is the goddamn way of the Strega Ilmalo to follow this pattern, this twisted cycle of death and revenge, death and revenge. When Matteo and I were in the apartment getting rid of the evidence, all I kept hearing were the words of my people. *You must seek revenge. This will not go unpunished.* And I thought to myself, that is their way. Does it have to be mine?"

I shuddered at the memory of that night.

Matteo and I had opted to burn the bodies in the fireplace. With a little magickal assistance, there would be no trace of them when we were finished. Matteo had been mopping up the blood, his pants splattered with reddish pink each time the mop had hit the floor.

"Katarina, you must be prepared to follow Alessandro tonight," he'd urged.

"Matteo, please, not now. I don't want to discuss this," I replied. "We've just disposed of the bodies of our friends. Please excuse me if I'm in no mood to strategize."

"You don't have the luxury of time. Not anymore," he shot back. "It's our way, the way of the Holy Strega Ilmalo, to act swiftly in times such as these. Especially when it's one of our own who is causing such chaos."

"And did you ever consider that I do not choose our way?" I snapped. "That our way is not my way?" I took a beat to gather my emotions. "Don't you see how much has been lost here tonight? Is it not enough that you've lost your own brother and our friends, but now you want to add to the body count?"

I shook my head in disapproval.

"No, no. I refuse to continue this ... this ... game that Alessandro has forced us all to play for the past four hundred years. Enough! How many more have to die before we realize that his death will never be enough to bring back the ones we've already lost?"

Matteo blanched.

"Are you renouncing the ways of the Strega Ilmalo?" His voice was steady. "How can you turn your back on your ancestral right, your place in our clan? How can you stand there and let all this death be for nothing?" he shook his head. "Why bother coming here at all? Why even put Patrick and Willem in this position to begin with?"

It was a question I couldn't answer that night. Still couldn't. It was a question that haunted me at this very moment where I now stood with Gio in his small studio apartment, above Claire's shop, and would most likely haunt me every day for the rest of my earthen life.

Why had I been so quick to seek revenge? Why had I taken innocent people with me? It had been a point of contention between Matteo and I for the few days back at his house and in our travel back up to Freestone. It was the reason he'd left promptly after our visit with Rose.

Matteo wanted revenge. To avenge his brother's death. I wanted to seek solace in releasing our friends to the Goddess in peace.

"I'm just … tired, Gio," I began. "I'm tired of it all. None of this makes sense to me, what we're doing, chasing after him, putting everyone's lives in danger. This isn't the sixteenth century anymore. I've lived more lives than anyone ever should and I'm different because of it. I … I'm …"

I brought my hands to my face. Tears began slipping through my fingers. "I'm so sorry for all the pain … the death … the suffering … I'm sorry for it all," I said, my voice muffled by my hands.

I felt his hands on each side of my face. He kissed my forehead, his lips lingering on my skin.

"Then let's take a break from all this," he said softly. "Let's just pack up our stuff and get the hell out of here … disappear for a while."

"But what about Claire?" I questioned. "We can't leave her. She needs us now more than ever."

"Then we'll take her with us," he replied. "She needs to get away more than we do. And I doubt she'll argue, considering how Rose has been breathing down her neck lately."

"And Alessandro?"

Gio's crystal-blue eyes darkened to the color of the sea after a storm. His voice grew grim.

"We won't forget about Alessandro. His time will come. And believe me when I say that he *will* get what is coming to him."

A chill raced up my spine at the severity of his meaning. This wasn't the same Gio that I had known when he was human. This part, this new Strega part, was something I was still getting to know.

What I did know was that he was right. Alessandro *would* get what was coming to him, but not at the expense of any more of our friends. We needed a break, time to get away, to get far away and perhaps, live a simpler life ... for a while, at least.

"I do believe you" I said. "And if Claire agrees to come with us, then I think we should leave. Just get out of here and see where we land. This town holds nothing for any of us anymore."

"Then it's settled," he agreed. "We leave as soon as Claire is on board."

"Speaking of which," I said. "I should go check on her. I'll be back in bit."

"Here, let me go," he offered. "You need your rest. You've been tending to her since we returned, and you're still looking a bit pale. Stay here and lie down. I'll go check on her."

He tried to direct me to the bed, but I resisted.

"No, I'm fine ... really," I replied. "I want to check in with her. She'll be expecting me anyway."

He gave me a sideways glance but didn't argue. He stepped aside and let me pass, but not before pressing his lips to mine. A fire burned in my belly as my body responded to his heat. His kiss went deep inside me, and I felt a stirring between my legs as he fully engaged me by stroking my hips with his hands.

Reluctantly, we parted, and I headed downstairs. I'd set her to rest on the sofa bed in the small office in the back of the store. Under typical circumstances, it wasn't the safest place for her to be, but right now, Rose had no less than ten of her senior Watchers posted all around the store, ready to unleash all kinds of magickal hell if any unidentified person even *thought* to approach her granddaughter's shop. Not to mention the ward she had placed on the entire damn town.

It was the only way Gio would let me go alone. Even if Alessandro had been bold enough to attempt to make contact, there was no way he could get by undetected and without a serious fight. Considering that he was a coward, the odds were well within our favor.

I entered the store from the front and headed straight to the back, not even stopping to turn on the front lights. I passed through the hanging beads that separated the front space from the back space and walked a couple dozen feet more before I got to the door of the back office.

It was closed.

I knocked four times and waited.

"You don't have to knock, Katarina." Claire's voice came from behind the door. "I know it's you. I heard your thoughts since you walked in."

Turning the knob, I entered, a smile spreading across my face. She sounded like her old self. I closed the door behind me and examined her face.

She was sitting up in bed, her feet dangling from the edge. Her short-cropped hair stuck up every which way, the streak of pink pointing up prominently to the sky. She wore an oversized grey T-shirt and a pair of red flannel pants. Her eye make-up was smudged from sleep.

"Hey, how are you feeling? You hungry?"

"Ugh, I can totally see what I look like in your mind. Gross."

"Stop. You've been through a lot," I responded. "More than most people. Honestly, I'd be worried if you *didn't* look like shit."

She shot me a look.

"It still doesn't feel real," she said after a minute. "I still think he's going to walk into the room and ask me about some plant that grows around here or something. And Patrick ... I've known him my entire life. I ... I ..."

She didn't complete her sentence. She didn't have to.

"No one is asking for you to be on terms with this now. It's going to take time. A lot of time. And still, it will never completely go away."

Claire breathed steadily, each rise and fall of her chest an intentional movement.

"Look, you don't have to listen to me, but I'm hoping you will. I do understand a little bit about loss. As someone who's been forced to remember past lives and relive many deaths in my memories, I do know that it will never go away. Time will make it more bearable, allow you to breathe again so that it doesn't hurt so intensely. But the pain? It never fully leaves."

"How am I going to do it? You know, handle this?"

"If there's one thing I know about you, Claire, it's that you're full of surprises. You're resourceful and smart and loyal and unpredictable and good. However you do it, you *will* get through it. And trust me when I say you will not have to do this alone. I'm here. Gio's here. We're both here for you whenever you need us."

Claire's face relaxed for a moment, then turned to concern when she picked up on a thought that had been floating through my head.

"What do you mean, leave?" she asked. "You just said that you'd be here for me. Now I hear that you and Gio are leaving?"

Her tone grew panicked. I walked over to her and sat down.

"Calm down, we are not leaving," I assured. "At least, we're not leaving without you."

She looked at me confused.

"Are we heading after Alessandro?" she asked.

I shook my head.

"No," I answered. "Not yet, anyway. Gio and I were talking about everything upstairs and we think that maybe we could use some time to gather ourselves together before we attempt to chase that bastard down.

"Freestone has nothing in it but tainted memories," I continued. "We both think that some time away, somewhere else, would allow us to heal ... to rebuild ... to release a teensy bit of the pain and collect our focus. But most importantly, getting out of here would give us the space we need to have a chance at being *us* again ... to heal.

"And we want you to come with us. You're just as much a part of us as we are of each other. You're not just Gio's Watcher and my closest friend. You're our family."

She listened as she sat quietly mulling it all over.

"If you don't want to go, if you'd rather stay close to the other Watchers, we'll stay. We're family now, and family doesn't leave. But we really hope you'll consider going. What do you think?"

She was silent for a few minutes before she spoke with a new resolve.

"When do we leave?"

Two days later we stood in front of Rowan's Prius with our bags piled high on the curb outside Claire's shop.

"I can't believe I'm saying goodbye to you, girl," Rowan said, giving Claire a monstrous hug. "I'm going to miss you so much."

"You're welcome to come along," Gio called from the back of the car, where he was throwing the bags in.

"Thanks, but my place is here," Rowan replied. "Besides, who'd run the shop? And someone's got to be here to deal with Rose. She's been all up in arms since you told her you're leaving."

"She'll get over it," Claire replied. "She always does."

"Yeah, but in the meantime, we all have to hear it," Rowan smiled knowingly.

"Thank you," Claire said giving Rowan one more hug before the redhead walked back into the shop.

"All set?" Gio asked as he came around to the driver's side.

Claire nodded as she climbed into the back seat of the car.

"How about you?" he asked, leaning in for a kiss.

"I've never been more ready for anything in my life ..." my voice trailed off. "Lives?"

Gio smiled at my attempt at humor, rolling his eyes for effect. I swatted his backside before running around the car and getting in on the passenger side.

With Gio at the wheel, Claire and I sat in the car and waited for the question we knew he was about to ask.

"Where to?"

Claire glanced at me before answering. I nodded.

"North?"

"Seems as good a direction as any," he said, nodding and starting the car.

As we headed out of the city limits, I glanced around once more at the town that had been both my home and my prison for so long. I was finally leaving ... potentially for good. The excitement ran through my body at the finality of the possibility.

We got on the freeway and headed north on Highway 101, beginning the long drive to an unknown destination. The excitement was palpable. It wasn't so much that we had someplace to go as it was that we were finally going. After a while, Claire spoke up.

"I know that right now we're taking a break from ... everything, but what happens if Alessandro finds us first? What happens if we're the ones being chased?"

Gio and I were both silent at the question. We'd considered

this to be a very definite possibility. With only the three of us, would we be able to defend ourselves, or would it be just a matter of time before we joined our friends in the next life?

"Then let him chase us," I said boldly. "Let him come. We'll fight him, no matter where it is. But for right now, I choose me. I choose us. I choose not to play his little games and continue this madness. I choose not to let him run our lives."

"It's the right thing to do," Gio added. "I felt it the moment I put the bags in the trunk. We need to be on the road right now. And there's a reason why we're heading the way we are. Can anyone else feel it?"

I opened my heart to the universe and asked for a sign, a feeling, anything to affirm that we were making the right decision by heading out of town. Before I could speak, Claire answered his question.

"I feel it," she responded. "I didn't know how to identify it this morning. I've been so out of touch, but now that you say it, it all makes sense. You're right, Gio. And it's not a coincidence that I suggested we head north, is it? It feels ... safe."

"Yeah, it does," he agreed. "And also— there's something up there for us to do ... or find ... or see. I'm not sure, but as soon as you said north, I felt it. I knew that we were being guided by a divine presence."

"Then let's not waste any time," I suggested as I turned on the music. "Let's see how fast this little thing can go."

We sped through much of Northern California, only stopping for the restroom and snacks once. Always on high alert. It was six o'clock before any of us became hungry for a more substantial meal.

"Where are we?" Claire asked as we drove through a hamlet.

"Looks like we're heading into Crescent City," I said as the Prius entered the small, incorporated city.

The sky was overcast, dark and lightly sprinkling, making everything look fuzzy from the windows of the car. As we drove along the main road into downtown, I was able to make out the historic buildings and shops.

We pulled into a parking spot on the main street and walked into an old mom and pop diner. Sitting down, we ordered some food while perusing through some of the brochures we found at the hostess station.

"How about this place?" I offered, placing the rack card in the center of the table so everyone could see it. "Casa Robles. Sounds cozy ... and interesting. It says here that it's located right on the beach, has in-suite kitchens and offers weekly rates."

"Sounds like a great place to start," Claire said.

"Just what we're looking for," added Gio.

We finished our meal and headed just southwest of the town toward the ocean.

Casa Robles was exactly as the brochure described, situated on the beach just yards from the ocean. The sun was setting and low in the sky. As I got out of the car, I watched it fight to break through the grey clouds far off on the horizon.

Standing at the edge of the parking lot, looking out into the sea, a icy gust of wind wrapped around me, its sharp talons clawed at my clothing and left gooseflesh on my skin. It was so cold. I shivered as Gio came up beside me and wrapped his arm around me.

"A little bit colder here," he said rubbing his hand up and down my arm.

"It feels alive, though."

"I've always liked the smell of the ocean," Claire added as she approached us. "There's something about the salt water that leaves the air smelling fresh."

We found the office and purchased a suite for the week. A week of isolation. After that, we'd figure out where to head next.

The small bungalow was more than comfortable for the three of us. The main room was spacious and decorated in a classic beach style of light blues and Shaker paneling. Chunks of driftwood were strategically placed between the two plush-looking couches in front of oversized French doors overlooking the beach. Though it was quite dark outside by now, I could still make out the large shapes and outlines of the natural landscape.

The kitchen was small but had all the essentials, with a three-quarter-size refrigerator, a small oven, a portable dishwasher, and a deep sink.

I entered the living room and flopped down on one of the couches. It was good to know that we'd be out of the car for a while. I stretched my body, placing my hands on my lower back. Gio sat next to me and rubbed its length.

"Long ride?" he asked. When I nodded, he added, "Are you feeling all right? Something's up, I can tell. What is it?"

I turned to face him. I spied Claire over his shoulder; she busied herself by unpacking the few grocery items we had picked up after we had eaten and putting them away in the cabinets. Now she stopped and raised her eyebrows at me.

"I'm just worn out, that's all," I responded, ignoring her. "Nothing that a long hot bath, a glass of wine, and a good night's sleep can't fix."

We brought in the rest of our bags from the car and settled in for the night. We had a fire going in the fireplace within the hour. Claire found an old newspaper in one of the end table drawers and was working on the crossword on the rug next to the hearth. Gio found a book to read, and I was content to lie down on the couch and stare out into the darkness of the night, a blanket draped over me, my head resting on his lap.

Other than the comforting crackling of the fire, it was peacefully silent.

My eyes grew heavy, and as I drifted in and out of sleep, I felt myself being pulled to a restful state. Gio had his hand on my hip, every now and then caressing it. It felt good to be somewhere other than Freestone. It felt *right*.

I heard the distant blare of the foghorn from the lighthouse, its far-away bellow warning ships off the rocky shore. I let myself fall further into sleep, deeper into the subconscious, letting my mind find its natural rhythm.

Before I knew it, reality blended into a dream state, and I no longer rested on my lover's lap but walked along a forest path. My feet were bare, and as I looked down at the ground, I could see them leaving imprints in the soft, brown earth with every step. The lush green forest fell like a curtain on my left side. To my right, a steep ledge overlooked a small brook, water trickling along the stones and tree branches that had fallen in its path.

I spread my arms out to my sides and inhaled deeply as I walked through the greenery. Everything around me was quiet … peaceful … as it should be. I lifted my skirt and started to run, not out of fear as I had in so many dreams of my past, but out of joy, out of happiness.

Suddenly, I stopped. In front of me stood an old, rusted iron gate. Its pickets were ornate with spear-like tops, the largest ones decorated with fleur-de-lis. I reached out to open the gate when a shadow from above caught my attention.

Looking up to the sky, a giant great horned owl flew in circles above me. Its wings were fully spread as it glided overhead, revealing its deep caramel-colored feathers speckled with black. I watched as the owl screeched above me, its high-pitched tenor echoing through the trees as if to reassure that it'd be with me as I crossed the threshold into the gated forest beyond.

Looking back down at the gate, I lifted the latch and pushed it open. The hinges creaked as it swung. I lifted one foot and cautiously stepped over the threshold into the unknown.

"Katarina," Gio said as he softly shook me awake. "Katarina, let's go to bed."

I opened my eyes to a darkened room. The fire was now just a small pile of embers.

"Where's Claire?"

"She went to sleep hours ago."

"Have you been sitting here long? You should have awakened me sooner."

He smiled.

"And disturb what's been one of the few peaceful sleeps you've had these past couple of weeks? The only reason I'm waking you now is because you'd probably sleep better in the bed, not crunched up on the couch with my lap as a pillow."

He gently helped me sit up.

"I think your lap is the perfect pillow, thank you very much. I'm not sure I'd trade it for anything," I replied yawning.

"Well, either way, we're moving to the bed now, Sleeping Beauty," he said taking my hand as he stood up.

We entered the bedroom, and he switched on the bedside lamp. A soft glow illuminated the room. Like the rest of the cottage, the space was simply decorated. There was a primitive white dresser on the wall closest to the door with a shabby chic coat rack affixed just to the right of it. A queen-sized bed sat against the wall opposite the door and was covered in a fluffy white comforter that looked like a giant cloud. I automatically smiled when I saw it.

I peeled off my clothes and climbed into bed.

Gio climbed in next to me. His body was warm. I could feel the heat radiating off his skin as it rubbed up against mine.

"Mmmm, you feel so good," I purred.

I turned to face him. Looking at him in the soft glow of the lamp, a wave of emotion flooded into me. Tears welled in my eyes.

"What's wrong?" he whispered, his fingers catching my tears as they slipped from the lids.

"I'm just ... happy ... scared ... confused," I replied. "I'm so happy to be here with you. It still doesn't feel real. To touch you and feel you so close to me. And at the same time, I feel guilty that I have you, that I have this happiness. I'm scared that it'll all end. And I'm confused about why *I* get to have this when Claire is in the next room and Willem is in the next life. I ... I ..." I choked on a sob.

He kissed my cheeks.

"I know exactly what you mean," he said. "I feel the same way. But I also know that we are meant to be together. I've seen too much to let this gift ... us, here ... go unappreciated."

He leaned in, his lips barely touching mine. I instantly responded. Pressing up against him, my breasts crushed into his chest, his belly was flush against mine as his hand found its way around my back and pulled me firmly into him. His hot hand seared my skin in the best way possible. I wound my leg over his hip and back between his legs. His hardness pressed into me as our bodies grew more excited with each passing second.

Holding me close, he rolled onto his back, and pulled me on top of him, our mouths never parting. I repositioned myself so I straddled him, my body open for the taking.

A soft moan escaped his lips as I pulled and tugged at his flesh with my mouth, an insatiable need to consume him rising in me. Never had I felt so hungry for him. Never had I wanted him so much.

My tongue grew restless as he teased me with his. The urgency in my movements grew, and he responded to my need.

His energy gathered and I knew that he would wait until we were both heightened until he released it to me. I squirmed in anticipation, wanting more and more of him, anticipating the moment when he would be inside me.

My breathing grew ragged, uneven, and I moaned in waiting. Gio, took his time, gently breaking our kiss.

"You're so beautiful," he whispered. "So amazing." His voice held nothing but the same pure raw love I felt for him. "You're my life, Katarina. Forever. For always. In this life and in the next and the next and the next. I'm yours."

I pushed myself up and looked deep into his eyes. The man lying beneath me was the only man I'd ever give myself to, the one man who would do anything for me. The only one who understood me at a level no one else could ... ever. The only man I'd ever trust. If there was ever a moment to let him know what I was keeping from him, now was the time.

My expression must have hinted a shift in my thoughts because he looked at me with a furrowed brow. My heart raced and I felt the blood drain from my face. My fingers grew cold, my lips tingled, my stomach fluttered. I opened my mouth to speak, but the words got caught in the dryness of my throat. I closed it again.

"Talk to me, please," he coaxed. "What's going on? What're you thinking? Please, my love, you can tell me anything. There's nothing you can say that can ever change how I feel about you. Do you understand? Nothing. So, please, trust me. Tell me."

I swallowed and opened my mouth once more, my breathing shallow as the words slowly, quietly slipped out.

"I'm pregnant."

Chapter One Death Before Dying

COMING NOVEMBER 2026

Katarina

The sun clawed its way over the horizon far too soon. Or at least, that's how it felt. In reality, it could've been the dead of night, and my head would've still throbbed with the same bone-deep exhaustion. I pressed the heels of my hands against my temples, kneading away the dull ache. My eyes burned, raw and gritty from a restless, fractured sleep. Turning my head, I squinted at the nightstand. The clock's red digits blinked back at me—eleven thirty-two a.m. Nearly noon. A sharp inhale tightened my chest as I tried to shake the fog from my thoughts. The last time I'd slept this late, I had been under the influence of something far stronger than fatigue, an enchantment, laced with dark intent, courtesy of my husband, Alessandro.

Bastard.

Even thinking the name sent my stomach into vaulting

spasms. I inhaled deeply once more and let the oxygen calm the urgency to hurl. I pushed my hair back off my brow, noting the clamminess of my forehead.

Jesus, I had slept like the dead.

It still didn't feel real. Any of it. I swallowed hard, my throat tight, my mind refusing to accept the truth. That Alessandro would go to such extraordinary, no, monstrous, lengths to keep me from following my heart. That he would sink to something so vile, so unforgivably brutal, just to keep Gio and me apart.

I sat up in bed and rubbed the sleep from my eyes. Four hundred years. The shock that Alessandro had succeeded in keeping my consciousness locked away for so long, left me numb. Though, I didn't know why I was surprised. He always had placed his faith in the dark sorcery woven into the Ilmalo practice. And his bloodline, rooted deep in the Manushe, practically ensured his allegiance. How could I have been so naïve?

I squeezed my eyes shut. My head pounded like four hundred years had actually passed overnight. And with all my memories releasing like a tsunami these past weeks, it pretty much had. But was the headache really necessary? Why hadn't my powers kicked in? I pressed my eyelids in an effort to relieve the pain. Enough was enough.

Fucking Alessandro. How could he have surrendered his soul to darkness? I was Ilmalo, too, and I had been able to control my most feral inclinations. And my mother had been the most powerful of her time. Alessandro and I both carried the blood of the clan's greatest elders, yet somehow, I had found a balance, a way to walk the fine line between right and what was... questionable. My father had seen to that. He was Strega Onesta, after all. Without him, I dared not imagine who I might have become. Would I have turned out different?

Alessandro never had that choice. Never had a chance.

The thought curled through my mind like a ribbon of ink unspooling from a typewriter. My heart softened. My eyes snapped open.

Wait, what?

I scrubbed my face with my hands until the hatred for him began to harden in my chest. Much better. I took a deep breath and stretched my arms above my head, my back arching like a cat's. Goddess, how could I have ever conceded to Alessandro's offer of marriage so long ago? Even four centuries ago I knew, as I knew now, I didn't love him. Not only in my heart, but my bones as well. In my soul. I relaxed the stretch and slumped back down into the thick down pillow, my head cushioned in the soft, white marshmallow fabric.

"It wasn't all your fault," I whispered into the empty room.

It was true. It wasn't *entirely* my fault. At the time, there was no other choice. I'd accepted Alessandro's offer of marriage only to save my father from eminent death. Little did I know he would pass away shortly after, and, by that time, it was far too late. Everything had been set into motion. I had no other option but to follow through with the proposal.

But then Gio came.

And I suppose, then, it was my fault. I rolled over on my side and rubbed the empty spot in the bed where he had slept last night. My connection to him told me he was just in the other room. Unsettled. Uneased.

Same here, my love.

My fingers traced an invisible outline of his body on the bed sheet. I didn't know falling in love with him would lead us into a four-hundred-year-old nightmare. I should've known, but I didn't. Magick always comes with a price.

I tilted my head and listened intently trying to pick up on

the voices murmuring in the next room. Claire's high voice balanced out the low tenor of his. They were talking about me. About our situation. About the baby. My stomach rolled and my hands flew to my midsection in reflex. Tears stung my eyes. How could a life so small leave me questioning my every–

"Stop it," I hissed to myself. "You are strong. You are powerful. You can handle this."

Just like you handled Alessandro?

Inner doubt jabbed at my most exposed spots. How many times had Alesandro killed me? The scenes flipped through my head. Too many to count, but the feeling was undeniable. Each time, the slow fading of life as it slid out of my body in a hot, smooth river. While Gio watched. Every. Single. Time. If Alessandro couldn't have me, no one would. And so, the never-ending game of *Capture the Katarina* began.

It was all the same. Every reincarnation. Except this one. This one was different. Not even Alessandro could've anticipated the outcome. I don't even know what would've happened had Claire not been with us this last time. Well, actually, I do.

He would've kept me this time, bound me to him, and let me live in ignorance of who I really am. He'd continue to have his way with me and I'd be none the wiser. He would've won. Until death do us part. I shuddered. He got dangerously close.

But he didn't.

He didn't and now Gio and I have a chance at a life together. A family. I turned over on my back and looked up at the ceiling.

And baby makes three.

"It certainly does," I whispered. I rested a hand on the softness of my belly. Then, placing both hands on either side of my stomach, I pressed inward ever so slightly.

"Who are you in there?"

I closed my eyes and quieted my mind, reaching out with something deeper than thought, trying to listen to the life growing inside of me. My chest rose and fell in a slow, steady rhythm.

C'mon, just little sign . . . something small. I know you can sense me.

Nothing.

"Ugh."

I scrubbed my face with both hands and forced back the tears stinging my eyes. Gio hadn't said anything last night, but the way he had looked at me told me everything I needed to know.

Whose baby was it?

Flashes of my anniversary weekend flickered through my mind. Alex had come home, and I'd been asleep in the bathtub. There was the fight. Goddess, I'd been so scared. And then, we had sex. Unprotected, of course. It was always unprotected. Why wouldn't it be? We'd been husband and wife for nearly a decade. And, it hadn't just been that night. Bile rose in my throat as the images of the following two days played like a grotesque slide show behind my eyes. I had tried so hard to make up for the fight *he* had started.

My breathing quickened. I remembered walking around on eggshells, willing to do anything to please him that weekend. And it was always sex.

Fucking Strega and their sex magic.

I clamped both hands over my mouth, stifling a gag. How could this be happening? For nine years, Alessandro had kept up his ruse. I squeezed my eyes shut, trying to force the memories away. But there was no hiding from the truth. It always caught up to you—eventually.

Instant rage surged within me, ready to be unleashed, but I shoved it down. There would be a time and place to unleash that monster. But not now. Not with Gio and Claire just a room away. I focused on my breathing.

Inhale. Fill the chest.

Exhale. Let it out.

Again.

My hands instinctively went to my stomach again and panic erupted through me like an electrical current.

No. No. Stay focused. Keep breathing. Push it down. Push it away.

I pressed my fingertips to temples and squeezed.

After a full minute, I sat up, my head in my hands. I swung my legs over the edge of the bed, stood, and walked to the doors that led out to the deck. Silently, I turned the knob and slipped outside.

The ocean air struck me full in the face. Gooseflesh rippled across my arms as I stood in the early chill. Fog curled on the horizon, mist settling like a veil. I lifted my face to the sky. A light drizzle kissed my cheeks, clung to my lashes. I rolled my lips together, tasting the briny mist that collected there.

"What have I done to deserve this?" I whispered to the heavens. "Dear Aradia, Goddess of All, Queen of the Strega and my true ruler, tell me please... why now? Why do I carry this child? Whose child do I carry? What can I do to stop this?"

Tears streaked down my face. My heart was open, raw. Goddess, I wanted it to be Gio's. I *needed* it to be his. There could be no other way. How could it not be? For nine years, Alessandro and I had been husband and wife. And in all that time, out union had never led to a child. Why now? How?

Because the curse had been weakened. The curse had been broken.

A sharp gasp caught in my throat. My heart flipped in my chest.

No, it couldn't be.

I counted on my fingers, trying–desperately– to map out the timeline. When had Alessandro last touched me? When had Gio and I broken the curse? Was it possible? Goddess, was it *actually possible* that Alessandro could be the father? How long had it been from when Alessandro had sex with me to when Gio and I'd broken the curse? An intrusive thought, once easily dismissed, now sat stone-heavy in my chest.

Fuck.

If only my mind wasn't so clouded, maybe I could think clearly. At the very least, count the goddamn days.

Focus.

Anniversary weekend. That was the last time. Sunday. Yes. Sunday had been the last time Alessandro touched me. I ticked the days off on my fingers.

Monday.

Tuesday.

Wednesday.

Thursday.

Friday.

Shit.

I'd slept with Gio on Friday.

Five days.

"Fuck," I muttered to myself shaking my head. "No. No. This isn't happening. It . . . no. Alessandro can't be the father. He. Just. Can't."

I buried my face in my hands and wept, openly, violently, no longer trying to control the grief detonating in my chest.

I could be carrying Alessandro's child.

The life growing inside me might have shared energy with a manipulative, murderous psychopath.

Everything blurred. My head swam. My knees gave out beneath me.

I collapsed onto the deck, the wood hard beneath my

body, but I didn't feel a thing. Any physical pain was eclipsed by the storm tearing through my from the inside.

My fingers clawed downward, from my neck, past my breast, until they found my belly. I pressed hard into the center of it, as if pressure could force the truth out of me.

It could be Alessandro's baby...

It could be Alessandro's baby...

Son of a bitch.

About the Author

A California native turned Pacific Northwest dweller, SC Alban thrives in the moody Fall vibes and endless rainstorms that are the perfect backdrop for her storytelling. When she's not writing, she's out hiking trails, kayaking on misty waters, or chillin' at home crocheting cozy projects.

Her trusty fur baby and dedicated familiar, Mateo, is always by her side making every adventure whether outdoors or in the world of words that much better.